D0752748

"I'LL GIVE YOU A
HUNDRED-THOUSAND
DOLLARS TO
SEDUCE MY HUSBAND."

IT WAS THE MOMENT OF TRUTH

Clea stared at Brandon, torn between her wish for him to stay, just because *she* wanted him to, and her knowledge that she was trapping him in Tiffany's web if he did. But it wasn't Tiffany's needs that prompted her. It was her own.

"Sit down," she said, pulling him into a chair.

She went behind him, and began to massage his shoulders. A slow moan escaped him. "That feels nice," he whispered.

He rolled his head back and looked up at her. "You're a woman of many talents, Clea."

She wasn't sure if it was Brandon who made the first move, or if it was she . . . whether he raised up or she bent down, but slowly, gently, sweetly, their lips came together.

Also by Terri Herrington

Silena
Her Father's Daughter

Available from HarperPaperbacks

Harper
Monogram

ONE GOOD MAN

Terri Herrington

HarperPaperbacks
A Division of **HarperCollins***Publishers*

If you purchased this book without a cover, you should be
aware that this book is stolen property. It was reported as
"unsold and destroyed" to the publisher and neither the
author nor the publisher has received any payment for this
"stripped book."

This is a work of fiction. The characters, incidents, and
dialogues are products of the author's imagination and are not
to be construed as real. Any resemblance to actual events or
persons, living or dead, is entirely coincidental.

HarperPaperbacks   *A Division of* HarperCollins*Publishers*
                 10 East 53rd Street, New York, N.Y. 10022

Copyright © 1993 by Terri Herrington Blackstock
All rights reserved. No part of this book may be used or
reproduced in any manner whatsoever without written
permission of the publisher, except in the case of brief
quotations embodied in critical articles and reviews. For
information address HarperCollins*Publishers,*
10 East 53rd Street, New York, N.Y. 10022.

Cover photography by Herman Estevez

First printing: September 1993

Printed in the United States of America

HarperPaperbacks, HarperMonogram, and colophon are
trademarks of HarperCollins*Publishers*

❖ 10 9 8 7 6 5 4 3 2 1

To Ken,
the one good man in my life

1

"*I'll give you fifty thousand dollars* to seduce my husband. That's my first offer." Tiffany Donovan angled her amused gaze on Clea Sands, enjoying the sense of power the young woman's reaction gave her. Clea had a lot of nerve looking the slightest bit shocked, after her week-long trial for shooting a man in the testicles. But that was what Tiffany liked about her. She needed someone with nerve.

"Did you hear me?" Tiffany asked. "I told you I'd give you fifty thousand dollars to—"

"I heard you." Clea's fathomless eyes snapped back to her with sharp disgust. "You want me to seduce your husband. I have to tell you, that's about the most unusual request I've ever heard."

Tiffany noted the slight Texas drawl, though the inflection had more to do with the lazy way she held out her words than with her pronunciation of them. She didn't like admitting that it gave the woman a soft air of warmth that contrasted drastically with her cold facade.

"I want a divorce," Tiffany said, as matter-of-factly as

she might have explained her choice of nail color. "But I need to catch him at something. Something big."

Clea's face reddened infinitesimally, and she reached for her purse hanging over the back of her chair. "I'm not the call girl type, Mrs. Donovan," she said in the deep, almost-hoarse voice that had struck Tiffany when she'd spoken to her by phone. "I don't know where you got my name, but you've come to the wrong person." Pushing back her chair, she started to rise.

Tiffany caught her arm, and Clea stopped. "I know exactly what type you are."

Clea's eyes grew even colder, suggesting more silver than blue, though Tiffany wouldn't have ventured a bet as to which color the woman claimed on her driver's license. "I know why you were dismissed from law school," she said. "I know all about the banker you exchanged favors with to pay your way, as well as the little shooting incident."

Although those eyes gave the impression of innocence, there was a savvy world-weariness about them, too. "Everyone in Michigan who can read knows about the trial. Nothing in my life is a secret. Including the fact that it was self-defense and I was vindicated." Her voice broke, Tiffany's second clue that she was getting somewhere.

"You slept with him for money," Tiffany said, without out a trace of distaste or judgment. "Why is my offer so different?"

The young woman's face remained expressionless. As if it held some sustenance to get her through this, Clea reached for the drink she had ignored until now and brought it to her lips. Setting it down again, she focused on Tiffany. "Don't believe everything you read, Mrs. Donovan," she said. "My only sin was being desperate. I hope you never have to learn about that firsthand."

Tiffany wondered if Clea was still desperate. She hoped so, for that would give her the leverage she needed. Her years on the board of Donovan Concepts had taught her a few things about playing on people's weaknesses.

She sighed and stared down at the barely touched lobster on her plate. Tiffany never ate anything that required saturation in butter, but she'd ordered it for both of them to impress the girl, since rumor had it that she was practically destitute. Clea hadn't touched hers, though.

"Desperation," she repeated, as if the word was an old friend. Her eyes were intentionally weary looking as she brought them back to Clea. "I already have learned about desperation," she said. "That's why I need you."

Clea sat rigid as she held the woman's gaze for a few beats longer than was comfortable, searching for the punchline, the booby trap that would blow up in her face at any moment. She had learned the hard way how to look into a man and see the selfish secrets and daggers they hid just below the surface of their phony smiles. Enough of those daggers had been aimed at her, and she had the scars to prove it.

With women it wasn't so easy, for in the world where Clea had been raised, it was the women who struggled and cried and picked up the shattered pieces the men left behind. But Tiffany Donovan was known for her fairy-tale marriage to the automobile tycoon, Brandon Donovan, and Clea found it hard to believe there were any pieces there to pick up.

"This doesn't make sense, Mrs. Donovan. I have to know why I'm doing something before I set out to do it.

By all accounts, you have the perfect husband, the perfect marriage. Why do you need me?"

Tiffany's posture suggested intimate woman-to-woman secrecy, and she fixed her brown eyes on Clea—eyes that hardened as the words spilled from her lips. "Despite what you may have heard, Clea, my husband is a cruel, heartless, self-centered bastard who treats me like chattel. I've suffered this marriage for twenty years, but I've had enough."

For the first time since Clea had walked into this restaurant, she found something about Tiffany she could relate to. "That still doesn't answer my question," she said. "Where do I fit in?"

Tiffany sat up and glanced to her right and then to her left, as if about to disclose some earth-shattering secret that would do her in if she were overheard. "Despite his other vices, Clea, my husband is monogamous. He doesn't fool around. The other things are too hard to prove, but infidelity . . . that's something I could fight him with. You're my ammunition."

Tiffany's face tightened, and she went on. "We signed prenuptial agreements when we got married ensuring that we had no claim to each other's money in the event of a divorce." Clea watched as she paused, finished off her wine, then ran her long silk nail along the rim of the glass. "*My* family was the one that had money. Brandon had nothing. The agreement was to protect *me,* not him."

A waiter appeared to refill her glass from the bottle chilling beside the table, and mechanically she took another fortifying sip and then set it down. "How did I know he would wind up one of the richest men in the country?"

Clea found it difficult to understand the financial

woes of a woman who wore a diamond on her finger priced higher than Clea's mother's house in Texas.

"I want a divorce," Tiffany went on, her voice packed with finality. "In order to fight that prenuptial agreement in court and get my share of his assets, I have to have ammunition. And you're it."

"I see."

"I want witnesses," Tiffany said. "I want pictures. The more wronged I look, the better. And then the court will throw out the agreement, and I'll get what I deserve." A smile crept across her face. "More importantly, Brandon will get what *he* deserves. A little of the hell he's dragged me through."

Clea stared at Tiffany. The woman didn't look like she'd ever been dragged through anything in her life. Despite the cool edge to her face—a face that looked at least a decade and a half younger than it rightfully should have—the woman had an elegant aura of luxury about her. That, she supposed, was why the media loved to photograph her. To the world, she looked like the fairy princess who had stood behind her man as he catapulted himself to the top of his industrial ladder. What Clea saw now was a beautiful schemer with a wicked glint in her eye. Her just-coiffed coffee-colored hair hung around her face, framing eyes that were round and aware, a nose that the finest doctors had improved upon, and collagen-injected lips that gave her the serious, pouty look that distracted from her eyes.

Tiffany's beauty was the kind that only lots of money and idle time could maintain, and Clea had never been impressed with women like her. Still, there was a part of Clea's mind that reached for other impressions, other clues, other signs that there was more to the woman. It was common knowledge that she was the daughter of old Philadelphia money and that her father was a renowned law professor at the University of Pennsylvania. Tiffany was highly educated, flawlessly groomed, and her background fit her perfectly into her role as a CEO's wife.

Yes, she was a schemer, but if Clea's experiences had taught her anything, it was that right and goodness had no place in a man's world. To recover . . . indeed, to survive, one had to scheme. Maybe she could learn something from Tiffany after all.

"Fifty thousand dollars," Tiffany said again, withdrawing a long cigarette from a gold box in her purse.

Clea breathed a laugh.

"What would it take then?"

What would it take? Clea asked herself. Would more money help to banish the memories of all the things men had taken from her over the years? Would it help her to never need a man again? Would it give her back the dignity that had been snatched so cruelly from her in the past few months? Would it help her finish law school, when not a university in the country would touch her now?

She sighed. "I'm sorry, Mrs. Donovan, but money doesn't mean a lot to me anymore. I needed it for law school before, but it won't do me much good now."

Tiffany stared at her for a long moment, turning wheels in her mind, and Clea knew she hadn't given up yet.

She tapped her cigarette on a marble ashtray, studying the ashes as they fell. When she looked up at Clea, her eyes were alive with amusement. "Did you know that my father is Theodore Holland, one of the country's most respected law professors?"

"I may have read that somewhere."

Tiffany stubbed out her cigarette. "Try this on for size. A hundred thousand dollars, and I get a letter of recommendation from my father that will get you admittance to any law school you want."

Clea laughed. "Let me get this straight. You want me to stir up a scandal that will break up your marriage, and you think your father will help your husband's mistress get into a law school?"

"He'll do it if I ask him to," Tiffany said. "And he won't ask questions. The bottom line is that I come out of this marriage with my fair share."

"And what kind of school would accept someone who caused trouble everywhere she went?"

"We could keep it quiet," Tiffany said. "I don't plan to drag the press in on this. All I need is a few pictures and your name to use in court. I would do everything within my power—and within my father's power—to keep the press from getting your name. Besides, even if it did get out, lawyers are supposed to be shrewd and opportunistic. And no one could deny that you had that going for you."

Maybe, Clea thought. "Well, I have to say, that's an intriguing offer," she said.

Tiffany smiled. "You're not stupid. Brandon will like that about you." Her frosty eyes assessed Clea. "I'll pay you in thirds."

"Thirds?"

"Yes," Tiffany said. "A third when I place you in my husband's office as his secretary. A third when I have photographs and public witnesses to your affair . . ."

"And the other third?"

Tiffany took her time reaching for her glass, finishing off the Dom Perignon, setting the glass back down.

When she brought her eyes back to Clea, they glistened with a hardness that never showed up in her photographs. Clea wondered if Brandon had put it there. "And the final third when I get my divorce and half of Brandon's fortune."

"Sounds fair."

Tiffany studied her nail and reached for another cigarette. "It'll take time, you understand. He won't take the bait right away. You have to take things very slowly, or he'll fire you. You have to make him think he's making the first move. That could take a very long time."

Something about the woman's smugness cut into Clea. She had never yet taken on a job that she hadn't excelled at, and despite her distaste for this one, she didn't intend to break her streak now. "Don't underestimate me, Mrs. Donovan. And don't overestimate him. Men have one basic weakness. It isn't that hard to penetrate."

"You don't know Brandon. He's been offered the best. The very best."

"Not yet, he hasn't."

Clea wondered whether to attribute the redness on Tiffany's neck to anger or indignation, but she decided it wasn't worth figuring out. She didn't like the woman much, and she especially didn't like what she was about to agree to do for her.

"I don't know about working as his secretary, though," Clea said before the woman could respond. "After two years in law school at the top of my class . . ."

"You don't have to worry," Tiffany cut in. "This isn't an ordinary secretarial job. You'll be Brandon's right hand, and he'll pay you extremely well. And that's in addition to what I'm paying you."

Clea wondered if Tiffany really hated men enough to sell out on such a monumental level. But if what she had implied about her husband was true—and Clea had no reason to doubt her—then he deserved whatever he got from a woman. Maybe even more than the men in Clea's past did.

"I need your final answer now," Tiffany said.

Clea braced her arms on the table and regarded the woman who would change her fate . . . one way or another. "All right, Mrs. Donovan," she said. "It looks like we've got a deal."

2

Clyde Sands *was the kind* of man who had a keen sense of smell when it came to two things: money and sex. Neither of these was a problem to find in Beaut, Texas, in 1968, for the town was rich with oil and virgins. Unfortunately, his was one of the families who had no claim to any oil wells—which should have made the virgins inaccessible.

Daddies all over Smith County forbade their daughters from dating him, which made him all the more attractive to most of them. But after he'd looked down the barrel of a gun one too many times, and been rather violently warned by most of the patriarchs of the community that if he didn't keep his fly zipped in their parts of town, they'd see to it that he was on the next plane out to Vietnam, he had to start looking elsewhere for his amusement.

Elsewhere was pretty much the side of the tracks where girls grew clean and pretty but held no promise of future wealth or family prestige. But Clyde was quick to learn that in the backseat of his Chevy, it didn't really matter who had money and who didn't. Satisfaction felt the same no matter who gave it to him.

That was when he made sex his top priority, and pushed money down his list a bit. That was also when he met Myrna Thompson, the prettiest girl without money he'd ever met. Myrna had silky, golden blonde hair that trailed down to the small of her back, and huge round eyes that could turn from blue to silver, depending on her mood. Her biggest asset, however, was the size of her breasts. Clyde calculated that they were much more than a handful—and he had big hands—and he made it his business to get a clearer measurement at his first opportunity. That she was a devout Baptist and confirmed virgin didn't bother him; it only made the challenge greater. He'd learned long ago that the hardest earned pleasures were the best ones, at least where his libido was concerned.

Myrna told him she would never sleep with a man she wasn't married to, to which Clyde replied that he'd have been married two hundred times if he kept such standards. He was quite sure that such a count of his exploits would make her hungrier for a taste of her own.

He was wrong.

So when all else failed, he did the only thing a self-respecting Texan stud could do to get in her pants.

He found religion.

Feeling as if she had been single-handedly responsible for leading him to the light, Myrna told him she was in love with him, which he returned with all the fervor he could muster, and during their spiritual bonding one night after church in the school parking lot, he managed to get her blouse unbuttoned and his hand inside her bra.

"No," she had whispered, horrified. "I can't do this in the backseat of a car."

"Why not?"

"Because it's sinful, that's why."

He tried not to let on how annoyed that particular statement made him. He didn't want to destroy the mood.

"And where *wouldn't* it be sinful?"

"Well . . . it's sinful anywhere if we're not married. But it has to be more sinful in the backseat."

"What about out beneath the stars?" he whispered. "Just you and me, on a blanket, holding each other . . ."

When she didn't answer, he took that to be a yes. Always willing to accommodate, he snatched the blanket he carried in his trunk for just such occasions, laid it out on the grass next to the football field, and pulled her down with him.

"I love you," he told her, as he groped at her bra, trying to get it unfastened. "I've never felt this way about anybody before."

And because Myrna believed every word, and thought there must be no greater feeling on earth than that of Clyde's hands moving over her body, she gave him her virginity that night beneath the stars.

Within three weeks, Myrna knew she was pregnant. She knew because her breasts grew painful to Clyde's touch, because she was nauseous all the time, and because her conscience had begun to haunt her with the force of all hell's angels. Her stepfather, Cletus Tiegs, a mechanic who showed her absolutely no interest except to yell at her when she tripped over one of the spare parts he sometimes brought home and left on the kitchen floor, found her crying hysterically in her bedroom one day. When she let it out that she was pregnant, he saw the opportunity to have one less mouth to feed, and told her to hightail it over to Clyde's and tell him immediately. They'd plan the wedding for the following weekend, he said, and if Mr. Sands had any qualms, he'd deal with him himself.

Myrna suddenly felt better. Maybe there was a bright side after all. She would be getting married to the best-looking man in Smith County, a man who'd dated some of the richest and prettiest girls in town. She wondered if her mother still had her wedding gown from her first wedding up in the attic. She wondered if the church would be available on Saturday. She wondered where he'd take her on their honeymoon.

Euphoric now that the initial dread had passed, Myrna went to the hardware store where Clyde worked to tell him the news. Her eyes were bright with tears and excitement when she found him in the warehouse cutting two-by-fours. "Clyde, I need to talk to you," she said. "It's real important."

"Can't right now," he told her. "I'm busy."

"But Clyde, it can't wait," she said. "We have to talk."

Clyde finished measuring out the two-by-four he was cutting and began to saw. "All right, Myrna. Talk."

She waited for the sawing to stop, but the moment the pieces fell off, he began measuring out another section. The sawing started again. Taking a deep breath, she realized she'd have to talk over the noise. "Clyde, I'm pregnant."

The sawing stopped immediately, and without moving a muscle, Clyde moved his suddenly hard eyes to Myrna. "Come again?" he asked through his teeth.

"I'm going to have a baby," she said. "Clyde, we have to get married as soon as possible, before it starts getting obvious . . ."

With slow deliberate motions, Clyde set the saw down on the cement floor, brushed the sawdust off his denims, and pulled a cigarette out of the pack he kept rolled in his tee-shirt sleeve. Lighting it, he drew the smoke deep into his lungs, then let it out slowly as he narrowed his eyes on Myrna.

Suddenly, he began to chuckle, and shook his head as if recalling some dirty joke the boys down at the pool hall had told him. "Look, Myrna, I don't know what kind of shit you're trying to pull here, but I ain't marrying nobody. Least of all you."

Myrna's hopeful expression collapsed, and she swallowed the lump obstructing her throat. "But Clyde, we have to."

"I don't have to do anything," he said, lifting his heavy brows in an expression of finality. He dropped the cigarette on the floor, stubbed it out beneath his foot. "But I'll tell you what I'll do. I know this woman over on Fifth Street who can take care of it for you. I can pay for it—"

"No!" Myrna's strangled cry reverberated through the warehouse. "Clyde, how could you even suggest such a thing?"

Clyde's jaw popped as he reached down and picked the saw back up. "Take it or leave it, darlin'," he said, starting to saw again.

Myrna stood there watching him, incredulous, for several moments before she turned and ran from the building.

Clyde didn't waste much time telling his boss that he'd had an emergency come up and needed to take the rest of the afternoon off. Then he got in his Chevy and gunned it down the back roads toward his house, cursing and banging the steering wheel as he went.

He'd had it with this no-account town, he told himself. He was too good for these petty little girls who thought a roll in the hay meant he was theirs for life. The bitch. It hadn't even been that good. Certainly not worth the wait. The only reason he'd kept going back was that she was so convenient, so willing, so eager, once she'd had her first Clyde-ride.

But damn it all, something like this always happened to ruin it.

He screeched into his driveway and noted with relief that his mother wasn't home. She was at the beauty shop, no doubt, which left the house to him for a while. Long enough to pack a bag, anyway.

What he needed was to get out of town for a while, maybe just long enough for Myrna to see that he wasn't biting, so she'd leave him alone and give up on her crazy notion about marriage. Who did she think he was, anyway? A fool?

He lit a cigarette, pulled a duffel bag out of his bedroom closet, and began filling it with enough necessities for a couple of weeks away. Who knows? he thought with a burst of bravado. If he could find a decent job somewhere else, he might just stay there. There wasn't anything keeping him in this one-horse town, after all.

He was back in his Chevy, on his way to the bus station before his mother ever got back home. He bought his ticket, one way to New Orleans, a town he'd been meaning to get to sooner or later anyway. He'd been told that whores lined the streets there—beautiful whores, who didn't get pregnant and sure as hell never thought of wedding bells—and he decided that was right up his alley. Besides, there was a lot of money to be made in New Orleans. He could get a job on one of those oil rigs, maybe, or a fishing boat, or maybe come up with one of those be-your-own-boss jobs where he sold things on the sidewalk of Bourbon Street. That sounded pretty good to him.

"Bus seventeen to New Orleans is now boarding. . . ."

He started toward the gate through which he could see Bus 17 idling in the drive.

"You goin' somewhere, boy?"

He swung around and confronted Cletus Tiegs. "Uh, I was just . . ."

The man's huge hand clamped over his as he turned him back around toward the front door. "Seems to me like you ain't got time to leave town, boy. Seems to me like I heard about a weddin' bein' planned for Saturday. Seems like you're the groom."

"No sir," Clyde said, his face mottling with red patches. "I ain't marryin' nobody. I told Myrna that. Now if you're worried about what's gonna happen to her, I told her I know somebody who can take care of things, but she wouldn't hear of it. But I ain't gettin' married."

"Oh yeah, you are," the man said, shoving him through the front door and toward his pickup truck. He reached in through the window and withdrew a rifle. "Get in, boy."

"Mr. Tiegs, I don't know what—"

"I said, get in," he bit out through his teeth as the nose of the rifle came up level with Clyde's Adam's apple.

Clyde got in and popped his jaw as the man went around the truck and got in, setting the rifle on his lap, aimed at Clyde. "Where are we goin'?"

"To get Myrna," he said. "And you're gonna tell her how sorry you were to hurt her feelin's like that, and then you two are goin' to city hall to apply for a marriage license. Then we'll start huntin' ya'll a place to live."

"A place to live?" Clyde threw back. "With her?"

"A man should live with his wife and child," Cletus said with a chuckle. "Don't you think?"

Clyde dropped his head back against the seat and closed his eyes. "Go ahead, Mr. Tiegs. Just shoot me. It's worth it."

"Much as I'd love to," Cletus said, "I believe I'll wait awhile. At least till after you've made an honest woman out of little Myrna and helped her save face with her church."

"Oh, come off it," Clyde shot out. "You just want to get her out of your house so you don't have to support her anymore."

"That'll be nice," Cletus said with another maddening chuckle. "That'll be your job now."

And as Clyde covered his face with a rough hand, Cletus gave a great belly laugh that made Clyde as sick as a kid who'd just guzzled a fifth of rye on an empty stomach.

3

Clyde and Myrna were married on a rainy Saturday in the justice of the peace's office. Just as he had done around the clock since he'd caught Clyde trying to leave town, Cletus kept a gun aimed at him throughout the ceremony.

Myrna had cried since the day she found out she was pregnant, for Clyde used every form of emotional cruelty he knew to make her back out of the wedding. When her pastor refused to marry them after finding out she was pregnant, she had to face the fact that her dream wedding would never be a reality. Instead of her mother's wedding dress, she wore a plain yellow lace dress, the dress she'd worn for Easter last year, and carried a spray of flowers her mother had picked from the little garden in their backyard. The justice of the peace's office was a far cry from her pretty little church chapel. The paint was peeling in places, the floor was warped, and the roof leaked.

But when he said "I now pronounce you man and wife," she supposed she was just as married as Princess

Grace was after her fairy-tale wedding. Only Clyde, in his dirty jeans and dingy tee shirt, was a far cry from Prince Rainier. She had a lot of work to do on him, she thought, but it was all right, for she had the rest of her life.

The fact that the baby born seven months later was a girl disgusted Clyde as much as it delighted Myrna. He left the hospital as soon as he was told and got drunk down at Al's Spirits. Instead of passing out cigars, he just passed out. When the bar closed, Al and one of the bartenders carried him as far as his pickup truck, where he slept the rest of the night.

He wasn't around when Myrna's anesthesia wore off and she held her baby for the first time. He didn't share her thrill when the child opened her round eyes and looked right into Myrna's.

"You're a beauty," Myrna whispered, holding the infant close. "Don't worry about your daddy. You'll win him over. Why, one look in those pretty eyes of yours and he'll be wrapped around your little finger."

Later that night, when Clyde didn't return, Myrna's spirits sank, in spite of the child she considered the pot of gold at the end of her rainbow. Cletus didn't bother to visit, but her mother came and brought the baby a homemade afghan she'd worked on for months and a lace headband with a little plastic faux ruby that dangled ridiculously on the child's forehead.

The next morning, when Clyde stumbled in with bloodshot eyes and smelling like a football locker room, she tried to make him laugh by putting the headband on the baby's head.

Clyde only gave some indefinable grunt that translated into indifference.

"I've been thinking of names for her," she said. "I have a list over there . . ."

"Name her whatever you want," Clyde said, sinking into a chair and throwing his head against the back.

Myrna tried not to look disappointed. "All right. I thought of Grace, after Princess Grace . . . She's so beautiful, she looks like she could be a real princess someday, don't you think, Clyde?"

Clyde answered in a caustic voice without opening his eyes. "She looks like Cleopatra with that shit on her head."

"Cleopatra . . ." She rolled the name around on her tongue, considering its implications. Images of power, wealth, control, and irresistible beauty filled her mind. All the things she wanted for her daughter.

"I like that, Clyde," Myrna said finally. "Even though she's a blonde, I think the name works for her."

He cracked his eyes open and peered at her through slits. "What name?"

"Cleopatra."

His eyes closed again. "You can't name her a fool name like that. People would laugh at us."

"No they wouldn't. They'd envy her. It's a beautiful fairy-tale name."

"Surprise, Myrna. This ain't a fairy tale. You name her that and she'll kill herself before she's four years old. Mark my word."

Tears came to her eyes, and she gazed down at the child sleeping so trustfully in her arms. The more she looked at that fake jewel on her forehead, the more appropriate the name sounded. Someday, this child would wear real rubies, and she wanted her to have a name worth growing into.

"I'll name her Clea," Myrna said. "Clea Patra Sands."

Clyde sat up, the look on his face the most reaction she'd gotten from him since she'd gone into labor. "Hell no, you won't," he said. "You leave off that Patra shit or I'll swear I was nowhere around when she was conceived."

"Clyde!" Myrna tried to tell herself—as she had a million times since she'd married him—that he didn't mean to hurt her. Men were just ignorant sometimes about the sensitivities of women.

"All right, but if we can't use Patra, we'll have to leave off her middle name. Clea just doesn't go with anything else."

"Whatever," Clyde muttered.

From then after, every time Myrna told the story of how Clea got her name, she swore that it had been Clyde's idea, that they had discussed at length whether to add the middle name of Patra, and that since her first day Clyde had pampered her as if she were Cleopatra herself. The more she told it, the more she believed it.

It just didn't do to believe anything else.

Clyde continued to treat his daughter with the same indifference he'd shown on that first day. In other words, he hardly acknowledged her at all, except to yell at Myrna to come shut the kid up when she was crying.

Myrna didn't ask questions when he left the house each evening after supper, for it was easier to handle the baby when Clyde wasn't home. Besides, she remembered that her own father had rarely been home, and Cletus, her stepfather, spent a lot of time away, as well. Men just weren't supposed to have to deal with the mundane details of family life, she told herself. They had more important things to think about.

Myrna didn't know that one of those things included

whose wife would be the greatest challenge to get into bed, and where they'd do it so they wouldn't get caught. If she had ever learned that he spent more hours at the Alamo Motel than he did at home, she would have found some way to glamorize it and redeem him for it. After all, he was just a man, and men were basically weak creatures. Hadn't her mother always told her that? It was their strengths that were important, and Clyde managed to put a roof over their heads, though it leaked when it rained and the pipes backed up often.

To keep her mind off her wandering husband's whereabouts, Myrna buried herself in sewing frilly little outfits for her daughter to wear to church, reading to her from the little children's Bible the church ladies had sent over when she was born, and following her as she toddled around the house, her intelligent curiosity getting her into anything and everything.

At night, when Clea was asleep, Myrna had to make a concerted effort to fight her loneliness, for that, again, was an emotion she wasn't entitled to feel. Clyde didn't deserve that, she thought. He was probably at this very moment slaving at some second job he was afraid to tell her about, to supplement his income and provide some of the luxuries Myrna and Clea deserved. The more she recited this fantasy to herself, the more she believed it, and at night, when he hobbled in at two in the morning and collapsed in the bed next to her, she told herself that his exhaustion was work induced, and she loved him all the more for it.

But Myrna never saw any extra money, and the alcohol on his breath was increasingly hard to ignore. Other tiny clues, like lipstick on his shirts, wadded phone numbers in his pockets, a hotel key in his wallet, began to assault her with a force she couldn't deny.

And just as she began to feel her world crumbling, something happened.

Clyde changed.

Suddenly, the interest he'd shown in church prior to their marriage was renewed, and he started going to Sunday school with her, frequenting training union at night, joining in the fellowships with other church families. Myrna was certain that her patience and quiet endurance of the rocky first two years of their marriage was finally paying off, and that he was transforming into the kind of husband that she had always dreamed of.

But dreams, unlike fairy tales, sometimes shatter in the end. One night after prayer meeting, Clyde disappeared with the pastor's wife. When Myrna went home that night, all of his clothes were gone, and in his closet he had left her a note telling her that the Lord had told him it was time to move on.

Neither Myrna nor Clea ever saw him again. Myrna never forgot the pain and humiliation he caused her. Clea never remembered knowing him at all.

4

Clea was three years old, the pass-around child of a working mother who had no skills, when Myrna was swept off her feet by Joe Don Wilson, the "Cowboy Car Salesman" whose commercials graced the screen of Channel 10 in Beaut, Texas, twelve times each day. She had met him working as a waitress in the donut shop across from the dealership, and because she was still pretty and at least twenty years younger than he, and because she didn't seem disturbed by the huge paunch that hung over a silver belt buckle with the word Bullshit written on it, he began showering her with little expensive trinkets such as Myrna had never known in her life.

"I think he's my Prince Charming," she told Clea one night when she was taking her from her daytime baby-sitter's house to her mother's, so that she could go out for the evening. "I think he's gonna ask me to marry him."

The fair-haired child looked up at her with huge silver-blue eyes. "Prince Charming has a wife."

Myrna shot her a disturbed look. "No, he doesn't. He's divorced."

Clea's eyes were unwavering as she considered that twist. "From Cinderella or Sleeping Beauty?"

Realizing they weren't talking about the same person, Myrna let out a long sigh. "From Thelma Wilson. Don't worry, darlin'. The real Prince Charming is still married and living happily ever after. Just like I'm gonna be."

She noted the child's pensive expression, as if she sorted out answers to questions Myrna could never grasp. It made her slightly uncomfortable that the child was so precocious, but only because she didn't quite know what to do with her. She didn't want her daughter's intelligence to go to waste, but there wasn't a lot she could do about that, considering that she had to work fifty hours a week in the donut shop and barely made ends meet.

What she really needed was a husband to rescue her from the drudgery and set things right in her life. And deep in her gut, she believed Joe Don was going to be the one.

Three months later, Myrna had the wedding she'd always dreamed of. She didn't wear her mother's wedding dress, however, because Joe Don didn't like old things and had decided that he wanted to buy her a dress. He picked out a tight white number in taffeta that was cut so low it barely covered her nipples. The taffeta stretched over her small hips, revealing every nuance of her still youthful body, and flared out around her knees.

White streamers decorated the room where the wedding was performed, and he even hired one of Channel

10's television cameras to be there in case there was
something he could figure how to use in a commercial.
They had three kegs of beer that they served to all the
guests at the reception, and then a long white limousine
with a longhorn on the hood whisked them off to the airport where they flew to Reno.

Myrna didn't leave the hotel room for more than ten
minutes a day, for Joe Don liked her best in sex garb and
tousled from bed play. She told herself the frequency of
his need for sex was in direct proportion to his affection
for her, so she didn't mind it. At night, after they shared
a champagne dinner in the room and romped in the bed
again, he went down to the casino to gamble and left her
there to "rest up for next time."

It never occurred to Myrna to be annoyed, for she
was so thrilled to be his wife after such a long year of
scraping by. As long as she kept him happy in bed, she
told herself, he would never stray as Clyde had done.
She just had to make sure she never told him no.

Clea was four years old when her mother gave birth
to another baby girl. Unlike Clyde, Joe Don whooped
and hollered—then belched profusely—when he was
told of his new daughter.

Immediately, he demanded that they name her Shalimar. Though he couldn't say where he'd heard it, he
declared that it was the prettiest name he'd ever heard,
so it should rightfully belong to his daughter. Myrna was
delighted at his interest in the child, so she didn't mind
when he told her he had to go celebrate with "the boys"
that night. She was tired, anyway, she told herself, and
she needed to rest.

Joe Don celebrated his first daughter's birth by tak-

ing all the boys of the local Moose lodge to Miss Bett's
Massage Parlor. As they partied with the "ladies" there,
the doors burst open and a flurry of policemen rushed
in, followed by television cameras and reporters from
Channel 10. Between two of his commercials that night,
the Cowboy Car Salesman was shown on the news coming out of a room with Miss Bett herself, wearing only a
pair of handcuffs that he held modestly over his private
parts, which had now been made public.

Clea saw the news at her grandmother's that night.
"That's Joe Don," she said matter-of-factly. "He's naked
with that lady."

Her grandmother looked up from her sewing and
muttered, "I'll be damned," breaking a forty-nine-year
record of not cussing.

In the hospital room, Myrna missed the news, but
she was quickly informed of it and "comforted" by a
string of phone callers who described the incident in
detail and asked if there was anything they could do.

Still woozy from the anesthesia, Myrna called a cab,
got dressed, and made her way out of the hospital without being stopped. She ordered the cab, the only one in
Beaut, Texas, at that time, to take her to the police
station, where she bailed out her husband.

She was back in the cab before the paperwork had
been processed, and back in her hospital bed before the
nursing staff even noticed she was gone.

When Joe Don came to visit the next morning, he
acted as jolly as if nothing had ever happened. Myrna
decided she should be grateful that he hadn't left her as
Clyde had done, and knowing that she couldn't make it
with two children and no man, she never brought the
subject up again.

Before he left to go to work that day, Joe Don kissed

her forehead, patted her hand, and said, "You're a real good sport, darlin'. You know that?"

Myrna managed to smile and convince herself that her patience with him would garner her his unfailing fidelity in the future.

Each time she realized over the years that she was wrong—that her patience only enabled him to cheat repeatedly without fear of consequence—her good Baptist upbringing and the year of struggling alone kept her from making any trouble. Joe Don was a good husband, she told herself. He never beat her, he was good to Clea, and he doted on little Shalimar as if she were a princess. He also had money, and didn't mind spending it, provided he spent it on things that would make him look good. Myrna had everything she needed, except for unconditional love and faithfulness. But by now she knew that those things weren't bestowed by many men, so she satisfied herself that what she had was better than nothing. And Joe Don was a far cry from Clyde.

The little humiliations along the way were almost worth it.

5

Shalimar came into the world with Joe Don's zest for life and his ability to float through embarrassing experiences and humiliating episodes without being embarrassed or humiliated. Yesterday faded like fog from her mind as soon as it was gone, but today presented a challenge that had no room for conscience nor concern.

Despite the fact that Shalimar made a mess everywhere she went and Clea made it her business to clean those messes up, Clea loved Shalimar's ability to laugh at her mistakes, then thumb her nose at their memory and forget them altogether. From the time Shalimar started school, Clea protected her from the people she carelessly angered, the teachers she agitated beyond control, the adults she pushed to the limit. And Joe Don didn't help matters any, for he doted on Shalimar as if she were royalty born by accident from his loins. From the time she could walk, he had called her "Lady Shalimar." He showered her with toys and clothes and candy and anything her little heart desired, and Shalimar never hesitated to tell him whatever that was.

Shalimar wasn't blessed with the beauty that Clea had, though she was cute and bubbly and wore a perpetually mischievous smile on her face. Her hair, a rich dark brown like her father's, was cut in a way that made it impossible for it to look unkempt, though Shalimar rarely bothered with it, and her eyes, dark brown and always laughing, were the kind of eyes that drew attention wherever she went.

But it was Clea's sultry blonde looks that drew the most attention. As soon as she entered the double digit ages, boys began dropping things and turning red in her presence, passing notes, and calling her and hanging up. Other girls gravitated toward her, vicariously enjoying the attention. Clea had to admit she enjoyed it as well, but she rarely gave the boys much more than a half lift of her full lips, like she'd seen Joe Don's secretary do to him whenever Clea visited him at the dealership.

About the time that she turned twelve, as Clea's body began to develop in places it had never occurred to her would change, she began to notice attention from older men, as well. Even Joe Don looked at her differently and began to show her more affection than he'd ever shown her in her life. His hugs seemed to reach all the way around her, allowing his fingertips to brush the small swell of her breasts, and she found herself getting uncomfortable whenever she was alone with him.

Clea's mother told her she was mature for her age. "You're lucky," she told her. "Men love big breasts."

But as she grew into her teens and experienced the lengths to which a man would go to glimpse them, she began to wonder if her mother wasn't mistaken about her luck. It was the night that she looked up from the bathtub to see Joe Don standing in her bathroom that she realized her breasts were not luck at all but a terrible curse.

Slipping under the water, which was clear and did nothing to hide her, she threw her hands over her breasts. "Joe Don, I'm taking a bath!"

"I see that," he said, his voice breathy and raspy. "You don't have to hide from me, darlin'. I've brought you up from a little girl. I've seen you naked more times than you could count."

Clea told herself that that was true, but somehow she felt it was different this time. Still, he was as close to a father as she'd ever have, and she wanted to believe she had nothing to fear from him. "I'm too old for that now," she managed to whisper.

Chuckling as if she were silly to doubt him, he reached out to move her hands from her breasts. Shaking, she allowed him to slide her hands beneath them.

"I do believe you're better endowed than your mother," he said, his eyes dilating at the sight of her nakedness. He reached for the soap, dipped his hand in the water, and lathered it. Then, slowly, carefully, he wiped a trail of suds across her nipple.

Her arms flew up to cover herself again, and she wished she had put soap bubbles in the water to hide herself from him. "Joe Don, you'd better go."

"Men are gonna like you, Clea, and you need to know what you're gettin' into."

Clea trembled from her shoulders to her feet. "What do you mean?"

"I mean, you don't want some hormone-pumped little punk to be your first, do you? You need someone more experienced . . . someone who knows you."

Suddenly she understood what he was suggesting, and something turned in her stomach. "Get out of here," she said.

"Just think about it," he whispered. "No one would

have to know. We aren't really blood kin, after all, so what would be so wrong?"

She sat up in the tub, hugging her knees to cover herself. "I said, get out!"

Shaking his head and sighing heavily, he dried his hand and went to the door. "Think about it, Clea. There's a lot I can teach you. Your mama's always real concerned about your education."

Clea sat motionless until the door had closed behind him, and quickly she got out of the bath and threw a towel around herself.

Later that night, when Shalimar and Myrna came home from a long conference with Shalimar's teachers, who were at the end of their rope with the child who did as she pleased, Myrna found Clea locked in her room. She knocked, but there was no answer.

"I don't think she's feelin' too well," Joe Don told her before he went out to one of his "meetings." "She's been keepin' to herself all afternoon."

Myrna shrugged it off to adolescence and turned her attentions to the fact that Shalimar was about to be kicked out of school for the third time.

Clea never made the mistake of being in the house alone with Joe Don again. Her education with him was complete, she told herself. That one episode in her bathroom had taught her everything about men she cared to know.

On her sixteenth birthday, Joe Don drove home a brand new lemon yellow Camarro with a big red bow tied on the roof. The family made great ceremony of luring Clea outside to confront what Shalimar told her was the "best present anybody ever got in the world."

She allowed her sister and mother to drag her out the door, and when they told her to open her eyes, she absorbed the sight of that Camarro, complete with Joe Don leaning against the fender like one of the bikini-clad models in his TV commercials. Taking his cigar out of his mouth, he swept his hand over the car.

"It's all yours. Happy Birthday, darlin'."

Clea gaped at the car, then at Joe Don, and knew instantly what the price would be. Her face went pale.

"Sweetheart?" Her mother nudged her. "Don't you want to try it out?"

"Uh . . ." Clea remained motionless, and looked from her mother, to Shalimar, to Joe Don again. "Uh . . . well . . . "

Tentatively, he stepped forward, and opened the driver's door.

"Clea." Her mother's tone was one of admonishment, and she knitted her brows together. "Honey, aren't you gonna thank Joe Don?"

Clea looked into her stepfather's eyes for the first time since he'd come into her bathroom, and a shudder went through her.

He was grinning at her like some alien who could see through her clothes. He was waiting for gratitude, she told herself. A lot of it. So much that she'd be ashamed to say no this time.

She fought the urge to throw the keys in his face, for that would require an explanation to her mother. And it wasn't Myrna's wrath that Clea feared, but her indifference.

Clea couldn't bear to see her mother turning her head on Joe Don's lust, so she did what was expected of her. Stiffly, she said, "Thank you, Joe Don." Then, standing on her toes, she pressed a quick kiss on his cheek.

Joe Don hugged her, crushing her breasts against him, dragging the full length of her body into a vulgar embrace that Myrna interpreted as genuine father love.

"I think I'm gonna cry," Clea's mother said through her laughter.

When Joe Don let Clea go, she stumbled back and eyed the door, wondering how soon she could get away from the smell of his tobacco and his cheap aftershave.

"Come on, darlin'," Joe Don said, opening the car door for her. "Let's take it for a ride."

Fear shivered through her as she got into the car, and she looked frantically at her mother. Did Joe Don intend to ride with her alone? He got into the passenger seat, his smell immediately mixing with the smell of new car.

Desperately, she turned to Shalimar. "Come on, Sis. I'll drive you by the high school and you can moon the football team."

Joe Don's grin collapsed as Shalimar's face lit up. "All right," she said, running around the car and slipping in behind her father.

The ride was uneventful, except when Shalimar took Clea at her word and tried to moon the football team, but her father wrestled her back down and threatened her with a whipping if she didn't "behave." When Clea pulled the car back up to their house, she thanked God that she had escaped Joe Don one more time.

But before they went into the house, he grabbed her arm and stopped her. "Later we'll go alone, darlin'," he said. "Then I can show you some of the special features. And you can show your appreciation."

Clea's face paled. She jerked away from him and rushed into the house.

She never drove that car again, despite Joe Don's

constant urgings, and finally, when he realized that his plan hadn't worked, he allowed his frustration to turn to anger.

Myrna tried to cool it by talking to Clea one afternoon when he wasn't home, about honoring your father and mother and how honoring meant driving the yellow Camarro he'd bought her, showing her gratitude, and treating him with respect. When Clea wasn't swayed, Myrna added that her only hope of getting him to pay for her college was if she changed her attitude.

"Darlin'," Myrna said quietly, "when are you going to wake up and realize that it's a man's world we live in? We're at their mercy, because we can't make it alone. Even your father was better than nothing, God rest his soul."

"He's not dead, Mama."

"Well, he will be someday, dear," she said wistfully. Then, she added, "It's true, what I was saying, though. Without them, we're nothing."

"I'm gonna be something without them," Clea said, lifting her chin high. "You just wait and see."

Myrna's soft laughter surprised her. "Oh, Clea. Don't you see how much like me you are? The first sweet-talking charmer who comes along is gonna get you just as bushwacked as I've been. Then it's you who'll see."

Clea told herself that her mother didn't know what she was talking about as she stormed out of the room.

Clea got her first job soon after that, for she realized that Joe Don wasn't going to budge anymore about college money. She wouldn't have taken it from him, anyway, but she would earn it herself if it took every drop of energy she had.

Because of her mother's predictions and Clea's determination to show her that she was wrong, Clea rarely went out with any of the young men who wooed her at school. What if they all thought of her the way Joe Don did? What if they overpowered her, and worse, what if she fell in love as deeply and foolishly as her mother had, only to be made a laughingstock?

Around the time she was eighteen, her body had caught up with her breasts, and she was no longer disproportionate, though she was still well endowed. Shalimar, who was now fourteen, mourned the fact that she wasn't as "blessed" as Clea.

"It's not fair," she said one day as she stood topless in front of the bathroom mirror, shamelessly assessing her own breasts. "By the time you were fourteen, you had a lot more than I have. What boy's ever gonna like me if I'm flat as a damn board?"

Clea smeared her eyeshadow across her eyelid and gave her sister a disgusted look. "It's not your breasts that's gonna turn them off, Shalimar. It's your mouth."

"Who cares about mouths when you have boobs like yours?" Shalimar said. "Do you think Daddy would pay for me to have a boob job?"

Clea's face reddened at the association of Joe Don with breasts. "Shalimar, you're fourteen. Give it a few more years."

"I don't *have* a few more years!" the girl said. "Chris Michaels is gonna wind up with that mousy little Susan Alandro if I don't do something. She has huge boobs, and she's my age. Why can't I have them?"

As frustrated as Clea often got with her sister, she couldn't help being amused at her logic. "So you think that if you had big breasts, he'd like you instead of her?"

Shalimar turned around and set her hands on her tiny

hips. "Tell me it isn't true, Clea. You can't, can you? You know it's true, because boys have been trippin' all over themselves around you ever since you were twelve. I don't know what you think, Clea, but it's not the hair that's makin' them so horny."

"Shalimar, you're starting to sound like one of those girls who works over at Miss Bett's."

"Fat chance," Shalimar said, turning back to the mirror. "She'd never hire someone as flat as me."

Clea stopped trying to change her sister's bizarre way of thinking, but she never gave up on Shalimar herself. She was just misguided, she thought, and whenever she bailed Shalimar out of trouble—which happened more often than anyone but Clea knew—she told herself that one of these days Shalimar would outgrow that wild streak.

But Shalimar never learned to curb her behavior, just as she never managed to grow breasts. So when she was sixteen, she talked Joe Don into letting her get a "boob job." When the surgery was over, Shalimar was even bigger in the chest than Clea, and suddenly her outlook on life changed. She was a bombshell, she convinced herself, and she would let it take her as far as she could go.

Joe Don soon hired Shalimar to "star" with him in his commercials, and by the time Shalimar graduated from high school, her bikini-clad body was a fixture in the minds of all the boys in Smith County, Texas.

Joe Don Wilson died in the bed of Wanda Malone, the widow who fixed Myrna's hair every Thursday morning. The coroner's report claimed that he died of natural causes, but no one in Beaut thought there was anything natural about his being in the widow's bed in the first place. They also thought there was nothing particularly unusual about it.

Clea heard about the place of his death before Myrna did, and she tried to keep it from her mother. But it was all over town, and the first dowager Myrna spoke to at the funeral home broke the news to her.

Myrna accepted it as stoically as she had accepted every other indiscretion in her marriage, and she mourned genuinely for the man she had given most of her adult life to. Clea knew then that, despite everything, her mother truly had loved the dirty old man who didn't know the meaning of fidelity.

The day of the funeral, Myrna—with a hairdo that had seen better days, since she hadn't been able to keep her appointment with Wanda that morning—cried profusely over his open casket, over the hands clasped reverently over his chest, over the awkward smile the mortician had massaged onto his face. Around his waist, Joe Don still wore the big belt buckle with the word Bullshit printed on it. Shalimar fought with Myrna and told her she wanted that belt buckle to remember him by. Myrna insisted that the buckle be buried with him. Clea couldn't help echoing that sentiment.

Shalimar cried and wailed until she had to be sedated, and some of the aunts had to take her out of the funeral home to lie down before the service began.

For the first time since her sixteenth birthday, Clea drove her lemon yellow Camarro to watch them lower Joe Don Wilson into the ground. In all her years with Joe Don, she had never enjoyed a gift from him as much as she did that day.

6

John Carmichael was on his third date with a first-year law student with long, luscious legs and a mouth that never stopped, when he saw Clea Sands for the first time.

She was waiting tables across the restaurant from him, her long, goldish-brownish hair swaying around her waist and feathering out from her face like Farrah Fawcett's. He was struck by the insular way she carried herself around the other fast-track law and M.B.A. students who hit on her at every opportunity, and the way she kept going back to the book she was studying from when things slowed down.

Unlike the other women he'd seen carousing around lately, looking for a future lawyer or doctor or executive to hook, she was self-contained, as if she had her own agenda and her own purpose. The waitress outfit she wore only enhanced her small, though curvaceous shape, and when he forced his eyes back to his date, he wondered what he'd ever seen in her in the first place. Feigning a headache, he took her home, then dashed back to the restaurant, hoping to catch the waitress when she got off work.

The restaurant was almost empty when he came back in, and he ran into the waitress who'd just served him— the one who was still smarting over the meager tip he'd left. "I just want another cup of coffee," he said, "but I want a table over there."

The waitress gladly seated him in Clea's station, bidding good riddance to the hot shot who couldn't put his money where his clothes and looks and mouth were.

He watched Clea look up from her book and sigh at the fact that her shift was expected to go on for the duration of another meal. No recognition passed over her eyes, and he realized she didn't know he'd even been there earlier. The fact chagrined him somewhat, but it only made the challenge greater.

Reluctantly, she came toward him. "I'm sorry, but the kitchen is closed. I could get you some coffee . . ."

"Coffee's fine," he said with his most charming smile. "Just a little something to get me through the night. I have a killer torts exam tomorrow. Have to study all night."

She slid her pad into her apron pocket and nodded without any hint of being impressed that he was a law student. When she came back with a cup and a pot of coffee, he nodded toward the stool she'd been sitting on behind the counter, and said, "I see you're studying, too. What is it?"

"Twentieth Century History," she said. "I snatch every minute I can get just to keep up."

"So you're a freshman?"

"Sophomore," she corrected.

"Test tomorrow?" he asked.

She shook her head. "No, but I never like to wait

until the last minute." She poured his coffee, then offered him a cursory smile and started away. "Let me know if I can get you anything else."

"How about some company?"

That smile tugged a little harder at the edges of her mouth. "No, my boss wouldn't like that."

"What about after work? You must get off pretty soon."

Clea breathed a laugh, and a strand of hair stuck to the wet lip gloss she wore. Unselfconsciously, she flicked it away. "I don't even know your name."

He held out his hand. "John Carmichael."

She took it, and he closed his other hand over hers. Slowly, she withdrew it. "I'm Clea Sands."

"Clea," he whispered, rolling the name across his tongue as if it were some magical chant. "Clea. That's beautiful."

She cocked her head and gave him a look that said she'd been propositioned before, and she knew all the lines and moves. He would have to be better to turn her head.

"Come on, Clea. The truth is that I was in here earlier and I saw you from over there. I've been watching you all night, and I honestly don't think I'll be able to sleep if I don't get to know you a little better."

"Gee," Clea said with a coy smile. "We wouldn't want you to lose sleep. Especially with that killer torts exam tomorrow."

John wondered if she was at all touched by his admission that he'd been watching her. None of her responses was as he expected.

He gave her a narrow look and reached out to take her hand from her apron pocket. It was small and smooth, and her nails were filed short with a clear base coat of polish over them. For a moment, she didn't pull away, and he found himself encouraged by that.

"Look, maybe we could just leave here and go over to Shoney's for a bite. You must be hungry."

"Actually," she said, "I'm just tired. I'd really like to get some sleep."

"But I wouldn't keep you out long. Come on, Clea. Don't send a guy home to lick his wounds. What if I never see you again?"

"We'll both live," she said with a smile and withdrew her hand again. "Besides, I'm here every weeknight. I'm not that hard to find."

She pulled his ticket out of her pocket and set it on his table. Feeling like a wounded puppy, he picked it up and read it as she walked away. There was no cryptic note written below the total, no phone number, nothing. Just the price of a cup of coffee.

Before he left the restaurant, he shot one look at her over his shoulder, hoping for one more moment of eye contact, one sign that he'd moved her at all.

She was as deeply engrossed in her history book as she might have been in a Stephen King novel. It was as if he'd never even been there.

As he walked across the almost empty parking lot to his BMW, he told himself that it wasn't over yet. Clea Sands hadn't seen the last of him.

Clea told herself over the next few weeks that the meager attraction she felt for John Carmichael was just a sign of weakness. The last thing she needed in her life was some sex-crazed man trying to distract her from her goals. Right now it took every ounce of energy she had to keep up her studies and work enough hours to keep herself in school.

Still, she couldn't ignore the tiny leap she felt inside each time John came into the restaurant and insisted on sitting in her station. And she couldn't deny the tiny thrill of pleasure she got when she caught his eyes sweeping from her face down to the small opening at the neckline of her uniform.

She fantasized about him at night when she was alone, reenacting romantic scenes from movies, and replacing Tom Cruise with John Carmichael. Would he be gentle? she wondered. Would he be passionate?

But she resolved that she would never find out, because she wasn't like Shalimar, willing to roll in the hay with the lover of the week—or her mother, who still believed every line every man with a smile sent her way.

For years she'd heard tales of her father's exploits before he was married, and now that she was grown she'd heard too often how he'd vamoosed with the pastor's wife. Before she ever married, she told herself, she had to be sure that her husband had self-control, loyalty, and integrity. But most of all, she wanted him to love her, for in all her life, she had never been loved by a man. Lust, on the other hand, was something she'd grown accustomed to.

She couldn't test those qualities in a man if she slept with him, and the truth was, she was skeptical that any man could have them at all. So she vowed not to sleep with anyone until she was married, and if that day never came . . . then, at least she was better off than Myrna, who'd had her heart smashed two too many times, or Shalimar, whose restless, reckless spirit would no doubt cost her even more heartache than her mother.

Still, John Carmichael continued coming to her station at the restaurant, watching her with patient, kind eyes, baiting her with questions and bits of revelations about himself—some designed to impress her, others almost inadvertently expressed.

It was on one particularly trying Friday night, when he caught her out in the parking lot on the way to her Camarro, that she finally decided to put an end to it.

He had been waiting for her to get off work, after spending the entire evening at one of her tables. She couldn't complain about his tips—he always tipped her more than she'd earned—but the fact that he watched her with such unyielding scrutiny had begun to wear on her nerves. She found herself dropping things when he was around, forgetting things her customers asked for, delivering meals to the wrong tables.

As she made her way across the dark parking lot and saw him leaning against her car, she realized a confrontation was inevitable.

"Clea, when are you going to go out with me?" he asked her.

She fished her keys out of her purse and thrust them into her door. "Never, John. I've told you."

He grabbed her arm and swung her around, not violently, but with an eloquent frustration that forced her to face him. "Come on, Clea. I may not be the best-looking thing to hit the campus, but I'm not ugly. I've always been able to get dates. Why don't you like me?"

She almost smiled, but caught herself. "I do like you. I just don't want to date you."

"Why?" he asked. "Tell me and I'll leave you alone. I swear to God."

A small smile cracked the corners of her lips, and she swept her hair back over her shoulders. Other waitresses and cooks began spilling out of the restaurant, getting into their cars and pulling away.

"I don't want to go out with you, John, because . . . because . . . I'm just not interested in . . ."

"In what, Clea? Just spit it out."

"In going to bed with you," she blurted.

He caught his breath on an incredulous laugh, and she felt her cheeks growing hot. "Going to bed with me? I'm asking you to have dinner with me, and you think I want to jump your bones?"

She sighed and turned back to the car. "I know your type."

"What type is that?"

"Male," she said.

Again, his laughter cut through the night. "You think all men have only one thing on their minds?"

"Yes," she said. "I sure do."

He watched her open her car door, but he moved closer and stopped her before she could get in. He turned her around again, took both her hands, and she could see the challenge glimmering in his eyes. It would have frightened her, if it hadn't set a spark glowing in the pit of her stomach.

"Clea, there's nothing I'd like better than to get you into bed. But first things first."

"There's not going to be a first thing," she said, tossing her purse across to the passenger seat. "I'm not interested."

He caught her arm before she could drop into her seat, and drew her up close to him until her breasts grazed his chest. "Clea, I'm a man who believes in investments. If it takes a little celibacy to earn your trust, you've got it, babe."

"I don't want you to earn my trust," she said, looking

up into his eyes as if he didn't move her at all. "I don't want anything from you."

John saw through her facade, and decided that whatever it took, he had to have her. He was the kind of man who knew what he wanted and, given enough time, could usually figure out how to get it. Even at twenty-four and with limited means, he was the kind of man who didn't settle for much. And settling for less than Clea Sands was something he couldn't fathom.

"Yes, you do," he said, taking a gamble. "You want to trust me, and you want to let yourself go and fall in love with me. Do it, Clea. I swear to God I won't let you down."

Before she could turn away, he kissed her with the force of a hurricane sweeping through her insides, tearing at the walls she'd built from the inside out, racking the emotions she had so carefully enclosed. She felt the excitement whirl up inside herself, the adventure, the thrill of dangerous, reckless feelings that caught hold like a vise and wouldn't be shaken off.

Even as she melted in his arms and gave in to that first kiss, Clea resolved that she would stick to her guns if she had to turn them on herself.

What she didn't know was that Myrna had once had those same convictions and had felt that same excitement. And that was how she knew that all of the carefully preconceived ideas Clea had about her life weren't going to stand up any longer than sandcastles built at low tide.

Everything changed for Clea the moment she fell in love.

John's obsession with Clea grew the more she fell in love with him, for he had never known a woman to be so sensually sweet, so accidentally erotic, without sleeping with him. It drove him crazy and frustrated him beyond belief. Finally, he did the only thing he could do to ease the desire straining within him. He asked her to marry him.

They married when John was about to enter his third year of law school, and Clea was entering her junior year of undergraduate school. Proudly, she walked down the aisle wearing virgin white, while her maid of honor, Shalimar, made the most of her pale pink bridesmaid's dress by wearing it braless and letting the sleeves drop off her shoulders, with the tops of her breasts swelling just above the taffeta.

That night, John made love to her with all the fierce desire he had borne for her, and as Clea unleashed what she had been holding back for John, she discovered a new, profound dimension to their love.

Afterward, she lay in his arms, touching his face, nuzzling his jaw, breathing his skin. "I love you so much, John," she whispered. "I promise I'll make you happy."

"You damn well better," he said without opening his eyes.

She lifted her head and gaped at him, until he cracked his eyes and gave her a wry grin. She told herself that he had been kidding, and dropped her face back to his chest, where she hoped to sleep for the night.

"It's a little hot in here," he whispered, and shook her off.

Adjustments had to be made, she told herself, and she was one who had always made them. As long as he loved her, she could be flexible. Scooting to her side of the bed, she fell asleep, until John woke in the middle of the night and remembered that his desire could be sated any time he wanted now.

But as he moved against her warm body and watched her shiver to heights he hadn't imagined she could reach, he couldn't help suppressing a tiny tinge of disappointment.

For she was his now, and the challenge was gone.

John's father died two weeks after their wedding, and his mother, who had never worked a day in her life, suddenly found it impossible to finish financing his education. There would be no income from his father again, she told him in a panic, and she couldn't risk depleting her funds by giving all their savings to him.

He took a job at a law office in town, but could only work a few hours a day and keep up his studies. In order to keep him in school, Clea took two more jobs in addition to her waitressing one in the restaurant. On weekends she worked in the legal library on campus. And on weekend nights she worked a job in the movie box office a few miles off campus.

In between jobs she studied, desperately trying to keep up her own studies, for she wanted more than anything to go to law school and open a practice with him when they were both attorneys. Their hard work and exhaustion was an investment in both their futures, he told her often. And when he graduated and passed the bar, her ride through law school would be much easier than his.

In her senior year of college she applied for admission to law schools and was accepted not only at the one where John was going but also at several others in the state. But she never questioned where she would go. She would stay in Dallas where John was most comfortable, and he would work as a lawyer and put her through school as she had done for him.

But the night after he got word that he had passed the bar, Clea got off work early and rushed home with a bottle of champagne to celebrate. She found him naked on the living room floor with one of the freshman cheerleaders from campus.

And suddenly her world came tumbling down.

They didn't talk for two days, but finally, when he called her to meet him so they could decide what to do, John told her that his manhood had been compromised while she was working so many hours, never having time for him. He told her that he had grown lonely, that he had needed someone, that she hadn't been there for him. He didn't love her anymore, as hard as he had tried.

Clea didn't honor those excuses with an answer.

They ended their marriage in a Pizza Hut in Fort Worth, Texas, and throughout it all, Clea refused to cry. Because they had no children to fight over and few assets, she graciously conceded the pizza—pepperoni with extra-thick crust—which he took home to his cheerleader. She walked away from the marriage with seven thousand dollars worth of bills, no idea how to pay her own way through law school, and a bruise on her soul the size of Texas.

7

The ugly reality of divorce haunted Clea for the next two years, for she simply could not afford to go to law school. Instead, she went back home to Beaut, moved in with her mother, and took a job in what had been Joe Don's car dealership, which had been sold shortly after his death to pay off his debts. It was now named Stanley Supleman's Car Emporium, and Stanley was happy to hire Clea as a saleswoman.

"It's just a hunch, mind ya," he said, "but I wouldn't be surprised if some of our tougher customers forgot about the competitors the minute they saw you flashing those big eyes, shaking that glorious hair around, and smiling in that sexy way you have. Honey, you and me could make a fortune."

He suggested that she revamp her wardrobe to include blouses as lowcut as decorum would allow. Clea didn't argue, but she didn't change her wardrobe, either.

Clea was the top commissioned salesperson ten of the twelve months of the first year she worked for

Stanley Supleman, and she didn't have to reveal her cleavage one time the whole year. Not that Stanley didn't try to make her. Every few weeks he'd call her in for a "man-to-man," in which he'd tell her how well she was doing and how much better she'd do if she "used her assets."

That first year, she paid off all her debts from her marriage and still managed to save up over half the money she would need for her first semester in law school. The second and third years she saved enough to get her through two complete years. Then she set about applying for admission again, this time not just to the schools in Texas, but to the top law schools in the country.

She was accepted almost immediately by the University of Michigan, which was situated just outside of Detroit in Ann Arbor. The change of locale appealed greatly to her, for she told herself that maybe it was the southern "gentlemen" who were scum, and not just all men in general. Maybe eventually, if she ever tried dating again—which she vowed to put off until she got her law degree so that she couldn't be diverted from her goal again—she'd find a love that didn't end in disappointment and betrayal.

At the end of her third year at the Car Emporium, she resigned and packed her bags to head for Michigan. Myrna, who was getting involved with an oil man who'd lost his company during the recession, cried for days before Clea left. Shalimar was too wrapped up in her affair with Zeke Meride, who was a producer of several television commercials that ran on Channel 12. He had yet to feature Shalimar in any of them, however, but she hadn't given up yet. The day Clea left, she wasn't able to find her sister anywhere, so she left her a note telling her that she was welcome to visit her in Ann Arbor any time she needed to get out of Texas for a while. Then, bidding a tearful good-bye to her mother, she headed off for Michigan, with money in her pocket and much too much hope in her heart.

8

While Shalimar manicured her way into fast cars driven by faster men, Clea learned how to fight her way past rigid law professors who stereotyped her as a husband-hunter the moment she walked into their classrooms. There was no time for dating, though a day didn't go by that one of her classmates didn't ask her out. The money she had saved selling cars, along with her income from two part-time waitressing jobs, had gotten her through the first two difficult years, but after that she had to try to get a student loan from a bank.

She was turned down repeatedly by bankers who couldn't see past the smears John had put on their credit history without her knowledge, or the still unpaid college loans they'd both gotten to help them through school. She had what the banks considered an "adequate" income from the part-time jobs, but she needed to quit them to keep up her studies.

Undaunted, she went to every financial institution in town. Defeat was something that Clea had rarely accepted in her life, and she wasn't about to start now.

Still, with the word "no" coming at her from every angle, and registration just around the corner, she found herself feeling more and more hopeless.

It should be different, she told herself. She had worked and struggled to put John through school, expecting her own time to come as soon as he finished. But the last she had heard, he was opening his own practice and supporting his cheerleader bimbo instead.

But Clea had never deceived herself into thinking that life was fair. And she didn't deceive herself that December morning when she pulled herself out of the car in which she'd had a good cry, patched up her make-up and straightened her thrift shop outfit, and marched into the FidCo Savings & Loan, her head held high as if she had a million dollars worth of collateral and all the time in the world.

Richard J. Mills offered her a spark of hope when he appeared at the door to his office. He wasn't that much older than she, and he looked more accessible and receptive than any banker she'd met so far.

But he was a breast man, she noted instantly, for his eyes perused her shape beneath her sweater, then came back up to absorb her face.

It would be all right, she told herself. She had the edge. She was a woman, and that was obviously his weakness.

"You see, Clea . . . may I call you Clea?" he asked her after she'd outlined her need for a loan. "It's such a lovely name . . ."

She smiled. "Of course."

"And you may call me Richard." He sat back in his chair and chewed his pencil eraser for a moment, and Clea tried not to bristle at the way his eyes raked her over again.

Harmless, she told herself. He's just a man, and I'm immune.

"You see, as I was saying . . . it's difficult, you know, to come up with the kind of money you need without collateral. We do make educational loans often, but the clients we make those sorts of loans to fit a certain . . . profile."

"You mean they're men?" Clea shot out.

Richard smiled a slow, unscrupulous smile. "Now that isn't remotely what I said, is it, Clea? You know, I don't think I've ever quite seen hair your color before. What color would you say it is? Blonde or brown? I'd say it's both, depending on the angle of the light, wouldn't you?"

Clea felt the muscles in her neck constricting, and she wanted to throw something in his face and leave. But no one knew better than she that she needed him to get where she was going. As long as she thought of him as a rung on a ladder, and kept him beneath her feet, she would be all right.

"I brought a transcript of my grades, Mr. Mills," she said, deliberately avoiding his first name. "You'll see I graduated at the top of my class in college, despite the fact that I worked three jobs at the time. My law school record shows that I'm consistently at the top of my class here, as well. I'm going to be a lawyer, Mr. Mills, and I only need tuition for another year. After that I'll be liquid enough to pay back every penny . . ."

"Now, Clea," the man said, steepling his fingers and swiveling slightly back and forth in his chair. "You know it takes time to build a practice, and even if you sign on with the best law firm in the state, you still won't be making that much money at first."

"I'll make enough," she said. "I'll make as much as any man would in the same situation."

"It isn't a gender differentiation," Richard said, lowering his hands to the table and leaning into his elbows. "As a matter of fact, Clea, you might have certain . . . advantages . . . over a man."

For a moment, she didn't understand what he was implying. Was he telling her there was a chance that she might get the loan?

His eyes dropped again to her breasts, and she suddenly wished she'd worn a more blousy top rather than this sweater that clung to her shape. Anger swirled up inside her, and she felt her face growing hot. "Just what are you suggesting, Mr. Mills?"

"I told you, Clea. I prefer that you call me Richard."

His eyes had taken on the glisten of intimacy, and she held her breath to keep from covering her body with her arms. Her voice cracked when she spoke again. "Just what are you suggesting, *Richard*?"

He smiled. "What fragrance is that you're wearing, Clea? It's maddening. Enough to give a man lurid dreams at night."

Swallowing, she came to her feet. "I think I should be going now. Thank you for your time."

"Wait." He was up and around his desk, stopping her before she could reach the door. "I was trying to tell you, Clea, that I think perhaps we can do business. It's just a matter of working out the details."

Clea looked up at the man who towered over her. "What details would those be?"

"Why, the details of our relationship. I'd very much like to take you to dinner, get to know you better."

"And would that be a condition of my loan?"

He threw his hand over his heart. "You wound me, Clea. I would hope that you would be grateful enough to cultivate our friendship. As a matter of fact, I would think that if I could come up with a loan of this size, you'd be very grateful, indeed."

Clea held his eyes for a long moment, measuring the extent of what he suggested, but there was no doubt in her mind that he wanted the same thing Joe Don had wanted when he'd given her the Camaro. It only took a moment for her to make up her mind.

"Thank you for your time, Mr. Mills," she said. "But I'll get my money from somewhere else."

His smile faded, but that intimacy in his eyes and voice didn't. "You may change your mind when you exhaust all your other possibilities," he said. "I'll hope to hear from you again."

She reached for the doorknob, but he put his hand over hers. "You know, you really are quite beautiful."

The words sent a shiver through her, and without another word, she hurried back through the bank to her car.

That night, after a grueling day of rejection, Clea lay on her bed with a cold washcloth on her forehead to fight the headache that had sunk its claws into her, and realized that she had very few doors left open to her.

Why was it, she wondered, that women like her who struggled to do things the legitimate way, without hurting anyone, always wound up on a defective ladder with faulty rungs that slipped the closer you got to the top?

She thought of Richard Mills, and the suggestions he'd made about the terms of her "gratitude." Her headache throbbed harder as the idea dawned on her that maybe that was why men got further ahead than women. Maybe it was the conscience thing. The ethics. The morality involved.

The thought set a burning knot in her stomach, and she realized that she was running out of time. Tuition for the spring semester would be due in three weeks, and she had to get the money by then or give up on law school entirely.

What she didn't know was that Richard Mills was a man who liked nothing better than a challenge, and Clea Sands was the biggest challenge he'd ever faced.

He began to call her daily, asking her to dinner so that they might talk about her loan, but each time, she told him that she had to work at that silly little waitressing job she had, as if that would put a dent in the kind of money she needed. If she wasn't working, she claimed to be studying or to have "other plans." If he hadn't known better, he would have thought she didn't like him.

He had called her every day for a week when it occurred to him that he was taking the wrong approach. He had to woo her with romance—charm and shit like that that women loved—then *tell* her they were going to dinner. Not taking no for an answer—that had always worked for him before.

He started by setting a long-stemmed red rose on the windshield of her Camarro every day for a week, with a note attached saying that it was from him. None of that secret-admirer crap, he thought, for he didn't want her mind wandering off in the wrong direction.

He waited outside the diner where she worked each day, watched her as she approached her car and found the rose clamped beneath her windshield wiper. Was it confusion or suspicion in her face? he wondered, as she looked around for him, then spotting him, held up the rose, as if in a toast, and got into her car.

Not a word, not even a smile, he thought with chagrin. Only that deep, penetrating look, then she evaporated.

Then he started sending the cards, those long drawn-out, heart-wrenching cards that sat in the drugstore between the tampons and hemorrhoid medications. He signed them all, "Crazy for you, Richard."

Clea still got that frosty look in her eyes whenever she saw him, and she kept her calls from him short. But he didn't give up hope, for he knew that she'd have to write that check for her tuition some time very soon. Then she'd be begging him for help.

He waited until the day before registration, when he knew she'd be a nervous wreck, and showed up at her diner with a check in the exact amount she needed. When she looked up at him, he slid the check across the counter.

She read it quickly, then brought her startled eyes back to his. "What's this?"

"You know what it is," he said. "I've decided to give you the loan."

Her expression didn't crack at all. "And what's the catch?"

"Dinner," he said. "That's all. Just have dinner with me."

He knew that look—that, gee I don't want to like him, but I can't help it look. He was scoring. Big time.

He propped his chin on his hand and grinned that sexy grin again. He had great lips, he reminded himself, and his teeth were perfect. His father's money had assured that years ago. "Come on, Clea," he said. "Would that be so bad?"

By degrees, her cold facade crumbled, and finally she laughed under her breath, then looked back down at the check. "All right," she said finally. "I'll have dinner with you."

He refrained from screaming "Yes!" and kept that smile turned on full volume. "I'll pick you up at seven."

"Tonight?" she asked. "I didn't mean . . ."

"Why wait? I happen to know you're off work tonight, and you'll need that money tomorrow. There are papers to sign, terms to work out. Besides, you wouldn't want to make a guy suffer anymore after he's waited this long, would you?"

Her smile faded, and he saw the uncertainty there. She was a tough one, he thought, but that was what excited him so much about her.

"All right," she said, but there was an air of coolness in her tone. "Tonight. Seven. I have to be home early, though."

He slid back the chair and stood up, his perfect teeth still flashing for her. "I'm gonna show you such a good time, Miss Clea, that you may not ever want to go home."

As he left the diner, he couldn't help noticing that her smile faded. A surge of excitement shivered through him again, as he planned his strategy for the evening. By the time he was finished with her, she'd be begging him for more.

And then he would be the one to be indifferent.

Clea couldn't escape the uneasy feeling that she was the prey for some terrible beast as she sat through dinner with Richard Mills, but she didn't want to feel that way, for she might have liked him if not for the leverage he had over her. Maybe she was being too hard on him, she thought. Maybe he really did just want to spend time with her, without a payoff at the end of the date.

He took her in his brand-new Lexus to the most elegant restaurant in town, one in which she could not have afforded a tip, much less an entree. The dinner lingered on for more than three hours, as he talked and talked and talked, and appeared interested in what little she revealed about herself.

When they finally left the restaurant and he asked if he could come in to her apartment for a nightcap, she had forgotten that uneasy feeling she'd had earlier and invited him in.

Her apartment was warm, so when he took off his jacket and dropped it on her couch, she didn't worry. She kept the heat too high, and there was no reason he shouldn't be comfortable, she told herself.

"I'll go get you a drink," she said, starting to the kitchen. "What would you like?"

He caught her wrist and stopped her. "I'm not thirsty," he said.

She looked into his eyes and recognized the lust there, for it was the same look Joe Don used to get when he looked at her, the same look John wore when he asked her to marry him. "Richard, I didn't ask you in here to—"

"Come on, Clea," he cut in, in a soft, urgent voice. "I dropped a wad on you tonight, not to mention writing your ticket for law school. Quit kidding yourself and stop playing these games."

She stiffened as he drew her closer, and she set her hand hard against his chest to hold him back. "What games?"

"These hard-to-get games. I've seen how you look at me. I know you want it as much as I do."

"Richard, I told you—" Her words were muffled as he closed his mouth over hers to quiet her.

She shook her head free and began to push him

away, but he only gripped her tighter. She tried to wrench free, but he swung her around and flung her down on the couch.

She screamed and tried to get up, but in an instant he was on top of her, his weight crushing her into the cushions. Her scream cut through the apartment, and he reared back and hit her with his fist. Blood began to seep from her lip, which throbbed with pain, but he only wrestled her harder.

"You . . . son . . . ofa . . . bitch . . . !" she screamed as he tore at her clothes, but she knew no one would come.

She felt his hand groping at his zipper, and knew without a doubt that he was too strong for her to fight. He was going to rape her.

A burst of adrenaline shot through her, and suddenly she thought of the gun she kept in the end table next to the couch. As he rose to release his zipper, she channeled all her energy into slipping out from under him long enough to reach the gun.

He grabbed her and tried to pull her back, but before he did, she managed to slide out the drawer and put her hand over the cold barrel of the pistol.

It's too little, not even big enough to do much damage, her mother had told her when she gave her the gun. *But it might scare somebody.*

He turned her back over, and she saw his readiness for her. He hadn't seen the gun, didn't know she had it, so he wasn't prepared when she held it between them and pulled the trigger.

His body went rigid for a moment, and he fell off of her, clutching his crotch. Blood began to dribble through his fingers, and she heard a muffled cry escape from his throat. "Ho . . . ly . . . shit . . ."

She got to her feet and stood over him, still holding

the gun in her trembling hands, watching him bleed.

"Bet you won't ever try that again, will you, you bastard?" she asked.

"Am . . . bulance . . ." he grunted. "Please . . ."

She stood over him for a moment longer, then finally, went to the phone and dialed 911.

The ambulance was there in ten minutes, and Richard Mills was taken to the emergency room where he was told that his "equipment" had been severely damaged for life. Clea had been right. He would never be able to try that again.

The police booked Clea for assault with a deadly weapon. Her mother had to come all the way from Beaut to bail her out, and she was suspended from school until the trial date.

It would be months before she would realize just how much of a turning point that one date with Richard Mills had been.

The first Clea heard of Richard's devoted, pregnant wife—a fact he had hidden each time she had seen him—was in the newspaper accounts of her alleged affair with him. The trial became even more of a sensational nightmare, as the prosecuting attorney dug up everything he could to condemn Clea and sanctify the name of the Mills family, which was prominent in Detroit society. There was a Mills on the Michigan supreme court, a Mills who was a former governor, a Mills who sat in the U.S. Senate. Richard's own father was a prominent attorney in Detroit, and his uncle sat on the board of directors of the University of Michigan. Clea, on the other hand, was the no-account stepdaughter of a Texas used-car salesman who had allegedly believed that Richard Mills would be her ticket to the top. When she realized he wasn't as interested as she hoped, she shot him for revenge.

The story played well, except for the cuts and bruises evident on Clea's face in her mug shots. Not only that, but one neighbor reported to have heard her screams that night before the gun went off. The jury took note of all of this, even if the general public did not.

Myrna and Shalimar appeared daily at the trials, propping up Clea and letting her know she wasn't alone. But on the third day, when the prosecutor began introducing all his "evidence" that Clea had had a long-running affair with the banker in exchange for his promise to finance her education, she felt the world closing in on her again.

Creative details came out for the world to see. Fellow workers testified to the roses she had on her windshield each day, the "secretive" phone calls at work, the cards with suggestive little messages inside. Then the prosecutor came up with bogus dates on which they had supposedly met at a sleazy motel Clea had never seen in her life, and witnesses who claimed to have seen them in compromising positions. She sat defeated and deflated as the world heard things about her she had never even imagined, and she had the miserable feeling that no one believed her testimony that she had never been out with Richard Mills before that night. When the trial ended that afternoon and she turned to her mother, she found that Myrna was gone.

Shalimar told her that her mother had been too upset and embarrassed by the evidence, and had had to leave.

"Personally, I'm proud as hell of you," Shalimar said as they waited for the verdict. "I never thought you had it in you to sleep with a married man for money."

"I did not sleep with him," Clea whispered viciously. "I had dinner with him, but I had no idea he was married."

Shalimar laughed and studied her fingernails. "And to shoot a guy in the balls . . . I love it."

"It was rape, Shalimar. I shot him out of self-defense."

"Runs in the family, I guess," Shalimar went on, fluffing her dark curls. "Driving men to tear off your clothes, I mean. Happens to me all the time. 'Course, I've never really wanted to shoot anybody for it. That's where we're different, I guess."

Miraculously, the jury came back with a verdict of not guilty on the grounds of self-defense, and for a moment Clea felt a mountain of worries fall off her shoulders. But the victory was short-lived: Her mother packed up and went back to Beaut without a word of good-bye, and soon after that, Clea got word that she had been dismissed from law school on ethical grounds, due to her alleged affair with the banker.

But the dismissal didn't make that much difference, since she didn't have the money for law school, anyway. She was broke, humiliated, and ruined, and she didn't have a clue to where to turn.

It was a week after that, when Clea was at the lowest point she'd ever reached in her life, that she got the call from Tiffany Donovan.

9

The sound of the rotary engine cutting the outer edge of the curve a mile away split the air, and Brandon Donovan raised his binoculars to his eyes and caught sight of the new model "THD" flying down the hill and tearing at 150 miles per hour through the hairpin curve that had been specially placed there to enhance the grueling test run. The driver he had on contract to test his cars—Ned Blackstone, a two-time Winston Cup winner who ate, drank, and breathed sports cars—had given him a list of flaws that morning, none of which was major but all of which needed to be attended to right away.

But Brandon wasn't satisfied that the prototype was that sound. He always liked to get a second opinion, and until this year, he'd had another hot-dogger under contract—Bill Barrett, one of the top racers in the country. But Bill had been killed last year after taking a turn a hair too wide while qualifying in Indianapolis.

"Steven's having more trouble with those corners and bends than Ned had," muttered Lawrence Henderson, who had been Brandon's chief styling engineer before he took over as president of Donovan Concepts. "Is it the car or . . ." His voice trailed off, as if he'd thought better of voicing that particular question, and Brandon dropped his binoculars and gave him a sidelong look.

"You can say it, Larry. Is it the car or the driver?"

Lawrence shrugged. "No offense, Brandon, but he's reckless, even if he is your kid."

Brandon considered Lawrence his most trusted colleague, not to mention his closest friend. He'd always had a lot of faith in Lawrence's judgment . . . so much, in fact, that when Brandon had wanted to spend more time on the THD, he'd turned most of his duties over to him. This enabled Brandon to remain CEO of the company but still "demote" himself to project chief over the THD so he could be involved with it from the ground up. Since his first days in the company, Brandon hadn't had this much fun being in the trenches. Without Lawrence's cool head and administrative skills and his way of shooting from the hip, Brandon couldn't have had so much freedom.

"Thanks for the tact, Larry," Brandon said. "But don't worry. He just wanted to drive the car. We don't have to carve his ideas in stone, but we could listen. He might have an idea or two."

"Waste of time if you ask me," Lawrence said. He pulled away from the fence and smoothed back his hair. Brandon smiled at his friend's vanity. For someone with the looks of George Hamilton, he sure worried about his appearance a lot. It was rare to see the man without full coat and tie, and even when they played golf, he'd never known Lawrence to sweat. "I already have Blackstone's list," he added, patting the report he'd put in his pocket earlier. "I doubt Steven has a lot to add."

"Oh ye of little faith," Brandon said with a grin. He turned back to the racetrack and realized that if anyone else had spoken that way of his son, he would have been offended. But the truth was that Larry was just as fed up with Steven as Brandon should have been, after his short-lived, volatile career at DC and his decision to quit without a moment's notice to pursue his dream of conquering the racetrack.

"Damn, the car looks good, though," Lawrence said, watching through the binoculars. He watched until the car was out of sight, then grinned at Brandon. "We're going to make a fortune on it."

"That's the plan," Brandon said, "and we'll have a hell of a lot of fun while we're doing it."

They started toward the track, where Steven would be passing momentarily, and for the thousandth time, Brandon wondered at the wisdom of letting his son give the prototype a test run. Secrecy was vitally important, and there had already been leaks attributed to Steven. Besides, it was standard procedure to have the cars test-driven by world-class racers, and Steven definitely didn't fit that bill. But he had won his share of races, and was going to attempt to qualify to run the Winston 500 in Talladega next month. He was on his way up. The facts that he was Brandon's son and had the money to pour into such a hobby, not to mention the sponsorship of Donovan Concepts, were his greatest qualifications.

They watched as the car blew past again, and Brandon peered through his binoculars as Steven took a turn too wide and sent the car into a skid. Seconds later, he righted it and kept going.

"Mmmm," was all that Lawrence said, but the monosyllabic sound was packed full of meaning.

Brandon dropped his binoculars and looked at

Lawrence. "Don't say it, Larry. I know what you're thinking."

"I'm just hoping he doesn't crash the car," Lawrence said. "He's just too inexperienced."

Brandon let out a heavy sigh and rubbed his eyes. "I know he is. But I feel like I should involve him in the company somehow. Someday he'll inherit all my stock, and he'll be calling the shots."

Lawrence's smile was something close to a smirk. "Never thought that Harvard education would prepare him for this, did you?"

"Hell no." Brandon braced his arms on the top of the railing separating them from the track, and watched his son and his prototype disappear behind the trees. "But his butt got kinda chapped when I wanted him to come into the company at entry level. Guess he had delusions of sitting in the president's seat or something. Damn, how'd he expect to run a company if he didn't know the workings of it from the bottom up? He didn't even get through his junior year of college, for God's sake."

"Things have changed, Brandon," Lawrence said. "Not like when we were young."

"Damn right." He propped his chin on his hand, and looked over at his dearest friend. They had known each other since their college days at M.I.T., and had both been second-generation Ford engineers. When Brandon's frustration with his limitations at Ford drove him to start his own company, he convinced Lawrence to come to work for him. Brandon had the vision and the perseverance to brainstorm such a venture, and Lawrence had the practical expertise to help execute it. "Did I ever tell you what my dad gave me on my sixteenth birthday?"

"Didn't he give you that Mustang you've got on the

fourth floor? I got one, too. All the Ford execs gave their sons cars on their sixteenth birthdays, didn't they?"

Brandon laughed. "Yeah, but my dad was different. He gave me that Mustang, all right, but it was in a box."

"In a box?" Lawrence's ample brows drew together in confusion. "What do you mean, in a box?"

"I mean, disassembled. Thousands of pieces that I had to put together myself."

"You're kidding."

"Nope." A nostalgic smile twinkled in his eyes, and Brandon rubbed his rough hand through the wind-tousled brown hair that needed a cut. "I worked on it the whole summer, and within two and a half months, I was driving that baby. That's why I'm displaying a Ford on the fourth floor. Every time I step off the elevator, it reminds me not to let myself get too far above the nuts and bolts."

Lawrence chuckled and gazed out over the track. In the distance, the prototype tore up a hill, zigzagging with every bend in the road. "What did you give Steven for his sixteenth?"

"Wanted to do the same thing," Brandon said, his smile fading. "But Tiffany wouldn't hear of it. Hell, she didn't even want me giving him an *assembled* Donovan. Not sporty enough. So he wound up with a Porsche. Totaled it six months later. Since then, he's had five others."

"Well, I'll bet the THD will be sporty enough for him."

"Yeah," Brandon said. "Ought to be. And when he gets tired of racing, maybe he'll give college another shot. Maybe by then he'll know enough to know he's got a lot to learn."

"You think he has the head to take your place when you retire?"

Brandon looked insulted. "Forty isn't exactly retirement age, you know. I've got a long way to go before I step down. But yeah, he has the head. He just needs a little motivation and a little humility. Neither of which are trademarks of his generation, but he'll learn his lessons just like we did. He'll just take a different road."

As he spoke, he watched the THD rounding the last bend toward them, slowing its speed like a plane making a smooth landing. Finally it came to a halt in front of them.

Steven got out, pulling off his helmet, and wiped the sweat from his brow. "That was great," he said, breathless.

Brandon rounded the car and took his clipboard from Lawrence. "We noticed you taking those corners a little bit rough. Any problems?"

"There might be too much understeer," Steven said, raking his long fingers through the ebony hair he had inherited from his mother.

"Might be?" Brandon asked. "You were the driver. Is there or isn't there?"

Steven's expression hardened. "There is, okay?"

Brandon made a note on his clipboard. "I'll have George check that out when I get back. Maybe we need to take another look at the A-arms."

"What else?" Lawrence asked.

Steven stood back and looked at the car, as if he could see the inner workings from the outside. "Did you lower the suspension mounts since I drove it last?"

"A couple inches," Lawrence said. "Why?"

"I thought so." Steven looked at his father, rubbing his beard as he spoke. "It squatted a little on acceleration, but dived when I hit the brakes."

Brandon looked at Lawrence, frowning. "Didn't Ned mention that, too?"

Lawrence nodded. "Yeah. We'll have to take another look."

They walked back toward the trailer that had transported the car. It was carefully covered and hidden so as not to give any of the media or other spies that might be lurking about, waiting for a picture of the new Donovan project, a chance to preview the unfinished model. The transport crew began preparing to reload the car and get it back to DC.

"Dad, it felt great other than those little things," Steven said. "Why can't you get it out in time for next year's models? I'm ready for one of my own."

Brandon laughed. "That would be rushing it a little. We still have several clinics lined up, and there are too many glitches. If I'm going to market a car in this price range, it has to be flawless. Besides, the anticipation won't hurt anyone. You can't rush perfection, Steve."

Steven shrugged. "Seems pretty close to perfection to me."

"Pretty close has never been good enough." Brandon patted his son on the back. "Wanna have lunch?"

Steven grinned. "Are we talking a corn beef hash on rye eaten in the car while you dictate letters over the phone?" Brandon gave him a guilty look, and Steven laughed. "Sorry. I can do better than that."

"I have to economize with my time if I'm going to get home in time for dinner tonight. It's Thursday. You'll be there, won't you?"

"I'm not sure." Steven unzipped his jacket as he reached his Porsche and, slipping out of it, tossed it into the passenger side.

"If you have nothing better to do, will we see you?"

"Maybe." Steven gave him his most charming twenty-year-old smile, the one that had the greatest effect on the women he dated—the ones whose hearts he broke on an hourly basis. As hard as Brandon had tried to instill in him a sense of commitment and loyalty, Tiffany insisted that his fickleness was just characteristic of his age and not his personality.

"I'd appreciate a report of your whole impression of the car on my desk this afternoon," Brandon said as he started to his own car. "I want to get started on the refinements before the clinic in Georgia."

"No problem," Steven said, but Brandon wondered if he would really have it in time. Usually he came up with excuses about secretaries being busy and his having to "think things over" more carefully. But Brandon learned to work that way with Steven. As long as his son wasn't actually a staff member, he supposed he couldn't hold the delays against him.

He felt good about the THD as he got into his own Donovan Executive, the top-of-the-line luxury car that his company had been producing since its inception fifteen years ago. This was the first time Donovan Concepts, or DC, as it had come to be called, had ventured into the sports car market. He had to admit, it was tempting to rush the car into the marketplace, but there had been too much hype about this car already. He wasn't about to come out with something the critics could tear apart.

Besides, he wouldn't have let his wife talk him into naming it after her—or at least her initials—if he hadn't expected it to be the best sports car in the world. Despite her pride over the gesture, however, Tiffany still referred to it as his "Yupmobile." He didn't know how many times he'd told her that the THD was not a car for yuppies. The advertising campaign they were planning would tell people, truthfully, that the car was

"For a New Generation of Millionaires." The average yuppy wouldn't be able to afford it.

Of course, if they didn't get all the bugs worked out, not even a yuppy would want it. The gull-wing doors had just recently been pulled from the design, and there were still problems with the windows, the cooling system, and the amount of space in the cockpit. They had a long way to go before the prototype could go into production.

He pulled out into the Detroit traffic, and immediately picked up his cellular phone. Damn, he thought, he needed an assistant. It had been three days since he let his previous one go after she'd had a run-in with Tiffany, and he'd been regretting it ever since. But disrespect for his wife was something that couldn't be tolerated, and when Tiffany told him what Edith had called her, well, what else could he have done?

Still, he wished personnel would hurry up and get him somebody reliable. He needed someone with him right now to jot notes as he returned phone calls, list orders to be carried out when they got back to the office, plan meetings he needed to call to get all the teams on the THD working together. He needed someone with a brain, someone who could field his ideas and point out problems he was too busy to see.

He punched in the number to his office, and his secretary picked up the phone. "It's me," he said. "What's up?"

"Hi, Brandon. You have a call from *Motor Trend,* and Mr. Fielding at the Department of Transportation returned your call, and your wife wants you to get in touch with her as soon as possible. She might be in her car."

"All right, Evelyn. Thanks. I'll be in in about thirty minutes."

He punched the End button to cut off the line, then dialed Tiffany's car phone. "Hello?"

Her voice always amazed him, for it had that Wellsley above-it-all quality of the debutantes who never would go out with him when he was younger. He supposed that was part of what had attracted him to Tiffany. She was the unattainable beauty who was out of his league. Even after all these years, he wasn't sure he was any closer to "attaining her" than he ever had been. He supposed he'd given up trying long ago. That superiority in her voice irritated him now, however, for he didn't like it directed at him.

"It's me, Tiffany," he said. "Did you call?"

"Darling, yes," she said, her tone growing the tiniest bit warmer. "I have some news for you."

"Let's hear it," he said, checking his watch and wondering how long he'd have before Fielding went to lunch.

"I have your new administrative assistant. Oh, Brandon, she's perfect."

He winced and raked his hand through his sandy hair, a habit that left it perpetually mussed. He hated it when Tiffany tried to pick his employees. It never worked out, and half the time he wound up making everybody mad by firing them. Of course, whenever he hired his own people, particularly women, Tiffany always found something wrong with them and some reason to fire them herself. He couldn't win, he thought, so he might as well allow Tiffany her input from the outset.

"Who is she?"

"Her name's Clea Sands," Tiffany said.

"Clea?" he asked. "Somebody actually named their child Clea?"

Tiffany laughed. "Don't you remember that woman who got kicked out of law school after that nasty trial?"

"No," he said. "What trial?"

"You know," Tiffany pressed. "She shot that guy in the crotch." He heard her laugh again, something she only resorted to when talking about others' misfortunes. "It was priceless, really, and she got off, but she still got kicked out of law school. And she happens to be looking for a job."

Brandon rolled his eyes and shook his head, and wished that Tiffany would get involved in one of her charities and leave the hiring and firing to him. "Honey, I'm really not interested in a woman who goes around shooting guys in their crotches. I've grown kind of attached to mine."

"So have I, darling," she said. "But yours is safe. Unless you force yourself on her, she won't pull that trigger. Seriously, Brandon, it really was self-defense. The jury even said so."

Brandon looked at his watch again and rounded a corner. "So what makes you think she'd be right for this job?"

"Because she's hungry," Tiffany said. "And she's smart. Oh, and she grew up in the car business. Her father owned a dealership or something, and she spent several years selling cars. Please, Brandon, I want you to at least meet her."

Brandon sighed and wondered if there was any way out of this, but finally he decided there wasn't. Tiffany was a very determined woman when she had her mind set on something. He pictured this Clea Sands as someone with a tight chignon and sour lips, someone who carried her six-shooter in a big purse and wore stockings that bagged around her ankles. Well, maybe that was for the best, he thought. Tiffany got jealous easily. If they eliminated the potential for jealousy right from the start, maybe he'd keep this assistant longer than he'd kept the last one.

"All right," he said with a sigh. "I guess I could give her a few minutes. I'm on the way back to the office now. Can you have her there, say, in an hour?"

"The sooner the better," Tiffany said. "I'll bring her myself."

Brandon pressed End and set the phone back on its stand, wishing he'd put her off until tomorrow. There was too much to do today, much more than he could handle alone, and no time for bullshit sessions. The aerodynamic flow profile on the THD should be ready today, he thought, and that was something he needed to concentrate on.

He didn't try to return any calls or make any plans, and instead, he gave himself a quiet moment. It wasn't very often that things were quiet in his life anymore, but that was all right, because it wasn't something he had expected in adulthood, anyway. He'd planned on a lot of children in his life, children of all ages running up and down the stairs, congregating in a homey kitchen beside a fireplace, eating cookies, and swapping school stories. That was how his family had been, but adulthood had dealt him another hand altogether.

It wasn't that he minded that they lived in a penthouse instead of a big house out in the country, and that Tiffany considered the kitchen a place where only the servants were supposed to be. He'd gotten used to her ways, her preferences, her tastes. That they weren't his own wasn't that important, for he spent most of his time at the office, anyway.

But he was still disappointed that they'd only had one

child. After Steven's birth so soon after their marriage, Tiffany had flatly refused to conceive again. The baby had done too much damage to her waistline, she'd said, and besides, it would be harder to travel and do all the things they wanted if they had more than one child.

So Brandon had put all the energy he would have expended on those other offspring into Steven, his only son. Everyone at Donovan Concepts knew how proud he was that his son was going to Harvard, but when he dropped out in his junior year in order to keep from flunking out, Brandon kept that news to himself. It was just a matter of time, he was sure, before Steven would abandon his racing passion and go back to school, and then he would turn his talents toward the company, regardless of how low his father expected him to start.

Brandon himself had gone in at the bottom, when his father had worked for Ford, and after engineering school, he learned the business from the assembly lines all the way to the fourteenth floor. Perhaps he shouldn't have been so lenient and flexible with his own son, Brandon thought, and Steven wouldn't expect so much today.

It would work out, though, as soon as Steven grew up a little bit and outgrew his wildness. He was sure Steven had the makeup to be a great leader, and he knew he had the ambition. It was just a matter of teaching him balance.

He pulled into the Donovan Concepts parking garage, then went into the lobby and waved at the receptionist in the middle of the floor, surrounded by current models of all the Donovan cars. "How's it going, Linda?"

Linda shrugged. "Hi, Brandon. I'm okay, I guess."

"Still getting married next week?"

"Yeah," the girl said, "if I don't kill his parents first."

"Hang in there," he said as he whizzed toward the elevators.

"Hey Brandon," she called after him. "Thanks for the gift."

Knowing she referred to the three-hundred-dollar check he'd sent her yesterday, he winked. "Yeah, enjoy it."

The elevator opened, and he stepped into the glass car and leaned back against the wall. As he passed each floor, he saw the intense work going on, as everyone, from secretaries to design engineers, went about the business of improving on the five models of Donovans already on the market.

Each floor represented another level of operation at DC. The second floor, which contained the marketing department, was decorated in burgundy and gray, and from the elevator, Brandon could see the futuristic life-size clay models of concept cars displayed there, most of which were so impractical that they'd never even reach the market.

The third floor, decorated with an old airplane relic that took up half of the front floor space, but demonstrated nicely the relationship between the aerodynamics of air flight and the aerodynamics of a Donovan ride, held a mix of design engineers and artisans, whose job it was to develop new styles and improve on old ones.

The fourth and fifth floors held several of the various engineering teams required to perfect everything from rear suspension to alternative fuel sources, and through the glass he saw his own first Mustang, his most prized exhibit. It reminded him of his childhood, and the pride he'd taken in building something from nothing. He wished he could give his son that same pride, but Steven had shown very little interest in being involved in designing the THD. It was only now that most of the work was done that he showed any interest at all. But designing it had brought back all of Brandon's youthful fervor, all his exuberance over going to work every day, all his excitement at what the future of Donovan Concepts held.

The elevator stopped at the sixth floor, where a life-size portrait of himself leaning against the first Donovan prototype filled the back wall.

Brandon stepped off the elevator and saw a cluster of engineers huddled around the water cooler, where much of the brainstorming took place from day to day.

"Hey Bruce," he called to one of them heading back to his office. "You got that baby home yet?"

"Yeah," the young engineer told him. "Note the bags under my eyes."

Laughing, Brandon went on, waving as he went past offices where men and women congregated around drafting tables and computers. One of his vice presidents fell into step with him. "Brandon, you got a minute to take a look at the new color my staff is proposing?"

Brandon took the color sample and gave it a cursory examination. "For which car?"

"Could go for all of them, but if you want it exclusively for the THD . . ."

"No, it's not flashy enough," he said. "Nice, though. Give it to Larry and tell him I like it for everything *except* the THD."

"Uh . . . that might be a problem. I've been trying to show it to him for three days, but I can't get in to see him."

"He's busy," Brandon said, just as he saw Lawrence stepping off of the elevator. "Look, I'll hand the sample to him right now and tell him I like it. Call him tomorrow and he'll see you."

"Thanks, Brandon," the VP said, punching the air in victory and turning back to his office.

Lawrence made his way to his office, and Brandon called across the floor, "Hey, old man. I need to talk to you."

Lawrence paused in the doorway and flashed him one of those Hamilton-like smiles that didn't look quite real. Brandon always kidded him that he belonged in Hollywood rather than Detroit.

"Take a look at this," Brandon said, tossing him the color sample. "I want it on all the new models next year."

Lawrence took it and gave it a glance. "Brandon, you can't free up your time to concentrate on your project if you keep letting those guys trouble you with details."

Brandon shrugged. "No problem. I was just delivering it to you. You're getting a reputation for being unapproachable. You should watch that, you know."

Lawrence seemed chagrined at the suggestion. "Brandon, when I took over here, we agreed that I had a style different from yours. I don't have time for every two-bit idea that crosses the mind of every engineer here."

"It's those two-bit ideas that make the difference between a Pinto and a Porsche," he said, punching his arm. "Lighten up, pal. Don't take yourself so seriously." He started across the floor to his own office, then swung back around, walking backward. "Hey, mark off some time for me first thing tomorrow morning. We need to put our heads together about a few things, okay?"

He noted the way Lawrence's eyes frosted, but it didn't bother him. The man was moody. Brandon had known that for years, and he'd learned to live with it. "Whatever you say."

"See you later."

Stopping outside his office, he picked up the messages his secretary had on the desk for him and flipped through them, mentally prioritizing them.

He went into his office and saw that the computer profile from yesterday's wind-tunnel test was waiting for him. Taking off his coat to reveal a beige golf shirt tucked into his khakis, he plopped down in his chair and picked up the profile.

The phone on his desk buzzed, and he pressed the speaker button and asked, "Yes, Evelyn?"

"Brandon, Mrs. Donovan is on her way up."

He smiled at the formal way she referred to his wife, and wondered again what difference it made to Tiffany what they called her. She had long ago insisted that everyone in the company, except for George and Lawrence, who had known her for years, speak to her in formalities. It was one of her quirks, but he guessed it wasn't that big of a deal. "Already?" He checked his watch and saw that she was twenty minutes early. The thought irritated him, but he shoved that irritation aside and rubbed his temples. "All right, Evelyn. Tell her to come on in when she gets here."

Clea tried to absorb the sights of Donovan Concepts as she followed in the wake of Tiffany's perfume. The woman breezed past the receptionist, ignoring her "Good morning, Mrs. Donovan." Clea smiled at the girl, but noted the way she rushed to pick up the phone, as if warning those on upper levels that the boss's wife was in the building.

"These damn elevators are never here when you need them," Tiffany said as they reached the glass enclosure. "Pull your hair over your shoulder . . . yes, like that. And don't smile when you meet him. You look too young when you smile."

"I know how to make a first impression," Clea said quietly. "I didn't just ride in on a hay truck."

"A Texas first impression is somewhat different than a Detroit first impression," Tiffany said, smoothing back her hair as she caught her reflection in the chrome surrounding the elevator.

"Texans can be as professional and cultured as those from Michigan, Tiffany."

The use of her first name seemed to irritate the woman, and she turned her cool eyes to Clea. "It would be wise to take my advice without arguing at every turn," she said in a voice as sweet and calm as if they were talking about the weather. "Don't forget where your checks are coming from."

The glass doors of the elevator opened, and biting back a retort, Clea followed her on. Since Tiffany had picked her up an hour ago, Clea had faced one criticism after another. First Tiffany had made her change her hair, which she'd originally worn in a French twist. Tiffany said it was too severe and that Brandon liked hair. She had made her wear it down, a style that Clea had always rejected when she was in a business setting. It reminded her of Stanley Supleman's suggestion to wear low-cut dresses to sell more cars. But even as she felt the repulsion at looking so bimbo-esque, she realized she had no right to feel that way. She was taking money to play the part of seductress, after all.

Then, as they'd driven across town, she had listened to Tiffany extol her virtues to Brandon on the phone, and she had bitten her tongue at the part about shooting Richard Mills in the crotch. Tiffany had a special talent for making things sound sleazy, she had thought, even when she was trying to convince Brandon that Clea was the busy executive's dream.

Absently her eyes took in the various floors as the elevators passed, and she noticed a hubbub of activity on every level. Because Tiffany had punched a special code into the elevator's computer, it didn't stop for anyone else. When they reached the top floor, they stepped off, and again, Tiffany floated past the workers, ignoring their greetings and never making eye contact with any of them. The huddle of people at the water cooler seemed to disperse as they approached, and those chatting in the halls disappeared into their offices as Tiffany made her way through, with Clea on her heels.

They reached the executive area, where double oak doors with a sign reading Brandon Donovan, CEO, closed off Brandon's office. Across the way, another elegant office sat with its door opened, and a man got up and came to the door. The first genuine smile she had ever seen on Tiffany's face brought it to life, and Clea wondered if she was a consummate actress or just the moodiest individual she'd ever met.

"Tiffany, what brings you here?" the man asked, kissing her hand with all the charm of a French prince.

"I came to see Brandon," she said. "I have someone for him. You know, as his assistant?"

The man lowered Tiffany's hand and gave Clea a once-over. "Yes. I think she might do nicely."

Clea's face reddened at his intimate scrutiny, and she wondered just what they did look for in assistants here. Was it the size of her brain or the size of her breasts? Would she be a part of the DC team, or the DC harem?

Since she hadn't been introduced, she extended her hand. "I'm Clea Sands."

He took her hand in his, and she felt that it was too soft, too pampered, and his grip was almost condescending. Yet he was handsome in a Lyle Wagner sort of way, a little too good-looking, too groomed, and too polite. "Good luck, dear. I know he'll like you. He has exquisite taste in women."

She saw the amused looks pass between Tiffany and Lawrence, and she wondered if the comment had something to do with the abusive behavior that Tiffany had described in Brandon. Perhaps Tiffany wasn't the only one who hated him. If he was truly unlikable, she thought, it would make her deception easier. The physical part of her job, however, might be more difficult.

Neither Tiffany nor the man volunteered his name or position, so she glanced at his door and read the sign that said, Lawrence Henderson, President.

Tiffany turned around to the secretary sitting nearest Brandon's office. Without a word of greeting, she said, "Tell him I'm here."

"He knows, Mrs. Donovan," the older secretary said with a placating smile. "He said to go right in."

Tiffany touched Lawrence's hand and said, "Good to see you, darling." Then to Clea, "Wait right here for a moment."

Clea waited as Tiffany fluttered into Brandon's office, no doubt preparing him for meeting her. For a moment she thought of running away as far and as fast as she could. It wasn't too late. She wasn't in too deep yet.

But then she remembered her father and Joe Don and John and Richard, all the men who had used her and intimidated her. She thought of all they had cost her. She thought of all the destroyed dreams, the massacred hopes.

And instead of running, she held her head higher, and prepared to do what was expected of her.

Brandon looked up as Tiffany flew in, the scent of her perfume wafting around her like a pleasant breeze. As always he got up and went around his desk. "Hello, darling," she said, popping a kiss on his cheek.

"Hi, honey." He smiled as he looked her over, relishing the fact that she looked beautiful, though he knew what that beauty cost him. The crimson color of her suit looked fabulous with her dark, full-bodied hair grazing her shoulders, and those red, flawless lips. Her eyes still distracted him, for they still held that deep, aloof quality that had so enchanted him years ago, that quality that made her seem as if she had a secret that gave her some kind of edge, a secret she would never disclose even to those she loved the most. To this day, he couldn't say that he had learned it yet.

"Brandon, I've got the woman outside, and before you invite her in, I want to tell you to please keep your mind open. She's quite a catch, and I'm rather proud of myself for finding her."

He sighed and went back around his desk. "Tiffany, I appreciate your trying to help. I really do. And I'll give her as much of a chance as I would anyone personnel sent me," he said. "Go ahead and bring her in so I can talk to her."

Tiffany went out, and he looked back down at the printouts on his desk. He had barely had the chance to read the first line before she sailed back in with her candidate.

The woman was too pretty, he noted instantly. He needed a powerhouse, not an empty cottage. What must Tiffany be thinking?

He was struggling to find a nice rejection that would waste the least of his time without hurting Tiffany's feelings—since she obviously didn't intend to let him conduct the interview alone—when the woman smiled at him.

Instantly, that smile struck him, for it was confident yet innocent, and it had a sweet, sexy air that disturbed him more than he wanted to admit. He looked from her to his wife and frowned. Had Tiffany even looked at her? As jealous as she'd always been, did she really want him working side by side at least twelve hours a day with a woman who could have put Kim Basinger to shame?

Tiffany beamed as she made the introduction. "Brandon, this is Clea Sands."

Clea, Brandon thought, coming slowly to his feet and stepping around his desk. The name sounded like something a hooker would make up. No self-respecting, intelligent woman would have a name like Clea. He reached for her hand, shook it quickly, then let it go.

"It's nice meeting you," Clea said, her voice containing a husky quality that disturbed him even more. "I've followed your climb since your Ford days. When I was working in a dealership, we used to fight over the Donovan demos. It's the best car I've ever driven. Unfortunately, I haven't been able to afford one."

Surprised at her forthrightness, since she didn't look like she had any brains at all under all that hair, he cleared his throat and cast his wife an annoyed look. "Well . . . I suppose Tiffany has told you a little about the job?" he asked in a lackluster voice, gesturing for her to sit down.

Clea lowered herself into the chair next to Tiffany's, as Brandon went back to his own. He noted as he sat down that she was dressed quite tastefully. Her dress, though inexpensive, was tailored and professional, and not at all provocative. Still, a lot of women could dress for success. It didn't mean she had anything under that blonde mane of hers.

"Yes," Clea said, leaning forward and looking into his eyes in a way that demanded his full attention. "I was a little concerned about taking a secretarial job when I was at the top of my class in law school . . ."

"The top of your class?" Brandon asked. "Really?"

"Yes," she said, lifting her chin. "Another year and I would have taken the bar exam. I'm not really interested in a gofer job, Mr. Donovan."

He studied her over his steepled fingers. "This is hardly a gofer job. And it's not a secretarial position, either. In fact, this job is easily one of the most important jobs in this company. At least as far as I'm concerned."

Clea sat back and cocked her head, her eyes—which were guarded, though riveted on his every word—holding him captive. "I'd like to hear more."

He glanced at his wife, again wondering why in the world Tiffany would want to thrust him together with someone who looked like a centerfold in a men's magazine. "Well, it's a very demanding job. Whoever fills it will have to be capable of doing almost everything I do . . . sometimes more. It requires extremely long hours . . . sometimes fifteen or sixteen hours a day. There will be a lot of travel, a lot of ulcer-provoking problems that come up, a lot of missed meals, and a hell of a lot of stress. I don't believe in sugar-coating things, Miss Sands. I don't have the time to waste on someone who'll quit when the going gets tough."

"I'm not a quitter, Mr. Donovan," she said. "I've come as far as I have despite great personal obstacles."

"Looks to me like you haven't come anywhere except

to a dead halt," he said. "I don't watch the news, and if I read about your trial in the paper, it didn't register. But my wife tells me you got thrown out of law school for shooting someone."

She seemed undaunted, and he could see that she was used to defending herself against rumors and accusations. "I protected myself, Mr. Donovan. Just as anyone else would have done."

Despite his reluctance to like her, he had to admit he did. She was tough and assertive, and he could almost see her pulling that gun on that weasel who tried to rape her. "Still, I don't think many people realize just how grueling a day of work with me can be. I don't have time for someone who can't keep up."

"I can keep up," Clea said. "I worked three jobs when I was in college to put my former husband through law school, and I still graduated summa cum laude. I know what it means to work hard."

He had to admit she was impressive, but he still couldn't figure his jealous wife not being jealous of her. It didn't add up, unless Tiffany had finally outgrown her claws. As he considered this, it occurred to him that, except for her run-in with Edith, she hadn't shown those claws in quite some time.

"Do you have a résumé with you?" he asked Clea.

Clea reached into her small briefcase and pulled one out. "I think you'll find everything you need there."

He nodded and stood up, dismissing her. "All right. I promise to read it over and get back to you, maybe for another interview. The job pays pretty well, so I don't need to tell you that a lot of other people are vying for it."

"A lot of other people weren't handpicked by the boss's wife," Tiffany said, winking at Clea.

Clea didn't react as he'd expected. Instead, she came to her feet and reached out for his hand. "Mr. Donovan, I don't want you to hire me because your wife likes me. I want you to hire me because I'm the best person you're going to find for this job. I'm intelligent, I'm a hard worker, and I know a lot about the automobile business already. I realize there's a lot more to learn, but I'm a fast learner."

Brandon looked into her eyes, and saw that, despite the confusing blend of colors and the enchanting quality of their depth, they were bright with purpose and a rare integrity. Still, they had that same aloofness that had attracted him to Tiffany . . . and they were just as guarded as Tiffany's had been as she stared up at him, waiting for his answer. "I'll take all that into consideration," he said.

"I do appreciate your taking the time to see me," she said, starting for the door. "I hope to hear from you soon."

Brandon watched as she left the room, his mind whirling, and finally he turned back to his wife, who seemed to watch his face with intense interest.

"Didn't I tell you she was a catch?"

"She seems more than adequate, but I'm surprised that you'd want me working so closely with her."

"Oh, because she's gorgeous? Don't worry, Brandon. My jealous days are over. If you were going to cheat on me, you'd have done it by now. Heaven knows the *crème de la crème* has come after you." She stood on her toes and pressed a kiss on his lips, and he felt something flutter down to where he reacted most strongly to her. "I want you to have someone who'll make your job easier so you can come home earlier to me each day, darling, and I think she's the one who can do it. Hire her, darling. I really like her."

Brandon still didn't make any promises. "I'll think about it," he said.

But it wasn't until that night, when he finally got home from the office, that he began to think about it again. He had read Clea's résumé carefully, and had immediately ordered the private detectives he hired from time to time to do a check on Clea in case there was some skeleton in her closet that would suggest she could be a spy for a competing company. The initial reports he'd gotten back late that day had left him duly impressed by her credentials, despite the scandal she'd endured lately. She seemed like someone who didn't easily waver from her goals, and he needed someone like that. Still, he couldn't quite get past her looks.

Women who looked like Clea generally made a living with their looks. They became models or actresses, or they sold cosmetics. They didn't work in think tanks, and they didn't sacrifice sleep to keep up with the demands of the day. His instinct was to tell Tiffany no, that Clea wasn't what he was looking for. But it was always hard saying no to Tiffany. It was the one thing he had never become good at.

He went into the bedroom to shed his coat and look for his wife, but she wasn't there. And then he caught her scent, cool and sensuous, and shamefully expensive, and he turned and saw her waiting in the doorway leading to her dressing room. "I thought you'd never get home, darling," she said.

She had bought a new negligee, and while it was long and flowing, its transparency left little to the imagination. She was trying to manipulate him, he thought instantly, for she never tried to seduce him unless she wanted something. He'd seen it so many times that it had little effect on him anymore. "Tell me, darling. Did you think about Clea?"

"I read her résumé."

She grinned as his eyes swept the length of her. "And what did you decide?"

"I decided not to decide," he said.

Her face fell dramatically, and she dropped her hands to her side, almost spilling the glass of brandy. "Oh, darling, don't tell me that. I was feeling so proud of myself for helping you."

She came closer, brushed her breasts against his chest, and began to unbutton his shirt. He stopped her hands and gave her a cold look. Manipulation was the biggest turn-off he could think of, but she hadn't figured that out yet. The last time she'd done this it had been for that little villa in Paris. The time before that, the yacht. This time it was Clea.

Pushing his anger aside, he dropped a chaste kiss on her lips and looked into those onyx eyes that photographed so well. Long ago he'd stopped hoping for some vulnerability in those eyes. He'd learned to accept that about his wife. "Tiffany, we haven't even had dinner yet."

"Can't dinner wait?" she asked.

"But isn't Steven coming?"

"He couldn't make it," she said, pulling his shirt out of his pants, "so I thought we'd have dessert first."

With a coolness he hated, but couldn't seem to help, he grazed her lips. Why couldn't he take advantage of this little performance, he asked himself, and turn on even the slightest bit? Years ago, he couldn't get enough of her. But something had changed. Was it her, or him?

After all these years, she still had a terrific body. Liposuction hadn't hurt matters any. Who was he to complain? He liked her body, but not as much as she liked it herself.

"So let's talk some more about Clea," she said, sliding her hands up his chest and circling a fingertip over his nipple.

"I told you, I haven't decided about her."

"You're evading," she whispered. "I hate it when you evade."

"And you're obsessing."

She dropped her hands to her sides and stepped back. "Obsessing? Darling, is that really how seriously you take my opinion? If I have strong convictions about something, I'm obsessing?"

"No," he said. "I just don't like feeling like you're trying to manipulate me into giving you what you want, for God only knows what reason. It's my decision."

"Fine," she said, picking up her brandy glass again and taking a bigger gulp. "Just go on working every waking moment, doing the job of four people. Go on trying to do everything yourself, because you're too busy to even think rationally about hiring anyone. And you say I'm obsessing."

She raked her fingers upward through her hair and let it fall in soft cascades around her face. Pouting, she came closer again. "You don't take me seriously. Clea's the best person you're going to find, and you know it. And you'd hire her in a second if I hadn't been the one to bring her to you."

"That's not true."

"Then prove it." Her hand lowered to his belt, and she began unbuckling it. Again, he stopped her hand.

"Come on, Brandon," she whispered, slipping her hand inside his pants. "Prove that I count for something."

"Prove it by pretending that this little show is because you want me, or because you want me to hire Clea?"

"Both," she said, setting one foot on her vanity stool and sliding the filmy fabric up her thigh. He watched her move again, watched that hand slide up her smooth leg, her head arching back, her eyes smoking. He wondered how long it had been since she'd done anything like this, and he realized it must have been two years. Usually she was too tired or too busy or too aloof for him. Brandon had the same desires as any other healthy man, but he'd learned to control them long ago. Despite how she thought she was making him feel, he felt next to nothing.

Suddenly, it didn't matter if he hired a lobotomy patient with a background as a stripper to work as his assistant, as long as he didn't have to endure this controlling game of hers any longer.

"All right, Tiffany, you can stop the theatrics," he said. "I'll hire her."

The smile creeping across Tiffany's full lips, and her sudden, appeased withdrawal, made whatever he'd promised worth it. Mission accomplished, he thought sadly. Once again, she'd gotten what she wanted, and as he'd suspected, it wasn't him at all.

"You will, really?" Tiffany asked.

"Yes," he whispered.

"Oh, Brandon, I love you," she said, surprising him since he couldn't remember the last time he'd heard it. "And I've had Cook make your favorite tonight. Cornish game hen, made with your mother's recipe . . ."

He didn't have much appetite, for her or the hen, but he couldn't pinpoint what would satisfy the hunger that had been growing in his soul.

And as she glided out of the room, he followed. He forced his way through dinner and Tiffany's small talk, and tried to hold off his desire to bury himself in work as she lingered through dessert, putting brandy away like it was Kool-Aid.

Maybe they needed counseling, he thought, to get some feeling back into their marriage. Maybe he was the one who needed to do some adjusting, some trying, some rejuvenating.

Tomorrow he would try to come up with a plan, he thought, because he didn't know how much longer he could go on like this. He was committed to his wife, but he just didn't know if he loved her anymore.

10

It was a done deal, as Joe Don used to say, and the moment Clea hung up from Tiffany's call, she sank onto her bed and wondered if she had the stomach to pull this off. She'd never seduced anyone before . . . never even wanted to. Especially not a married man.

Feeling heavy with the weight of the task ahead, Clea went to her closet and searched through it for the right thing to wear on her first day. The sooner she seduced him, the sooner she could collect her money, finish law school, and get on with her life.

So should she wear a low-cut short dress and bend over a lot? Tears sprang to her eyes, and she told herself that she wasn't hurting anyone except a man who probably deserved everything that was coming to him.

She pulled out a spandex dress that Shalimar had given her for Christmas last year. It was skin tight and way too revealing, and Clea had never worn it. She wondered if it was something she should risk wearing tomorrow.

Again, she sank onto her bed and thought about how

she didn't really want to be caught ten feet from her door in that dress. It wasn't her, and if she wore it, she'd be a nervous wreck all day. Shalimar was the actress, not Clea. But then Shalimar wouldn't have been able to land the job in the first place.

Take it slow, Tiffany had said, otherwise he'd fire her. He was a faithful husband. That was the problem.

Clea laughed under her breath, knowing that her bitterness was a little too obvious these days, and told herself that there wasn't a man alive who didn't cheat on his wife. Tiffany just hadn't learned that yet. He probably had a cheerleader stashed in every closet and a bimbo or two already on his staff.

She lay back on the bed, still clutching the dress, and thought about the offices she'd seen that afternoon. They were plush and busy and exciting, just the kind of place she would have loved to work, under different circumstances. She didn't like going in the back door to do Tiffany's dirty work. She'd rather be herself, make a contribution.

She tossed the black dress aside and took out one of her business suits hanging at the back. She hadn't worn it since she'd stopped working for the dealership in Beaut. It was coral colored and attractively tapered, and the white silk blouse she wore with it was conservative, yet alluring.

Torn between wanting to be taken seriously as an employee, and wanting to get this filthy job over with, she sat back on the bed and looked from one outfit to the other. Maybe the suit would be best for the first day, she thought, until she could feel him out and see if he was the kind of man who would work side by side with a woman in a skin-tight dress every day. If he had any class, it would embarrass him, and he wouldn't have time for it. But she didn't have much faith in that.

Growing impatient with herself, she tossed the dress aside and decided once and for all on the suit. Tiffany may think it was too conservative, but if Clea was going to be the one to bring Brandon Donovan down, she wanted him to know he'd been brought down with class.

Later that night, she crawled into bed and lay there staring at the ceiling and found that sleep was as elusive as the dreams she had tried to conquer. It was her damnable conscience—the same conscience that had made her wait for sex with John until she was married, the same conscience that had made it impossible for her to see Richard Mills on his terms. It would fade more as time went on, she assured herself. And one day, like Clyde and Joe Don, she wouldn't have to deal with it at all.

Until then, she could grow used to sleepless nights. It was a small price to pay, after all, for getting her life back on track.

11

Brandon's office door was open when she got to work the next morning, and Evelyn, his secretary, told her to go in. Pausing in the doorway, she knocked tentatively.

Brandon didn't look up. "Your supplies are on that table over there."

Slightly chagrined at the cold greeting, Clea stepped inside the office and set down her briefcase, then glanced from Brandon to the oak conference table he referred to. That he was cold was no real surprise to her, for Tiffany had warned her at that first meeting. He was cruel, heartless, and self-centered, she'd said. Steeling herself, she decided not to let him intimidate her.

"What's the matter?" he asked, still not looking away from the monitor on his desk, into which he was typing numbers furiously, though he stood as if at any moment he would break and run. "You do know how to work a laptop, don't you?"

Clea reminded herself that she held the ace in this game. "Of course. It's no different from a regular PC, is it?"

The telephone buzzed, and he snapped his hand over the button that turned the speaker on. "Yeah." His other hand didn't miss a beat as he continued punching numbers into his computer.

"Brandon, it's Lawrence on line one. He's at the plant and wants to know—"

"Tell him we're on our way over. We'll be there in ten minutes."

The woman on the speaker laughed. "Brandon, it'll take you twenty to get there, at least."

"Tell him ten so he'll wait," Brandon said. "You know how impatient he is."

Clea took a quick inventory of the supplies he'd laid out for her on the table: the laptop computer, a stack of legal pads, a full Rolodex, a tape recorder, and a thirty-five-millimeter camera. "Where's my office going to be?" she asked.

For the first time since she'd walked in, he looked up at her, and she was certain it was amusement she saw in his eyes. "Right here, kiddo. You're my official sidekick, didn't you know that?"

"Here?" Clea looked around at the huge, elegantly appointed office—the antique desk he worked at, the sofa against the wall, the polished table surrounded by leather chippendale chairs. There was no place to stash a box of tampons or extra pencils, no place to kick off her shoes and relax when there was a lull. But it shouldn't matter anyway. She wasn't going to be there that long. "We're going to share this office?"

"Share?" Brandon threw his head back and laughed aloud. "That's pretty good."

She thought of snapping back at him that she didn't like being laughed at, but she thought better of it. There was plenty of time to turn the joke back on him.

"I don't intend to *share* my office with anyone. But as my assistant, you'll be here with me a lot of the time. It's your job to be my shadow, to anticipate my every thought and act on my every order."

"Hmmm," she said. "And we don't even have a marriage license."

For a moment he stood still, a moment that Clea imagined would be very rare, and an appreciative grin stole across his face. "I have a wife," he said. "Right now I need a right-hand man. You're it. Now get your coat."

"I'm going with you?"

"Yep. Grab the laptop, something to write on, and the camera. Hope you have your walking shoes on."

She looked uneasily at the heels she wore and wished she had time to run home and change. He was at the door before she'd gathered the things. And as she picked up what he had told her she'd need and followed him out, she told herself that she'd been crazy to worry about seducing him on the first day. At this pace, she'd be lucky to get him to look at her more than twice.

But she couldn't suppress the soft smile breaking across her face as they reached the elevator. She didn't have a clue what the day would hold, but she was certain that it wouldn't be boring.

She was good. He had to hand it to her. Brandon glanced at Clea's reflection in the window of the prototype Lawrence was inspecting after a few changes had been made, and he couldn't help chuckling under his breath at the way she struggled to keep up with him. As hard as he'd pushed her today, she'd held her own.

Damn it.

He watched a strand of tawny hair slip from where

she'd piled it in a loose bun on top of her head, and realized that Tiffany had been right. There was more to this Clea woman than fluff, he thought. She had brains and stamina and an ability to concentrate on the tiniest details. But her best recommendation was her ability to follow his own sometimes fragmented thought patterns, something he hadn't found in many other employees.

"George suggested trying to lighten it a bit for better performance," Lawrence was saying, "but he's had his team working on it, and nobody can come up with anything else."

"If we could just shave off ten or fifteen pounds, it would make all the difference," Brandon said. "But we're already at the barest minimum."

"So was the RX-7."

Brandon glanced at Clea over his shoulder, shooting her a look that asked where in the hell that observation had come from.

Clea looked up from the clipboard she jotted Brandon's notes on. "Don't you remember 'Operation Gram Per Head'? Mazda's attempt to shave off the weight of the RX-7?"

Brandon's frown slowly faded. "That was at least ten years ago. Didn't they mandate that each engineer had to find one gram of weight that could be cut out?"

"Mmm-hmmm," Clea said, dropping the camera. "They took a prototype apart piece by piece and laid all the pieces out in a big room."

"I remember something about that," Lawrence said. "The engineers went from piece to piece trying to decide where they could replace steel with alloy materials."

"And just looking for any expendable weight," Clea added.

Brandon's frown cut deeper into his forehead, and he

stared at her as if he'd just seen her for the first time. "How did you know about all this? You couldn't have been selling cars then."

"No," she said, "but I read a lot. My stepfather always had car magazines around the house. And later the dealership I worked for had an imports division, and I sold RX-7s. I believe in doing my homework."

Brandon didn't quite know what to say to that, so he turned back to Lawrence, who was studying the car pensively, turning Clea's suggestion over in his mind. "What do you think?"

"It's worth a try," Lawrence said. "God knows we're bound to shave off something that way."

"Call a meeting for tomorrow and we'll plan out the steps," Brandon said. "We could award the engineer who saves us the most a free car. Maybe even one of the first THDs." Growing warm, he slipped out of his coat and started back toward the office part of the building. "It's almost ten. We have a board meeting in half an hour. Clea, fax those letters I dictated in the car back to HQ, and call Evelyn to get my messages. I have to stop by marketing, but I'll be at the car before you finish." He reached into his pocket and tossed his keys to her.

She caught them in the air, and the look in her eyes spoke of victory.

"Good catch," he said as he started away. He was in the elevator before he let the smile overtake his face.

12

Tiffany Donovan tapped her long, silk finger-nails on the telephone receiver she held to her ear while she paced the apricot carpet on the floor of her bed-room. "It's after ten," she said, "and I can't help thinking that's good. He didn't work that late with Edith."

The voice on the other end of the phone was deep with boredom. "Of course he did, darling. Otherwise you and I never would have had time to be together."

"Well, not all that much. Besides, Edith didn't look like Clea Sands."

"Do you think your plan could have worked this quickly?"

Tiffany went to the huge window overlooking the city, and confronted her reflection there. She was still beautiful, even if she did have to work at it more than she used to. "Well, I'll know soon enough. I told her to call me the moment she got home tonight. I doubt if she's gotten him into bed yet," she said, rubbing a smudge off the glass with the sleeve of her kimono. "But that doesn't mean it hasn't crossed his mind."

"I don't know," the voice said. "Brandon has a one-track mind, and he's not easily swayed on anything. My bet is that they're just working." He paused for a moment, and his voice dropped to a more intimate pitch. "It's going to take time, darling, but you know it'll be worth it. I miss you."

"When can I see you again?" she asked, bringing her other hand to clasp the phone, as if he could feel the gentleness passing through the line.

"Tomorrow," he said. "I have a meeting near the Westin at ten. Can you get us a suite there and be waiting for me afterward?"

In the glass, Tiffany saw the way her eyes became effervescent with the thought of being with him, and she cursed herself for being that vulnerable. She liked being on top, but somehow, ever since they'd begun their affair, she'd been like a sick kitten craving his attention.

"I'll be there," she whispered. "I'll leave the suite number on your machine."

She could almost hear his smile as he breathed into the phone. "I can't wait, darling. Wear the teddy I gave you last week. I want to take it off of you."

A crimson heat tingled through Tiffany's body, and she smiled. "You're the most exciting thing that's ever happened to me," she whispered.

His laughter rippled over the line. "Wait until tomorrow," he said. "Good-bye, darling."

Tiffany hung up the phone and caught her reflection again. Her hair brushed her shoulders in a gentle, rich ebony wave, and her eyes looked serene and sexy. It was an effect she'd worked hard at, and the facelift last year hadn't hurt anything. Brandon had told her not to get it, that she didn't need it, but she had known that he would love to see her face withered and wrinkled so that other men wouldn't notice her. Brandon had never been comfortable with the way she turned men's heads.

She, on the other hand, had thrived on it.

And she could still turn them. But there was only one man she wanted to please now, and she would do almost anything for him.

The phone rang, startling her as if she had been caught with her wayward thoughts, and she brought it back to her ear. "Yes?"

"Tiffany? It's Clea."

Tiffany noted the fact that the girl had used her first name again, a liberty she had not offered her, but she let it go. "Did you just get home?"

"Yes," Clea said. "It was a grueling day. We worked until ten, and I swear I don't think the man even noticed that it was dark until then. He could have gone all night."

"Speaking of going all night," Tiffany cut in impatiently, "what kind of progress did you make?"

Clea hesitated. "Well . . . none. To tell you the truth, I was so busy, I hardly thought about it all day. And he certainly didn't. His head was always buried in paperwork, designs, correspondence . . . or he was on the phone . . ."

Tiffany's neck reddened, and she touched it with her crimson fingernails. "Are you telling me that nothing happened at all? Not even a look? Not even a little flirtation?"

Clea sighed. "Tiffany, you said yourself that he wouldn't be easy. I'm working on it, okay? You can't expect it to all happen the first day."

Tiffany flung herself away from her image in the mirror and went into her bathroom, where her vanity table was lit with professional-quality lighting. Examining her image in that mirror, she touched a faint line beneath her eye. Not so bad, she thought. Christie Brinkley had more wrinkles than she had.

"It's your clothes," Tiffany said, pouring a dot of perfume on her finger and touching it to the swell of each breast. "When I came by the office this morning, I realized instantly that you had dressed too conservatively today. You should have worn your skirt shorter, or your neckline lower. And don't wear your hair up like that again."

She heard Clea issue a long breath. "Your husband is a man with class, Tiffany. He isn't going to take the bait if I look like I'm trying to lure him. Besides, I don't exactly have a sexy wardrobe. I've been in law school, not modeling school."

"Then I'll have some things sent over to you tomorrow."

Again, Clea hesitated. "That won't be necessary. I can pick out my own clothes."

"There isn't time for you to wait until you have a weekend to shop, Clea. Brandon likes to work weekends, too. I'll buy some things tomorrow and have them delivered to your apartment. And damn it, I expect you to wear them."

Clea could hear Tiffany's chagrin over the line. Finally, she whispered, "Whatever you say, Tiffany."

"And make a strategy tonight. Before you go back there tomorrow, I want you to have some moves planned. Innocent touches. Close brushes. Flirtatious comments. Let him know you're open to the idea of an affair. You need a strategy, Clea. Do you understand me?"

"Yes," Clea said.

The front door opened, and Tiffany heard Brandon

rustling in. "He's home. Call me tomorrow," she said, then hung up.

Clea felt completely powerless as she stared at the telephone she still held in her hand. She began to regret that she had ever gotten into this in the first place.

The truth was, today had been the best day she'd had in months, since before her fatal date with Richard Mills. Brandon had expected the world from her, and she had delivered. Unless she had read all his signals wrong, he had been happy with her work.

But whom was she kidding? she thought, kicking off her shoes and falling to her bed. She wasn't supposed to make him happy with her work. She was supposed to make him miserable with her body.

But he hadn't even given her a suggestive look today. She could have been a sixty-year-old grandmother, and he wouldn't have treated her any differently. All she had gotten from him was respect.

For the life of her, she didn't know why that satisfied her so much more than what she was getting paid for.

Brandon Donovan acted like a husband—someone else's. He acted like a man who had turned off the "roving eyes" and flirting mode long ago. Was his fidelity genuine, or was he just good at hiding what most men couldn't?

She didn't know, but she decided that she'd worry about it tomorrow. She pulled herself up off the bed, and took the phone again. Slowly, she dialed and put it to her ear.

"Hello?"

"Mama?" Her voice was soft, cautious, for she never knew these days just how her mother would treat her.

"Yes?" Her mother's answer was crisp, curt.

"It's me, Clea. I just . . . wanted to see how things are."

"Things are just fine, Clea," she said. Her Southern accent sounded like home, for Clea didn't hear it much in Detroit. Hers was almost gone . . . she'd learned in law school that pretty women with Southern accents weren't taken seriously.

But that warmth that she had imagined disappeared as her mother went on. "Thank you for calling, but I have something in the oven."

Clea's heart sank, and that old familiar pain shot through her again. "Mama, when are you going to get over being so mad at me?"

"The damage has been done," her mother said. "I was embarrassed when you shot a man in the groin, for heaven's sake, but that I could have gotten over. But when it came out about the affair you'd had with him . . . Clea, you've made this family a laughingstock."

Her face grew hot, and she felt like a child caught at shoplifting. "Mama, I told you it was all a lie. And even if it hadn't been, this wasn't the first time Beaut laughed at us, Mama. We're due every few years." Immediately, she regretted what she had said, and pinching the bridge of her nose, she tried to hold back the tears.

"I have tried to lead a decent, good life, Clea. I can't help the humiliation the people I love keep causing me, but I certainly haven't brought any of it on myself."

No, Mama, you never made a bad choice, did you? Clea wanted to cry. *What about Clyde Sands and Joe Don Wilson? What about the oil bum who dropped her when he realized Joe Don had left her nothing, or the sixty-year-old crop duster who traded her in for a twenty-year-old aerobics teacher?* But it didn't help matters to rub her mother's nose in her past mistakes, the way she insisted on doing with Clea. If she only knew about Clea's present ones . . .

Clea shuddered, and took a deep breath. "That's right, Mama. But we can't all be as upright as you. Is Shalimar home?"

She could tell instantly that Shalimar was another sore subject. "Shalimar's disappeared again. My guess is that she's gone off somewhere with Joseph."

"Who's Joseph?" That Shalimar had disappeared was of no great concern, for Clea's sister had always come and gone as she pleased.

"She's been dating him for a couple of months now. Seems serious. I'm hoping he'll propose. He has money, you know."

Money. The only thing Myrna put higher than her faith. "Well, that's good, Mama. I hope things work out for her. By the way, I got a new job. I'm administrative assistant to Brandon Donovan. You know, of Donovan Concepts?"

Her mother's tone changed suddenly. "Brandon Donovan? The multimillionaire? You're his secretary?"

"No, Mama. I'm his assistant. His right-hand."

"Well . . ." The word came out in the tone her mother used when she was most impressed and was considering just how to word this latest news when she related it to the ladies in her Bible-study group. The Bible may have warned against pride, but Myrna just liked to "share the news" of her children. If it topped Dot Holmes's news about her children, well, couldn't help that. She never set out to brag, after all.

"How did this come about?"

"I heard he had lost his assistant," she said, "and I applied. He was impressed with my background in law, and he thought I'd be good for the job."

"Oh, Clea. You'll meet so many interesting people. The 'pretty people.' Not like the ones rotting down here where I am. And the money . . . you might meet Mr. Right working for him. Mr. Donovan's married, isn't he?"

"Yes, Mama," Clea said, her spirits sinking the warmer her mother became. It was something to have her speaking to her again without condemnation in her voice, but she would have preferred that unconditional kind of love she'd always heard parents were supposed to have toward their children.

"Tiffany Donovan, isn't that his wife? I read about them in *People* magazine last month. She's beautiful, isn't she?"

"Yes, Mama. She's very attractive."

"Maybe you could make friends with her. She could introduce you to some nice, rich young man."

"I'm not looking for a nice young man, Mama," Clea said, taking off an earring and tossing it onto her bed table. "I'm not convinced nice is an adjective that can be used to describe any man."

"Don't be bitter, Clea. After all that's happened to me, no one can ever say I'm bitter."

"That's good, Mama. I guess I'll outgrow it one of these days."

"I'll pray for you," her mother said.

Clea smiled. If her mother would pray for her, that meant she had forgiven her. She cast aside the feeling that the forgiveness only came because of her new job with Brandon Donovan, and decided she'd take it any way she could get it. "Thanks, Mama. If you feel like you need a vacation, you could come here for a few days. I'll be working long hours for a while, though."

"Clea, don't you worry about me now, you hear? I'm

just fine here. You just concentrate on Mr. Donovan."

"I am, Mama." She wondered what her mother would think when her "affair" with him hit the newsstands, and Tiffany used it as a weapon to destroy him. Would she be proud of her then?

A tear suddenly fell from her eye, and she wiped it away. "Well, I'll let you go. If Shalimar comes back any time soon, tell her to call me and fill me in on her love life. It makes for good entertainment."

"I will, Angel." Angel. Now she was "Angel." "Byebye, now."

Clea hung up the telephone and dropped back onto her bed. She wasn't sure whether it was the conversation with Tiffany or the one with her mother that had taken so much out of her, but she didn't have the energy to worry about it. She was too tired.

And before she had time to dwell further on the shame of the scheme she had embarked upon, she drifted into a deep sleep.

13

Brandon was waiting for her when she arrived at work the next day, and for a moment, she wondered if she was late. Then she remembered she'd actually arrived an hour early, hoping to get a jump on the paperwork she didn't like doing beneath his scrutiny.

He smiled at her as she came in, a far cry from yesterday when he had ignored her. "I would have come earlier if I'd known you'd be here," she said.

He shrugged. "No need. I'm an early riser."

"So am I." Awkwardly, she folded her arms and regarded him openly. He stood leaning against the outer edge of his desk, his polo shirt open at the collar and tucked into freshly creased khakis. From a distance, she thought, he could pass for Mel Gibson, but up close, the ruggedness seemed more confidently polished, and the look in his eyes was fathoms deeper than any she'd ever seen in the actor's. And his grin, as it inched across his face, was at the same time playful and guarded.

So different was this demeanor from the reluctant one she had faced yesterday that she couldn't help being a little suspicious. "Well . . . ," she said, turning back to her briefcase and pulling out reports, legal pads, and her laptop. "I guess I should get started."

He watched her try to get organized on his tabletop, using as little area as possible so as not to clutter his office, and all the while he grinned at her as if he knew something she didn't.

Finally, when she had sat down and turned on the computer, he said, "Wouldn't it be just a little bit easier to work in your own space?"

She looked up at him, wondering if this was a trick question. "Well yes, but since I don't see you surrendering your desk any time soon . . ."

He laughed, and she allowed a soft smile to creep across her lips. "No, you can't have my desk. I meant one of your own."

She sat back in her seat and crossed her arms, regarding him with disbelief. "You said I was supposed to be your shadow. That I had to work here."

"That's because I was trying to make it tough for you. I figured you'd leave by noon yesterday."

"Leave?" she asked, not surprised. "Why? It was the best day I've had in months."

"Running the heels off your shoes, listening to me and my orders all day, keeping up with all the unexpected glitches? That was fun?"

"Well . . . yes."

Again he laughed and ruffled his hair back, and for a moment she thought he looked like any man off the street who might catch her eye. Not the multimillionaire whose wife wanted to destroy him.

"Since you feel that way, and since I can see that you are suited for this job, despite my suspicions about Tiffany's motives . . ."

"Suspicions?" she asked too suddenly.

He paused. "Yes. My wife rarely takes an interest in my business. And to bring in someone like you . . ." His voice trailed off, and awkwardly, he went around his desk and began flipping through papers.

"Someone like me," she repeated, her heart fluttering. "Meaning . . . my history? The scandal?"

"No," he said, still not looking at her. "Meaning . . . your looks."

"Oh." The word fell like a lead weight, and she realized she was beginning to perspire beneath the silk blouse she had worn. He was about to suggest that she had been hired by his wife to bring about his downfall.

"Anyway," he said, "I have a surprise for you."

Her mouth went dry. "A surprise?"

"Yes. Come with me."

She stood up and felt her legs growing weak, felt her heart sprinting at a runaway pace, felt her breath getting trapped in her lungs. Was he going to spring her own sins on her like it was Judgment Day? Was he going to humiliate her first privately, then publicly?

As he opened a door and led her into a short hall, she faced the startling conclusion that she wasn't cut out for deceit.

He opened another door, flicked on a light, and turned back to her. "Your new office," he said.

A thousand pounds of pressure escaped her lungs, her heart slowed to a nonthreatening pace, and her legs regained some of their vigor. "My office? I thought you said . . ."

"I lied," he admitted. "But you proved yourself yesterday, so what the hell? You've got to do all that work somewhere. I have to warn you, though, you won't be in it much."

She set down her briefcase on the polished mahogany desk and looked around. It was modest, nothing like his, but it was more than Clea had hoped for. "Thank you, Brandon."

"Don't thank me. It's the same office Edith used. It comes with the job." Clea checked the drawers and saw some of the items his former assistant had left. A picture of an older woman with two grandchildren lay at the bottom of one of them, beneath a box of paper clips, some random rubber bands, and some pens. Pulling it out, she asked, "Is this Edith?"

Brandon took the picture. "Yeah. Sure is. She must have forgotten it. I'll get Evelyn to mail it to her."

Clea watched him drop the picture into his shirt pocket. "Could I ask you something?"

"Shoot."

"What happened to Edith?"

"I had to fire her," he said. "She spoke disrespectfully to my wife, and when I heard that, there was really not much I could do. Hated to lose her."

Clea averted her eyes to a bookcase full of books on the car industry, government standard reports, and other business publications. She was quite sure that *she* was the reason Edith had lost her job. Tiffany had cleared the way. She was smart, Clea thought uncomfortably. Too smart. And now that woman—that sweet-looking, competent assistant Brandon had depended on—was unemployed.

"Well, look around, familiarize yourself with everything. Take your time." He started out of her office, then turned back with a grin. "As long as you're back in my office in fifteen minutes. We have a meeting to prepare for."

*   *   *

At seven o'clock that evening Brandon told Evelyn she could go if she ordered them some sandwiches first. When the food arrived Clea finally stopped working and collapsed on the sofa in his office. Having an office hadn't helped her much with her work load, although it had made her a little more productive and less fragmented during the times when she'd found a few minutes' refuge there.

"Tired?" Brandon asked with a grin.

She smiled slightly. "I'll make it."

"I should tell you that I don't always keep these long hours. It's just that since I lost Edith I've gotten behind. Usually, I try to get home and eat with my wife. She understands when I go through a spurt now and then of working late."

"Don't worry about it," Clea said. "I don't have anyone waiting for me."

"No?" He took a bite of his sub, and considered her for a long moment. "Why not?"

She shrugged. "I've been too busy for the last few years. And the truth is, relationships and I don't go very well together."

"I know. I read your dossier."

Clea shot him a look.

"Don't look so surprised. You don't think I'd hire anyone without doing a thorough check on them, do you? Anyway, I saw that you're divorced."

"Yeah," she said, suddenly losing her appetite. She set the sandwich down and turned back to the paperwork stacked on the cushion beside her.

"I'm sorry. I didn't mean to bring up a sore subject."

"It's okay. I'm over it. Besides, I suppose I deserved everything that happened."

He let out an astonished laugh. "Why? You put him

through law school, and worked three jobs. How could you deserve it?"

Pushing back the pain that she didn't like to feel, she said, "Anyone who has the audacity to feel secure in a marriage deserves to have it fall apart."

"Wow," Brandon said on a whisper. "That's a tough statement."

As if he had lost interest in his sandwich, he set it down and leaned forward, settling his elbows on his thighs. His eyes cut into her like those of an old friend. "If I'm getting too personal, just tell me to shut up, but I can't help wondering what he did to make you feel that way."

Clea gave out a harsh laugh and wondered if enough time had passed for her to talk about it without that damnable constricting in her throat and that unexpected mist in her eyes. It had been five years, after all, and if she wasn't over it now, she never would be. "He fell for some platinum bimbo and left me with all our debts and not one damn thing to show for it."

"You didn't use adultery as grounds," he said.

Clea squinted in disbelief. "You read my divorce papers?"

"Matter of public record," he said.

"Yeah, in Texas."

He smiled. "My people are thorough. As much weight as Tiffany's recommendation carried, I still had to be satisfied that I wasn't letting some schizo into my operation." He took another bite, watching her as he ate. "So why didn't you use adultery? He would have gotten the debts, and you might have been able to make him help you cover your tuition."

She laid her head back on the couch and shook it from side to side. "I was proud. I told myself I didn't want or need anything from him. So I let him off the hook."

She noted the chastising look in Brandon's eyes. "Don't look at me like that. I outgrew my pride long ago. If law school taught me anything, it's that you should take the edge when you have it. So much would be different if I'd just sued him for adultery."

He watched her as someone who had cared about her for years would, and she realized it didn't make her uncomfortable to confide in him, as it had with so many others in her life. He was an easy man to talk to. "What would have been different?" he asked softly.

She sighed. "I wouldn't have had to beg, borrow or . . . "

"Date the banker?"

Her face grew as hot as if he'd slapped it. "Yes," she said after a moment. Her mouth trembled, and she struggled to fend off the emotions that did her no good—the emotions that Brandon had so easily pulled out of her.

"But the shooting might still have happened. You can't pin that on an adulterous husband."

"Oh yes, I can," she said. "If he'd stayed faithful to me, I never would have met that banker. You see, I've put a lot of thought into this. Every evil in my life has had its root in infidelity."

The words coming out of her own mouth startled her, for she hadn't meant to reveal quite so much. But how true those words were, she thought. From Clyde Sands, to Joe Don Wilson, to John Carmichael, to Richard Mills . . . Even now, her efforts were focused on creating a new infidelity. One that might take the most out of her yet, for it involved cheating herself.

"You sound bitter."

"Funny, that's what my mother called me last night,"

she admitted, meeting his eyes directly. "But that's okay. Bitterness can be used to my advantage. It helps me to do what I have to do."

"And what is that?"

"Take care of myself," she said. But somehow the words didn't reinforce her as much as they broke her down.

Brandon stared at her for a moment, and she wondered what he was thinking. Had she revealed too much and given the impression that she was inaccessible? Had she shamed any interest he may have had with all her talk about infidelity? A swirl of fear rose inside her, and she rebuked herself for forgetting her mission. Already she had deposited her first check from Tiffany. She was locked into the game and couldn't jeopardize it now.

Stretching, she took off her shoes and straightened her legs out on the coffee table in front of her. She noticed his eyes flitting to her legs, then back to her hair, long and swirling around her breasts. Then their eyes met in a moment of utter awareness, a lightning bolt of a second in which they both seemed to consider acting on the impulses drawing them in.

But then it passed, and Brandon quickly jerked his eyes away and got to his feet. "Back to work."

Clea dropped her feet and watched him retreat to his desk. Part of her thought she had moved him just a little, but another part told her that that might just have driven him away. Brandon Donovan didn't *want* to be attracted to her. And as long as it meant the culmination of Tiffany's scheme, she couldn't say she really wanted him to be, either.

Tougher than the job Tiffany had hired her to do was the image that she wanted her to keep. When Clea got home and discovered the boxes of clothes that Tiffany had sent over for her, she felt her spirits sinking again.

There wasn't a skirt there that hung longer than mid-thigh, a style Clea had never worn and could never imagine herself feeling comfortable in. All of the blouses had low—though tasteful—necklines, and the jackets were all fitted to enhance her small waist and the size of her breasts. She thought of the amount of bending over she had to do in his office and realized that all he'd have to do was look in order to get a clear picture of either her breasts or her underwear each time she did.

Tears stung her eyes and something in her stomach revolted. Getting up, she went into the bathroom, bent over the sink, and splashed cold water on her face. Then, looking into the mirror, she confronted the face she was growing increasingly uncomfortable with. The face of the woman who'd sell her body for a buck.

There's a high price for low living . . .

Her mother's sanctimonious words scraped through her mind, and the conscience that was becoming her enemy rebelled in the truth of them. But another part of her cried out that not everyone paid. Joe Don hadn't paid, and John had been allowed to walk away without a look back. And Richard Mills, damaged goods that he was, had still gotten the last laugh when she lost her shot at the bar.

Damn it, why was it always she who paid?

The doorbell rang, and she hesitated, hoping the visitor would go away. All of her law school friends had abandoned her after the trial, and the only visitors she had now were Jehovah's Witnesses and salesmen, both with the same high-pressure pitches to get them in the door.

The bell rang again, followed by an urgent knock. She reached for the towel and dried her face, then headed for the door. "Who is it?"

"You're not gonna believe this."

The voice was unmistakable, and the phrase, one she'd heard so often, made Clea throw open the door. "Shalimar?"

Her sister stood before her in a black stretch knit dress that conformed like a body stocking to her shape, in heels that made her stand virtually on the tips of her toes, and with her black permed hair falling in loose curls all over her face. Her brown eyes were puffy and red, and Clea could see that she'd been crying.

"Oh, Sis, it's been awful," she said in her heavy Southern drawl as she clomped into Clea's apartment. "Joseph promised me the world and didn't deliver dirt."

Clea ushered her sister in and closed the door behind her. "Shally, what happened?"

"He dumped me, that's what!" she cried. "He didn't understand my career demands. The things I have to do to get where I'm headed."

Clea noted that Shalimar's despair was real, something she always doubted when Shalimar came crying to her. Her sister cried just as many fake tears as real ones. It was a gift. "What career demands?"

"Oh!" Shalimar tossed her purse on Clea's couch and kicked the foot of it. "That damn agent. Said he could get me a part in a national commercial for lemon juice. Just wanted to get to know me better. Oh, Clea, I didn't sleep with him because I *wanted* to. I just did it to advance my career. Can I help it if I'm ambitious?"

Clea fought the smile tugging at the edge of her lips. Only Shalimar could say that with a straight face and mean it from the bottom of her heart. "Don't tell me, let me guess. Joseph caught you?"

"In the act. And it was so awful. I mean, I've been caught with my pants down before, but he made such a *scene*. I'll bet that agent gets somebody else to do the lemon juice commercial."

Clea's smile tugged harder. "I'll bet he will, Shally, if there ever was one in the first place."

Shalimar wiped at her eyes and tossed her sister a look. "So you think he just wanted me for my body?" The thought sent a devilish grin scurrying across her face. "Aw, hell, I guess I can live with that, too."

For the first time, she looked around her, and saw the boxes of clothes scattered across the floor. "Oh, God, Clea. Look at all these clothes! They're gorgeous. What did you do? Win the lottery?"

"In a manner of speaking," Clea said as Shalimar dropped to her knees and began pulling out the outfits. She held up a tight blouse that opened to the cleavage. "Oh, I love this!"

"You would," Clea said.

"But lord, Clea, I can't believe you're gonna show your knees. That's a big step, you know. First it's the knees, then the thighs, and next thing you know you'll quit wearing panties altogether."

Clea picked up a skirt and threw it at her sister. "I have a new job, Shally, so I needed some new things. They're all in style."

"But these are so sexy," Shalimar crooned. "I've never known you to wear *anything* sexy."

"Shally, we haven't lived in the same town in years. How do you know what I wear?"

"I *know* what you wear, Clea," she said. "Anything to cover up that great bod. I'm glad you're finally bringin' it out of the closet. So tell me about your job."

Clea's smile collapsed, and she got up and began to

gather up the clothes. The less she told Shalimar about her job, the better. "Well, it's working for Donovan Concepts, as an administrative assistant. To Brandon Donovan."

"No!" The word burst out over the room, and her sister got to her feet, tugging her dress down, and grabbed Clea's arm. "You're working for Brandon Donovan? Clea, he's rich. Not to mention fine-outa-his-mind. Oh, I get hot just thinkin' about him."

Clea didn't like Shalimar's assumption that she would entertain the notion of sleeping with a married man, but then the whole world thought she had slept with Richard Mills, and she had never forgotten how proud Shalimar had been of the news that her sister wasn't perfect. "He's all business, Shally. Nothing's gonna happen."

"Well, if it does, Clea, try not to shoot him in the balls this time. It would be a shame to let those go to waste."

"How do you know?" Clea asked as she gathered up the clothes and started back to her room, with Shalimar's heels clomping behind her.

"I can only imagine." Shalimar breathed a sigh as she lay down on the bed. "Mmmm, this is comfortable. I had to sleep on the bus last night. You are gonna let me crash here for a few days, aren't you?"

"Stay as long as you want, Shally. I probably won't be here all that much."

"Off with old Brandon, huh? Never let it be said that I interfered in somethin' that important. By the way, if for some off-the-wall reason you don't want him, steer him my way. Men of power really turn me on."

"What about Joseph?"

"What about him?"

"A minute ago you were crying over him."

"So sue me if I got off the subject. The truth is, I'm

sick over it. I loved him, Clea. He could have done so much for me."

Tears filled her eyes again, and Clea told herself it was good to have Shalimar here. As shallow as she had begun to feel, it was nice to know that someone else was worse than she.

"So how's the new girl working out, darling?" Tiffany asked as Brandon stripped down to his underwear and crawled under the covers.

"Fine," he said, and she noted that his voice was a little quieter than before. "She's very nice."

"Isn't she, though? She's also very beautiful, don't you think?"

He shot her a curious look, and she realized that she was trying too hard. "Why would you ask me a thing like that?"

"Because, darling," Tiffany said. "I'd like to fix her up with somebody. Whom do we know?"

"Nobody," he said. "I don't know anybody."

"Oh, come on, Brandon," Tiffany said. "Just this once you can put aside your aversion to matchmaking. Someone would be indebted to you forever. All that long, flowing blonde hair, and those eyes . . .are they gray or azure?"

"Both." His voice had a soft, pensive quality as he spoke, and Tiffany looked at him. He was staring off into space, in another world . . .

Suddenly a pang of jealousy shot through her, but she told herself that it was irrational. Her plan was working, after all, if he could get so lost in thought about the color of Clea's eyes.

She sat for a moment, watching him staring off, and finally, she got out of bed.

"Where are you going?"

"To get something for my headache," she said.

Brandon watched her disappear, ashamed that he was glad she'd left. He couldn't remember the last time they'd had a meaningful conversation, and their physical relationship had been just as bland lately. He lay in the bed staring at the ceiling and wondering if every marriage was as lacking as his. It had been years since they'd had anything in common. She couldn't care less about the things that were important to him. He doubted if she even knew that the THD was made of aluminum or that the roof's hardtop could slide away at the touch of a button. He doubted if she would have been able to pick out the design among any others.

But it wasn't that way with Clea. He thought of the way her eyes had lit up the first time she saw the prototype, the suggestions she'd had for shaving the weight, the input she'd had into what the consumer really wanted. Her intelligence hadn't yet ceased to intrigue him. In fact, it interested him more than he wanted to admit, and tonight when she had bared her soul, then kicked off her shoes and stretched those long legs out on the coffee table . . .

He snatched his thoughts back and rebuked himself for the thought. If Clea was to be his right-hand, he'd have to stop thinking of her legs and her hair and her eyes . . . He'd have to stop daydreaming about her even when she was in the room.

Brandon rolled over, trying to find sleep before Tiffany came back to bed. The fact that he'd rather sleep than make love to his wife sent a surge of guilt through him. It had been a long time since he felt attracted to her in that way.

But he supposed all marriages went through those kinds of ups and downs.

Anyone with the audacity to feel secure in a marriage deserves to have it fall apart.

Clea's words disturbed him for the second time that day, and he told himself that she was wrong. Despite its problems, his marriage was one of the only constants in his life. Divorce had never been an option, and neither was looking elsewhere for satisfaction. Not even when Clea Sands was right under his nose.

He heard Tiffany coming back and closed his eyes. She crawled into bed next to him and stayed on her side of the bed. And not for the first time, Brandon realized that the loneliest he ever felt was at night, in bed next to his wife.

14

For some reason that Brandon couldn't pinpoint, he felt the sudden need to talk to his father when he woke the next morning. Before light had marked the emergence of dawn, he rose and dressed, leaving Tiffany to sleep.

Quietly, he sat at the breakfast table in the kitchen, for the live-in staff hadn't awakened yet, and ate a bowl of corn flakes, which he'd asked LaTanya to keep stocked for him. As he ate, he wondered if Tiffany had ever had a corn flake in her life, or if she even knew what a corn flake was? He doubted it, and something about that saddened him. On the heels of that doubt came the certainty that Clea had probably grown up on them.

He finished the bowl, but continued to sit there, staring at a stain on the table, wondering absently how that particular imperfection had gotten past his wife. She didn't like spots in her life. And he couldn't say he cared much for them, either.

Yet there were some. There were spots and stains he

had been careful to hide, imperfections in his life and his marriage that he had ignored for years, as if refusing to confront them meant that they didn't exist. He didn't want them to exist.

He was supposed to have a wonderful, loving home like the one in which he'd been raised. He was supposed to have children who doted on him and emulated him. He was supposed to have a wife who cherished him.

A deep, gnawing craving started in his soul, and his desire to talk to his father turned into urgency. What would his father say if he knew he'd had a dream about his assistant last night, a dream that a married man ought never to dream?

Go to confession, son. Hand it over to God.

That's what his father would have said, as if he knew, as if he'd suffered the same weaknesses and temptations himself. Yet that couldn't be, for as far back as he could remember, his father had been a boisterously happy man who put his family above everything else in the world and right beneath his allegiance to the Almighty.

He looked at the phone, then at the clock, and wondered if it was too early for him to call. He knew the old man rose early these days, especially since Brandon's mother had died two years ago. He started early figuring out ways to fill up days that had grown too long and too dull.

Picking up the phone, he dialed the number that meant home to him, the number he'd always called to tell his mother he'd be late getting home from football practice, or to ask his sisters to wash his blue shirt so he could wear it on his date that night, or just to hear his parents' voices when he was in college feeling homesick.

"Hello?" The voice was old and rugged, but had the same familiar cadence that Brandon had always loved.

"Dad? Did I wake you?"

"Brandon, my boy," his father said with a chuckle on his voice. "I've been up for some time. Is everything all right?"

"Fine, Dad. Fine. I was just thinking about you, and I thought I'd call."

"How's that new project going?"

"Great," he said. "Why don't you plan to come to Georgia with me for the clinic I've scheduled? You can check it out firsthand and see if you have any ideas on improvements."

"I might do it, at that," his father said. "This old man might still have a few ideas up his sleeve."

"I'd bet my whole company on it," Brandon said.

"So how's your new role working out? In the business, I mean. It's a big step going from CEO to Project Chief."

Brandon smiled. His father had been the only one to understand when he reached the burn-out point last year from running such a huge operation, with its four models of cars and all the headaches that went along with them. Over a glass of wine in the little mom-and-pop restaurant where his father ate dinner every night, Brandon had recounted how he missed the days when he worked for Ford, running just one department, and using his engineering skills the way he had been trained to. "By the time the reports and graphs and profiles work their way to me," he had said, "the engineers have all had their input. I'm a pencil-pusher, Dad. An administrator. It was fun starting Donovan Concepts, but now it's turning into a grind."

"You're the boss," his father had said. "If you don't like your job, change it."

It wasn't until that moment that it occurred to Brandon that he didn't have to administrate every detail of the company. He could "demote" himself, if he wanted, name himself project chief of the THD, and use his talents as an engineer. Other people could do the pencil pushing.

"It's great, Dad. I've been involved in every phase of the production of the THD. I'm loving every minute. And I've just delegated a lot more responsibility to Lawrence and my VPs. It's working out better than I imagined."

The old man laughed. "Good, son. Then you did the right thing."

Suddenly the melancholy fell over Brandon again. "Hey, Dad, do you ever go to confession anymore?"

His father's voice was solemn now. "Every Wednesday morning. My big regret, though, is that I don't have anything interesting to confess. I have a hunch that poor Father John watches Alfred Hitchcock videos on a portable TV with headphones while I talk. Can't say I blame him."

Brandon smiled. "I was thinking of going today. I haven't been in a while."

"Go, son," his father said. "Confession is good for the soul. It's a cliché because it's true."

"I know."

He knew his father sensed the quiet in his voice, and he felt like a kid again, struggling with the questions he needed to ask his father about sex, but unable to find the words. The old man had known then, too.

"How's Tiffany?"

Something jolted inside him, as if he didn't want his father probing that close to his problems, but he didn't try to hide it. "She's . . . the same. Busy. Distracted. Moody."

"Still as beautiful as ever."

"Yeah." The compliment bothered Brandon, for his father had never considered outward appearances to be worth much. He only used physical compliments when he couldn't find anything nice to say about what was inside a person. "She really works at it."

"And Steven?"

"He's fine. Still driving, though. He has a race in Talladega the same week of the clinic. I'll be going early to catch it. Part of me can't stand it if he doesn't at least qualify, but if he doesn't, I'll have a better chance of convincing him to finish school."

"He'll come around. It'll all be all right. Don't give up on him, son. Family is the most important thing. It's the greatest gift our Maker gave us. The harder we cling to it, the happier it will grow. You know that's true, don't you, son?"

Brandon chuckled under his breath. "Sure, Dad. I know." He sighed, the breath tearing out what felt like a hole in the center of his spirit. "I miss the good times when Mom was alive and everybody lived at home."

"So do I," his father said. "But there are lots of other good times, and you have your own home. Tiffany and Steven . . . they're your home now."

"Yeah. Listen, be thinking about going to the clinic with me. It wouldn't hurt you to get away. And no kidding, I could use your input."

"I will," his father promised. "Take care now. And Brandon, if you have something interesting to confess, don't talk yourself out of going. Those poor priests need something to brighten up their days."

Brandon laughed along with his father before he hung up.

The church where Brandon went to mass at least three Sundays a month smelled of old wood and candlewax, and the pews creaked beneath his weight. This wasn't one of the Catholic churches where the rich went to worship. Instead, he drove forty-five minutes to the other side of town, where working men and women came with their children to pray. Tiffany preferred to sleep late and meet her friends for brunch.

In a way, it was just as well, because if Tiffany had had any inclination toward going to mass, he would have had to go to the elite church on their side of town, the one where only cars costing forty-thousand or more filled the parking lots, and talk centered around what so-and-so's wife was wearing, rather than the service itself.

He didn't see how anyone could worship in a building like that one, which had cost several million dollars to build and where people went only every once in a while because it was the civilized thing to do. He preferred the rustic look of this old building, the warped places in the floor, and the way the sun shone through windows that were unadorned with color. There was no stained glass he'd ever seen that could outshine the sun's own glory as it beamed through at this hour of morning.

He walked into the sanctuary and saw that no one else was here. Even the confessional was empty.

Quietly, he walked to the front and lit a candle for his mother, then knelt at the altar, pulled out his rosary, and began to pray. When he was finished, he looked up at the statue of Mary holding her divine little baby.

Tiffany had never looked like that when Steven was born, and he supposed that was the biggest disappointment he'd faced as an adult. He had compensated for Tiffany's lack of maternal instincts, however, and doted on Steven himself since the day he was born. The child had run to him when he was hurt or upset. But whenever Brandon administered the flip side of that love and attempted to discipline the child, Tiffany always intervened and undid whatever progress Brandon had made.

He heard a door open at the side of the church, and saw the priest across the floor toward the confessional. Quickly, Brandon stood and made his way to the booth.

He stepped into the anonymous darkness of the confessional and waited for the priest to acknowledge him. When he did, he whispered, "Forgive me, Father, for I have sinned . . ."

The priest listened to the mundane sins Brandon threw in a bag at his feet, sins of anger, sins of omission, sins of white lies . . . He kept thinking of more and more, dreading getting to the one that had really brought him here. But finally, he drew in a deep breath and spat it out. "There's a woman I keep thinking about . . . I had a dream about her last night. But I love my wife, and I would never carry through on these . . . thoughts."

There, he thought. It was out, and the uttering of it made it less of a monster to deal with. As the priest absolved him and gave him his penance, Clea didn't seem as much of a temptation anymore. He could deal with it, the way his father might have.

He left the confessional, knelt at one of the benches, and began canting the prayers that the priest had given him for penance. When he came back to his feet, he felt refreshed, freed from the bondage that the dream had locked him in, and ready to face the day.

And Clea.

But when he arrived at his office and saw her standing at her desk, bent over the computer as she typed in some data, her golden-brown hair draping around her arms, and wearing a short plaid skirt and tall heels with those long, perfect legs, he felt angry at himself again. It was going to take more than a priest's absolution for him to deal with this.

Maybe he would just have to fire her.

There was a strain between them today, Clea thought, and for the life of her, she couldn't figure out what she had done. From the moment Brandon had walked in that morning, he'd been barking out orders. She would have blamed the clothes, but she could swear he hadn't laid eyes on her yet today.

Unwilling to "stew in her own juices," as Joe Don used to say, she finally confronted him in his office after a particularly clipped exchange between them.

"Brandon, I realize I haven't known you long enough to decipher your mood swings, so would you mind telling me if I've done something to upset you, or if you just woke up on the wrong side of the bed?"

Brandon seemed to tear his eyes from the pile of parts he'd poured out of a bag on his desk, and regarded her for what she was sure was the first time that day. "You didn't do anything."

"Then why do I feel like I've been on the chopping block all day?"

"I wasn't aware that you felt that way." He went back to the report that had come with the parts.

"Well, I have." She watched his face change as he scanned the report, and he frowned and looked up at her.

"Did you read this?"

"Yes," she said, stepping toward the desk. "They've been able to shave four pounds off the THD so far."

"Thanks to your idea." His eyes cut through her, as if he was still angry at her, and she felt genuinely confused.

"Well . . . that's good. Isn't it?"

"It's damn good." He frowned down at the parts again, looking as if he couldn't decide whether to fling the bag of parts against the wall or hurl them at her.

"So . . . why do you look so . . . angry?"

He dropped his forehead into his hand and massaged his temples, feeling the opposing forces of desire and commitment at war in his mind. Damn it, he couldn't fire her, not when she was so competent, so smart, and so conciliatory. He needed her, and it wouldn't be fair to fire a woman just because he was attracted to her. That was as bad as firing someone because he wasn't.

He looked up at her, trying not to absorb the fact that her loose hair was sexy as hell and had its own scent that wafted across the room when she breezed by, not like a perfume, but like a breath of fresh air. And he tried not to see the way her skirt hugged her small hips, or the length of those long legs encased in black stockings.

"We have a clinic in Georgia next week," he said, knowing that the announcement didn't answer her question but unable to help it. "We'll be gone for at least four days. That won't be a problem, I hope."

Clea shook her head. "No, that's fine."

"Evelyn's making the travel arrangements. Check with her for details. Steven, my son, has a race there, which is why I want to go a couple days early. Oh, and pack something formal. We'll be entertaining some of the dealers in that area. You do have something, don't you?"

Clea racked her brain for what was in her closet, and realized that there was nothing that could be remotely considered formal. "I'll come up with something."

The tiniest hint of a smile burst into his eyes. "You don't have anything, do you?"

"Well . . . no. But that's not a problem. I can—"

Before she could finish her sentence, Brandon picked up the phone, flipped through his Rolodex, and dialed a number. "Sharon? This is Brandon Donovan. Yeah, listen, I'm going to send my assistant over there today, about five o'clock, and I'd like for you to have some evening gowns ready to show her. Help her pick out a couple, and then put it on my account."

Clea caught her breath and frowned as he hung up the phone. "Brandon, I can buy my own clothes . . ."

"This is a business expense, Clea. It's in my best interest to have you wearing the best, and Sharon knows what I like. I buy all my gifts for Tiffany from her." He jotted down an address, and Clea saw that it was a designer's studio, not a store. "Don't be late. She gets a little crazy when people waste her time."

"All right."

"Now, back to business. They're suggesting we start making each of these parts out of alloy to cut the weight. What I need to know is how much more that would cost and whether it's worth it."

Clea loaded the parts into the bag and took the report. "No problem. I'll take care of it."

"And we have a meeting in an hour with the design team. Problems with the interior space." He leaned back and shot her a grin. "Got any ideas about interiors?"

She grinned and started out of the room. "Tons of them. But I have to hear the problems first."

"If something comes to you during the meeting, Clea, spit it out. Don't be shy."

"Me shy?" she asked, flashing a grin that made something inside him stir. "If I have something to say, Brandon, I'll always say it."

Clea could have sworn that he was still watching her as she left his office.

15

Clea struggled to balance her briefcase and the two formal dresses hanging over her arm and dig for her housekey at the same time. She had knocked as hard as possible with her knee, but Shalimar didn't answer. Maybe she'd left already, Clea thought. Maybe she'd decided to buck up and go home and try to pull her life back together. Or more likely, Joseph had whisked back into her life. It was all just as well, she thought as she dug for her keys, for she had those price comparisons yet to work on before she could go to bed tonight, and there was too much whirling through her mind. Shalimar was a distraction she couldn't afford right now.

She found the keys, fished them out, and jabbed one into the lock. The moment she opened the door, she realized Shalimar hadn't gone anywhere. She was just too busy to answer the door.

Clea stepped over the blouse Shalimar had dropped on the living-room floor, and turned down George Strait's voice droning about a better class of losers on the stereo. She turned back around and saw the high heels lying beside the couch, along with a pair of men's shoes . . .

"Shalimar!" Clea's voice cracked out over the apartment.

"Yeah?" her sister yelled from the bedroom, as if she'd been caught folding laundry. Clea had to admit that, for Shalimar, what she was doing was more natural than any domestic chores she might have engaged in.

Clea set her briefcase down and, still holding the gowns, went to her closed bedroom door. "Am I to assume that you aren't alone in there?"

Shalimar laughed. "Damn, Sis, you're good!"

Clea felt her cheeks reddening, and through her teeth said, "Shalimar, may I speak to you alone, please?"

"Can't it wait?"

"No," Clea bit out. "It can't."

She heard Shalimar cursing, and in a moment, her sister, wrapped in Clea's robe, came to the door and peered out. "Damn it, Clea, what do you want?"

"This is my apartment, Shally. I don't like coming home and finding strange men in my bed."

"He's not strange!" Shalimar said. "He's my friend."

"I don't care *who* he is! Get him out! Now!"

"Damn it, Clea, you're such a prude!" Rolling her eyes, she turned back to the bed and shoved the door closed behind her.

Clea went to the living room, sat down on the couch, and tapped her fingers on the sofa arm as she heard the muffled voices in the bedroom.

Then the door opened, and the man came out. Without looking at him, Clea handed him his shoes over her shoulder.

"Thanks," he muttered.

Shalimar walked him to the door, whispered something about being sorry, then closed it and turned back to her sister.

"All right," she said, "hit me with your best shot."

Clea sprang to her feet and glared at her. "How dare you?"

"How dare I what? Oh God, Clea, where did you get those dresses? They're gorgeous! They must have cost a fortune!"

"Don't change the subject!" Clea shouted. "I told you you could stay here for a while, Shally, but you've got to respect the fact that this is my apartment. I don't want you bringing men into my apartment and my bed! Do you understand what I'm saying?"

"Well, I didn't *plan* it or anything. It's just that I was at the mall buyin' some plants to brighten up the place, and this guy and I struck up a conversation, and he was really good lookin', and soooo nice, and well, the next thing I know, I'm invitin' him back for a drink . . ."

"Shally, how could you sleep with someone you just met?"

"Well, I didn't plan that either, Clea, and don't worry, we took precautions. One thing you can always say about me is I'm careful. I don't believe in takin' chances, you know."

"I'm not even talking about that, Shally. I'm talking about the intimacy. How could you do that?"

Shalimar smiled and sashayed forward, taking one of the dresses from Clea and holding it up. "Oh, Clea, I'm just a romantic, I guess. Men are so nice to me sometimes, and it's just so hard to say no. Oh God, this is beautiful."

Clea fixed her eyes on her sister and realized there was no way a lecture was going to change her. "I had to get it for a trip I'm taking to Georgia next week."

"But how did you afford this?" Shalimar held the dress up to her, then moaned over the other one, and took it from Clea, too. "Clea, these cost thousands and thousands of dollars."

"Yeah, they must," Clea said. "I didn't see the bill."

"You mean to tell me that Brandon bought these for you?" Her eyes came to life. "Clea! He's buyin' you presents?"

"No," Clea said, though she had to wonder at the indignation in her own voice. "They weren't presents, and the company paid for them, not Brandon himself. Don't start reading things into this, Shally."

"Well, if he isn't smitten now, he will be when he gets a load of you in this!"

Clea felt her heart sinking. The dress *was* sexy, though appropriate to Clea's own taste, and she knew that it was very likely that her job would come to fruition next week in Georgia. The thought made her want to quit, for she honestly didn't know if she could go through with it. "I have to hang them up," she said quietly.

Shalimar went back to the stereo and turned the music back up as Clea went to clean up the mess her sister had made of her bedroom.

Later that night, when the telephone rang, Clea knew it would be Tiffany, waiting to lambaste her for not making more progress. But tonight she had news for her.

Somehow, she just didn't want to tell it.

She let it ring three times before Shalimar shouted, "I'll get it!"

Clea jumped up and grabbed the phone. "No, I've got it!"

She took it into the bedroom before she answered it. "Hello?"

"Clea, Tiffany."

"No kidding."

She could hear the chagrin in Tiffany's voice. "I hope there was some progress today."

"You might think so," Clea said, her voice as dead as it had ever been. "We're going to Georgia next week."

"He's taking you with him? That's wonderful!" Tiffany said. "That'll be perfect. If you don't make your move then, Clea, you're not trying."

"You know I'm trying," Clea said. "It's just not as easy as I thought it would be."

"I thought you said you were the best." Tiffany's amused tone made Clea's teeth clamp tight. "Don't worry, Clea. I told you he was faithful."

"Then why do you want to leave him?" Clea asked quietly.

She could tell immediately that the question disturbed her. "I don't have to justify myself to you, Clea. You're the hired help. Just do your job."

The phone clicked in her ear, and Clea sat staring at it.

"So who's leavin' who?"

Clea jumped and swung around to see her sister leaning in the doorway, still wearing her robe.

"Were you eavesdropping?"

"Hell, no. I was *listenin'*."

"Why?"

Shalimar shook the curls around on her head and threw up her hands. "Well, what else is there to do around this place? It's as excitin' as a morgue in here, Clea. Who's leavin' who?"

"A friend of mine . . ." Clea stammered. "She's leaving her husband. It's . . . it's not important."

"Sounds like the girl needs to talk." Shalimar dropped down on the bed and examined a fingernail. "Maybe you should get us together. Heaven knows I know all about man troubles."

Clea wanted to laugh for she knew Shalimar didn't have a clue what real "man troubles" were. Man troubles were when your stepfather stalked and lusted after you. Man troubles were when your husband got all he could get out of you, then moved on to fresher pastures. Man troubles were being arrested for shooting someone who was trying to rape you. Man troubles were when you were getting paid to do a dirty job on someone you were beginning to like more than you had planned.

Tears came to her eyes, and she shook her head and lay back down on the bed. "I'll ask her if she needs advice," Clea said in a monotone.

"Great. You know, I could use a friend or two around here. Course, I don't usually get along as well with women as men, 'cause there's that jealousy factor I always have to deal with. Hey, you're not gonna believe this! I got a job today."

Clea sat up straight. "A job? I thought you were just visiting Detroit."

"I like it here, Clea," Shalimar said, grabbing Clea and throwing her arms around her. "And I like being here with you instead of listenin' to Mama yell and nag at me all the time. So I got a job at that little hair place, the Hairem Scarem, and I'll be doin' nails and makeovers. Hey, Clea, this is a big opportunity, you know, cause there's always rich people goin' in and out. I could get discovered, you know."

"Discovered doing what?" Clea asked, irritated.

"Well . . . you know. I could have just the look some-body's lookin' for or somethin'." She saw the look on

Clea's face, and stamped her foot. "Don't be so gloom and doom."

Clea raked her hair back from her face. "Where do you plan to live?"

"Well, here with you, if it's okay. It is, isn't it, Clea?"

Clea regarded her sister for a long moment, struggling between telling her she could stay as long as she wanted and asking her to move out tomorrow. Shalimar was so flighty that someone had to watch out for her. Besides, Clea was hardly ever home.

"Of course it's okay," she said. "You can stay as long as you need to. Just . . . let's try to respect each other's privacy, okay?"

"Sure," Shalimar agreed quickly. "That means we have some kinda signal so we don't come bargin' in on each other when we have men over?"

"No," Clea said. "That means you don't *have* men over."

Shalimar looked stricken. "Not at all?"

"Well, at least not in my bedroom. It's mine, Shally. I don't want people parading through it."

"Well, gee . . . If we can't go into a room and close the door, there's no tellin' what you might walk in on." A devilish grin lit up her face. "'Course, that could make it more excitin'.'"

Clea's temples began to throb. "Shally, can't you cool it for a little while? I'm not asking you to be celibate, for heaven's sake. But you don't have to be so promiscuous."

"I'm not promiscuous," Shalimar protested. "I'm just friendly."

"Well, how about if you aren't so friendly in my apartment? If you can't handle it, maybe you'd better get your own place."

"Can't do that," Shalimar said. "Have you seen the

prices in this city? Nope, I think I'll just stay here awhile."

Clea smiled slightly at the realization that Shalimar had no intention of sharing the rent. But that was all right. Her sister probably wouldn't be there long enough for it to matter. Within a week or two, she'd be onto something new and flit away like a confused little bird.

Besides, Clea could use a friend right now.

"Come on," she said. "Let's see what I've got to eat. Then I've got some work to do."

"Work, work, work," Shalimar said, scuffing out behind her. "Don't you ever have any fun?"

"I don't have time for fun," Clea said, as those familiar barriers began rising between them again But even as she spoke, she wasn't sure if those barriers were keeping the truth out or the lies in.

16

The King Air plane with the name Donovan on the side was a far cry from the coach seats Clea usually flew on Delta, just as the limousine ride to the airport was miles above the yellow Camarro that was finally beginning to show its age.

As she approached the plane, that old apprehension welled up inside her again. What if they were alone in the cabin? What if this was the moment Tiffany had been waiting for? And what if she couldn't go through with it?

She reached the steps leading to the cabin, took a deep breath, and started up the steps into the open door of the plane.

Immediately, she saw Brandon sitting on a sofa in the middle of the plushly appointed cabin, reading the paper. He glanced up at her and smiled. "Right on time."

"Hi there," she said. "You didn't tell me we were going in a private plane."

Brandon got up and took her briefcase. "Yeah, well.

It's my one indulgence. I hate wasting time in airports.
And this way my luggage never gets lost."

He reached around her and closed the door, locking
them in, then opened the door to the cockpit and told
the pilot they would be ready to leave as soon as their
luggage was loaded on the plane.

When he had closed the door again, assuring their
privacy, he turned back to her. His eyes swept down
her, from the hair that she wore long and loose, as
Tiffany had instructed, to the open-necked blouse that
only hinted at her cleavage, and the short, fitted skirt
that Tiffany had bought.

She swallowed and tried to hold his gaze a moment
longer than her comfort zone allowed, longer than she
would have if she hadn't had a mission. "This is nice,"
she said. "Real private."

Again a moment of silence passed between them,
and he stared at her, as if trying to decide exactly how
much significance to hang on her words. She should
step closer to him, she thought, and touch his chest. She
should wet her lips. She should make some kind of
move . . .

But strangely, she only stood still.

And then, as Brandon stood there, also still, she
wondered if he was going to make one.

A door at the back of the cabin opened, and Clea
jumped.

Brandon smiled toward the door as an older man
emerged from the rest room. "Clea, I don't think I told
you my father would be traveling with us. He didn't tell
me for sure until last night."

Relief flooded through her that they wouldn't be
alone, that she wouldn't have an opportunity to do
what Tiffany wanted, that she could enjoy Brandon's

company rather than plot his demise. "Your father?" she asked, extending her hand. "It's so nice to meet you, Mr. Donovan."

"The pleasure is all mine, dear," the smiling old man said as he took her hand in both of his. "My, my, son, she's lovely. Why don't we get her a date with Steven?"

Brandon smiled but looked uncomfortable. "No, Dad. I don't think so."

"Why not?" He looked at Clea again, laughing as if he'd known her for years. "Steven has a definite eye for a pretty lady, and you mark my words, he'll like you."

Clea noted Brandon's tightening face and shook her head. "I appreciate that, Mr. Donovan, but I'm probably too old for your grandson. Besides, I'm too busy to date much."

"Too busy? My dear, you have to make time."

"Don't worry about her, Dad. I keep her pretty busy, but somehow I don't think she sits at home too much," Brandon teased.

"The truth is, I really do. When I was in law school, I studied all the time. And now . . ."

"And now I work you like a slave, is that it?" Brandon asked with a smile. "Come on. You're going to make my father think I'm ruining your life. I'll never hear the end of it."

"Well . . . I like keeping busy."

"Oh, my, this will never do," Peter Donovan said. "We'll have to show her a good time in Georgia, son. Can't let her go on leading such a sheltered life."

"She won't, Dad. I have plans for Clea."

Their eyes met like two magnets crashing together, and she wondered if he was warning her of something, feeling her out, testing her for a sign as to whether she would comply if he made some kind of move. He held his gaze a second too long, and a soft smile curled across his mouth.

Peter only shook his head and gestured for Clea to sit down. "Well, I guess Brandon has his reasons for not wanting to fix you up with Steven. Conflict of interest, and all that, you know. He's a real stickler for that kind of stuff. The age shouldn't be a problem, though. My grandson knows value when he sees it."

Clea laughed as Brandon shook his head and pulled some diagrams out of his briefcase. "Come here, Dad. Leave Clea alone and look these over. See what you think."

The two men launched a two-hour exchange on the THD. Clea watched the respect and friendship with which they treated each other, and envied it, for she'd never had that from either parent. By the time they landed in Georgia, she had grown very fond of the old man who had raised Brandon.

And she had a new perspective on Brandon. One that she liked very much. As they landed, it suddenly hit Clea that the more she liked him, the less she liked herself.

Tears sprang to her eyes, and quickly, she blinked them back. Her choices had been made, and there was nothing left but to do what she was being paid to do.

17

The smell of exhaust and burning rubber wafted through Steven Donovan's cockpit, and he pulled himself out of his car and jerked off his helmet.

"Some asshole forgot to pull the pin out of the grid!" he shouted to his team manager. Surrounding him, the pit crew scrambled around his car looking for the reason for his loss of control on the track.

"Damn it, the skirts aren't down. There's no down-force!"

"We got it, Steve," his manager said. "It's not too late."

"Whoever is responsible is fired," he said. "And if I don't qualify, you're all fired. Now get your thumb out of your ass and refuel me so I don't have to lose another lap."

His crew set to work refueling, and he sat in the cockpit again impatiently, waiting to screech out of the pit the moment it was ready. He *had* to qualify to enter the Can-Am race, he thought. But so far it wasn't looking good.

His father would love this.

He bit the inside of his lip until he almost drew blood, and scanned the idle people who had pit passes, most of them half-dressed groupies hanging out waiting for him or one of the other drivers to look their way. Hell, there was never any shortage of women in this business, he thought, even when he lost. They lined up after the races, like a litter of dogs waiting to be picked over, and were happy to go with anyone who chose them. He could have his pick of them, and he had, for some of them followed the series from one racetrack to another. He saw a cute little platinum blonde in a pair of shorts that defined her cute little derriere, and tried to recall her name. Diana, Dierdre . . . something like that. Not that it really mattered.

And then he saw past her, to his father standing against the railing, out of the way, watching him. Shit, he thought, moaning aloud. He hadn't expected his father to come for the qualifying round. He'd expected him tomorrow, when the real race started.

He doesn't think I'll qualify. The thought sent a chill of rage through him, and he pushed it down and told himself that he'd just have to show him. His father expected him to fail, probably hoped he would so he'd have no choice but to go back to DC with his tail between his legs.

He'd just have to show him.

And his grandfather! What was this? A family reunion, for God's sake? It was all he needed. A bandstand of Donovans waiting to see him lose. They probably expected to take him out and console him tonight, as if he would enjoy their company more than the ladies waiting for him in the stands.

And then he saw Clea standing between his father

and his grandfather, and he lifted the face of his helmet and peered closer. His father saw him staring and lifted his hand in a wave, and Steven wanted to yell to him to move aside, that it was the woman he was looking at. The woman with the hypnotic golden hair and the body that almost made him wet himself.

Damn it, Dad, he thought. Where'd you find her?

Suddenly it didn't matter if he had to hang around his father tonight. Suddenly there was nothing he'd rather do.

His crew yelled at him, and he shook his thoughts free and realized his car was ready to roll. Snapping his faceplate down, he waved toward his father, and pulled back out onto the strip again, ready to show them, ready to show her, that he was the fastest son-of-a-bitch ever to hit this track.

By the time he got her alone tonight, she'd be so hot for him, she'd be ripping his clothes off. Which was all right with him, he thought, for he performed best without his clothes.

Laughing, he gunned his engine, and slipped back onto the speedway.

Clea held her breath as Steven made the last lap of the qualifying race, and counted the cars clustering around him. There were too many front-runners to count, and behind him, she had watched six others crash or skid out of the competition.

They made the last curve, and she watched Steven's car brush dangerously against the one next to it. Peter yelled, and Brandon came to his feet. The cars smoked in toward the finish, neck-in-neck, behind a cluster of winners.

Clea stood up herself, caught up in the excitement of

the moment. She heard herself yelling right along with Brandon, until finally the race was over.

Steven's car was one of the last to cross the finish line, and he failed to qualify to run the Can-Am.

The three sank down into the stands, disappointed, and tried to catch their breath.

"He drove well," Peter said. "It's not that he didn't give it all he had."

"No, it isn't," Brandon admitted. "He did his best."

"What now?" Clea whispered.

"Now he licks his wounds and I try to forget all the money I've put out on that car." Brandon was quiet for a moment before he said, "Well, there's always another race. He'll get better each time."

Steven climbed out of his car and kicked the door in, leaving a footprint in the almost invincible metal. "Damn it, you asshole," he told his crew manager. "It was those tires. They started sliding on that last lap."

"There's nothing wrong with the tires," argued the man who had fifteen years' experience. "You just weren't fast enough. But don't sweat it, Steven. You almost qualified, and that's about the best you can hope for until you get a little more experience."

"Damn it, *almost* doesn't cut it! There were people here—"

He cut himself off and flung around, ripping his helmet off and flinging it across the pavement. Out of the corner of his eye, he saw racetrack reporters coming toward him. They'd want to know how it felt to be a frigging loser when you had everything going for you.

Feels great, man, he'd say. *My car's a piece of shit, and my team is a bunch of assholes.*

He saw his father approaching him, with that woman trailing behind him. They would probably laugh. His father had never wanted him to race, anyway. He'd wanted him to finish school and join the business. Learn how to assemble rear suspension and install doors. He might as well start him on the assembly line. Now he'd use this loss as leverage to control him.

The reporters passed him by, and he felt the sting of being ignored. That was worse than having his nose rubbed in it, he thought. As his father approached, he saw the girl better, and something in his groin tightened again. Damn, she was good-looking. And the way those breasts bounced slightly when she walked . . .

"You did great, son," his father called out. "You're getting better all the time."

Steven bristled, but decided against the sarcastic quip that came to mind. He didn't want to scare off this little piece.

"You always bring me something, Dad," he said, "but this is the best you've done yet."

It took a second for Clea to realize he referred to her, and as he leered at her and extended a gloved hand, she fought the urge to tell him she couldn't be his in his wildest dreams. She bit back the lines she'd spent years cultivating as a waitress, fending off unwanted advances from men who expected her to fall to her knees, and took his hand.

"Steven, this is my new assistant, Clea Sands."

Steven brought her hand to his lips and kissed it. "Your assistant, huh? She's a far cry from Edith, isn't she, Dad?"

"I told you he'd like her," Peter Donovan put in, patting his grandson—who hadn't yet acknowledged him—on the back. "You drove great, boy. I'm proud of you."

Steven shot his grandfather an unappreciative look without releasing Clea's hand. "Can the fake sentiments, all right, Gramps?"

Peter looked as if the biting retort didn't surprise him at all.

She started to take her hand back, but he tightened his hold. "You like fast cars, honey?"

Clea's ire rose, but she told herself it would serve no purpose to insult Brandon's son. "I like cars," she said, forcing her hand free and crossing her arms in front of her. "I wouldn't be working for your father if I didn't."

He grinned and winked at his dad. "Oh, I don't know if that's a natural assumption. I can think of a lot of reasons to hire you, and none of them would have anything to do with cars."

Her heartbeat tripled its pace, and her eyes took on that sharp glare she got just before she hit a man with her most lethal barb. But she couldn't do it here.

"You're absolutely right, Steven," Brandon cut in. "The two years of law school, the past experience in a Texas dealership, and your mother's recommendation are among them."

"Mother? Really?" He eyed Clea again. "Now there's a new twist." He raked his hands through his black hair and turned back to Clea. "Well, I hope you'll have dinner with me tonight. Sort of a consolation prize. I might come out a winner, after all."

"No, I can't," Clea said quickly.

"Oh, but you have to eat. And my father surely couldn't have any objections, unless he wants you all to himself."

"Steve, that's enough," Brandon said. "We have a dinner tonight with my dealers in the area. I was hoping you'd join us."

"Dad, my idea of a good time is not swapping transmission stories with a bunch of car salesmen."

"Those car salesmen are the ones who keep you in Porsches and race cars, son. It's a black-tie dinner with a live country band that one of my Atlanta dealers lined up. I'd love to have you there, but—"

"Is she coming?"

"Yes," Clea said, refusing to be talked around. "I'll be there."

"Then I'll come," he said, resuming his grin. "And Clea and I can burn up the dance floor. Being from Texas, you probably have shit-kicking in your genes."

Brandon rolled his eyes. "Steven . . ."

"It's all right, Brandon," Clea said with a smile. "I can hold my own on a dance floor, if that's what you mean."

Peter laughed his hoarse chuckle that warmed Clea's heart, and he squeezed her shoulder. "I'll bet you can, Clea. Maybe you can teach this old man a few steps."

"Watch it, Gramps. I don't plan to share her much tonight."

Something worrisome stirred in Clea's heart as they left the racetrack, for she realized that she had garnered the wrong Donovan's attention. And how she would wiggle out of this, she wasn't entirely sure.

18

The ballroom of the Waverly Hotel in Atlanta exuded money and success, and all the Donovan sales teams in Georgia, Florida, and Alabama were turning out for the blowout with the Donovan brass. Clea caught her breath as she walked into the room and saw white-suited waiters scurrying about setting tables and putting last minute touches on party favors that would go on every table. She scanned the room for Brandon, and caught her own reflection in the ten-foot mirror across the room.

She doubted there were many times in her life that she had looked better, and there certainly weren't any times she had worn a dress that cost as much as this one that Brandon had paid for. It was at once sexy and conservative, flashy and tasteful, simple and beautiful.

She wore her hair up tonight—regardless of Tiffany's orders for her to wear it down at all times, and the soft wisps of curls that hung loose from her French twist contrasted well to the black sequins at her shoulders. Examining herself further down, she wondered if the black netting down the center of the dress, revealing the shadows between her breasts and part of her stomach, was too bold. What if Brandon was embarrassed by her?

Nervously, she looked away from the mirror, and immediately her eyes collided with his. He stood across the floor, one hand in his trouser pocket, staring, stricken, at her.

He didn't like it. She could feel his disapproval, and a warm blush spread from her neck all the way up her cheeks.

He started toward her, his expression still carefully guarded. She swallowed as he approached, and opened her mouth to blurt out an apology for her mistake.

"This dress is all wrong, isn't it? I think I'll just run back up and put on the other one."

"Don't you dare."

The force of his reply startled her, and a soft smile tugged at the corner of her mouth. "Then . . . it's okay?"

"Okay?" He cleared his throat, and his eyes glittered with the slightest hint of a grin. "Clea, if I weren't a married man . . ." His voice faded, and finally, he said, "The dress is lovely. *You're* lovely."

Again, she struggled against the blush. "Thank you, Brandon."

"No, thank you. For bringing some color into a life that was getting a little dreary." As soon as the words were out, she could tell he regretted saying them. "Our table is over there," he said, nodding toward it. "Why don't you check with the hotel people to make sure everything is ready?"

With that, he walked away, as if he hadn't just seared her with one of the sweetest proclamations she'd ever had from a man.

       °   °   °

The dance floor filled up later that night as the band played "Achy Breaky Heart," and hundreds of salesmen and their wives packed the dance floor, their liquor-induced joy apparent in the way they moved and laughed.

"Well, honey, let's do it."

Clea looked at Steven and wondered where on earth he'd gotten his particular brand of charm. She wasn't sure, but she suspected he'd gotten it along the racing circuit. "Excuse me?"

"I said, let's dance. Come on."

Clea shook her head. "No, you go ahead. I'd rather just watch."

"Tell her, Pop," Steven said across the table. "She has to do what you say."

Brandon, who had just joined them after a short speech of appreciation to his dealerships and a morale-boosting pep talk, shrugged. "If the lady doesn't want to dance, Steven . . ."

"Come on, Clea," Steven said, leaning flirtatiously toward her and coaxing her with a smile that might have brought a younger or less experienced woman to her knees. But Clea knew his kind.

Still, she saw the irritation on Brandon's face and knew that Steven wasn't going to give in. It wasn't worth a battle, she decided. Steven wasn't a man who was used to hearing the word no.

Reluctantly, she got to her feet. "All right, Steven, but I can't promise anything without my boots."

Flashing his father a victorious grin, Steven led her onto the dance floor, and she was instantly stricken with the fact that he did know how to dance. She wondered if Tiffany had put him in lessons when he was younger or if he'd picked it up in all the bars along the racing circuit too. He laughed and pulled her against him, confining her movements, and forcing her pelvis to move with his in a rhythm not suited for country dancing.

Clea tried to pull away. "I prefer not to dance so close."

"Hell, honey, it's not like I told you to throw a leg over my shoulder." His eyes sparkled with whiskey and humor as his hand slid down her back and held her against him. "I just like to be close."

"We *are* close," she said. "Too close. Now let go of me or I'm going to sit back down."

Steven loosened his grip and allowed her a little more room. "Damn, you're tough. Don't you like men?"

"Some better than others," she said.

He laughed. "Well, with those you like, do you ever just get naked and roll around in satin sheets? Do you ever let a man get lost in all that gorgeous hair?"

She felt her face reddening. "Do you ever think with anything other than the brains you have packed in your jockey strap?"

Steven's grin widened. "See there? I knew you noticed."

Clea turned slightly away, trying to ignore him as they danced.

"Do you ever think that the way your breasts move when you dance like that and how much that dress reveals might have some effect on what's packed inside my jockstrap?"

Clea stopped dancing cold. "I think I've had enough dancing for tonight."

"We just got started," he said, grabbing her wrist.

She started to pull away, but a flash of warning glimmered over his eyes.

"Come on, Clea," he said. "You don't want to huff

back to the table and pout the rest of the night. My
father might think you're being obstinate to a member
of his family, and you know how he hates that. Might get
you fired."

Clea glanced back to the table and saw that Brandon
was watching them, and suddenly she realized that what
Steven threatened was true. She had to be civil to Brandon's son, no matter how much of an animal he was.

Planting a smile on her face, she whispered, "Your
father won't even have to know, Steven, because when I
ram the heel of my shoe into a very vulnerable place on
your anatomy, you'll be making a beeline for the bathroom to check the damage. I've made sopranos out of
better men than you."

The words only seemed to please him more, and as
she headed back for the table, still smiling, he followed.

She sat down and saw that he wasn't going to run
away licking his wounds. He was going to sit there and
hound her all night. And at the table, in front of
Brandon and his grandfather, there was nothing she
could say to put him in his place.

The band struck up a heel-kicking tune by Clint
Black, and Clea reached across the table for Peter's
wrinkled hand. "Come on, Mr. Donovan. Why don't you
dance with me?"

The old man laughed aloud, and Brandon's face
brightened. "Come on, Dad. Go show her what you're
made of."

"I haven't danced in fifteen years, at least," Peter
said.

"Then it's time you did." Clea scraped her chair back
and went around to him. "Come on, Mr. Donovan. I'll
go easy on you."

Laughing heartily, the old man got to his feet and

took her hand. And as she led him to the dance floor, Clea looked back over her shoulder. Brandon was laughing as if he personally felt his father's enjoyment. Steven, on the other hand, gave her a small, threatening grin, and leered at her as if she were about to do a striptease instead of the cotton-eyed Joe.

She laughed with Peter as he fell into the rhythm of the song, but as she watched the father and son sitting at the table, watching every move she made, she realized that Steven's interest added a new dimension to the plan she had embarked upon. Not only would Brandon lose his marriage and his business, but he would lose his relationship with his son. She had never set out to pit Brandon against Steven, but what if it came to that?

She saw Brandon refill her glass of champagne and decided that maybe she should drink as much as she could tonight. It was, after all, their first night in Georgia. This might be the night she needed to accomplish her mission. Already, the few tabloid photographers who had slipped into the function had gotten pictures of them together, but she doubted there was much they could use, since she'd looked more like Steven's date than Brandon's.

The song came to an end, and she and Peter stumbled back to the table, the old man laughing and gasping for breath.

"I don't know when I've had so much fun," he wheezed. "Brandon, it's your turn now."

"I don't think so," Brandon said. "I don't know any of those country dances."

"All you have to know how to do is move, Dad," Steven said. "But if you don't want to, I'll spin her around the floor a few more times."

Clea picked up her drink and gulped down the champagne.

"Son, get out on that floor," Peter said. "You need to have a little fun for a change."

Brandon shifted back his chair and started to get up, surprising Clea. "All right," he said, "but we head for the middle of the dance floor. That way the photographers can't find us, and maybe the dealers won't notice me making a fool out of myself."

Clea nodded and started for the place he had indicated, and as she did, the band struck up a new song, a Reba McEntire song about a broken heart. It was slow, too slow, just slow enough that Tiffany would have been jumping for joy, pushing Clea to go for it.

And as the dancers surrounded them, Brandon smiled and pulled her into his arms.

Clea had danced with many men, and some had been too tall or too clumsy, or too short or too awkward. Some had sweated too much or worn too much cologne. Others had clutched her too tightly, or made a seduction out of a simple dance.

But none of those things applied to Brandon. He held her right hand against his heart, and she settled her other hand on his shoulder, trying not to press too intimately against him. But his hand on her back was insistent.

"What's the matter?" he asked with a soft grin. "Haven't you ever danced with your boss before?"

"No," she said, smiling, and realizing how brightly the blue flecks in Brandon's eyes sparkled when the light hit them just right. "I wouldn't have been caught dead with any of my other bosses."

"Gee, I guess I should be flattered."

He pressed his chin against her crown, in such a natural gesture that she assumed he danced like this with everyone. It wasn't just her.

Still, when he let her go and spun her unexpectedly, then laughed at the surprise on her face, her heart fluttered. She was more attracted to Brandon than she was supposed to be, she realized. She was charmed and enchanted, and she liked having him hold her more than she ever had a right to.

And she had to admit that it was a dangerous feeling. A tragic feeling. For there was no way it could come to any good end.

She looked up at him, desperate to say something, anything, to get her out of this mess she was in, but when their eyes met, she was struck mute. There was something in his eyes, something as profound as what she felt in her heart, something that frightened him as well.

Something that she didn't want him to feel.

Quickly, she stepped back, and touching her forehead, pretended to be dizzy. "I . . . I'd better sit down. I'm a little light-headed."

He bent down and touched her forehead, testing her for fever. "Are you all right? You seem a little flushed."

"Just the champagne and the smoke," she said. "I'm not that used to it."

"Come on," he said. "You need to sit down for a while."

"But I didn't have the chance to teach you the two-step," she said, recovering her smile.

"Another time," he said as he led her back through the crowd.

Steven bristled all the way to his car after saying good-night to his father and grandfather. Hard as he'd tried, he hadn't been able to get Clea alone again. She was elusive and uninterested, and something about that attracted him more than he could stand.

Something in his groin stirred. He decided to go back into the hotel, wait until his father was in his room, and then go to Clea's room. Maybe if she wasn't being monitored by her boss, she'd let loose and invite him in.

He pictured himself peeling off her clothes, uncovering those perky breasts that had teased him almost to the point of madness when they were dancing earlier. He pictured slipping her skirt over her hips, feeling the texture of the soft skin of her buttocks, the smoothness of her thighs.

Closing his eyes, he imagined himself inside her, full and explosive, as her hair swept over his face, his chest, swinging with her movement . . .

He forced his eyes open, and told himself that he would have her tonight if it killed him. And once he was there alone with her, she would want him. He knew she would.

He would make her want him if it was the last thing he did.

19

Clea closed and locked the door to her suite and collapsed against it, wondering if her heart had been playing tricks on her downstairs or if Brandon and she really had shared a moment of awareness. A split second of mutual longing.

But then he had left her in the hotel lobby, telling her to meet him for breakfast at seven so they could get a couple of hours' work done before they had to be at the site of the clinic. As if she were Evelyn, or anyone else on his staff, he'd said good-night and headed to his suite.

She kicked off her shoes and fell back on the bed, staring at the ceiling. This was getting out of hand, she thought. She was falling for a man she wasn't even supposed to like. She wanted him to hold her, but he was married, and the permission—the command, rather—from his wife only tainted the idea more. The moment she got him into bed—and gave Tiffany the proof she needed—her association with him would end.

The telephone rang, startling her, and she picked it up. "Hello?"

"It's me." The voice was unmistakably Tiffany's, and Clea closed her eyes and sat up straight. "I want a status report."

Clea sighed. "The status is the same as it was yesterday."

"Nothing? Do you mean to tell me you've been with him all day and all night and nothing has happened?"

"How do you know he isn't with me right now?"

"Because he just called home," Tiffany said. "Don't bluff me, Clea."

"I wasn't bluffing," Clea bit out. "I was just trying to make a point. Just because you don't have some incriminating pictures in your hand doesn't mean that I'm not making progress."

"What did you wear tonight?"

Clea frowned and came to her feet. "Why?"

"Because it's important. Were you alluring enough, or did you look like some Victorian schoolmarm?"

Clea's chest felt heavy, and she drew in a deep breath. "I don't think you would have hired me if I looked like a schoolmarm, now would you?" When Tiffany didn't answer, Clea went on. "I was alluring enough to make your son drool all over me."

"Steven?"

"Yes. I had to threaten him into keeping his hands off me."

"Clea," Tiffany said, suddenly more ruffled than Clea had ever heard her. "Steven cannot figure into this picture. If Brandon has an inkling that he's interested in you, he won't bite."

"I thought of that."

"You'll have to make him lose interest."

Clea gave out a heartless laugh. "Fine. You tell me how to be alluring enough for Brandon while still turning off Steven."

Tiffany sighed. "Just stay away from him. Once you're back here in Detroit it won't be a problem. Steven keeps a house here, but he's rarely in town."

"Thank God," Clea whispered.

"What?"

"This may come as a surprise to you, Tiffany, but I don't like your son."

Tiffany hesitated, and Clea smiled. "I suppose I should warn you not to let Brandon see you insulting him. He's very protective of his family."

"I've already figured that out," Clea said.

"Back to business," Tiffany cut in. "I want you to make a move on him tonight. Find some reason to go to his room. Ask him for aspirin or something. Then slip in and make your move."

Clea's face reddened. "Tiffany, I'm tired. It's been a long day. Neither one of us—"

"I'm not paying you to sleep all safe and cozy in your own suite, Clea. Just do it."

Clea checked the clock, realized it was after midnight. The thought of knocking on his door and trying to arouse him at this hour terrified her. "Tiffany, I'm beginning to think I'm not cut out for this job. It's not the way I envisioned it at all."

"That's too bad, Clea. I suggest you just grin and bear it. Brandon's not an unattractive man, after all. It can't be that bad."

"No," Clea said, her voice falling with her spirits. "He certainly isn't unattractive."

"Then go in there and do something," she said. "And Clea, if you need a little confidence, try this. He hasn't had sex in weeks. His willpower will be very flimsy by now."

Clea was silent for a moment, and finally, Tiffany

said, "I'll check in with you tomorrow. And Clea, you'd better have something to tell me by then."

Clea dropped the phone back in its cradle and raked her fingers back through her hair. She thought of packing her bags and taking the first flight home. She thought of cutting her hair and gaining weight so that no one ever hired her to do such a fool thing again. Plain women didn't have the problems she had had in her life. To her, beauty had been more of a curse than a blessing.

A knock sounded on her door, and something in her heart fluttered. Was it Brandon, saving her the trouble of following Tiffany's order? She went to the door, looked out the peephole, and saw Steven standing there.

Quickly, she went to her makeup bag in the bathroom and grabbed a pair of scissors, stuffed them into her pocket, and went back to the door.

"What do you want?" she asked when she'd opened it.

"You," he said, pushing the door further open and squeezing through.

"I don't want you," she said. "Get out."

Smiling, he closed the door, and she backed away, unwilling to make a scene for fear that Brandon would hear. "Steven, I'm not interested in you. Why don't you go back to that bar and pick up one of those cute little bimbo types? You'd be so much better off."

He started toward her, his eyes smoky with desire and a wicked grin inching across his face. Any resemblance he had to Brandon slowly disappeared, and as he came toward her, she realized that he was his mother's son, not his father's. There wasn't much of Brandon in him.

He hemmed her against the wall and took her arms,

and she clutched her hands around the scissors as he dragged her against him. "Kiss me," he ordered. "And then I'll undress you. Slowly."

Clea turned her face away. "I don't want you, Steven. How can I get that through your head?"

"You can't," he said. "Because I know better. I saw the way you looked at me all night. Those deliberate little moves when you knew I was watching. The way you bent over to show off those breasts that would make the strongest man crumble."

"I didn't do any of that!" She tried to wrest free of his grip, but he caught her mouth with his and tried to pry her lips open with his tongue.

Finally, she stopped wrestling, and allowed him to kiss her, blindly, viciously. As he did, she pulled the scissors from her pocket, and slowly slid her hand down his stomach, until the blade was poised just below his testicle. As the kiss ended, she brought the dull side of the blade up just enough to call his attention to it.

"Do you feel that?" she asked through her teeth.

He started to back away, but she whispered, "I wouldn't move if I were you. You might lose something."

His grin surprised her. "You wouldn't."

"Oh, but I have. Only last time it was a bullet. You can read about it in the papers."

He dropped his arms, releasing her, and slowly backed away.

Clea smiled, but didn't drop the scissors. "That's better."

"You know, I don't give up easy," he said, his eyes delighting in her defense. "I'm used to getting what I want."

"I'm sure you are, Steven," she said. "But we all have

to grow up sometime. I'm the wrong person to test. Now get out of my room."

Still smiling, he went to the door, and turned back before opening it. "You're going to be begging for me someday, Clea," he said. "You're going to want me so much it'll make you crazy."

"We'll see," she said.

He closed the door behind him, and quickly she rushed forward, locking the deadbolt.

Men were scum, she told herself for the ten thousandth time. They were all alike.

Except for Brandon. And ironically enough, he was the one she had been hired to *make* into scum.

Which, she supposed, made *her* scum.

She looked back at the telephone, where Tiffany had told her moments ago to get into Brandon's room tonight and seduce him, and she thought of calling her and telling her to forget the whole thing. That she wanted to give the money back. That she wouldn't be her puppet anymore.

But before she could make it to the phone, someone knocked again.

Still clutching the scissors, she went back to the door and peered out. Brandon stood there, in his tux pants, sans cummerbund, and a tee shirt. Quickly, she opened the door.

"Brandon?"

He stepped inside, and she closed the door behind her. "I was afraid I'd wake you," he said. "But your briefcase got put in my suite by mistake today. I thought you might need it."

She took it and set it down. "Thank you."

He shrugged. "I thought you might have personal items in there that you needed. Makeup or something."

"Yes," she said. "I appreciate it."

It was the moment of truth, she thought, the moment Tiffany had prayed for. The moment when she had Brandon alone and vulnerable, when she thought he might have the same thing on his mind that she had on hers.

"I . . . I really had fun dancing tonight," she said, knowing her words sounded lame, but unable to do any better. "Would . . . would you like a glass of wine? The bar's pretty well stocked."

She started toward it, but he shook his head. "No, I can't. I have a headache. I should probably just go back to the room and lie down."

She stared at him for a moment, torn between her wish for him to stay, just because *she* wanted him to, and her knowledge that she was trapping him in Tiffany's web if he did. But it wasn't Tiffany's needs that prompted her as she acted. It was her own.

"Sit down," she said, pulling him into a chair. Complying, he sat.

She went behind him, and began to massage his shoulders, and a slow moan escaped him. "That feels nice," he whispered.

She worked her massage up his neck, to the base of his skull, behind his ears, up to his temples. She could feel the tension seeping out of him, and the relaxation taking hold.

"How did you learn to do this?" he whispered.

"When I was selling cars I used to get pretty tense sometimes," she said. "So I went to a masseuse once a week. I picked up a few things."

"You sure did." He rolled his head back and looked up at her. "You're a woman of many talents, Clea."

She stared down at him, her hair falling on each side

of his face, and for a moment he stared up at her, as frozen in the moment as she.

She wasn't sure if it was Brandon who made the first move, or if it was she . . . whether he raised up or she bent down, but slowly, gently, sweetly, their lips came together, parted. Their tongues swirled and made a brief play at mating.

And as quickly as it started, it was over.

Brandon came to his feet, raking his hands through his hair, breathing heavily and shaking his head. "I'm sorry."

"No, I'm sorry," Clea said. "I don't know what came over me . . ."

He started to the door, then turned back to her, his face anguished. "I'm not a monk, Clea. I have the same hormones that pulse through every other sane man on the face of the earth. But this can't happen."

"I know," she said.

His face twisted, and he came toward her, almost reaching for her, then clutching his hands just before he did. "I'm a married man," he said. "A happily married man. And I believe in my marriage vows."

"You . . . don't have to explain that," she said. "I of all people can appreciate a man who can say that. I would never . . ." Her voice trailed off as she thought of telling him that she would never sleep with a married man. But could she leave off the *unless I had enough incentive* part?

"You're a sweet woman, Clea. And so beautiful . . . You have the potential to drive me crazy. I know that. But maybe if we just define this right now, so that we both know that nothing is ever going to happen . . ." He rubbed his eyes and looked over his fingers at her. "Clea, I'd rather fire you than do something that would make it hard for me to look myself in the mirror."

"I would rather you did, too," she said.

He nodded and touched her shoulder, frowned intensely into her eyes, and then backed away. "We'll pretend that nothing ever happened. And from now on, I'll stay out of your suite at night."

"That's not necessary," she said. "I'll keep my hands to myself from now on. You can't avoid me if I'm working for you. We need to go on like we have been. Brandon, you have nothing to fear from me."

"It's myself I'm afraid of," he whispered, and before she could say anything else, he was gone.

20

Steven paused at Clea's door in the hotel, and decided against knocking. She had made herself clear the night before. She didn't like him, but that only made him more determined to have her. She didn't yet know what he was made of. He would just have to show her.

He walked further down the hall to the suite his father occupied, and did a rhythmic little knock on the door. After a moment, Brandon opened the door, his hands full of papers.

"You got a minute to talk?" Steven asked.

Brandon took the pencil out of his mouth. "Sure. Clea and I were just taking care of some things."

Steven looked past his father to Clea, who sat at a table with work spread out in front of her, and quickly, she gathered her papers into a stack and got to her feet. "I'll go make these phone calls while you visit with Steven, Brandon."

"Yeah, you do that," Brandon said. "And call Evelyn for messages. And when George calls tell him to call me immediately so I can inspect the cars. And call

Lawrence to find out the latest on that door problem we were having."

Steven watched as Clea took notes, unruffled, then started out of the room.

"Don't work too hard, Clea," he said.

Over her shoulder, she tossed him a look that made him feel like an idiot throwing out a child's cliché. "I won't."

Her smile was false—he knew it was, for it was strained and admonishing—as she closed the door behind him.

Brandon dropped his own papers back on the table and turned back to Steven, offering him his undivided attention. "What's up?"

Steven dropped onto the sofa and let out a long sigh. "This racing business, Dad. I guess I'm disappointed that I didn't even qualify."

"There are other races."

"Maybe not for me."

Brandon looked startled. "You're twenty years old, son. It's time you learned to stick with something even when it gets tough."

Steven leaned forward and planted his elbows on his knees. "I am learning, Dad. That's why I want another shot at DC."

Brandon's eyebrows lifted suddenly. "You want to come to work for Donovan Concepts?"

"Yeah. I might keep racing some on the side, just for fun. But I guess I feel like it's time to start my climb."

"Your climb to what?"

"To the top, Dad. It's your job I'm after, you know."

Brandon threw his head back and laughed. "CEO, huh? You have a long way to go, Steven. And you won't get there by skipping steps."

"I realize that. That's why I'm willing to come in at any level you say. And then, next fall, I could finish school . . ."

Brandon frowned and stared at his son, knowing that something wasn't right. Was this the same man who just six months ago told him he could shove college and his entry-level job offer up his ass? "Any level?"

"Well . . . I don't want to work on the assembly line. I kind of picture myself in an office, making decisions. I think I could make a difference, Dad. You know I have the education, and now my racing background would enhance that."

"It might, at that," Brandon said. He rubbed his chin, which was beginning to stubble, even though he'd shaved that morning. "Maybe you could make a contribution to the THD."

"Hell, you've got Gramps in on it. You might as well sign me up."

Brandon sat back for a moment, considering where his son might best fit. "I could talk to George about putting you on his staff."

"Would I be in the DC building?"

"Most of the time," Brandon said.

Steven nodded. "Then it sounds fine."

"It would do you good to watch the evolution of the THD from the inside out. The more you can learn at the lower levels, the better suited you really will be for my job one day."

"I'm counting on it," Steven said.

Brandon extended his hand for his son to shake. "Then I guess we've got a deal. Provided George agrees."

"He wouldn't dare turn you down," Steven said smugly. "Hey, by the way. You wouldn't mind throwing

Clea in as a perk, would you? I'll need a secretary."

Brandon narrowed his eyes at his son and wondered if this was an offhanded comment or his entire motivation for this decision. "Clea's not a secretary. She's my assistant. And no, she doesn't come with the job."

Steven snapped his fingers. "Damn. Oh well, I guess I can manage without her. But when it comes to hiring, I want someone with legs like hers and breasts at least as big. Do they have an agency you can call for secretaries like that?"

Brandon's smile faded entirely. "Steven, despite what you might think, I did not hire Clea for her legs or her breasts."

Steven stood up, laughing. "Come on, Dad. You can be straight with me. They couldn't have hurt any."

Brandon turned back to the papers on his desk. "I'll talk to George when he gets here with the cars. Meanwhile, you can start tomorrow. It won't hurt you to be at the clinic and see what kind of feedback we get."

"Yeah, I'll be there," Steven said, meandering to the door.

When he left, Brandon sat back down, staring at the door, wondering if Steven would really change careers for a woman. Was it Clea who had finally gotten him into the company, when all of Brandon's persuading hadn't done it?

No, he thought. It couldn't be. Steven had women lined up, and he usually liked cheaper women who dressed extravagantly, the kind that could go from a thousand-dollar-a-plate dinner into a stripteasing session without batting an eye. No, it wasn't Clea that motivated him, he told himself, but pragmatism. Donovan ambition. He was ready to start being groomed to take over the company someday. That was all there was to it.

He reached for the phone, dialed Clea's room, and asked her to come back in. Strange how hard it was to get any work done these days without her, he thought. Strange how comforting and exhilarating her company had become.

Maybe too comforting, and too exhilarating. He hadn't missed Tiffany at all during this trip. When he'd called her, she'd seemed so distracted that he hadn't even kept her on the phone long. She was probably planning some fund-raising event or writing a speech for one of her women's groups. She couldn't care less about Steven's race or the clinic for the car that bore her initials.

But Clea did. In everything she said, he could read her excitement about the clinic, where they'd hear from ordinary people what they thought of the car, what their favorite features were, what items they preferred over others.

Clea understood his own excitement. The car was becoming as much hers as his. But sharing that was a little too intimate. He would have to pull back even more if he knew what was good for him. Last night was too close a call. He'd have to make sure it never happened again.

Clea watched the clinic participants enter the arena where the THD prototypes were parked in a circle and meander among the cars, looking at one with gull-wing doors, another with hydraulic sliding doors, and another with standard doors. One of the THDs had a sun roof, another had alloy wheels, another had a bigger cockpit to include a one-passenger backseat.

The consumers' input that day would help determine

which of the features would wind up in the final version
of the THD, or whether the whole concept of the car
was a failure or success. Also on the lot were a Lotus, a
Porsche, and a Lamborghini, unmarked, to be com-
pared to the THD. If the majority of the clinic participants liked the other brand cars better, the Donovan
team would have to come up with something better than
what they already had.

Clea caught Brandon's eye across the lot, and he
smiled as clusters of people milled around the THDs.
She smiled back and started toward him, but someone
caught her arm.

"Hey, beautiful lady."

Swinging around, she confronted Steven. "Oh, it's
you. I didn't know you were coming."

He smiled at her indifferent reception. "Didn't my
father tell you? I've joined the company."

A look of alarm passed through her eyes, and she
glanced uncomfortably toward Brandon. He was
embroiled in a conversation with a group of people.
"No, he didn't mention it."

"Well, you'd better get used to it, darling, because
I'm going to be around a lot from now on."

"What about racing?"

"Giving it up," he said with a knowing grin. "I've
decided to join the ranks of Donovan execs. You won't
be able to avoid me, you know. I'm going to be everywhere you look."

"Is that why you're doing this?" she asked suddenly.

He laughed, an almost bitter laugh. "Why? To stalk
you? Oh, Clea, isn't that question a little self-centered?"

"Yes, it is," she said. "I'm sorry. It's just . . . after last
night, I didn't know . . ."

"Dad's been working on me for months," he said.

"It's a business decision, not a sexual one. Although, if you have something like that in mind, I wouldn't run from it."

"I don't," she snapped. "And if we're going to be working together, I hope we can learn to act like associates rather than a hunter and his prey."

Steven grinned. "I do love the hunt."

"Well, I don't like being hunted. I have my own agenda. I don't have time or energy for you."

His smile faltered a degree, and she realized she'd hit a nerve. "Give it time, Clea. You'll realize eventually that you want me."

"No, I won't, Steven. I can't get involved with you."

Steven glanced across to his father, and Clea followed his gaze. Brandon was watching her again, but he quickly looked away.

"Is that why?" Steven asked. "Are you interested in my old man?"

"No, of course not," she said, too abruptly.

"Because if you are, you can give it up. He's the most married man in the universe. My father would rather be hung by his toenails and beaten than cheat on my mother."

"I know that."

"Oh, do you?" His smile was a little too perceptive, and she wished she had kept her mouth shut. "Sounds like you've learned firsthand. What did you do, Clea, give it a shot? Is that why you wear your skirts so short and your blouse open enough to make a sated man hard?"

Her first instinct was to slap him, but she retained enough presence of mind to realize that Brandon would require an explanation. "Brandon is my boss," she said through her teeth. "Nothing more. You, on the other hand, are just another piece of scum who thinks he can woo a woman with sleazy little suggestions."

"You've got that right."

"Then you're about to get an education, after all."

His smile slipped wider across his face. "Maybe you're the one who has something to learn."

"We'll see about that," she said, and left him standing there grinning. He caught his father's eye again over the cars and lifted his hand in a wave. Damn, that woman could spar, he thought. Already he was enjoying this job even more than he had expected to.

21

The message Clea received when she got back to the hotel was unmistakably Tiffany's, though there was no name assigned to it. "Call me immediately," it said. And in the "From" section, the operator had written, "a woman who said you'd know who she was."

Clea wondered what on earth could be wrong now. She glanced awkwardly at Brandon, who was waiting for his messages as well, and shoved the paper into her pocket.

"Problem?" he asked.

"No," she said. "Just a call from my mother."

"Oh. Well, go on up and call her. Don't take too long, though. We have a lot of work to do before we can call it a day. The rest of the staff is meeting me in an hour, and I have several things to process before then."

"I'll just be a minute," she said. She headed for the elevator, her heels clicking on the marble floor. The moment she was in her room, she went for the telephone.

It rang three times before Tiffany picked it up, and

her voice was thick, as if she'd just been awakened.

"Tiffany? It's me."

"What the hell is going on?" Tiffany demanded without prelude. "I picked up the newspaper this morning, and there in the society section is a picture of you with my son!"

"Really?" Clea asked, undaunted. "That soon?"

"Clea, you don't seem to understand the gravity of this. I'm paying you to be photographed with Brandon, not Steven. If they think you're Steven's girlfriend, no one will connect you with Brandon."

"Tiffany, don't you think you're overreacting a little? Just because somebody got a picture of us doesn't mean they assume we're lovers."

"Well, they'll be more likely to assume you're lovers with Steven than Brandon. I'm warning you, Clea. If you're trying to play both sides against the middle, you're dealing with the wrong person."

"What do you mean both sides against the middle?"

"I mean, if you think you're going to get Steven as a consolation prize, I've got news for you. He's off limits."

Clea allowed a half-smile to creep across her face, and shaking her head, asked, "What makes you think I'd be interested in your son, Tiffany?"

"Why wouldn't you be? He's handsome and rich."

Clea sighed. "You don't have to worry. It takes more than handsome and rich to interest me. Having some semblance of a personality doesn't hurt."

"Excuse me? Are you insulting my son?"

"No, Tiffany. I would never deliberately insult your son. I'm just saying that if the man put half as much energy into his personality as he does into his technique, he might get along better."

"His technique? Has Steven made advances?"

"If you can call bulldozing his way into my suite an advance."

There were a few seconds of silence, before Tiffany asked, "Have you slept with him?"

Clea laughed. "No, Tiffany. One man per family is all I can handle. I threw him out. And as for anything happening in the future, forget it. He's not my type."

"You remember that," Tiffany said, her voice even frostier than when she first called. "Your association should only be with Brandon. And if you're going to be photographed, make sure you're with him instead of my son."

"Whatever you say," Clea uttered.

It was nearing ten o'clock by the time the meeting with the DC executives broke up, and assignments had been given out for incorporating the changes they'd decided to make to the THD. Only Clea, Steven, and George remained in Brandon's room when he decided to uncork a bottle of champagne and pour everyone a glass.

"Here's to our success today," he said, extending his glass in a toast. "We beat out the Lamborghini, for God's sake. It was almost unamimous that the THD was a better car."

They all laughed at his look of exhilaration and touched glasses. When she drank, Clea's excited eyes met Brandon's across the glass.

"I have an announcement to make," Brandon said. "And I wanted to tell it to all of you first. I've decided to unveil the prototype at the New York Auto Show. It's only three months away, and I think we can have it finished by then."

George straightened up. "Are you sure? That's pretty short notice. There's a lot to do yet . . ."

"Not that much," Brandon said. "If we really turn the heat up on the engineers, I think they can have it ready by then." He finished off his drink, too quickly, and poured another glass. "I'm anxious to debut the car, George," he said. "I can't wait until the public gets a hold of it. The press will go nuts. It'll be the pinnacle of my career."

It was at that moment, as she saw the dream in Brandon's eyes, that Clea realized she was falling in love with him. Brandon was a dreamer, but not just any dreamer. He was a man who knew what he wanted and maneuvered everything to get it. He was a man who didn't settle for second best, a man who didn't give up until he'd gotten the job done.

"What do you think, Clea? Can you see it?"

Clea smiled, her eyes glistening with too much adoration. "I can see it, Brandon," she said. "It'll be the biggest hit since GM unveiled the Corvette. But after the debut, I think you should make the public wait awhile before it's mass produced. Build up expectation. Get the dealers to start waiting lists. And ask top dollar."

Brandon filled her glass again and turned back to Steven. "What do you say, son? Is it the most exciting thing you've ever been involved in or not?"

Steven grinned, but his eyes were on Clea rather than his father. "Oh, it's exciting, all right."

"When those people were getting in the car, their eyes got as big as saucers. And these were sports car owners. We deliberately invited sophisticated drivers so we could have the toughest criticism."

"They loved it, all right," George said, coming to his feet. He set down his glass, and put his arm around Brandon's shoulders. "Congratulations, Brandon."

"Don't congratulate me," Brandon said. "The victory's at least half yours."

"It was your brainchild," George said, laughing. He turned back to Clea and, grinning, added, "You think he's excited now. You wait until the auto show. We'll have to anchor him down to keep him from flying out of the building."

He started for the door. "I'd better go down and get those data sheets out of my trunk. I want to look over them before I turn in tonight."

"Yeah," Brandon said. He glanced at his son, who was refilling his glass again, and said, "Steven, go help your new boss carry those things up."

Steven frowned. "Can't you get the bellboy to do it?"

"No," Brandon said. "These things are not for just anyone's eyes. I'd feel better if you and George did it."

Reluctantly, Steven got to his feet. "All right," he said. "Anything else?" The question came on a sarcastic note, but Brandon didn't seem to catch it.

"No, you can turn in after that. I'm going to finish up a few things here and hit the sack myself."

Steven stood still, and looked from Clea to Brandon, then back to Clea. "All right," he said finally. "You two don't work too hard."

As he ambled out the door behind George, Clea had a foreboding feeling that he could see right through her. And he knew her intentions with Brandon were anything but pure.

The door closed, and Brandon, not noticing anything unusual, refilled Clea's champagne, then his own again, and grinned like a little boy who'd just been declared MVP in Little League. "Did you hear what that guy asked at the end of the clinic?"

"The one who wanted to know where he could get his name on a waiting list for the car?"

"Yeah, that one. The man has owned four Porsches, and it looks like we've converted him."

"He won't be the only one, Brandon. I saw true lust in the eyes of some of those drivers today. When they saw the instrument panels, you would have thought they were standing at a gourmet feast after starving for six months. One guy told me he was selling his Ferrari the minute the THD came out." She sipped her champagne. "Have you thought of any names for the car?"

Brandon sat down beside her and shifted to face her on the couch. "I've thought of several things. I was thinking of something to do with lightning . . . I don't know. Another one that keeps coming up is the Donovan Streak, but that isn't glamorous enough."

"You could make it a contest. Let all the Donovan employees enter ideas, and give some prize to the one who comes up with the winning name."

"Yeah, I could," he said. "But you know, I didn't name it after Tiffany the first time for nothing. I wanted it to signify excellence, beauty, sophistication, wealth . . . And I realized those were qualities my wife had. Maybe I should keep following that plan and call it the Tiffany."

"Sounds too feminine," she said, tracing the perimeter of her glass. "No self-respecting macho sports car driver is going to want to drive something called Tiffany."

"Yeah, you're probably right."

"How about the Brandon?" she asked with a smile.

He leaned his head back on the sofa and smiled at the ceiling, as if he could picture it. "Nah. Lacks pizzazz."

"Depends on your perspective," she said with a smile.

He brought his eyes back to her, and for a moment, she saw something move deep within them, something she had put there, something she didn't yet know whether she'd planted deliberately or by accident. He was breaking down, despite his efforts not to.

After a moment, he reached for his glass again, bottomed it, breaking the spell of the moment. She knew that was exactly what he had intended.

Disappointment filled her, and she realized she wasn't ready to let the moment end just yet. "Brandon," she ventured, choosing her words carefully, since it suddenly seemed important for him to understand her. "I really enjoyed today. The whole trip has been so much fun for me, but today when I saw those people looking at the THD, I just felt a little tinge of propriety for it. Like I'd been in on designing it. I know I wasn't, but it's all so exciting . . . I can't help getting caught up in it."

He leaned his head back, and his eyes met hers again, and she thought how magnificent they looked when they were off guard and relaxed. They were the kind of eyes that made innocent women have sweet dreams at night—the kind of dreams that involved their hearts and not their hormones. Knight in shining armor dreams. Prince Charming dreams. Brandon Donovan dreams.

But he wasn't there to sweep her off her feet. She was there to knock him off of his.

This time, she broke their eye contact, and leaned forward, setting her glass down.

He reached out and caught her hand, and made her look at him again. "You're fun, Clea. I enjoy working with you. Beyond that, I consider you a good friend. It's fun to see someone get as excited over my car as I do."

She felt a blush come to her cheeks, and kicking herself, realized that it was ludicrous that she could still blush after signing her soul over to Tiffany. She was tainted now, and no matter how far she stretched her imagination, she would never be innocent again.

Brandon continued holding her hand, fondling her fingers, stroking her palm with his thumb. The room seemed to grow hot, and her head felt light. Did Brandon feel that, too? He'd been drinking champagne— one glass after another—so many that she'd lost count. It would be the perfect opportunity to break down his defenses . . . in this close moment, this time of intimate appraisal. He wouldn't be as willing to turn her away tonight. All she would have to do was touch him, and her mission could be fulfilled. All she would have to do was nudge him just a little . . .

She pulled back her hand and got to her feet. "Well, as exciting as the day has been, Brandon, I guess I'm just that tired. If you don't need me anymore tonight . . . I'll go on back to my suite."

He looked up at her silently with eyes that spoke volumes, and she hated herself for making him face a moral decision such as this one. She looked back at him, her eyes full of a pain whose origin he could never know.

"Clea . . ." The word came on a soft whisper, and he rose from the couch and looked down at her with smoky eyes. "I . . . I wish you wouldn't leave."

"I wish it, too," she returned softly. "But we both know I have to."

He dropped his hand to his side, and nodded. "Yeah, I guess so."

Smiling a truly genuine smile since she'd just done something that would enable her to look in the mirror tomorrow, she started out of the room, knowing he watched her until she was gone.

22

Shalimar *slipped her feet* into the backless heels she had found in Clea's closet and sashayed down the hall in her sweetest silk teddy. It was the one that cowboy from Omaha had given her last year . . . Billy Bob, or Bobby Joe . . . something like that. She was terrible with names, but she never forgot a face. The cowboy had had a mustache that tickled her when he kissed her . . . or was it a beard? Oh well, she thought, waving off the thought. The teddy was nice, anyway. And Mitch was wild about it.

"Don't you have to go to work today?" he asked, pulling on his work boots.

Shalimar shrugged. "Not for a while. I don't like to schedule appointments before noon. I have to get my beauty sleep, you know."

Mitch caught her by the waist and pulled her across his lap, and she laughed like a little girl. If there was anything she loved, it was manly playfulness. A man who could keep her surprised.

"Sleep, shit," he said. "You don't sleep. You play all

night. I'm gonna have to sleep the whole weekend to
catch up on the last few days."

Shalimar's face fell. "Really? But you'll call, won't
you?"

Mitch laughed and shook his head. "No, baby. I can't
call you on my days off. My wife watches me like a
hawk."

"Wife?" Shalimar sprang off his lap. "You didn't tell
me you were married."

"Well, hell, honey, you didn't ask."

"But you're not wearin' a ring. A man ought to wear a
ring if he's married."

"Not if he fools around, he doesn't," Mitch said on a
chuckle. He stood up, his shirt still unbuttoned and the
tails hanging over his jeans. "Now don't go pouting on
me, honey. You're the one who seduced me, remember? I was minding my own business, fixing the refrigerator, and the next thing I knew you were making all
those little suggestive suggestions . . ."

Shalimar swept her fingers back through her curls
and told herself that he was right. It had been her come-
on, but she hadn't expected him to be married.

"But I'll call you next week. Maybe I can tell my wife
I'm going to Ann Arbor to see my brother again. That's
where she thought I was the last couple of days."

"No," Shalimar said with a heavy sigh. "Don't bother.
I don't mess around with married men."

Mitch laughed again and dragged her against him.
"Honey, you know you'll mess around with anything in
pants. And it doesn't make one ding-damn's difference
if he has a ring on his finger or not."

"That's not true," she said, slipping out of his grip. "I
do have principles, you know."

Mitch chortled, as if he didn't believe a word. "Well,

do me a favor and save a few of 'em for me next week. This was the best sex I've had in weeks."

He started for the door, but it opened before he could reach the knob. Clea confronted them both.

Shalimar gasped. "Clea! You're back early."

Mitch grinned that sexy grin that had gotten Shalimar in trouble in the first place. "Damn, it just gets better and better." He looked back at Shalimar over his shoulder and winked. "If you'll both be here, maybe I can get one night away from my wife this weekend, after all."

Shalimar shoved him out the door and turned back to Clea like a kid who'd just flunked the third grade and didn't care who knew it.

Clea glared at her. "What are you doing?"

"Sayin' good-bye to my friend," Shalimar said, sweeping her hair back again and clomping into the kitchen, as if she had every right to be wearing her sister's shoes.

"Your married friend? In your teddy?"

"Look, don't start with me," Shalimar snapped. "I'm in a bad mood." She grabbed a yogurt out of the refrigerator and stuck a spoon in it. "You weren't even supposed to be back until tonight," she muttered.

Clea took the yogurt away from her. "Shally, I told you not to bring a parade of men through my apartment!"

"I didn't!" Shalimar cried. "He was here fixin' the refrigerator, which, incidentally, is gonna cost you two hundred dollars. Since he was here, anyway, I figured . . ."

"You figured you could hop into bed with him and it wouldn't make any difference?" Clea slammed her purse down on the counter and massaged her temples. "Damn it, Shalimar, why do you have to be so promiscuous?"

"Damn it, Clea, why do you have to be such a prude? I didn't do anything wrong! I didn't know he was married until a few minutes ago."

"What *did* you know about him? His last name? Where he lives?"

"Well . . ." She looked around the kitchen, found the receipt, and grabbed it up. "It must be on here . . ."

Clea snatched the receipt away. "Shalimar, you're starting to scare me. There's too much at stake for you to pass your body around like you do. You're too good for that."

"What's wrong with my takin' affection when it's offered?" Shalimar asked. "What's wrong with my respondin' when some guy is nice to me?"

"Try smiling, next time," Clea said. "Try saying thank you. You don't have to strip off your clothes."

"I didn't," she said with a pouty grin. "He took them off for me."

Clea groaned. She opened the door and realized Butch—Brandon's driver—had brought her luggage up while she was fighting with Shalimar. Already he was gone, and she hadn't had the chance to thank him.

She grabbed her suitcase and garment bag and started back to her bedroom. When she got there, she saw that the bed was unmade and the sheet lay on the floor. Furiously, she jerked the fitted sheet off the bed, flung it to the pile on the floor, grabbed the bundle up, and thrust it into the hall. "Wash these sheets, Shalimar!" she shouted. "Wash them now!"

"I was goin' to!" Shalimar called. "But you got home early." She clomped up the hall and stopped in the doorway. "Why did you get home so early, anyway?"

"Brandon decided he wanted to leave earlier. Would you please put something on? Your friend may have liked watching you parade around in that, but I don't."

"Oh," Shalimar said, looking down at herself as if she'd forgotten what she was wearing. "Sure." Clomping in, she grabbed a robe from Clea's closet and slipped it on.

Clea collapsed on the bed and covered her face with her hands. "Shally, we've got to work something out here. I've been by myself for too long to put up with all this."

Shalimar's face filled with remorse. "I won't do it anymore. Don't make me move out. Please, Clea. I don't make enough to pay for my own place."

"If you ever went to work, you might!"

"Can I help it if I haven't built up enough clientele, yet?" Shalimar asked. "Just because I don't have some cushy executive job like you doesn't mean I'm worthless."

Clea took a deep breath and told herself it wasn't even worth the fight. People like Shalimar could never comprehend mere logic. "I just wish you'd do more around here. Stop raiding my closet, for one thing, and stay out of my bed."

"And what else?" she asked. "I'd cook you supper, but you're never here. Just tell me what you want me to do, Clea. I'll do the grocery shoppin', or run errands . . . hell, anything to get me out of this dump."

Clea shot her another look, and Shalimar winced. "Sorry."

Join a support group, Clea thought. *Nymphos Anonymous*. "Don't worry about it, Shally," Clea whispered. "Just have a little respect, all right? For me, as well as yourself."

Shalimar clapped her hands together, as if they'd solved all their problems, and plopped stomach-down on the bed. "So how was your trip? Did anything happen?"

"Anything like what?" Clea asked, weary.

"Between you and Brandon."

"I'm really tired, Shally," Clea said, her voice turning sharper. "Please . . . I don't want to talk right now."

"Oh." Disappointed, she got up and sashayed toward the door, then turned back to her sister. "Geez, you're grumpy, you know that?"

Clea fell back onto the bare mattress and only then realized that Shalimar hadn't done a thing with the sheets she'd thrown on the floor. Eventually, she'd have to do it herself.

She tried to clear her mind, concentrate on one thing at a time. Brandon wanted her back at the office later this afternoon. She just had a few hours to decide what to do about Tiffany.

Pulling herself off the bed, she gathered up the sheets and started toward the washing machine, bent on cleaning up someone else's mess, simply because she wasn't adept at cleaning up her own.

23

  Tiffany pulled out her gold-plated cigarette box, withdrew a cigarette, and with marked ennui, scanned the faces of the diners at Opus One. She had already spoken to the few people she recognized and counted worthy of a moment's attention, but the others she'd breezed past without notice. Many of the diners frequently glanced her way. She was an enigma to them, she thought with amusement. A woman easily admired. A woman who inspired jealousy and envy, and that was just fine with her, for it meant she was still on top.

  Even if that didn't impress Clea Sands, it meant a lot to Tiffany. She felt that anger rising within her again at Clea's inaccessibility since she had returned from Georgia. She hadn't called her once, and every time Tiffany had called her, she had gotten her machine. Something was going on, she thought. Clea was holding out on her, and she intended to get to the bottom of it.

  That was why she'd insisted that Steven meet her for lunch today. Maybe he had some light to shed on the way things had played in Georgia.

A waiter lit her cigarette, and she snapped her box shut and dropped it back into her purse as Steven came into the restaurant. Several of the women at various tables turned around, straining their necks to glimpse the Donovan heir. She smiled and waved at him, feeling a surge of pride that her son was so strikingly handsome, even with that beard. But then, what else could she and Brandon have produced? Plainness wasn't in either of their gene pools.

Steven made his way to her table. "Hello, Mother," he said, kissing her on the cheek. "Sorry I was late, but I was entangled in manual labor and couldn't get away. I can feel my collar turning blue as we speak. And I can't eat. There isn't time."

Tiffany laughed. "Manual labor? You? I couldn't believe it when your father told me you had capitulated and decided to join the company." She brought her long cigarette to her lips, inhaled slowly, then released a thin trail of smoke. "It was a wonderful move, darling."

"I didn't capitulate," Steven replied. "I only decided the time was right."

"You'll never know how right," Tiffany said. "It could never be better." She took her son's hand, a gesture that she knew made him feel awkward. "Mark my word, darling, you'll climb a lot higher and faster than your father told you."

"I don't know about that," he said. "Dad would be thrilled if I wallowed on the assembly line for a few years. He nurses some idiotic illusion about my learning how to piece a car together myself. Hell, that's not what helps you succeed in the board room. It's shrewdness, negotiation, confidence. I have those. I don't care whether I ever learn how to install a carburetor."

"Don't worry, darling," Tiffany said again. "You'll

have it all on your terms. Before you know it, Steven, things are going to change drastically."

Steven looked at her with keen eyes, and she wondered if she had said too much. "Why would you say that?"

She squirmed slightly, something she rarely did, and tapped her cigarette on the ashtray. "Well, I am on the board of directors now, you know. I have a say in what goes on."

"Not that much, Mother," he said. "Don't kid yourself."

"We'll see, won't we?" She sat back, nursing that smug smile of hers. "So tell me. How have you enjoyed being back in the company?"

"It's been okay," he said. "I can't say I've minded working with Dad these last few days. Clea sticks like glue to him, but she's something to look at."

Tiffany smiled. "She is very beautiful, isn't she?"

Steven gave his mother a suspicious look. "Why aren't you jealous of her?"

"Should I be?" she asked innocently.

"Well . . . yes. Frankly, I'm not comfortable with the amount of time Dad spends with her. Mother, she's a very sexy woman. And Dad is a normal red-blooded man."

"You don't have to tell me that," Tiffany said. "But I trust him. He's a devoted husband, and I have utmost faith in him."

"Famous last words of millions of innocent wives across the planet," Steven muttered.

Tiffany set down her cigarette and leaned forward, fixing her eyes into his. "Steven, are you trying to tell me something?"

"Mother, I'm just saying that there were times in Georgia when I got the distinct impression that Dad was trying to get rid of me so he could be alone with

Clea. She stayed in his suite for hours after I'd gone. You can't tell me they were working all that time."

Tiffany brought her cigarette back to her lips. "I'm sure that's all they were doing."

"Then why do his eyes light up when he sees her? Why does he watch her from across rooms? Mother, forgive me, but he doesn't look at you that way."

Tiffany wasn't sure what to name the emotion twisting in her chest, the irrational, illogical jealousy that made her uncomfortable with the fact that Clea was succeeding at her job. She should be happy, secretly dancing in her heart. Instead, she felt the sting of competition, for she couldn't deny that it had been a very long time since her husband had looked at her that way.

Still, it only assured her that she was that much closer to her goal. If Steven had noticed such things, others had, too.

She sighed. "Well, if there's anything going on, it's probably one-sided. Maybe I should fire her."

"No, don't do that." Steven's outburst came too abruptly, and he forced himself to relax and sip his wine. "I mean . . . there's no need. I'd just keep an eye on them. In fact, I can do it now that I'm there all the time."

"And if there's anything else I should know, you'll tell me?"

"Of course." He checked his watch, scooted back his chair, and made ready to leave. "Sorry, but I really have to get back to the office. George has some more menial chores for me to do this afternoon. It gives him such a rush to put his boss's son to work."

Tiffany blew him a kiss, then motioned for the waitress to bring her check. As she watched her son leave, her mind strayed to Clea and Brandon in Georgia. Had something happened between them? If so, why hadn't

Clea told her? Could it be that Clea was holding out for a bigger prize, now that she had Brandon's affections? The thought sent a jolt of rage shooting through her, and she vowed to find out as soon as she could. Clea Sands may have a scheme of her own, but she would be making a big mistake if she crossed Tiffany Donovan.

Clea knew she couldn't hold off Tiffany any longer when the woman showed up at work that afternoon and warned Clea that she'd better get in touch with her before day's end or she'd be sorry.

Clea made an excuse to Brandon about having to pick a friend up at the airport, and he allowed her to leave early. As she hurried through the parking garage, searching through her briefcase for her keys, she saw Steven leaning against her car. Her step slowed.

"What are you doing here?"

"Waiting for you," he said. "I heard you telling my father you were leaving early today."

"Yes," she said. "I have to be somewhere." She checked her watch. "I'm late, as a matter of fact . . ."

He stood up straight and blocked her car door. "How about having dinner with me after you do what you have to do?"

"I can't," she said. "I told you I'm not going to go out with you."

She started to go around to the other side, but he caught her arms and jerked her back in front of him. "Damn it, Clea, you enjoy this, don't you? Prancing by me every time I see you, that haughty look you throw me, that daring stab with your eyes."

"I'm not doing anything like that," Clea said, trying to wrest free. "Now let me go. I'm in a hurry."

"So am I," he said. "I don't like to be kept waiting."

"Then *stop* waiting," she said. Freeing her arms, she stepped back. "I mean it. There's nothing that will ever happen between us. Now let me get in my car or I'll scream for security."

"What?" he asked. "No scissors in the groin? No gun play? Come on, Clea. You can do better than calling security."

She was beginning to tremble, and she went around her car and jabbed her key into the lock.

"Are you just frigid, Clea?" he asked across the roof. "Or is my father keeping you satisfied?"

Her look cut right through him. "I find my job to be very satisfying."

"I meant in bed."

"I know what you meant." She got into her car, slid across to the driver's side, and cranked the engine.

Steven stared after her as she pulled out of the garage.

He didn't like being evaded that way, especially by a woman like her. But then, he didn't know what kind of woman she was, Steven thought, for he couldn't say he'd ever met a woman quite like her before. She was an enigma. Tough, independent, unwavering.

And yet she was so powerfully sexy that he couldn't get her out of his head.

He went back into the building and decided that he'd find out everything he could about her so he could crack her shell more easily. It would be his new goal . . . getting into her pants. It would be the ultimate ride, he told himself. The ultimate victory. She would be the ultimate possession.

He saw the personnel director walk across the lobby, leaving for the day, and an idea occurred to him. He would start with her file, and if that wasn't enough, well, he'd just dig a little deeper. As deep as he had to to understand what it would take with a woman like her.

He had all the time in the world, and he was more than willing to do whatever it took.

She had to get out of this. It was all getting out of hand. Steven's perverted interest in her, Brandon's turmoil over his own feelings, the fact that her heart was getting much too entangled with his . . .

There was simply no way around it. Somehow, Clea had to convince Tiffany to let her out of the scheme, take the money back, and forget any of it had ever happened.

The trick would be to convince Tiffany to let her keep working for Brandon. The possibility was remote, but what did she have to lose?

She drove to the building where Tiffany and Brandon lived. He was working late tonight, and there would be time to tell Tiffany, listen to her rant and rave, and then get out before Brandon ever made it home.

A guard stopped her at the front desk, and she told him she was Brandon's assistant, and that she had to deliver a message to his wife.

She got clearance to go up and found Tiffany waiting for her the moment she reached the penthouse.

"What are you doing?" Tiffany hissed. "How could you come here like this? It's stupid!"

Clea strolled in and glanced around. Everything in the penthouse, from the rose-colored accents to the life-sized portrait on the wall, was Tiffany. Nothing, not one thing, would she have expected in Brandon's home. She couldn't help wondering if he found any comfort here at all. "You're the one who told me I'd better contact you or else."

"I meant on the telephone! What if Brandon came home and found you here?"

"He won't. He has a meeting tonight."

"Clea, I don't like it! Someone could—"

"Get off it, Tiffany," Clea cut in. "Sit down and listen. I'm going to do the talking for a change."

Tiffany caught her breath, but something told her that Clea meant business. She didn't like this, but she was smart enough to know she'd better do what Clea said. The woman held some powerful cards, and she had dealt her every one of them herself. "All right, Clea. Why don't you tell me what's so important that you would risk everything to come here?"

"I want to quit this . . . this fiasco I agreed to stage with you. I've had enough."

Tiffany's face revealed her confusion. "Wait a minute. Which is it you want to quit? The job with Brandon, or the affair?"

"There is no affair," Clea said. "And there's not going to be. He's probably the one good man left on the face of this earth, and I've decided that I can't help you bring him down."

Tiffany's laughter was the last thing Clea expected to hear. "So let me get this straight," she said, strolling to the bar and pulling out a bottle of scotch. "So far, I've paid you thirty-three thousand dollars to do this, but you figure you can just bail out any time you want? Clea, you just don't understand, do you?"

Clea watched as she poured the scotch into a tall glass, dropped several ice cubes in, and brought it to her lips. "I understand plenty," Clea said, reaching into her purse for her checkbook. "I'm giving the money back to you."

"Forget it." Tiffany bottomed the glass, and turned back to the bar to refill it. "It doesn't work that way, Clea. You would never have gotten that job if you hadn't been working for me first."

"But I've got it now," she said. "Brandon's happy with me. Why should he have to train someone all over again?"

Tiffany glowered at her, her eyes as sharp and chilling as a blade sheathed in ice. "You're in love with him, aren't you?"

Clea tried to hold Tiffany's gaze, but found it wasn't easy. "Of course not. I just don't want to be a part of your scheme. The more I've thought about it, the more difficult it's been for me."

As if she hadn't heard a single word, Tiffany asked, "How do I know you haven't slept with him already?"

"Because I haven't! I told you I hadn't."

"And if you're so bent on protecting my husband, how do I know you'd tell me the truth?"

Clea stepped up to the bar and faced the woman who had created such black holes in her life. She could be sucked into them at any moment, she thought, and lose herself forever. "You don't know," she said. "That's why you shouldn't trust me anymore. That's why you should let me out of this. Get somebody else."

"Right," Tiffany said, "and risk your warning Brandon. No, Clea. You're in too deep now. You can't get out. That isn't one of your options."

Clea's face reddened and a sense of panic rose inside her. But it was that same panic that empowered her and forced her into taking her stand. No one—not even Tiffany—could knock her down if she didn't allow it. "Tiffany, you're the one who doesn't understand. I came here to inform you, not to ask you. The ball's in my court."

"And how is that?"

Clea drew in a deep breath. "I could tell Brandon everything. Wouldn't he be surprised to know what his wife is up to? You'd get your divorce, all right, but nothing else."

Tiffany's face slowly drained of its color. Her nostrils twitched, and her perfectly painted lips became stiff against the strain. "How dare you threaten me?"

"How dare *you?*" Clea asked, suddenly feeling the upper hand. "I would have never gotten into this if you hadn't droned on about Brandon being some low-life wife-beater who deserved what was coming to him. It's you who's abusive and conniving, Tiffany, not Brandon. He doesn't deserve you!"

"You *are* in love with him!" The words came on a whisper.

"What difference does it make?" Clea asked. "I'm never going to sleep with him, because if I do, I'll help bring him down. Nothing you can do or say will make me do it, Tiffany."

Tiffany's face reddened, and she bit her lip. "You're in over your head, Clea. And if you think you're going to hold out for Brandon's fortune by hooking him entirely, you're out of your mind. Brandon would never marry someone like you. He may sleep with you, but he has more class than to ever make you more than his casual mistress."

Clea's heart sank, but she made herself answer. "I'm not after Brandon or his money. I just want to be able to go on making a living."

"And what a living it is. A job gotten under false pretenses. You know, I have enough on you already to make a case," Tiffany bit out. "My own son will testify that you spent hours alone with Brandon in his hotel suite. All of his business associates and friends are beginning to talk already. It's enough to get him, Clea."

"No, it isn't, Tiffany, and you know it. It may be enough to turn public opinion, but it isn't enough to make a court case. On the other hand, it wouldn't take much at all to make an airtight conspiracy case against you."

Tiffany came around the bar and faced Clea with rage in her eyes. "You breathe one word of this, and I'll drag you through the deepest part of hell."

"There's nothing you can do to me, Tiffany. I haven't done anything."

"Don't underestimate me, Clea. I can tell them all how you set your claws for Brandon and went after him like a barracuda. Given your reputation, anyone would believe it. My word will carry a lot more weight than the word of some gun-slinging bimbo who's already filled the newspapers for the last year."

Clea's lips trembled as she glared at the woman who had introduced more corruption into her life than any man ever had. "I'm warning you, Tiffany. You leave me alone or you'll regret it for the rest of your life. I have nothing else to lose."

"And you have nothing else to gain, either," Tiffany said. "Nothing at all."

They stared at each other for a murderous moment. "I won't let you ruin this for me, Clea. Too much has gone into this already."

Clea tore out the check she'd written before she came in and tossed it to her. "And I won't let you manipulate me. You've seen my cards, Tiffany. Don't push me."

And before the woman could reply, Clea left the penthouse.

24

Shalimar switched the channels with the remote control, until she came across "Hard Copy." It was about a blonde Southern girl who left home for Hollywood, "only to find love in all the wrong places and murder lurking just around the corner."

Chomping her celery stick, she kicked off her heels and pulled her feet up onto the couch. Damn it all, she thought as the show broke for commercial. There was nothing on tonight, and she didn't have a date. And Clea would probably be working till ten or eleven. She'd hoped for some nice cowboy-type to meander into the salon today, but for the life of her, no one did. Cowboy-types and movie producers were hard to come by in Detroit.

The doorbell rang, and she hopped up, her eyes coming to life, and slid back into her high-heeled pumps. Maybe Clea had come home early and forgotten her key, she thought. Maybe she'd feel like a game of cards, or renting a good juicy movie, or maybe they could go shopping . . .

She swung the door open and gasped. A tall, dark

hunk with brooding eyes and a close-cut beard leered at her, and for a moment, she considered falling down and worshiping him. "Well, well," she said, sliding a hand up the casing and striking her sexiest pose. "I certainly hope you've come here for me."

The man smiled, a decidedly striking smile that would have gone fine with a cowboy hat. "Uh . . . I may have the wrong apartment. I'm looking for Clea Sands."

"She's not here," Shalimar said, "but will I do?"

His grin sauntered further across his face. "I suppose so, until she gets home. This *is* her apartment, isn't it?"

"You got it," Shalimar drawled, extending her hand. "I'm her sister, Shalimar."

"Sister?" Laughing, he took her hand and brought it to his lips. "Shalimar, huh? I didn't even know she had a sister. I'm Steven Donovan."

Shalimar gasped again. "*The* Steven Donovan? Son of Brandon and Tiffany? Oh, God, come in!" She pulled him in and closed the door. "I have some beer in the fridge. Miller Lite, if that's all right, and Clea keeps some ancient bottle of wine in there that she never touches. Want some?"

"Yeah, I'll have a beer," he said. "So when will she be home?"

"Probably not till real late," Shalimar said with a suggestive grin. "We could be sittin' in here alone for a real long time."

Steven didn't miss what Shalimar was getting at, and he decided right then that the girl might be a nice diversion from Clea, not to mention a good source of information. But he knew that Clea had gotten off work early tonight. He'd have to make it a point to take advantage of the offer another time. Tonight he had other things on his mind.

° ° °

Clea caught her breath when she walked into her apartment and saw Steven sitting next to Shalimar on her couch, entangled in a necking session that would have embarrassed a hooker. The only redeeming fact was that they both still had their clothes on.

"Steven! What are you doing here?"

Steven looked up and flashed her a wicked grin. "Came to see you. You didn't tell me you had a sister."

"And you didn't tell me Brandon's son looked like that Greek god . . . what's his name? Apache?"

"Apollo," Steven corrected, catching Shalimar's hand as it slid up his chest.

"I knew his daddy was somethin', but lord, Clea, how could you keep this to yourself?"

Clea's face reddened as she set down her briefcase. "Steven, I think you should leave."

"Oh, now, Clea," Shalimar crooned, "you don't want to be rude to our company, do you?"

"He's not company, he's an intruder," Clea bit out.

"Your sister let me in," Steven said.

"My sister lets anything in pants in. We've talked about this, haven't we, Shally?"

Shalimar stood up and stomped her bare foot. "What's the matter with you? He's your boss's son, Clea. Treat the man with a little respect."

"When he starts treating me with some, I will," she said. "Now get out, Steven."

"Come on, Clea," he said, as if her rejection only made his game more stimulating. "I found out some things about you today. The dossier in your personnel file was incredibly interesting. I just wanted to talk to you about it."

Clea compressed her lips and opened the door, waiting for him to walk through it. "Fine, Steven. Then you know about the man whose equipment I shot off, don't you? If you were a thinking man, that might have scared you off."

His grin held even more delight. "Oh, I'm a thinking man, all right. And I think maybe you feel things you don't want to show."

"Not for you, I don't."

"Methinks the lady doth protest too much."

"Methinks the man is a slow learner."

Shalimar shook her curls. "What's all this methinks stuff? Is this poetry or somethin'?"

Neither of them answered her. "Steven, I'm perfectly willing to be cordial to you in the office, but I won't tolerate you stalking me in the parking garage or bulldozing your way into my apartment. Now leave or I'll call the police."

Steven's smile faded by degrees, and he slid his hands into his pockets. "All right, Clea, but you may regret this someday. I don't like rejection. Especially from you."

"I can live with that," Clea said.

He started through the door, his mouth set in a hard line, and Shalimar gaped at her. "I can't believe you, Clea." She quickly grabbed her purse and started out the door. "I'm leavin', too."

"Where are you going?" Clea asked.

"After him," Shalimar whispered. "You may be able to turn some millionaire hunk away like trash, but I won't."

"You can have him," Clea bit out, and slammed the door behind them both.

*　　*　　*

The last thing on Steven's mind tonight was Clea, Shalimar thought as she lay satiated and naked in his bed. No, he hadn't been thinking of her sister, she told herself. The only thing he'd had on his mind tonight was her.

He was a good lover, she thought, pigeonholing him quickly. He was what she'd categorize as an obsessive lover, almost an angry lover, one that was almost absent mentally and emotionally, but one that could hold up the physical end better than most people. Yes, it was nice to be held and stroked sometimes, but she could live without it, especially for someone with as much money as he had. And there was something about that impenetrable distance she liked. Masculine arrogance. It was a trait she'd always liked in her daddy.

She snuggled up beside him, even though he'd fallen asleep almost immediately after they had sex. It was only ten o'clock, she realized, but hell, she'd rather be here than at home watching the news with Clea.

Eventually, she drifted to sleep herself. It was pitch black in the room when she was jerked awake.

"What the hell do you think you're doing?" Steven asked.

She sat up, sleepy-eyed. "I thought I was sleepin'."

"Not in my bed." He got up and picked her clothes up off the floor, thrust them at her. "Here. Get dressed and go home."

"But it's the middle of the night."

"I don't care," he said. "I didn't invite you here, and I'm not going to share my bed with you all night. Go in the living room and call a cab."

"Boy, you're sure a romantic guy," Shalimar said, stepping back into her pants and snapping on her bra. She slipped her shirt over her head. "Damn it, Stevie, you didn't act like you hated me last night."

"Look, I'm tired, and I don't feel like getting into one of these emotional female conversations. Go home."

Tears came to her eyes as she slipped into her heels and grabbed her purse. "Well . . . are you gonna call me sometime?"

"Yeah, sure, I'll call you," he said, but she'd heard that tone before. He wouldn't call, and she didn't know what she'd done wrong.

Quietly, she went into the living room and phoned for a cab.

Clea avoided Steven every time she saw him the next day, for she didn't trust herself not to lash out at him in front of Brandon and jeopardize what was already a precarious position. She hadn't heard again from Tiffany, and that surprised her, for she had felt sure the woman would make at least one last-ditch effort to change her mind. It wasn't over yet, she knew, but she had no idea where the next bomb would drop.

When Brandon asked her to stay late that night to help with some reports he had to get ready for a board meeting the next day, she was relieved that she wouldn't have to go home and deal with the ghosts breathing down her neck. As long as she was with Brandon, she was safe. No one could get her here.

Tiffany waited until almost ten, when she surmised that Clea might have made it home, and dialed her number. It rang once before it was answered.

"Hello?"

"Clea, this is Tiffany. We need to talk."

There was no answer. Only silence.

"Now that you've had time to think over the fact that you have as much to lose if I expose you as I have to lose if you expose me, I was hoping we could come to some compromise."

"Compromise? What compromise?"

"I'm holding in my hand a letter of recommendation from my father that is guaranteed to get you into one of the most desirable law schools in the country. I'm also holding a check I'm prepared to send you today for sixty-six thousand. That'll make up for your little conscience fit the other day, plus the third I had planned to give you later."

Again, there was only silence. "Are you there?"

"Yes. Go on."

Tiffany sighed. Clea's silence was making her nervous. She hated being nervous, for it made her feel as if she were on a lower rung looking up. "Clea, I can have this check for sixty-six thousand dollars delivered to you tomorrow if you'll just go ahead and reel him in. You know you want to sleep with him, anyway. Just do it, and we'll all get what we want."

She held her breath, waiting for an answer, when finally, there was a click on the other end of the line. Feeling the rage rise inside her, Tiffany slammed down the phone.

Across town in Clea's apartment, Shalimar grinned at the phone she'd just hung up and bit her lip. What was her sister up to? Had Tiffany Donovan actually hired her saintly sister to seduce her husband? Could it be that Clea was human? Could it be that she'd agreed to something even worse than anything Shalimar had ever done?

She laughed aloud, and fell back on the couch, for she couldn't believe how wonderful life had just become.

25

Clea knew something was wrong the moment she came into the apartment and found Shalimar leaning against the sofa back with a wicked grin on her face. "Hello, Sis," she said.

"Good, you're home." Clea dropped her briefcase and gazed at her sister. The smile threw her. Had Shalimar already forgotten how angry Clea had been at her last night? Did she think Clea had gotten over it already? "Shally, I think maybe we need to talk."

"About what?" Shalimar asked innocently.

"About your sleeping with my boss's son."

"Oh, that. Is this where you chew me out for my low morals and try to make me feel like a gutter rat for having human impulses?"

"Shalimar, I have every right—"

Shalimar's laughter cut into her words, and Clea stared at her, startled.

"What's so funny?"

"You are, Sis. Miss High-and-Mighty. Miss I-would-never-do-a-thing-like-that. Miss Perpetual Virginity.

And if Tiffany Donovan hadn't called today, I would have gone on believin' it." She threw her curls back and laughed again. "It's really great, Sis. I love it."

Clea felt the hot blood of fear pulsating to her face, and her eyes seared her sister. But Shalimar didn't feel the heat. "What are you talking about?" she whispered.

"I'm talkin' about sex for money, Clea. I'm talkin' about sleepin' with a married man. I'm talkin' about your elaborate scheme with Brandon Donovan's wife so she could get a divorce."

Clea felt as if she'd been walloped in the stomach, and she sank down into a chair, breathless. "Oh, my God."

"Tough bein' found out, isn't it, Sis?" Shalimar asked. "It's a terrible thing when you pretend to be one thing and you're exposed for somethin' else."

"Why would she tell you?" Clea whispered.

"Thought I was you," Shalimar said. "You musta forgot to tell her your little sister lived with you. She never knew the difference."

Clea leaned forward, intent on making Shalimar understand. "Shalimar, it isn't what you think. I told her I wouldn't do it. I backed out yesterday."

"Well, I'm afraid Miss Tiffany has other plans. She mentioned sendin' you sixty-six thousand dollars now. Damn, you could have cut me in before you gave that first payment back. You knew I needed money."

"What else, Shalimar? What else did she say?"

"She said she had a letter of recommendation from her father that would get you into any law school. Damn, Clea, you know how to negotiate, don't you? Did you learn all that in school? Maybe I ought to go to law school. Might help when I become an actress, and start negotiatin' those real big contracts, you know? The ones that the press writes about?"

Tears came to Clea's eyes, and she stood up and faced her sister. "Shalimar, is that all she said?"

"She said to go ahead and reel him in, and everybody'd be happy. And personally, Clea, I have to say I agree with her. Reel the man in. Collect the loot, and we can go to Mexico and live it up when the shit hits the fan."

"The shit is not going to hit the fan," Clea cried. "I'm not going to do it. I gave the money back yesterday. All I wanted was my job!" She felt her hands trembling as they swept through her hair, and she looked around frantically, as if she might find some answer hidden somewhere in her apartment. Suddenly, it occurred to her that Shalimar had never effectively kept a secret in her entire life. She swung around and took Shalimar's arms. "Shally, you can't breathe a word of this to anyone. Do you understand? Not a word."

Shalimar removed Clea's hands from her arms and grinned like a child who finally had leverage over her parent. "Oh, I don't know, Clea. After you've made me feel so sleazy and so cheap. After all those lectures about my promiscuity. I plan to enjoy this for a while. I was thinkin' Stevie might like to hear about it, too."

"No, Shally! Think how he'd feel, if he knew what his mother had done!"

"Or his father." Shalimar laughed again, but the sound was brittle. "You don't expect me to believe that ole Brandon has turned you down, do you? Come on, Clea. You've already slept with him, haven't you?"

"No!" Clea's face darkened to the color of rage, and she smeared away the tears just beginning to fall. "Shally, nothing has happened. He's a good, good man. He's faithful to his wife. That's why I couldn't . . ."

"Oh, Clea, that's really lame. Nobody would believe it."

"Nobody has to believe anything unless you tell

them. Shally, please, you can't tell anyone. I haven't done anything wrong yet. It can all still be salvaged . . ."

"What can? Your self-respect? Your purity? Give me a break, Clea. Accordin' to the gospel accordin' to Clea, once that's gone, it's out the window. Never comes back. Isn't that what you've always said?"

"Shally, what do you want?"

Shalimar was amused as she considered that for a moment. "A piece of the action?" she asked. "A cut of the profit? Maybe a third?"

"A third of what?" Clea asked. "I told you I gave it all back! I told you I'm not taking any more."

"Well, damn it all, Clea, why can't you just go through with it? The worst part was joinin' Tiffany in the first place. You've already done that, so you might as well carry it through. I mean, you made a commitment, didn't you? And you are a woman of honor, after all."

"Damn it, Shally, I'm begging you to keep your mouth shut!"

"Why? So you can go on workin' with ole Brandon and keep drawin' that terrific paycheck? Or are you holdin' out—" A light bulb seemed to appear in Shalimar's eyes, and she gasped. "That's it, isn't it, Clea? You're holdin' out for more? Why should you stop at a little when you can get everything? All he has to do is fall in love with you, right? Oh, Clea, it's wonderful. My sister the billion-aire. You can buy me a house! Better yet, you can buy me a movie studio!"

"Shally, stop it," Clea screamed. "I don't want any-thing from Brandon." She caught her breath on a sob, and turned to the phone. "That's it. I have no choice. I'll quit my job tomorrow. I'll have my resignation on his desk first thing. Then nobody can manipulate me. It's the only way I can end this nightmare."

"Why?" Shalimar asked, becoming angry herself. "Clea, it was a great plan. I wish Tiffany had hired me. All you had to do was sleep with a fine-lookin' hunk of a billionaire, and it would be over."

"Along with my picture on every tabloid in the country as the femme fatale. And it would destroy him, ruin his company, cost him everything he's worked for. Besides, he never would have slept with me. He's too devoted to his marriage!"

She went to the phone, snatched it up, and began to dial.

"Who are you calling?"

"Tiffany. I'm going to tell her that her mouth just brought a third party in on our little secret, and that I'm resigning completely tomorrow. That she can't manipulate me anymore."

Shalimar snatched the phone away from her and pressed the plunger. "Clea, think before you do this."

"Give me the phone." She took it back, and dialed again.

The Donovan phone began to ring, and she took a breath, ready to let loose with both barrels, as Joe Don used to say, when someone picked it up.

"Hello?"

The voice was Brandon's, and suddenly Clea was speechless. Her finger found the plunger, and she cut him off. "It was Brandon," she whispered.

Shalimar looked at her more soberly now. "You're really gonna quit?"

"Yes," Clea said, smearing her tears and starting back to her bedroom. "I'm going to type my letter and deliver it tonight so it's on his desk when he gets there tomorrow. And it'll all be over."

"Damn it all," Shalimar said. "All in one night we go

from thousands of dollars, to a virtual fortune, to poverty. Go figure."

But Clea didn't see any humor at all in the situation. This mess was of her own making, and there was no neat way out of it.

Brandon reached the office at seven-thirty the next morning, poured himself a cup of coffee, and stretched before sitting down behind his desk. That was when he saw the letter, placed at the center of it.

Dear Brandon,

Due to circumstances beyond my control, I must offer my resignation as your administrative assistant, effective immediately. I have enjoyed working with you and regret having to make this decision. I hope it doesn't cause you any difficulties.

Sincerely,
Clea Sands

"*What the hell?*" Brandon grabbed the phone and dialed her number, but there was no answer.

Quickly, he hung up and punched out the number of the security guard downstairs. "Sid, how long ago did Clea leave here?"

"This morning?" the man asked, confused. "She wasn't here this morning, sir."

"Then check last night's log."

The man left the phone for a moment, and Brandon stretched the phone cord to the door that connected him to Clea's office. Her desk looked untouched, and he suddenly realized that she hadn't brought any personal effects with her in all the time she'd worked here. It was as if she'd known she would only be here temporarily.

But why? Was she a spy for some other company? No, he thought. That couldn't be. She'd made too many contributions, showed too much interest. And yesterday hadn't sent any lightning bolts of information that would send a spy home with a completed mission.

Sid came back to the phone. "Brandon, the book shows that Clea was in here around eleven last night. She left about ten minutes later."

"I see." Brandon dropped the phone and stared at the wall for a moment. How could she just quit, when they were so close to unveiling the THD? She had seemed as excited about it as he was.

Due to circumstances beyond my control . . .

What circumstances? Yesterday she had been fine. Everything was going smoothly, even though she'd been a little jumpy since their kiss in Georgia.

But hell, he'd been jumpy, too. They could get past that, he thought. She didn't have to quit over it.

Again, he picked up the phone and dialed Tiffany's chauffeur. "Butch? Brandon Donovan here. Listen, you were the one who took my assistant, Clea Sands, home from the airport the other day, weren't you?"

"Yes sir," Butch said. "I brought her to and from the airport."

"Good," he said. "Give me directions."

Butch instructed him how to get to Clea's apartment, and as soon as he'd hung up, he dashed down the hall to the elevator and hurried out to his car. In fifteen minutes, he was parked outside her building and running up the steps to her second-floor apartment.

He found her door with no trouble and rang the bell. There was no answer. Loudly, he knocked. No one came.

He dashed back down the stairs and came to the

manager's door, and banged more urgently there. A woman in a robe and rollers came to the door. "Yes?"

"Can you tell me if you've seen Clea Sands this morning?" he asked. "It's very important that I speak to her."

"Too late," the woman said. "She left a little while ago for Texas. She asked me to pick up her mail while she was gone."

"Texas?" he asked. "Why did she go to Texas? Was there an emergency?"

"Not that I know of," the woman said. "She just said she was going to visit her mother."

"Damn," he whispered, then to the woman he quickly said, "All right, thank you."

He walked more slowly out of the building, racking his brain to determine what might have happened. Had he made her angry yesterday? Had something frightened her away?

He drove back to the office, his mind groping for every possibility, until he finally decided that it had to be some emergency back home. Nothing else would have made Clea take off like she had.

He headed for personnel the moment he was back in the DC building, and looked for Clea's file so that he could find her dossier and perhaps her mother's phone number. Oddly, the file was missing.

"Damn!" he said, slamming the drawer shut.

Sharon Kavett, the personnel manager's secretary, looked up from her desk. "What's wrong, Brandon?"

"Clea's file. It's missing."

"It can't be. We keep them all right there."

"It is, though. Look for it, will you? Call me when you find it." Not waiting for a reply, he stormed back up to his office, ignoring greetings from other employees.

He saw Lawrence lurking around his secretary's

desk, and headed toward him. "Larry, can I see you for a minute, please?"

"What's wrong?"

"In here," Brandon said, pointing to his own office.

Frowning, Lawrence followed Brandon in. "What's up?"

"Close the door," Brandon said, lowering himself into his leather chair.

Lawrence hesitated a moment, looking at him like a man who didn't know whether to brace himself or find an excuse to leave. Slowly, he closed the door and sat down. "Sounds serious."

Brandon rubbed his forehead and picked up Clea's letter. "It is. Clea quit this morning. No warning, no explanation. Just this letter."

Lawrence took the letter out of Brandon's hand, and quickly read it. He looked up at Brandon. "When did this happen?"

"I found it this morning," Brandon said. "Do you know of anything that might have happened around here to drive her away? Did somebody say something?"

"No. You'd know better than anybody. You were still here working with her when I left yesterday."

"And everything was fine," he said. "I can't imagine why she would have made such a decision . . . "

Lawrence rubbed his jaw with his fingers. "Are you sure nothing happened? Last night, maybe, after everyone was gone?"

Brandon looked up at him, not following what he was getting at. "Like what?"

"Like . . . maybe a little intimacy? Maybe something that shouldn't have happened? No one would blame you, you know."

Brandon gaped at him. "I can't believe you'd ask me that."

Lawrence smiled. "Come on, Brandon. How long have I known you? You can confide in me. You know it won't go out of this room."

"As long as you've known me, Larry, have you ever known me to do something like that? I'm a married man."

"Married men are human, Brandon. Clea is a very beautiful woman."

"Yes, she is. But she was my assistant. That was all."

"To you, maybe," Lawrence said. "Maybe to her it was more. Maybe she quit because of her own feelings. Did she make a move, perhaps, one that might have embarrassed her after you rebuffed her?"

"No," Brandon said, too loudly. "Nothing happened. Everything was fine when she left last night, and then this morning I find this. It has to be an emergency in her family. But why couldn't she have come to me? I would have given her time off. She didn't have to quit."

He grabbed the phone, began to dial.

"Who are you calling?" Lawrence asked.

"Tiffany," Brandon said.

"Tiffany? Why?"

"Because she's the one who got me to hire Clea. Maybe she knows something I don't know. Maybe she can at least help me find Clea's mother. I don't even know what her name is."

Lawrence sat still, listening as Brandon got his wife. "Darling, I'm sorry I woke you. But I need to ask you something."

"What?" Tiffany asked.

"It's Clea. I found a letter of resignation from her this morning. Did she say anything to you about this?"

"She quit?" Tiffany's voice sounded instantly awake, and he could hear the sheets rustling. "She quit the job?"

"Yes. No explanation."

"She wouldn't dare."

Brandon frowned and shot Lawrence a vacant look. "Why wouldn't she? What's going on, Tiffany?"

"I just mean . . . she loved her job. She'd be crazy to quit. Why would she do that?"

"That's what I hoped you would know," he said, his voice growing more irritated.

"Why would I know?"

"Well, you knew her before I did. I found out she left for Texas this morning. Do you by any chance know her mother's name in Beaut?"

"You could probably find it in her file."

"It's gone. Someone's taken it."

"Who?"

"Got me. Who would want it?"

Tiffany was quiet for a moment, and he sensed her own frustration. It surprised him, for he hadn't expected more than mild annoyance that she had recommended Clea only to have her quit the job.

"Brandon, I'll find out her mother's name, and I'll let you know, all right?"

Brandon shrugged. "All right, if you have time. I could probably find it myself, but—"

"I'll do it," Tiffany said. "I'll get back to you."

She hung up, and Brandon looked at the receiver for a moment, then brought his eyes back to Lawrence. "Tiffany doesn't know anything either." He shrugged, then rubbed his troubled eyes. "Look, I'm sorry to take up your time with this. I just thought you might know something."

Lawrence got up and meandered to the door. "If you hear from her, let me know, all right? My curiosity is piqued."

"Yeah, I will," Brandon said. "Thanks, man."

He watched as Lawrence closed the door behind him and then slumped back in his chair. Slowly, he turned Lawrence's words over in his mind. Could there be some truth in his words? Had Clea been growing uncomfortable with her feelings for him?

Or, more likely, had she grown uncomfortable with his feelings for her? Had she realized he was thinking about her far too much, manufacturing reasons for them to work into the night, enjoying her closeness much too much? Had she exercised more wisdom than he, by removing herself from a situation that neither of them had the right to find themselves in?

But he would have been able to exercise control, he told himself. He knew his obligations to his marriage. He knew what his vows had meant, and it was against everything he believed in to be unfaithful to his wife.

That didn't keep him from thinking about Clea, though, remembering her scent when he went home at night, dreaming about her when he slept. It didn't keep his heart from getting entangled, despite his vows to keep his distance physically.

Maybe Clea knew that.

But she was wrong, for he couldn't remember ever having an assistant who contributed so much. It wasn't fair for her to have to walk away from it, just because of his feelings.

He checked his watch and told himself he had meetings, appointments, plans. He needed to get busy. But there was nothing he'd rather be doing today than tracking down Clea and demanding an explanation.

He hoped Tiffany would find her mother's number soon.

26

Clea sat on her mother's patio, the hot spring breeze sweeping through the screen that encircled it, as Shalimar babbled about her new strategy for breaking into stardom. Clea leaned her head back and closed her eyes, and wished she had come here without her sister. But she'd had to bring her, for she couldn't trust her to stay in Detroit and keep her mouth shut.

"I just wish you could stay longer," Myrna said as she set a tray of lemonade on the table and smiled longingly at her daughters. "I never get to see you anymore."

"Well now, we've got lives to live, Mama," Shalimar said, sprawling on the chaise longue and working her tank-top straps off her shoulders, just in case the sun hit them. "I have to be back at work Monday. Bills to pay, you know."

Clea almost laughed, for Shalimar had never paid a bill in her life, but somehow it didn't seem funny. "I might stay longer, Mama."

"Really?" Her mother's face brightened, then fell instantly. "Why? Don't you have to be back at work?"

"No," Clea said, leaning forward and getting a glass from the tray, as if the movement would cushion her words. "I'm between jobs."

"What?" Her mother's question came out as a wail, and she slapped her hands over her cheeks. "After I told everyone you were working for Brandon Donovan? Oh, Clea! Did he fire you?"

Clea's spine went rigid, and she brought her drink to her lips, took a long sip, and fixed her eyes on her mother's garden. The impatiens were in full bloom, and the rose-bushes were beginning to bud. She had forgotten how much she'd loved tending that garden. "No, Mama. I quit."

"Why on earth—?"

"Because she's a fool," Shalimar cut in, then looked away, as if she'd said all she intended to say on the subject.

Clea threw her sister a warning look. They had talked about this on the way here, and Shalimar had been threatened within an inch of her life if she told Myrna any of what she knew.

"I'm not a fool," Clea said. "I just felt it was best. There were some . . . personality conflicts. I thought the best thing to do was to leave."

"Personality conflicts?" Myrna's indignation was all over her face. "Clea, is it just me, or does it seem like you have a hard time getting along with people?"

Clea snapped a look at her mother. "I do not. I've never had a hard time getting along with anyone."

"Come on, Clea. You never got along with Joe Don, and your marriage fell apart for *some* reason."

"That reason happened to be a blonde bimbo, Mama. You know that."

"But why? A man fools around when things aren't right at home."

"Uh-oh," Shalimar muttered. "Here we go."

"Is that why Joe Don cheated on you with everything in skirts, Mama?" Clea flung back. "Because there was something wrong with you? Is that why my father left you for the preacher's wife?"

"Of course not!"

"Then don't dump my ex-husband's weaknesses on me. He was a spineless wimp with more testosterone than brain fluid."

"Then what about that Mills person? You shot him!"

Clea felt those old familiar walls go up around her, the ones she used to hide behind when home was a place where the enemy lived.

"I'm not even going to discuss this with you anymore," she said.

Shalimar looked at her mother. "Leave her alone, Mama. You know she wouldn't have shot a guy in the balls for no good reason. Would you rather she let him jump her bones?"

"I'm just saying that she has a problem getting along with people. Working for Brandon Donovan could have been the opportunity of a lifetime. And she gave it up because of a personality conflict?"

Clea wiped a tear that had fallen over her lashes. "I told you, I don't want to talk about it anymore."

"Well, Clea, maybe you should face up to the fact that—"

The telephone rang, saving Clea from her mother's diatribe, and sighing, Myrna got up and went inside to answer it.

After a few seconds, she came back out. "Clea, it's for you. Mrs. Donovan."

Shalimar's eyebrows shot up. "Uh-oh."

Clea felt a wave of misery sweep over her. How had Tiffany found her? And did she think she could track her down in Texas and force her to do something she refused to do?

"Tell her I'm not here."

"I can't do that! I already told her you were."

"Then tell her I won't talk to her," Clea said. "Tell her anything!"

"I will not!" Myrna bent over her chair and shook a finger in Clea's face. "You go in there right now and tell her you're sorry for whatever you've done, and you do whatever it takes to get your job back."

"Mama, you don't understand."

"Want me to talk to her?" Shalimar asked with a laugh. "If I limit the conversation to yes and no, she might think I'm you again. 'Course, I might say a few more yeses than nos, but I've always had that problem."

"Clea, she's holding, and it's long distance!" Myrna shouted.

Clea closed her eyes. "The woman has enough money to buy the phone company. Let her hold."

"Clea Sands, so help me God, if you don't go answer that phone I'm going to make your life a living hell."

Clea knew her mother meant every word. Myrna had done it before. Finally, she got up, but as she did, she realized she was responding like the little girl she used to be, the one who always did as she was told, the one who swallowed back all the idiotic orders that only she realized were idiotic.

"I'll go, Mama, but let me talk to her alone. I don't want the two of you listening to every word."

"You watch your mouth with her, young lady!" Myrna called after her.

Clea went to the telephone, sat down next to it, and realized that she had broken out in a cold sweat as she contemplated what she would say to the woman who was earnestly trying to ruin her life, along with Brandon's. But as long as she could help it, neither of them would suffer.

Taking a deep breath, she put the phone to her ear. "Hello?"

"What the hell do you think you're doing?"

"Tiffany. How nice to hear from you."

"You won't get away with this, Clea. I'm warning you, you're playing with fire."

"I'm not playing at all, Tiffany. That's what I can't seem to get across to you."

"I've paid you, Clea. We had an agreement."

"I *broke* the agreement, Tiffany. And I gave you a check."

"I'm not cashing it. You've screwed me, Clea. And I don't like to be screwed. I told you yesterday that I was sending you another payment. It's probably sitting in your mailbox right now."

"I won't cash it," Clea said.

"And the letter. I'm not sending that until you do your part."

"I don't want it," Clea said. "And for your information, Mrs. Donovan, it wasn't me you were talking to yesterday. It was my sister. Because of you, she knows everything. *That's* why I had no choice but to quit."

Tiffany was stunned into silence for a moment, and finally she muttered, "Are you telling me that she knows *everything*?"

"That's exactly what I'm telling you."

"Why the hell didn't you tell about her?"

"It didn't occur to me that it would matter," Clea said. "I never dreamed you'd spill your guts to anyone who picked up the phone!"

"Oh, my God. Can we trust her?"

Clea sighed. "I'd like to say yes, but I'm not sure. She means well, but sometimes her logic is a little screwed up."

"So where does that leave me?"

Clea closed her eyes. "It leaves you in a marriage with a wonderful, wealthy man, Tiffany. And if you take my advice, you'll count your blessings that someone like you could have wound up with Brandon Donovan in the first place."

"You've got a lot of damn gall," Tiffany said. "You mark my word. This is not over yet."

The phone clicked in Clea's ear, and she slammed it down. "Oh, yes it is, Tiffany," she said. "It's definitely over."

She took a deep breath, tried to still her trembling hands, and forced herself to go back to the porch. Her mother had gone out to the back of the yard to water her tomatoes. Shalimar sat up straight, waiting for the verdict. "What did she say?"

"What could she say?" Clea asked, dropping back down. "I quit, and there's nothing she can do about it."

Shalimar shook her head. "You're outa your head, Sis. You know that? A person who can turn down sixty-somethin' thousand dollars just like that is crazy. You need help. All you had to do was have sex with a hunk of a man, and the money could've all been yours. But noooo, not my sister."

Clea closed her eyes and tried to pretend she was alone.

27

Tiffany was drinking when Brandon came home, and from the looks of her, she'd been doing it for some time. Funny, he thought, drinking was just what he'd wished he could do for most of the day. Without Clea, nothing had gone right. And the joy he'd gotten from work before had seemed mundane today.

Where was she?

Tiffany rose when she saw him, and he watched her waver slightly and slosh her drink over the side of her glass. "I got her number," she said, as though he would know instantly who she was talking about.

"Whose number?"

"Clea Sands," she said, waving her glass in a flourish as she said the words. "I got her mother's number. Took some doing, but I did it."

He reached out and took the phone number from her, and gave her a suspicious look. "How did you find it?"

"Never mind that. I just did. Why don't you call her and talk her into coming back?"

Brandon stared at her for a moment, wondering what

in the world was going through Tiffany's mind. It wasn't like her to be so accommodating, so helpful. Not unless there was something in it for her.

"Tiffany, how much have you had to drink?"

"Who cares?" Tiffany said, shrugging the question away. "Call her, Brandon."

"Why?" he asked, hesitating. "Why would you be so concerned about this?"

"Why?" Tiffany asked him, her voice rising in pitch. "I'll tell you why. Because I brought her in there, Brandon. I got her the job. I convinced you to hire her. I don't like having my generosity thrown back in my face!"

Brandon sank down into a chair and rubbed his splitting head. "I can buy that, but it seems like you'd just want to chew her out. Why would you want me to talk her into coming back?"

"Because she was good," Tiffany said. "I mean, wasn't she? She seemed to be everything you wanted . . ."

He was silent for a moment, and he feared Tiffany would see the emotion passing over his face. Everything he wanted, indeed. But he was a grown man, and he was wise enough to know the grass wasn't always greener on the other side. He didn't have time for a mid-life crisis, like so many of his friends had experienced. Loneliness wasn't such a bad thing, when you looked at the cost of following your instincts.

"Yeah, Tiffany. She was good. And the thought of training someone else, starting over . . ."

"Then call her," Tiffany said. "You're a charmer, Brandon. Charm her into coming back. Offer her a raise, or a car or something."

Tiffany's overanxious state worried him, and he frowned and shook his head. "I don't get it," he said. When Tiffany only turned back to the bar to pour more scotch into her glass, he sighed and started back to the bedroom. "All right, I'll call her."

Tiffany didn't even turn around as he closed the door behind him.

In the bedroom, Brandon stared at the number for a long time before he made a move to pick up the phone. What would he say? That he needed her here, that there was little joy to be taken in the THD if she wasn't around to share it with him?

But none of that was appropriate. He was a married man, and he had no right to say such a thing to an employee. Clea Sands was no marriage-wrecker. She had seen trouble coming by the look in his eye, and she had run the other way.

What kind of man was he, anyway, to have adolescent fantasies about another woman? He would bet his father had never had feelings like that in all of his years of marriage. Peter Donovan had been head over heels in love with his wife until the day she died. If he hadn't, he'd done a good job of pretending to be.

But Peter had made a good choice in a wife, and from the abyss of his depression, Brandon wondered if he had been as wise. Tiffany was nothing like the wife he'd pictured having as he grew up. She was lacking in so many ways that Clea wasn't. He looked at the door and knew that Tiffany was probably still nursing her drink. He wondered what had set off this drinking spell. They didn't come very often, maybe two or three times a year, but when they did, she went into rages and fits, and he wondered why on earth God had ever put the two of them together.

And yet He had, and Brandon didn't pretend to

know more than God. This was his wife, and they'd been married in a church before the Lord, and his vows had been sacred and binding. As weak as he could be in his fantasy life, Brandon doubted he had it in him to betray her. His beliefs ran too deep. They were too permanent.

He looked at the phone number again and asked himself what he could say to Clea in light of those beliefs. He could only act as a confused employer who needed help running his business. Nothing more.

Slowly, he picked up the phone and dialed.

"Hello?" The voice almost sounded like Clea's, but was a little liltier. He hesitated, clearing his throat. "Clea?"

"No, this is Shalimar, Clea's sister. Who's this?"

"Brandon Donovan," he said. "I wondered if I might be able to reach Clea there."

"Well, well," the woman said. "Brandon Donovan. Listen, honey, if you need another secretary, I can't type, but I can do a lot of other stuff. I'm available."

Brandon laughed. "I didn't know Clea had a sister."

"Well, your son does. You might say the two of us hit it off the first time we laid eyes on each other. Sexy guy, old Stevie."

Brandon frowned. "He didn't mention it."

"No, I guess he wouldn't. Anyway, Clea's here, but I don't know if I can get her to talk to you."

Brandon's heart began to sink. "Why? Was there a family emergency or something?"

"No, nothin' like that," Shalimar drawled. "Here, I'll get her before my mouth gets me into any more trouble."

As Brandon waited he tried to sort through what she had said. How could Shalimar's mouth have gotten her into trouble? What was the big secret?

Several moments passed before Clea picked up an extension. "Hello?"

"Hi, it's me."

She was quiet for a moment, then in a gruffer voice said, "Shalimar, hang up."

He heard a sigh, then a click on the other end.

"Sorry," she said softly.

"It's okay," he said. "I didn't know you had a sister. Does she live there in Beaut?"

"No," she said. "Actually she's been living in Detroit with me. I guess I never mentioned her."

It suddenly occurred to him that Clea probably knew much more about him than he knew about her. She had always kept personal revelations to a minimum. "She said there wasn't an emergency in the family," he said quietly. "So that blew that theory. I'm sorry to bother you at home, but I did wonder what would make you leave like that."

"Personal reasons," Clea said.

He heard the catch in her voice and tried to picture her, sitting there on someone's bed with her legs crossed and her hair trailing down her arms and teasing the top of her breasts. He had spent many hours wondering what that hair felt like, but he'd never allowed himself to touch it.

"Personal reasons," he repeated. "Does that mean it's none of my business?"

"No," Clea said. "Of course it's your business. You're the one left holding the bag. It's just . . . I can't talk about it."

"Did something happen? Was it something I said?"

"Of course not," she said. "Nothing like that. I just had to make a decision, and I felt there wasn't anything else I could do."

She knows how I've begun to feel about her, he thought. *She quit to keep from getting involved with me.*

It was written all over my face. Even Larry saw it.

"I guess I have to respect that," he said, "but it doesn't make it easier to accept. You made a real contribution to DC, Clea. There are people right now who are suggesting you might have been a spy of some kind."

"A spy?" The surprise in her voice cast out any doubt he might have had. Still, he pressed on, hoping she'd offer some explanation, for self-defense if for no other reason.

"There are people who think it could be a possibility. That you got what you needed and dropped out of the picture before you were found out."

"That's absurd. Who would I be spying for?"

"Another company."

Clea's voice was more earnest when she asked, "You don't believe that, do you?"

He paused for a long moment, then said, "Not for a minute. But I have to admit I'm disappointed. I really enjoyed working with you."

"I enjoyed it, too," she said, her voice dropping almost to a whisper. "Maybe too much."

Why did his heart leap when she said that, he asked himself, and why was it pounding like an adolescent's? He cleared his throat again, wondering why it was so hard to get the words out, and he forced himself to go on. "Clea, I wish you'd reconsider. I really do. Is there anything I could do or say to convince you to come back?"

"I'm afraid not," she said.

His heart sank again, and he realized he was clutching the phone too hard. "Well . . . do you plan on coming back to Detroit?"

"Yes," she said. "I'll be back in a few days. I just need some time to . . . to refocus myself . . . decide where to go from here."

"Well, if I can help, let me know. You weren't with me very long, but I'd be happy to write you a letter of recommendation."

"I . . . I really appreciate that, Brandon."

The catch in her voice told him she was crying, and he wondered why that particular statement could have triggered tears. None of this made any sense.

"Well . . . I guess I'll let you go. Keep in touch."

"Yeah," she whispered.

But somehow he had a feeling he'd never talk to her again.

He hung up the phone and lay down on the bed, and fixed his eyes on the ceiling, as though he might see her face there if he tried hard enough. She was a lady, he thought, in every sense of the word. And she had left him because she realized his feelings were getting out of hand. Maybe hers were, too.

He supposed she'd done him some great favor, but right now he couldn't see it that way. Right now all he could feel was the desolate loneliness of knowing he wouldn't be seeing her again.

He heard a glass crash in the kitchen and got up and left the bedroom.

Tiffany was standing over the sink, her face raging red, with glass shattered all over the counter.

Brandon rushed forward and pulled her away from the counter. "What is it, Tiffany?"

"How dare she?" she asked. "How dare she throw my generosity back in my face?" She pushed her hair from her face with the back of her hand. "Did you talk her into coming back?"

"No, but if you're so angry at her, why would you want her to?"

"Because we need her!" she shouted. "You need her.

The family . . . the business . . . you can't do it without an assistant. Everything's screwed up without her . . ."

"Tiffany, you're not making sense. I'll get another assistant."

"Fine," she said, shaking him off and stumbling toward the bedroom. "Go get one, then. And the two of you can just go to hell."

"The two of who?"

"Clea . . . I mean, your assistant. Just go to hell. Both of you."

He stared at her, confusion causing a dull ache to throb behind his eyes, and he shook his head as Tiffany slammed the bedroom door behind her. None of this made any sense. And Tiffany's drunken fury made the least sense of all.

Fighting off his headache, he turned back to the counter and began picking up the pieces of Tiffany's drunken rage.

When he'd discarded all of the broken glass, he poured himself a drink and sat down in front of the barren fireplace, staring and trying to sort through the feelings he was having.

I enjoyed working with you, too. Maybe too much. She'd said those words as if they had had a bearing on her decision to quit. Had Tiffany accused her of something? That couldn't be, he told himself, otherwise she wouldn't be so adamant about his getting Clea back.

He gulped down his scotch and decided that as soon as she came back to Detroit, he'd make one final appeal. All he could do was give it one more shot, face-to-face.

He had nothing to lose, after all, except, perhaps, his heart.

28

Steven paced in his bedroom, where he'd entertained countless women, most of whose names he couldn't remember. Now his bed, beneath a canopy of mirrors, was covered with the pictures he'd found of Clea.

The first one had been in her personnel file. From reading her dossier, he'd learned of the trial. He'd then gone to the library, where he dug up every newspaper article that had covered it. He'd cut out all her pictures and put them in her file, and now he found himself with at least twenty. Pictures of her crying, pictures of her brooding, pictures of those icy eyes that he bet he could melt, pictures of her with her eyes closed, as though she were praying.

Damn it, why had she gone and quit and screwed up everything? He had developed a strategy in the last few days. He was going to lure her into his bed one step at a time. But she had bailed out before he had gotten to step one.

He went to his bed, chose his favorite of her pictures,

stroked her paper cheek with his hand, and then hung it on the wall over his headboard. She was beautiful, he thought, and now he could see her face every night when he went to sleep and every morning when he woke.

Maybe it wasn't over, yet, he thought. He still had Shalimar. She was a good tool, whether she was too stupid to realize it or not. He could use her to get to Clea. And he had to look at the bright side. If Clea wasn't working for Brandon anymore, she couldn't fall in love with him. He hated like hell having to compete with his old man over a woman. It was downright degrading.

Not that Brandon had it in him to compete. Steven suspected his milquetoast father wouldn't know sex appeal if it hit him in the face. He probably hadn't even noticed the shape of Clea's breasts, or the scent of her hair, or the length of her legs. He probably couldn't see past her computer skills . . . or whatever it was she did for him.

He picked up another of the photographs, hung it on the wall, and finally decided to put them all up. One was not enough. He needed to see as much of her as he could until he could make her fall in love with him.

He wondered what sex with her would be like. Would it be wild and angry, the way he liked it? Would that iciness translate into brutal passion? Would she scream with pleasure as his body slammed against hers?

He laughed aloud as the very thought hardened him, and he told himself that he had to get some relief soon. If he couldn't have Clea, Shalimar would do for a while. He could pretend he was sleeping with her sister, and find out all he needed to know about her. His hunger for information about her was as insatiable as his lust was.

He lay back on the bed and stared at the pictures making the sloppy thumbtack mirage on his wall, and smiled as his imagination stripped her clothes off little by little.

"Just you wait, my Clea," he whispered. "Soon enough, you'll be mine."

Sleep eluded him for the rest of the night, but his fantasies of Clea seemed as real as if she lay naked beside him.

The apartment smelled of fingernail-polish remover and hair spray when Shalimar got home, smells that she knew she had been responsible for, since she'd left the used cotton balls on the coffee table. Wincing at what she knew the consequences might be, she rushed across the room and peeled the cotton off. The polish remover had ruined the finish on the cherry table, and tiny fibers of cotton remained.

"Damn," Shalimar said, dropping her handful of mail on the couch and plopping down to scrape what she could off with her fingernails. "Clea's gonna kill me."

She kicked off her shoes and turned her attention from the spot on the table to the mail, and began to flip through. Bills, bills, bills . . . nothing to do with her, she thought. Clea paid for everything, but now that she was unemployed, Shalimar expected she'd start hitting her up for rent money. Shalimar sighed and sat back, and told herself that if it got too bad she could always go back to Texas and live with her mother.

She came to an envelope addressed to Clea with no return address, and an alarm went off in her mind. "Tiffany, ole babe, is that you?" she asked aloud, and quickly, she tore into the envelope. She pulled out the check in the amount of sixty-six thousand dollars and felt something leap in her heart, as if the money were hers. Closing her eyes, she breathed the scent of it, and despite the fact that it smelled only of paper and ink, she could have sworn that the very aura around it was intoxicating. So intoxicating, in fact, that she couldn't help the thoughts fleeting through her mind.

Clea had vowed to send the check back to Tiffany, but somehow Shalimar couldn't let her do that. Expecting her to sit by and twiddle her thumbs while her sister ruined her life was like asking a striptease to become a nun. Some things just went against the grain, and no matter how hard you tried, you just couldn't make yourself do them.

Besides, somebody needed to look out for her sister. Clea was too dumb to fend for herself. Imagine having sixty-six thousand in her hand and turning it down, all for a matter of principles? Clea had never learned that principles didn't pay the bills. Principles didn't hold you at night. Principles didn't buy you nice things. And principles sure as hell were bad company when all was said and done.

But Shalimar knew, for she had been born with car-salesman savvy, the kind that told her to do or say whatever needed doing or saying, and that the bottom line was how you came out in the end. Principles didn't amount to a hill of beans. What mattered was whether or not you got what you wanted.

Clea would never know that, because she needed someone to look out for her. Left to her own conscience, she'd wind up a destitute old maid. Lucky for Clea, though, she had a sister like Shalimar. One with foresight. One with street smarts. One who was willing to do what had to be done.

Feeling more motivated than she'd felt since she went to bed with that guy she thought was a movie producer, Shalimar got up and ran barefoot into Clea's room. She opened her closet and perused the shelves there for her box of checks. She found them at the back, and shoving everything aside, grabbed it.

It didn't take her more than a few seconds to make out a deposit slip for the check, less a thousand dollars which she could use until Clea got back. After forging Clea's signature, then endorsing the check herself, she slipped back into her shoes and headed for the bank.

She felt like a million bucks as she came back to the apartment gloating over the fact that she'd done Clea the biggest favor of her life. Clea had earned that money, after all, dealing with the likes of Tiffany Donovan, and if she hadn't yet, maybe the money actually sitting in her account would motivate her. Clea was dying to get into Brandon's pants, after all. It was obvious to everyone except Myrna, and that was because she was too naive herself. All Clea had to do was follow her natural instincts, and they'd be sitting pretty.

She bopped up to the door and found someone standing there waiting with his back to her. He was strong and sexy, and had cute little buns that made her heart skip a beat. And when he turned around, she caught her breath.

"Stevie!"

"Hi, there," he said with that sexy grin she'd fallen for the first time he came over. "I've been waiting for you."

Shalimar paused mid-step and flashed him her most welcoming smile. "You son-of-a-gun, I oughta just walk on past you without so much as a 'Kiss my butt.' You haven't even called."

"Well, I'm here now."

"You sure are," she said. She finished her climb up the stairs, and found herself eye to eye with him. Lordy, he was handsome, she thought. Lordy.

"So you wanna come in or would you prefer to just stand out here in the hall leerin' at each other?"

He laughed. "By all means, let's go inside."

She opened the door, and he followed her in, and suddenly she wished she'd worked harder on fixing the spot on the table.

"Are we alone?" he asked.

"Sure are, honey."

"So where's Clea?"

She smiled and took his hand, and led him to the couch. "In Texas." She pushed him down on the couch and plopped herself in his lap.

"Texas?" he asked. "When's she coming back?"

"Not tonight," Shalimar said. "It's just you and me."

"You and me?" he whispered, running a finger down her neck and teasing her cleavage.

"Yeah, you and me. We can get crazy and act like animals right here on the couch, or we can be a little more civil and go to the bedroom. Which would you prefer?"

He smiled and glanced to the back of the apartment, where there was only one door other than the bathroom. "Clea's bedroom?"

"You got it," she said. "Let me go change the sheets."

"No," he said, stopping her. His reaction was a little too quick, and she looked down at him. "I want you to leave Clea's room exactly as it is. And the sheets are fine."

"But she's slept on them for a week."

"Perfect," he said. "Leave them alone. I want to make love to you on Clea's bed just like it is."

Shalimar grinned as if she'd just been paid the highest compliment she could, for she knew that he was anxious to hold her, to make love to her. It didn't even matter if the sheets needed changing.

And as he picked her up and carried her back to the bedroom, she felt her heart slipping away like it had so many times before. Only this was different, she told herself. There was something about Steven Donovan. Something exciting. Something unpredictable.

Something that was going to be hard to extract herself from if she ever had to. So as she began to seduce him with all she had, she told herself she just wouldn't allow herself to have to. By the time she got through with him, he'd be thoroughly addicted. And he wouldn't be able to do without her for long.

Steven was different this time after the sex was over, for he didn't turn over and ice her away, and he didn't leave. Instead, he held her like someone who truly cared about her, and for the first time in weeks she felt completely cherished.

When he started talking about his job and his frustrations at work, and the way he missed driving, she felt as if he were sharing something vital of himself with her. And she found herself pulling closer to him.

"Then why don't you go back to drivin'?" she asked.

"My father's pretty insistent about my being in the business," he said. "And if I ever have any hope of taking over DC, I have to start now."

Shalimar smiled up at him. "Why? I always thought the boss's son could come in whenever he wanted and tell everybody else to move over."

"It's not like that," he said. "My father has this work-ethic thing. He's gonna make me grovel for it."

"Yeah," she said. "I could tell from Clea's hours that he's a workaholic."

He seemed to stiffen, and finally, he asked, "Is that why she left?"

"No," Shalimar said. "Clea's a workaholic herself."

"Then why?"

Shalimar knew better than to answer, for Clea would murder her if she knew she'd told Steven anything. Yet he wasn't just anybody. He was her new lover, and tonight they'd created a special bond, one she didn't want to break just yet.

"Well, if you promise not to get all upset or tell anybody or anything, I think she left because she was gettin' a little bit sweet on your daddy."

"What?" He sat up in bed and looked down at her, and she realized she'd gotten his attention.

"Well, I don't mean anything was happenin'. I mean, that was the thing. It couldn't. She has this Quaker attitude about married men, and so she dropped out of the picture."

From the look on his face, she instantly realized she'd made a mistake. But what could he do? Tell Tiffany? She already knew the whole story. And if he told Brandon, well, that might pique his interest in Clea even more, and force her to complete her mission whether she wanted to or not. The way Shalimar saw it, no one had anything to lose by knowing. After all, she hadn't told him anything about Tiffany's scheme. And she wouldn't. Secrets were secrets, after all.

"Has she slept with him?" The words were strained and clipped, and Shalimar laid her head on his chest and tried to stroke him back to relaxation.

"No. I told you my sister is a Puritan."

"She slept with that banker fellow."

Shalimar didn't question how he'd heard about that. Everyone knew. "Yeah, seems like she did, although she'll deny it till the day she dies. Who knows? Clea's value system is a mystery to me."

Steven didn't answer, but stared at the ceiling, turning her words over in her mind. Shalimar fell asleep before she'd had the chance to analyze his new mood.

Steven was still awake when the digital clock next to Clea's bed hit three A.M., and he glanced over at Shalimar, who was sound asleep. Burying his face in the pillow, he breathed in Clea's scent. It was the scent he'd smelled in her hair, the scent he'd had in his mind since the day he met her. Now he was surrounded by it.

He felt his groin stirring to life again, just at the thought of Clea's body sleeping on these same sheets. He wondered if she'd slept on them with his father, and something close to rage burned through him. *She's a little bit sweet on your old daddy.*

The thought made it impossible for him to lie still, so he got up and wandered around the room in the dark. He went to her dresser and peered at the pictures stuck in the casing. There was one of her and Shalimar standing in their underwear as children, their tops as bare and flat as if they were little boys. My how things change, he thought as he looked at the next picture. It was Clea's high school picture, with the photographer's velvet cloth draped around her bare shoulders, and her smile was sweet yet elusive. Did she have secrets even then? Did anyone know what went on behind those changing eyes?

He took the picture out of its slot on her mirror, then saw another one of her sitting atop a huge horse, her cowboy hat perched on her head. He took that one, too.

By the time he'd scrutinized all of the pictures, he'd slipped five from their positions and slid them into his pants pocket hanging over the chair.

He looked back toward the bed, realized that Shalimar was not a light sleeper, and looked around some more. There was a jewelry box with a few simple earrings and necklaces, a bottle of hand lotion, and a brush. He picked up the brush and saw some long golden strands trapped there. Pulling them out, he brought them to his nose. There was no smell, he realized, but it was Clea's hair nonetheless. Quietly, he stuffed the hair into his pocket as well.

Silently, he pulled out the top drawer of her dresser, and saw a neat stack of panties. His heart began to accelerate as he took the top pair in his hands and held them up, picturing the French cut as it might contour to her body. He felt himself growing hard, and he wadded the panties up and put them into his other pocket.

He pulled out another drawer, found some gowns folded there, and lifted one out. It was black and almost see-through, and he pictured the way her breasts would have been revealed through the skimpy fabric. He imagined her legs in black stockings, hooked to a garter, and her hips moving against him as he ran his hands down the silky fabric to the junction of her thighs.

Knowing he was pushing this too far, but for some inexplicable reason unable to control himself, he rolled up the teddy and put that in his pocket, as well. He hoped Shalimar wouldn't notice all the things bulging in his pockets, he thought. Maybe he could rearrange everything before he got dressed.

He stood in front of the mirror, looking at his own physique, his face, and the growing masculinity as he stood naked in Clea's bedroom. Women had grown addicted to him before. Some had chased him for months after sleeping with him once. Others had catered to his every whim until he grew tired of them. He had never been turned down by any woman who didn't eventually come around. And he knew that all it would take would be one time with Clea, and she would be his forever.

His lust grew unbearable, and he tried to imagine Clea walking in tonight, finding him standing in her bedroom naked and ready . . . What would she do? Would she turn and walk away, or would she come slowly into the room, unbuttoning her blouse, slipping off her skirt, peeling off her panties?

How would she feel when he touched her?

He felt his breathing grow thin, and he turned back to the bed. Clea wasn't here, but her sister was. It was dark, and he could imagine. There was no harm in that. His time with Clea would come soon enough.

He got back on the bed and reached for Shalimar, ran his hand over her breast, and felt her stir slightly. Slipping himself between her legs, he began to move, just enough to wake her.

Within moments, she was wide awake, and her body was responding to his as if she'd been in the middle of an erotic dream. And as their lovemaking heightened, Steven pretended it was Clea's body he held. And his release was greater than any he'd had before.

29

It was too late to call Shalimar when Clea reached the airport, so she took a cab to her apartment and carried her own luggage up the stairs to her door. Not bothering to knock, since she didn't want to wake her sister, she unlocked the door with her key and stepped inside.

The lights were off, but Shalimar wasn't on the couch. Clea flicked on a lamp and saw that her sister's shoes were sprawled in two directions, no doubt where she had kicked them. She was probably sleeping in Clea's bed, she thought, but she couldn't blame her. The couch wasn't something anyone would ever choose to sleep on, if given a choice.

Quietly, she tiptoed back there, hoping to get a clean nightgown out of her dresser, and in the darkness, she saw Shalimar sprawled out in her bed.

But she wasn't alone.

Clea caught her breath, and the sound woke the man in her bed. He sat up, looking groggily at her.

"Clea?"

It was Steven, and Clea stood gaping at him. "What are you doing here?"

Shalimar stirred to life and sat up, with no thought to cover her bare breasts. "Hey, Sis. You coulda told somebody you were coming back."

"I said, what is *he* doing here?"

"Who, Stevie?" Shalimar asked. "Well, what do you think?"

Steven got out of bed, revealing six feet two inches of naked male body, and Clea spun around and started up the hall. "Steven, you have ten minutes to get out of my house, or I'm calling the police."

"The police?" Shalimar squealed. "Geez, Clea. I invited him here. You can't call the police."

Clea spun around. "I can have them drag you out with him, Shalimar, so shut up! I told you I don't want him here!"

Steven appeared at the door in his jeans, his chest still bare, and grinned at her with sleepy eyes. "What's the matter, Clea? You jealous because your sister's getting some and you're not? We can take care of that."

Her face raging red, Clea pointed to the door. "Get out."

"Not until Shalimar tells me to."

"Shalimar has no say in the matter," Clea cried. "She's probably going to wind up on the street tonight, too."

Shalimar crossed her arms and stood naked, staring at her sister in horror. "What's the matter with you, comin' in here like this in the middle of the night and makin' a scene? Who do you think you are?"

"Go get some clothes on before I throw up!" Clea yelled. She stormed to the door and opened it for Steven. "Good-bye, Steven."

Steven's expression turned hard and cold, and he

pierced her with a look as he started out, his shirt thrown over his shoulder. "I'll be back, Clea."

"Well, maybe I'll be gone by then," she said.

His expression changed infinitesimally. "Gone where?"

"Back to Texas," she said. "For good."

She saw the surprise on his face for a split second before she slammed the door on it. When she turned back around, Shalimar was standing in her robe.

"How could you? Knowing what I've been through with that family, how could you get involved with Steven?"

"Hey, he came to me," Shalimar said. "What was I supposed to do?"

"Use your brains," Clea shouted. "Tell him to get lost!"

"I didn't want him to," Shalimar said. "Clea, he's been so sweet to me. He never gets tired of makin' love, and sends out for food so I don't have to cook, and he gave me money to restock the booze . . ."

Clea sat down on the couch and covered her face with her hands. "It's out of control," she muttered. "My whole life is out of control. I try to break ties with the Donovans, and you keep sleeping with their son." She shook her head, and looked back up at her sister. "Where's the mail?"

Shalimar hesitated, and slowly lowered herself to the couch. "Uh . . . well . . . Sis, we need to talk."

Clea's heart slowly constricted. "About what?"

"About that check Tiffany sent you." Shalimar pointed a finger at her, and raised her brows as their mother always did when she prepared a lecture. "Now you know that you haven't been in your right mind lately, what with quittin' DC and takin' off to Texas and all. And I didn't want you doin' anything that you might regret later, so I decided to just take matters into my own hands . . ."

Clea glared at her sister. "Shally, where is the check?"

Shalimar hesitated, and Clea felt her stomach sinking and the beginnings of a headache gnawing at her temples. "Shalimar, spit it out! What have you done with it?"

"Well . . . I deposited it. That way, it's safe until you have time to think."

"You what!" Tears sprang to her eyes, and she jumped up and loomed over her sister. "How could you do that? Once it's deposited, it means I've accepted it! Shalimar, how could you?"

"Well, if you don't want it, Sis, you can just write her a check back. I was tryin' to do what was right!"

"I *told* you what I wanted to do! Damn it, Shalimar, why can't you ever listen?"

"Well, hell, just hang me up by my fingernails and beat me, why don't ya? I did the best I could."

"You did shit!" Clea shouted. "You just complicated my life sixty-six thousand times worse than it was before. Damn you!"

She went for her checkbook, wrote out a check as fast as she could, and searched around for an envelope. When she found one, she stuffed it in, and hurriedly addressed it, as if each moment cost her more of her life.

"I have to get it back to her as fast as I can. She'll use this against me!" Clea cried. "She'll say I took the money. She could blackmail me. She'll try to make me out to be some kind of hooker."

"Well, takin' sixty-six thousand is no worse than takin' thirty-three. As far as I can see, nothin's that much different than before."

"It's different because I quit!" Clea cried. "I don't

want any part of her dirty money or her filthy scheme. I just want out!"

"Well, if she blackmails you, you can just blackmail her back."

"And who would listen to me?" Clea asked. "I'm just some woman who sold her soul for a buck. *Nobody* would listen! Shally, how could you?"

"Well, I wouldn't have if I'd realized it would make you this crazy."

"Crazy?" Clea asked. "I'll show you crazy." She went to her suitcase, opened it, and dumped the contents on the living room floor. "Take this, Shalimar, and pack your things right now. You're not welcome here anymore."

Shalimar gaped at her. "Clea, you can't throw me out. I'm your sister."

"I don't care who you are," she said. "Sisters don't destroy each other."

"You destroyed yourself, Clea. I didn't do anything except find out about it."

"You did plenty, and I want you out."

Tears came to Shalimar's eyes, and her bottom lip began to tremble, just like it always had on the rare occasions when her mother had punished her as a child. Slowly, she took the suitcase. "Where will I go?"

Clea went to her purse and pulled out a hundred dollar bill. "Here. Go get a hotel room, if you have to. Either that, or move in with one of your sleazy boyfriends. Steven's probably got plenty of room. As for me, I've had it with you."

"Oh yeah?" Shalimar threw back. "Well, I'm kinda sick of you, too. You deserve to be alone, Clea. You're not better than me, you know? You're just wrapped in a more expensive package! And you have Tiffany Donovan to thank for that!"

"Get out!" Clea shouted.

Shalimar stormed back to the bedroom, got dressed, and threw her clothes into the suitcase. Snapping it shut, she marched for the door. "When you get lonely and start wishin' you had somebody on your side, Sis, don't come to me," Shalimar said. "I'll be on the other side."

He should have taken her while he had the chance, Steven thought, slamming the door of his house and going straight to his bedroom, where pictures of Clea cluttered the wall above his bed. He should have taken advantage of his nakedness, his readiness, when she'd first seen him in her bedroom.

He dropped down on his bed, next to the black teddy he'd taken from her drawer, and buried his face in the filmy fabric. Erotic fantasies that only grew stronger each day whirled through his mind, making him dizzy. He had to fulfill them, but she treated him like he was the lowest form of pond scum. Didn't she realize who he was? What he was worth? Or was Shalimar right? Was she holding out for his father?

The thought made something snap inside him, and he flung the teddy across the room. He got up and kicked the wall beneath her picture, but suddenly his eye caught the image of her sitting in that courtroom, tears in her eyes. He had found it in color, on the front page of a back copy of the Sunday newspaper, and it had become the centerpiece of his Clea collage. He reached out and touched it, that muscle in his jaw twitching as he did. "You're mine," he whispered. "Somehow I'll convince you of that."

He went across the room and picked up the teddy again, brought it to his face, as if he could breathe in the scent of her. But it smelled only of detergent. Again, he thought of lying beneath her on cool sheets, her hair feathering across his chest, her tongue making wet tracks down his stomach . . .

The doorbell rang, and some illogical thread in his brain told him it was her. She had come here for him. The sight of his nakedness had plagued her, until she couldn't help herself . . .

He smiled, dropped the teddy on the bed, and headed for the front door. When he opened it to find Shalimar clutching a suitcase in her hand, a new rage filled him.

"What the hell do you want?"

"Stevie! Don't do me like that. Clea threw me out, too."

"So you expect me to take you in?"

"Well, I thought maybe I could bunk here for the night. You haven't minded stayin' at my house when you wanted to."

"That was Clea's house, not yours," he said. "And I don't want you here."

Tears sprang to her eyes, irritating him further. If women only knew how turned off he got by tears—they'd cut that act and find other ways to manipulate him.

"But . . . we're gettin' so close."

"We had great sex, Shalimar. There was nothing else to it."

She tilted her head as tears began to roll down her face, and stared at him like a little girl whose heart was broken. In many ways, he thought, Shalimar *was* a little girl. A bad little girl who never thought past the moment. And he was tired of her.

"Stevie, you can call it anything you want. We were good together."

"I've had better," he said, then started to close the door.

Shalimar reached out to stop it. "Stevie, where will I go?"

"I'll call you a cab," he said. "Go to a hotel. Go anywhere. Just leave me the hell alone."

He slammed the door and turned back to his bedroom, not giving one further thought to the woman crying outside his apartment.

Shalimar covered her face as a sob caught her, and finally, pulling herself together, she went back to the elevator and down to the first floor. She waited alone, just inside the foyer, with the security guard watching her like she was some dirty hooker. After a few moments, a cab drove up.

She got in and looked at the driver, a black man with a beret on his head.

"Where to, ma'am?" he asked in a Haitian accent.

Shalimar thought a moment about what she could afford, and remembered the thousand dollars she had in her wallet since she'd deposited Tiffany's check, besides the hundred Clea had given her. That could afford her a few nights of luxury before she was completely destitute, she thought. "Take me to the Ritz-Carlton," she said.

"The Ritz-Carlton?" The driver whistled under his breath. "Nice hotel."

"Nothin' but the best," she said with a smile. "My daddy always said that's what I deserved. Lady Shalimar, he called me."

All her despair vanished as they drove through Detroit, and a plan began to form in Shalimar's mind.

30

Brandon rose before dawn, in the hours when all of Detroit was silent, dressed quietly, and went into the kitchen for his bowl of cereal. He hadn't slept well at all since Clea had left DC, and the fact that it had affected him so worried him more than he liked to admit. He had caught himself during the day, staring off into space, thinking about her and the expressions on her face as she had said certain things to him, recalling her scent, hearing her voice.

But it was the other daydreams that caught him off guard and caused guilt to well up inside him. It was the fantasies of kissing her. Of touching her face. Of holding her so tight that she melted into him.

Could it be that he had fallen in love with her?

Again, that guilt shifted inside him, and he told himself that he was a fool for feeding such fantasies. He should forbid his mind from thinking of her. He should hire someone to replace her at work, preferably a man, and get on with things. He was a married man, and he was going to remain a married man.

He left his cereal without eating any, found his briefcase, and headed out the front door. Tiffany was still asleep, and from the way she'd been drinking the last few days, he figured she'd sleep very late today. It didn't add up. Her depression seemed almost as keen as his, even though he couldn't believe it had one thing to do with Clea.

Unless Tiffany suspected his feelings for her. But that in itself was hard to believe, for Tiffany had never been attuned to his feelings. She was a bottom-line, black-or-white person. She didn't read between lines, and she didn't see what wasn't obvious.

He rode the elevator down to the garage and told himself that he really should tell personnel to find a replacement for Clea today. But something kept him from it. Some hope that she'd call and want her job back. Some hope that it wasn't all over, even though it could never really get started.

The drive to work was lonelier than usual, and the dark, empty building was almost dismal as he rode to the top floor and made his way through empty workplaces to his office.

The telephone at the Donovan home rang incessantly until Tiffany dragged her head off the pillow to reach for it. Her head throbbed as if she'd been hammered with a gavel, and she knew she looked like death as she cursed the maid for following Brandon's orders not to answer their personal line. He didn't want to appear inaccessible to his office staff, even though Tiffany would have been happy to make it difficult for them to reach him at home.

"Hello," she said, not disguising the grogginess clinging to her with steely claws.

"Tiffany?" Tiffany's heart skipped, for she was certain it was Clea on the line.

"Clea?"

"Not hardly," the woman said, her Southern accent becoming more apparent. "This is Clea's sister, Shalimar Wilson."

Tiffany sat up and shoved back her tangled hair. "What do you want?"

"I don't know," Shalimar said. "I thought maybe you and I could make a deal, seein' how my sister stiffed you and all."

Tiffany clutched the phone tighter. "What kind of deal?"

"Well, I don't know. We'll have to put our heads together. But I'm in a position to help you, and I could use a little cash right now. Clea came back home last night, you know."

"She's back in Detroit?"

"Yeah, but not for long. She's plannin' to move back to Texas for good. So you don't have much time. But I've been thinkin', and there might be a way to get ole Brandon to pay her a little visit. Maybe I could get a picture or two . . . or hide a video camera in the apartment . . . or somethin' like that."

Tiffany's heart raced. "Yes, that would be very helpful. Do you have a camera?"

"Well . . . no. I just thought of this idea this mornin'."

"All right. I'll provide you with a camera that can be easily hidden." She gave her the name of the electronics store where she could pick it up, then asked, "When can you get it in place?"

"Probably by noon, if it isn't too hard. Clea and I aren't exactly speakin' to each other, so if I go in to get some more of my stuff out, I doubt if she'll hang around to chat."

"Perfect. Now about Brandon."

"I was thinkin' of callin' him myself and tellin' him that Clea's back. That she wants to talk to him. I could tell him she wants to give him an explanation for quittin'. Maybe hint that she'd take her job back if he'd give it to her. Do you think that would work?"

"With the right reinforcements, it might," Tiffany said.

Shalimar hesitated, then switched gears. "You do realize, don't you, that I'm not doin' this for free?"

"Of course. It's worth a thousand dollars to me."

Shalimar laughed. "Honey, I just deposited a sixty-six-thousand-dollar check you wrote my sister. You can do a little better than that for me."

A smile lifted one corner of Tiffany's lips. "You deposited the money?"

"In Clea's account. Which has a lot to do with why we're not speakin' to each other."

Tiffany's smile was full-fledged when she said, "Shalimar, I think you and I are going to get along just fine."

"How fine?"

"How does three thousand sound?"

"Ten sounds better," Shalimar said. "The way I figure it, I'm doin' you a big favor. I don't turn on my sister without good reason."

Tiffany expelled a heavy breath. "All right. Ten it is. When you deliver the videotape, you'll be paid."

She hung up the phone and smiled as she got out of bed, suddenly anxious to face the day.

Brandon was on his way out of his office when Evelyn stopped him. "Brandon, you have a call. She says it's Clea Sand's sister, and it's urgent."

"Clea's sister?" He checked his watch, then nodded. "All right. I'll take it in my office."

He went back in, closed the door, and set his briefcase on the couch. Picking up the phone, he said, "Brandon Donovan."

"Brandon? I'm Shalimar Wilson, Clea's sister. I hope I'm not botherin' you."

"No," he said, sitting down. "Is Clea all right?"

"She's fine," she said, "and I thought you should know that she came back to Detroit last night. She's been real depressed since quittin' her job there, especially for such a silly reason."

"Silly reason?" he asked. "What reason was that? She never told me."

"Oops," Shalimar said. "Guess I shouldn't, either. It's between the two of you, after all."

Brandon frowned. "Exactly what are you getting at?"

"Oh, I'm sorry," Shalimar said, as if frustrated with her own ramblings. "I don't express myself too well. What I'm callin' for is to tell you that Clea regrets that she didn't explain her reason for leavin'. She won't be in town very long. She's packin' to leave for good, but I think it would do her a lot of good if you'd give her the chance to explain."

"Well, of course," he said. "I admit the curiosity has eaten at me. She was a real asset to me . . . I mean, to the company. It's going to be hard to replace her."

"Well, you know . . . I shouldn't say this, since I can't speak for my sister, but personally I don't think it's beneath the realm of possibility for her to be convinced to come back. She's just got a lot of emotional stuff goin' on in her right now."

Brandon ignored her inarticulateness and tried instead to picture Clea dealing with "emotional stuff."

Could it have to do with him? Was it what he'd thought before, that she left because she recognized his feelings for her? Was she willing to give up everything her job could have meant, just to do the right thing?

"I'd like to see her and talk to her," he said.

"Good. She should be in the apartment packin' this afternoon. What time can you be there?"

He checked his watch. "I could probably get there around one."

"I'll see that she's there," Shalimar said. "Thank you, Brandon. It'll mean a lot to her."

Brandon hung up the phone and was staring at it when Lawrence knocked on his door and stepped into his office. "Could I speak to you a minute, Brandon, about the recall on the Executive carburetors?"

Brandon rubbed his brows and looked at his friend. "Could it wait? I've got a meeting with George and his staff in ten minutes."

"Sure. Block out some time for me this afternoon," Lawrence said. He looked at Brandon, noting the fatigue and distance on his face. "Are you all right?"

"Yeah," Brandon said. "It's just that I've been a little stressed out since Clea quit. Haven't replaced her yet."

"Well, if you need me to get personnel on it—"

"No," Brandon said quickly. "I'm not ready yet." He looked at the telephone, then back to Lawrence. "Too much to do to start interviewing people and then train someone all over again."

"Is there any chance of getting her to come back?" Lawrence asked. "It's a shame to lose someone of her caliber."

"True," Brandon agreed. "And I don't know. Maybe I can convince her to come back. I'm supposed to meet with her this afternoon. Question is, should I take another chance on someone who just disappeared without an explanation?"

"Maybe," Lawrence said, "if she had good reason." He leaned back in his chair and pulled his ankle over his knee. "You know, Brandon, we're all human. Every one of us is entitled to screw up."

Though Brandon knew his friend spoke of Clea's actions, Brandon felt the message shooting to his heart. Was he really entitled to screw up? Was he really allowed to disregard the "rules" every now and then, just because everyone else did?

No, he told himself. He wasn't. And yet he couldn't get Clea out of his mind. Already he was distracted, just knowing he'd see her today.

"I don't know."

Lawrence came to his feet. "Give her the job back, old boy. Give her a raise. Give her a good reason to stay. It sure is a hell of a lot easier than wading through a bunch of pathetic applicants and gambling on one of them."

"I can agree with that," Brandon said, standing up and retrieving his briefcase again. "Thanks for your ear, pal. I'll talk to you this afternoon."

"Good luck," Lawrence said.

Brandon flashed a thumbs-up as he went back into his own office.

Clea's reaction to her sister's showing up at her door was no surprise to Shalimar. She hadn't exactly expected to be welcomed with open arms.

"What do you want?" Clea asked.

"Don't be so mean," Shalimar said. "I just came to get the rest of my stuff out."

Clea glared at her. "Are you moving in with him?"

Shalimar laughed. "Who? Stevie? I might be."

Clea didn't move from the door. "Shalimar, you and I have nothing to say to each other. Absolutely nothing."

"Well, that'll be fine with me." She shoved Clea aside and clomped into the apartment. Boxes covered the living room floor, and she could see that Clea was busy working in the kitchen. "I'll just get my things and go, and you don't even have to hang around if you don't want to. As a matter of fact, don't you have some bankin' or somethin' to do?"

Clea bristled. "As a matter of fact I do, Shalimar. Thanks to you."

"Then you better get on it," Shalimar said. "The less I see of you today, the happier I'll be."

Clea's look shot a dagger through her sister, and she grabbed her purse. "I'll be gone about thirty minutes, Shally. That should be enough time to get your things and leave. I'd rather you weren't here when I get back."

"I'd rather I wasn't here now," Shalimar mocked. "But as Mick Jagger once said, you can't always get what you want."

After Clea slammed the door behind her, a grin crept across Shalimar's face. Kicking off her shoes, she ran to the window and peered out, until she saw Clea pull out of the parking garage in her car.

Then she ran back out the door to the end of the hall to retrieve the bag she'd hidden there. It had the cameras, and if she could remember how to work them, they'd be set up by the time Clea got back.

Feeling adventurous and a little mercenary—which didn't bother her a smidgeon since she told herself she was actually doing this to help Clea—she hid the camera in the foliage of a schleffera in the living room, and hooked it up so that she could turn it on by remote at exactly the right time. The plants were Shalimar's, so she knew they would be left alone until she could come back to retrieve the camera.

She laughed as she realized how easy the whole scheme was going to be, and pictured the papers tomorrow nailing Clea and Brandon. It served her right, she thought, but she wasn't doing it for revenge. The main thing, she told herself again, was that Clea would be able to keep the money she'd earned already, plus another thirty-three thousand if Tiffany could be trusted to keep her part of the bargain. Clea wouldn't be allowed to screw this up.

Someday, Shalimar thought, Clea would thank her. It might not be for a few years, when she was lying in the Bahamas somewhere sipping Fuzzy Navels, or whatever they drank in the Pacific or Caribbean or whichever ocean it was, and she realized that she'd still be broke and victimized if it weren't for her sister.

Hurriedly, she grabbed the rest of her things from the kitchen and the bathroom and stuffed all her clothes in the bags she had brought. Then she jotted a note that she would be back later that afternoon for her plants. "And that cute little camera that holds your future," Shalimar added on a laugh as she hung the note on the refrigerator.

Before Clea finished her business at the bank, Shalimar was long gone.

31

Getting Tiffany's money out of her account wasn't as easy as Clea had hoped. Writing a simple check was useless. Tiffany probably wouldn't cash it, just as she hadn't cashed the first one Clea had written her, for the money was the only smoking gun in the whole fiasco. As long as the money stayed in Clea's hands, Tiffany had as much blackmail power as Clea did. Wiring it to Tiffany's account was impossible, since she didn't have the woman's account number.

Finally, unable to think of a better idea, she got a cashier's check for sixty-six thousand dollars and had it messengered to Tiffany's door. By her calculations, Tiffany was smart enough to realize that it was out of Clea's account now whether she cashed it or not. Since the whole goal of her scheme was money, she couldn't imagine Tiffany throwing it away.

It left her uneasy, though, for Tiffany wasn't one to give up easily. She would stop at nothing to punish Clea for foiling Tiffany's plans.

Shalimar was gone when Clea came back to her apartment, and she sat down and looked around at the boxes that would be loaded into a moving van and moved to Texas tomorrow. There was nothing for her in Beaut. Nothing but Myrna, and Clea had come too far to be back under her mother's thumb now. But soon she would be out of money, and until she found a job, she had no choice.

Wiping a stray tear from under eyes that hadn't seen makeup in days, Clea grabbed an empty box and started toward the kitchen.

The doorbell rang, and Clea wondered whether to answer it. Was it Shalimar already, coming back to get her plants? There were only three, and they were all half dead. She wished her sister would let them die in peace so they could avoid another confrontation. She was too tired to fight with Shalimar, endure her barbs, or deal with the silent treatment.

The bell rang again, and dropping the box, Clea went to the door.

But it was Brandon, not Shalimar. He leaned against the casing with his hands in his pockets, wearing the look of a lover who had something to apologize for. "Clea, can we talk?" His voice was the gentlest she'd heard since she'd last spoken to him, and her heart stumbled into a triple-time cadence.

"Well, I was . . ."

"I can see you're busy," he cut in, "but this can't wait."

She stood paralyzed for a moment, staring at him as if he'd evaporate with her slightest movement. But he didn't fade away.

"All right," she said finally, her voice wavering slightly. "I guess I owe you that much."

Outside across the street, Shalimar had watched Brandon drive up and park in front of the building. She had given him enough time to get to Clea's door, and then she pushed the remote button that would start the camera reeling.

Biting her smile, she ducked into the café across the street and waited for Brandon to come out. In a couple of hours, she'd be ten grand richer. Then maybe Steven Donovan would stop treating her like white trash, good enough to sleep with but not good enough to acknowledge outside of the bedroom. One of the two sisters could be Donovan wife material, she thought, but it wasn't necessarily Clea.

Brandon felt like a kid approaching his high school sweetheart after months of estrangement, as he stepped into her apartment. She had been crying, he thought, and she didn't have a drop of makeup on, but somehow, she looked as beautiful as he remembered her. Something about being in her presence lifted his spirits to a level they hadn't reached since she'd left, and he dreaded the thought of never feeling that way again.

He looked around at the boxes carefully taped and marked, and said, "Why are you doing this?"

"Because," she said. "I'm going back to Texas for good. Detroit hasn't been very good to me."

He watched her pick up the tape and finish binding a box. Her hair was loose and fell across her face. Idly, she pushed it behind her ear. He had dreamed of touching her hair, burying his face in it, breathing its scent. But that was why he was standing here watching her pack, he thought. Those dreams were too obvious. And they were wrong.

"Clea, it's not Detroit that's driving you away. But I know what is."

Startled, Clea swung around to face him. "What do you mean?"

"I mean that I've been thinking about it for days, trying to figure out what could have sent you running. And it finally came to me."

Did her face turn pale, or was it just his imagination? He wasn't sure, but he could see that his certainty disturbed her. He lowered himself to the couch, braced his elbows on his thighs, and looking at the floor, said, "Come here, Clea. Come talk to me."

Tears glistened in her eyes as she came slowly toward him and sat down next to him. What would he do if she cried? he asked himself. Would he be able to sit here, keeping his hands appropriately to himself, or would he follow his dangerous instinct to pull her into his arms? He honestly didn't know.

"Clea, I think you did what you did out of a sense of nobility."

"Nobility?" she said on a laugh. "Brandon, I've made a lot of decisions in the last few months, but nobility wasn't behind any of them."

Her hands trembled as she laced her fingers together, and, without censoring his impulse, he reached out to take one. "Look at me, Clea."

Slowly, she brought those big, silver-blue eyes up to him, and he felt his heart burst and melt right into his bloodstream. She was so sweet, so vulnerable, so different from Tiffany. Just looking at him, she revealed so much about herself. Maybe too much.

"Clea, I know you left DC because my feelings frightened you."

She caught her breath and studied his face for a short eternity. "I . . . no . . . that's not it."

"I think it is," he said. "Anything else, I think you

would have felt comfortable telling me. But I've thought a lot about this, and I can't help thinking that my feelings were too obvious in my face and my actions, that maybe I let our work linger a little longer than it needed to some days, that maybe I liked being close to you a little too much . . ."

One tear spilled over her lashes, and she wiped it away. "Brandon, you don't have to say this. You really—"

He touched her lips with a finger to quiet her. "Clea, I need to say this."

She swallowed back the tears in her throat and looked at him, seeing love and goodness and honesty, but it was something outside her reach. She had done the unspeakable to him, and he didn't even know it.

Withdrawing her hand from his, she whispered, "Brandon, I don't want to hear it. You're a married man, and I'm . . ."

"A beautiful, sexy, very desirable woman," he whispered. "And yes, it's gotten to me. It serves no real purpose to lie about my feelings, but you're right, Clea. I am a married man, and I can't get past that no matter what I do. I will never be unfaithful to my wife. Never."

She brought her eyes back to his again, wet, unadorned lashes framing them better than any makeup ever could have. "I wouldn't let it," she said. "I couldn't."

"And that's why you quit."

She wiped her eyes again, and covered her face as a plethora of emotions passed across it, and finally, she managed to say, "That's part of it."

He looked at her so helplessly, so sweetly, that she thought her heart might break, but she couldn't stop the tears from racking her. Slowly, he reached out and touched her hair, stroked it with a gentle hand, and pressed his forehead to hers. "Don't cry," he whispered. "Clea, please don't cry."

She tried earnestly to pull herself together, but too much came rushing forward. Too much loneliness. Too much unfairness. Too many secrets. And a terrible, sick self-loathing that she feared she could never run fast enough to escape.

His arms closed around her, and he pulled her against him. Helpless to deny the touch she so desperately needed, she collapsed against him, allowing her despair to flood out on him.

And she realized it was the closest she had come to belonging in her life.

Brandon closed his eyes against the emotion assaulting him, as well, and held her, feeling not for the first time that this was where she belonged. Tucked against him, sweet and vulnerable, in the tight circle of his arms.

"Oh, Clea," he said, burying his face in the sweet scent of her hair. "I'm trying so hard not to fall in love with you."

Suddenly, she looked up, as if the words had stunned her out of her sobs. She shook her head. "Oh, no, Brandon. You can't."

"I know that," he whispered, still holding her. "That's why I'm fighting it like hell. I won't, Clea."

He pulled her against him, squeezing her as fiercely as if he'd never see her again.

"That's why I have to leave," she whispered.

It felt too good to hold her, and he didn't let her go as he whispered, "Come back to work for me, Clea. I swear to God I can control this. I'm a strong person. I don't break easily."

Clea shook her head. "The strongest people in the world can still be broken."

"But you're not out to break me, Clea. You're as determined as I am not to get involved."

"It isn't me you should fear," she whispered.

"I know. It's myself I should fear. And I do, Clea. But I also know my commitment to my vows. And I don't take those lightly."

Clea extracted herself from his arms and slipped back, putting some distance between them. "But here we are, right now, holding each other and talking about how nothing could happen between us. It could slip up on us, Brandon. I don't want to be responsible for ruining you."

She got up, putting ample distance between them. Brandon closed his eyes and buried his face in his hands. "I know you're right. I know in my head that you are, and that you're a bigger person than I am."

"No," she said, turning around and facing him again. "Don't think that about me, Brandon. You really don't know me."

"I know enough," he said. He looked up at her, his eyes as haunted and barren as she had ever seen them, but even through his own despair, he seemed to see straight to her soul. "Well, I guess you've made up your mind."

"Yes," she whispered. "I'll be leaving for Texas tomorrow."

Swallowing, he stood up and looked down at her. His arms longed to hold her again, but he jammed his hands into his pockets to keep from reaching out. "It won't be the same, unveiling the car next month, without you. I really looked forward to sharing that with you."

"I'll read about it," she said.

"And that letter of recommendation. I'll have it waiting for you when you get to Texas."

"Thanks. I appreciate that."

They stared at each other without touching for a long moment, and finally, he said, "Damn, Texas seems like a long way away."

Tears sprang to her eyes again, and suddenly he was pulling her back into his arms and squeezing the life out of her. He nuzzled his face against her neck, and she slid her own arms around him, hugging him with all the emotion she had no right to feel.

Finally, he let her go and moved away from her. "Take care," he said.

Clea only nodded as he left her apartment without looking back.

Outside, Shalimar saw Brandon leave the building and get back into his car, and her heart sank. He hadn't been in there long enough for much to have happened. What if she hadn't gotten anything good on the tapes? Would Tiffany still pay her?

She waited for him to start the car and leave, but he didn't. For several minutes, he only sat there, staring, and it suddenly struck her that *something* must have happened. Maybe something even better than sex.

She watched until he finally started the car, looked back toward the door leading to the stairs, then drove away. Clicking the button to turn the camera off, she paid her tab and headed across the street hoping Clea wouldn't find the camera before Shalimar could get it back.

She rang the bell once and waited several minutes before Clea came to the door. "Oh, it's you," she said when she saw Shalimar.

Shalimar shrugged and bopped inside, closing the door with her hip. "Who did you expect?"

"Nobody," she whispered.

Shalimar glanced at her and saw how raw, swollen, and red her sister's eyes were, and for a moment, she felt a little guilty. She had wanted revenge for Clea's insensitivity last night, she thought, but hell, she hadn't meant to make her cry.

It wouldn't have bothered her if it was a very common sight, but in all her life, she'd only known Clea to cry two or three times.

Dropping the empty boxes she'd brought with her to carry the plants, she went to her sister. "Hey, honey, what's the matter?"

Clea turned away. "Nothing. Just do what you came here to do and go."

Setting her hands on her hips, Shalimar shook her head at her sister. "Look, Clea, you and I may be at each other's throats, but we're still sisters. Nothin'll ever change that. And honey, it makes me sick to see you cryin' like this. What happened?"

"Everything happened," Clea whispered. "Nothing happened."

"I don't mean to criticize," Shalimar said, "but isn't that just a tad contradictory?"

"Get your plants, Shally," Clea said. "I have work to do."

Deciding not to pursue it further, since she had it all on tape, anyway, Shalimar gathered the plants, set them in the boxes along with the camera still hidden in the leaves, and got the vase from the living room and stuffed it in a bag of its own. She listened as Clea went into the bathroom to wash her face, and quickly, she checked the camera to make sure it had worked.

From the looks of it, the tape had rolled for about thirty minutes.

She was hiding the camera in the box when Clea came out of the bathroom. "So . . . you'll be goin' tomorrow, huh?"

"Yes."

Shalimar nodded. "Well . . . it's been nice bunkin' with you, Sis. I know I haven't exactly been a barrel of laughs." She stared at her sister, but Clea kept her eyes on the floor. "Honey, don't look so sad. Cheer up. I just know things are gonna get better."

"Maybe."

Shalimar set down her bags and went to her sister, arms outstretched. "Hang in there, okay, kiddo? Myrna's girls always bounce back."

Clea hugged her half-heartedly and wiped her eyes. "You be careful here, okay, Shally? Detroit's a tough town."

"Hell, I've been chewed up and spit out before. If things get bad, I always have you and Mama in Texas."

Clea let her go and opened the door for her as Shalimar picked up the bags again. "Try to stay out of trouble, Shally," she said as her sister started down the stairs.

"Well, hell," Shalimar said over her shoulder. "Just what fun would that be?"

Shalimar felt her sister watching her until she was out of sight. She felt sorry for her. Poor Clea never intentionally did anything wrong and kept getting into trouble. Shalimar did everything wrong and still landed on her feet. But that was okay, she thought, because she was going to get the wheels rolling for Clea.

She caught a cab and hurried back to Tiffany's building, told the guard she had a delivery for Mrs. Donovan, and waited to be sent up. Tiffany would wet her pants if she saw what Shalimar hoped was on them. For both Clea and Brandon to be so upset, there must have been a moment or two of intimacy. Maybe a kiss. One bare boob. A quickie on the couch. The possibilities were endless.

If things went as she hoped, she'd be a rich woman by sundown. And Clea would, too, with a clear conscience, for she would have earned every cent Tiffany had paid her. Hell, she might even wind up with Brandon after all was said and done.

And she would have Shalimar to thank for taking matters into her own hands.

Tiffany stood frozen in front of the television in her living room, watching the tape of her husband with Clea.

"Sorry the sound's not too good," Shalimar said, wishing they'd at least kiss or something. All that crying and hugging was real moving and all, but somehow she didn't think it was what Tiffany wanted. "They musta been whisperin' a lot."

"Doesn't matter," Tiffany said. "What matters is the pictures. And these are good. I think I can use them."

"In court?" Shalimar asked.

Tiffany smiled and clicked off the television. "Among other things. A picture of Clea in Brandon's arms was just what I hoped for. I'll have a few stills made of this and get this thing going once and for all."

Shalimar felt her heart take flight. If Tiffany was happy, then that meant she'd pay her.

Tiffany went to a drawer in a bureau in the corner of the room, withdrew an envelope, and handed it to Shalimar. "It's been a pleasure doing business with you," she said.

Shalimar opened the envelope and counted the money. She had never seen so much cash in one place, but somehow, she felt as if she'd been shortchanged. "Did Clea give back the money you paid her?"

"She sent it."

"Well . . . now that she's gonna serve the purpose you hired her for, don't you think she still deserves it?"

Tiffany laughed and took the videotape out of the VCR. "She doesn't deserve a dime."

Shalimar remained standing where she was. "Well, I was thinkin', since she did what she was supposed to do, with a little help from me, maybe I could take that money for her. Sorta hold it till she decides she needs it."

Tiffany's laughter rang out over the apartment. "You're great, Shalimar. You should try a career in comedy."

Shalimar took that as a compliment, though she wasn't sure where it had come from. "Thanks. Actually, I'm tryin' to get into pictures. I'm an actress. You wouldn't know anybody . . ."

Tiffany laughed again and, shaking her head, went to the front door. "Sorry, Shalimar, but I can't help you there. By the time I get through with your sister, though, she's going to be a household word. Maybe you can ride her coattails to notoriety."

Shalimar wasn't sure what she meant, but she figured that meant no. The sixty-six thousand wasn't going into Shalimar's pocket, but at least she had gotten ten. That could take her a long way. "Well," she said, sashaying through the doorway, "it was nice meetin' you. Call me any time I can help. You might catch me in a coopera- tive mood."

"Oh, I will," Tiffany said.

She closed the door before Shalimar could say good-bye, and Shalimar stood in the hallway waiting for the elevator. "Rich bitch," she said aloud. At least Steven had come by his superiority honestly. But some day, when she was rich, she was going to act just like they did. Slamming doors in peoples' faces, laughing openly at them, scheming behind their backs. She was cut out for it, she thought. She deserved it.

She looked at the money one last time, then stuffed it in her purse as the elevator doors opened. All she had to do now was wait for the shit to hit the fan and figure out some creative way to justify what she'd done to her sister.

Lucky for her, her conscience had a short attention span, and by the time the elevator came, she was thinking of the money in her purse and all the ways she would spend it.

32

Clea sat on the floor that night, taping up the last of her boxes, when the doorbell rang. An urgent knock followed, and she got up and rushed to the door.

The moment she opened it, a flash went off, blinding her momentarily, and someone stuck a microphone in her face. "Are you Clea Sands?"

"Yes," she said, blinking and covering her face from the light shining over the shoulder of the man with the microphone. "Who are you?"

"We're from the *Globe*," he said, and another picture flashed. "We'd like to ask you some questions about your relationship with Brandon Donovan."

"My what?"

Suddenly, she realized there was a television camera pointing at her and several other men standing in the hall, flashing pictures of her.

"We're running your story in tomorrow's paper, Ms. Sands, and we'd like a quote from you. How long has your affair with Mr. Donovan been going on?"

"There is no affair!" she shouted. "I used to work for him, but I quit. Now please, go away!"

She tried to close her door, but the man stuck a foot in, and the others pressed in against him.

"Did you and Mr. Donovan have a falling out? Is that why you quit?"

"No!" she screamed. "There was nothing between us at all. Nothing!"

She pushed the man back and managed to get the door shut, but the doorbell continued to ring. Locking the deadbolt, she backed away, staring at it in horror, unable to believe what had just happened.

A story running about her tomorrow? How could that be? She hadn't given Tiffany anything to use against them. There was nothing to write a story about . . . unless Tiffany had given them lies, something to hang on Brandon despite her lack of evidence.

She tried to catch her breath as the banging on her door continued, and thought of calling Brandon. But it was late, and he was probably at home, and she wasn't about to risk getting Tiffany. Still, she reached for the phone, which she was thankful wasn't being cut off until tomorrow.

Before she could pick it up, it began to ring.

"Hello?" she said, bringing it quickly to her ear.

"Clea Sands?" a voice asked.

"Yes."

"This is Scott Harold with the *National Enquirer.* I wondered if I could get a quote from you about your affair with Brandon Donovan."

"There is no affair!" she shouted, and slammed down the phone. Immediately, it started ringing again.

Her hands trembled as she picked it up and hung it up again, then listened for the dial tone and took the phone off the hook. It was happening. Just what she had tried to avoid. Just what she had feared.

She sank down on the floor against the wall and covered her ears as the doorbell rang again and again, while someone knocked incessantly, and the phone blared out its beeping tone. It was a nightmare about to begin, and there was nothing she could do about it. Her life was spinning out of control, and she was the one who had set it spinning. She deserved whatever happened.

But Brandon didn't. Pulling herself together and wiping the tears from her face, she reached for the phone again. She had to warn him somehow, she thought. She had to let him know what he was in for.

With trembling hands, she dialed his office, praying he was still there, and that the madness hadn't confronted him yet.

Brandon didn't hear the phone ringing in his office, for at that moment he was riding the elevator down to the first floor of the DC building. Before it came to a stop, he saw a crowd of reporters in the lobby, being held off by three security guards. One of them caught sight of him and ran to meet him.

"Brandon, we tried to call you in your office but you were on your way down. It's like a mob scene. They want to talk to you—"

"About the THD?" he asked, frowning. "There's no new news that would warrant this."

"Uh . . . I don't think that's what it's about," the guard said. "We can escort you out of the building, and I'll call for a police escort home if you want. That is, if you're going home."

Brandon looked at the guard he had known for ten years. "Jake, what's going on?"

But Jake didn't have time to answer, for three reporters escaped the blockade and came running toward him, flashing pictures. "Mr. Donovan, how long has your affair with Clea Sands been going on?"

"Did it start before you hired her, or since?"

"Is it true she's carrying your child?"

Brandon gaped at them. "What?" He caught himself and tried to recover, but suddenly realized there was nothing to do but hurry out the door as fast as he could.

"Mr. Donovan, do you plan to marry her after your divorce?"

"How is your wife taking it?"

He flung around, his face raging red, and shouted, "There isn't going to be a divorce because there hasn't been an affair!"

"How do you explain the pictures, Mr. Donovan?"

"What pictures? There aren't any pictures."

One of the reporters reached out to hand him an envelope that held the pictures. Brandon handed his briefcase to Jake and opened the envelope.

The reporters got quiet, but the cameras continued to roll and flash as Brandon opened the envelope and pulled out the snapshots. They had been taken that afternoon in Clea's apartment, as innocent as that encounter had been. The pictures of him holding her with his face buried against her neck made them look like lovers.

"Oh, my God," he whispered, then grabbed his briefcase and started the other way. "Get me out of here, Jake!"

Jake called for some more of the guards, who escorted Brandon around the back way to the garage and out to his car. Outside the garage, he could hear a guard shouting to hold off other reporters.

Raging, he got in his car, slammed the door, locked it, and barreled toward the reporters, who parted to let him out. He saw several cars pull out to follow him, but he put it in high gear and wove in and out of the traffic until he had lost them.

Racking his brain, he tried to think who could have done this. Was someone trying to set him up?

He thought of Clea, and how honest and sweet she'd been this afternoon, and how mortified and devastated she'd be to see that picture splashed across the tabloids. Quickly, he snatched up his phone and dialed her number.

The line was busy, and he closed his eyes and prayed that the reporters hadn't descended on her yet. Then he thought of Tiffany.

If the reporters had reached his office, surely they had reached his home. By now, Tiffany would have seen the pictures, and she would assume exactly what someone wanted her to assume. That he and Clea were lovers.

He dialed his home number, and the maid answered. "Donovan residence."

"Milly, I need to speak to Tiffany," he said.

"I'm sorry, sir," the maid answered. "She isn't feeling well. She asked me not to disturb her."

"Tell her I have to talk to her," he shouted. "It's urgent."

He waited as the maid left the phone, and after several long, excruciating moments, Tiffany picked up an extension. "Don't bother to come home tonight, Brandon," she said. "This marriage is over."

"Tiffany, wait. It's not the way it looks! Somebody framed me, and I wasn't—"

He heard the click in his ear and threw the phone across the car.

He drove for another twenty minutes, racking his brain for some course of action. When he felt calm enough to try Clea again he found her line was still busy, and he suspected she had taken it off the hook.

Helpless to come up with any answers, he called the Atheneum Suite Hotel and arranged to have a suite reserved without going through the front desk. Then, slipping into the hotel's garage like a fugitive in the night, he sought refuge before the real war began.

33

The photographs of Clea and Brandon were transmitted across the wires that night and by morning were headline items in some of the country's major newspapers. CNN added it to its news lineup, and even did a special feature on the fairy-tale marriage that was ending. *USA Today* gave a rundown of Clea's past, using high school pictures and photos from the newspapers during the trial. At the noon hour in Beaut, Texas, the "local girl made bad" story ran ahead of the weekend homicide, the closing of the town's biggest factory, and the governor's speech at the Civitan Club.

Myrna was livid when she picked up the phone to dial Clea's number, and the busy signal she continually got heightened her anger still. After having the operator verify that the line was not off the hook, she sat on the phone for two hours, dialing then hanging up, dialing then hanging up, until finally, by some miracle, she got the phone to ring.

"Hi, this is Clea. I'm not at home right now . . ."

Myrna waited for the tone, then spat out, "Clea, this

is your mother! Pick the phone up if you have one shred
of decency left in your—"

The phone was picked up, and she heard Clea in a
hoarse, whispered voice, say, "Hi Mama."

Something inside Myrna snapped, and she launched
into a high-pitch diatribe. "How dare you humiliate this
family again? Do you realize what this will do to my reputation in this town? They'll probably make me quit
teaching Sunday School, and I can forget about ever
being president of WMU." She paused for a breath, and
realized that Clea wasn't going to answer.

"So what do you have to say for yourself?" Myrna
prodded. "An affair with a married man? Again! A
famous one, at that? I have to tell you, a lot of things
make sense now. Your quitting. Your getting the job in
the first place . . ."

"I didn't do it, Mama." The words were so soft, so
matter-of-fact, that Myrna almost didn't hear them
through her own rambling.

"Well, the media says you did. They have pictures,
Clea. Pictures don't lie. And they couldn't print this
garbage about your rendezvous with him in Georgia and
late nights at the office if they weren't true."

"They're lies, Mama," Clea said. "Pure lies." Her
voice broke, and Myrna could hear Clea sniffing back
the tears. "I need your support right now, Mama. It's a
mess, and the only thing I can do is wallow through it
until it blows over. But you have to believe that I didn't
do this. I need you on my side, Mama. I don't have anybody else."

"Well, if you hadn't thrown your sister out in the
street, you'd have her, but I don't suppose it's easy carrying on a sordid affair with your sister in the apartment
all the time."

"I did not have an affair, Mama. Those pictures were the worst thing they could come up with, and it was only a platonic hug between us. I don't know how they got them. Someone must have been at my window or something. But they won't find anything else because there isn't anything."

"Well, you tell that to the media."

"They won't believe me," Clea said. "They're running with this as fast as they can. Mama, I still want to come home today. There are too many reporters around for me to move out, but I can leave the boxes here and come back for them later. I have to get out of here."

Myrna couldn't believe her ears. "You aren't coming anywhere near Beaut," she said. "It's bad enough what you've done to me without your being here to stir up more trouble. You stay put, young lady."

"But Mama, what am I gonna do?"

"You should have thought of that before. Your sister's at the Ritz-Carlton. If she can forgive you for throwing her out, maybe she'll help you. But I wouldn't hold my breath. She's probably as embarrassed to show her face around town as I am. It's disgraceful, the things we've had to endure from you."

"Mama, Shalimar's loving every minute of this."

"Your sister may be something of a free spirit, Clea, but she doesn't get in half the trouble you seem to." She paused for a moment, then switched gears. "Has he told you he's in love with you?"

"Who?"

"Brandon Donovan."

"No, Mama. I told you, there's nothing between us."

"Then how could you sleep with him? It would almost be forgivable if there was a chance for the two of you. . . ." She let her voice trail off. "You deserve this, you know it? Every bit of it. How could you turn your back on your upbringing that way? Just disregard all the values I've taught you?"

For a moment Clea was quiet, then finally she whispered, "I still believe in all those values, Mama. But some people are just tested more than others."

"And some people draw trouble like they draw flies."

"That's me, I guess."

Myrna pursed her lips and glanced out the living room window to see a car full of women drive up. "Oh, my lord, it's the Sunday School committee driving up. I knew it. I knew it was just a matter of hours before they asked me to quit. I have to go now, Clea, to clean up the mess that you've made of my life, and figure out some way to save a little dignity."

The line went dead in Clea's hand, and she closed her eyes as tears rushed out. She hadn't known she had so many tears. She didn't know where they all came from.

She pulled herself off the floor, erased the beginning of the message her mother had left, and listened as the phone rang again and the machine picked it up. It had rung nonstop since she'd turned on her machine that morning. And all day she had listened to the messages with hopes that someone who cared about her would break through and offer her some help. But until her mother called, she'd only heard from reporters.

She heard the machine beep, then a man's voice saying, "Clea? It's Brandon. I wanted to tell you how sorry I am about—"

She jerked the phone up. "Brandon?"

He hesitated a moment. "Clea? Are you all right?"

"Oh, Brandon, how could this happen?" she asked, her voice breaking.

"I don't know," he said. "My head is still spinning. I feel like I'm in the middle of some bad movie. Any minute now—someone will yell 'cut!'" He let his voice trail off, then said, "Listen, I'm going to clear you of this. I'll tell them there was no affair. That nothing happened."

"But they won't believe you," she said. "What about Tiffany?"

He paused, and she could see the words weren't easy for him. "She threw me out. I'm staying in a hotel right now. I expect to be served with divorce papers any time."

"Oh, Brandon!"

"It's almost like she's glad this happened."

Clea was silent, for she couldn't add to the confusion already apparent in Brandon's heart. He was innocent, and yet to all the world, she had made him into an adulterer. "I'll do whatever I can," she said. "If it goes to court, I'll testify. I'll tell them you were nothing but a gentleman with me. That nothing ever happened."

"It could have, you know."

Clea didn't know why his voice brought so much warmth into her heart, even when they were talking about something so tragic. "Brandon, no matter what you do, you won't talk yourself into being guilty of this. You didn't do anything wrong. And you had ample opportunity."

"It could be argued that you did, too. That there were times when I was vulnerable enough."

"We can all be vulnerable, Brandon. The bottom line is what happened. I worked for you, we became friends, and I quit. And I never once saw any evidence that you were anything but loyal to your marriage."

"It perpetuates the myth, you know. The one about the rich playboy. The one that gives men like me a real bad name."

Clea was quiet for a moment. Then, in a shaky voice, she said, "I used to think all men were like that. But then I met you. And I found the one good man who could restore my faith. I'm so sorry that knowing me has done this to you."

She broke down and covered her face, as if he could see her, and she heard him sighing. "Don't cry, Clea. It makes me feel so helpless."

"We're both helpless," she said.

"No, not entirely. I don't intend to roll over and play dead. And I don't want you to, either."

"No," she said, swallowing back her tears. "I haven't done that yet."

He held on for a moment longer, as if he didn't want to break the connection, and finally said, "Well, I guess I'd better go. I'm staying at the Atheneum, but I don't suppose it would be a good idea for you to call me here."

"No, I don't think so," she said.

"Are you going to be all right?"

"Fine," she said, her voice cracking. "I'll be fine as soon as I decide what to do. My mother doesn't want me to come home anymore."

"Look, if you need to get away from all this, maybe I could help you."

"I don't want your money," she said. "I can take care of myself."

"I didn't mean money. There's this cabin I have up on Lake Michigan. It's real little, not much, but I go fishing there sometimes. If you'd like to use it, no one would ever find you there."

"Really? What about Tiffany? What if she found out?"

"How would she? She's never even been there. If

you feel uncomfortable going there, it's fine. I just thought . . ."

"No, I'd really like that," she said. "It's just what I need."

"Good. You can stay as long as you want. Frankly, the less the press can reach you, the sooner this mess will die down."

"You're right," she said. "I'm not real interested in having my face splashed across every paper in the country."

"The problem is, how to get the key and map to you without being found out."

She thought for a moment. "You could send the map on my modem and have the key delivered to my sister. She's staying at the Ritz-Carlton. I could tell her it's from a Realtor who's trying to rent me some property. She'll never know where it is."

"Perfect," he said. "I'll messenger it over within the next hour."

She swallowed back her emotion. He was helping her, and never suspecting she had helped instigate the whole mess. "Thanks, Brandon," she whispered.

"Don't thank me," he said quietly. "What I want from you is forgiveness for dragging you into this."

"There's nothing to forgive," she said. "Nothing at all."

"Well, I'll touch base with you when you get there. There's a phone, but no television, so you'd better take one if you want it."

"No," she said. "I don't think I do."

"I don't blame you." He paused for a moment. "Don't worry, Clea. If it's in my power, I'll clear your name of this. I don't have any intention of dragging you down with me."

Clea couldn't answer for the emotion welling in her throat.

"Take care," he whispered.

"Bye." She held onto the phone even after he'd hung up, and wept into the earpiece until it began beeping restlessly. She hung it up and dropped her face to her knees.

The phone rang again, and she listened as a reporter gave her a name and number to call, but not before he'd offered her a thousand dollars for an exclusive interview. She waited until he hung up, then erased the message.

She looked outside her window and saw the crowd of reporters still gathered there. In a day or two it would thin out, once they realized that she had left town and wasn't going to talk.

Meanwhile, she had to pull herself together. She needed to get some sleep, but first she needed to eat. She hadn't been able to eat a bite since this had all started. In the last week since she'd quit her job, she'd lost about ten pounds, and her clothes were beginning to feel loose. She needed to eat, to keep up her strength, to find some resources deep inside herself, if she was to get through this. But there was no one to call.

No one except Shalimar.

Clea looked up the number of the Ritz-Carlton and began to dial. She didn't know if Shalimar would even talk to her, after the way she'd thrown her out. She was probably laughing at Clea's righteous indignation now. Her mother was right. Shalimar got into far less trouble than Clea. Now even Clea wondered which was the "good sister." Maybe they were both bad. Maybe it was in their genes.

The hotel desk answered, and then the room phone rang.

"Shalimar Wilson. We screw 'em, you sue 'em."

"Shalimar!" Clea shouted.

Her sister burst into laughter. "I knew it must be you. I just got off the phone with Mama."

"Shally, you haven't told anybody anything, have you?"

Shalimar laughed. "Of course not. I'd be embarrassed to tell anybody what a prude you are."

"I mean about Tiffany. You haven't told them about Tiffany, have you?"

"Hell no. I'm just gonna sit back and let the drama unfold. Have you heard from Brandon? I'll bet he's walkin' around in a daze."

"No," Clea lied. "Have you heard from Steven?"

"Not since all this hit. Wonder what he thinks of his dear old dad now?"

Clea's heart sank. "Look, Shally, I realize that you and I have been at each other's throats lately, but I need help. I probably don't have any right to ask."

"Ask away," Shalimar said. "You caught me in a good mood."

"I have someone delivering something to you within the next hour. It's real important. When you get it, could you bring it over?"

"Depends on what it is."

Clea thought for a moment. "It's just a key," she said. "A Realtor friend of mine is trying to sell me some property on Lake Michigan, and I'm going to look at it. I have to get away, just long enough to think. I can't stand this much longer. And . . . I need some food. I hadn't done any shopping since I thought I was moving, but . . . Mama won't let me come now."

"Never fear, Shally's here," her sister said. "I'll bring you the key, and a hamburger or somethin'. Don't worry about the reporters. I can handle them. What should I wear? Do you think my red halter-dress would look good in a picture? And should I wear my hair up? It always looks sexier up, at least that's what men tell me."

"Who the hell cares what it looks like?" Clea snapped.

"Well, I care, thank you very much. After all, if I'm gonna be linked with the barracuda who broke up poor ole Tiffany's marriage, I want to look the part."

"Shalimar, please don't do anything. Just say, 'no comment,' and walk through. There's a guard keeping the reporters out of the building, so tell him you're my sister. He'll clear it with me before you come up."

"You know, that red dress might not be low-cut enough," Shalimar said. "Maybe I need to accent my assets a little more. My little black number might look better in print, after all."

"Shally, did you hear a word I just said?"

"Yeah. No comment, guard, blah-blah-blah. I heard every word. I'll be there in an hour or so. Hang tight." She giggled. "Tell the truth, though, Clea. If you had to go through all this anyway, don't you wish you'd at least hopped in the sack with him once? I mean, hey, it might have all been worth it."

"I'll see you in an hour," Clea said. "Good-bye, Shalimar."

She dropped the phone in its cradle and decided to take a shower while she waited. She was down, she thought, but she wasn't completely defeated yet. She still had some dignity to uphold, and somehow, she'd have to pull herself together.

It wasn't going to be easy, but she'd done it before. It was just that she hadn't really known until now what a fine line there was between guilt and innocence.

◦　◦　◦

Clea knew immediately when Shalimar arrived, for the crowd outside the door of her building grew louder. She peered out her window and saw Shalimar standing in the midst of them, like a movie star on Oscar night.

"Oh, God," she prayed under her breath. "Please don't let her say anything stupid."

She had already told the guard to let her sister in, but it was several moments before she heard the knock on her door. Throwing it open, she pulled her sister in. "What did you tell them, Shally?"

Shalimar feigned an insulted look. "What makes you think I told 'em anything?"

"The fact that you stayed down there with them for ten minutes, smiling and chattering."

"You were watching," she said, dropping a grocery sack on the table and hurrying back to the bathroom, where she checked herself in the mirror. "Hey, I don't look so bad, do I? Do you think they'll put me in the paper? They took enough pictures."

"Damn it, Shally, what did you say?"

"Oh, Clea, don't worry. I just told them that even though Tiffany paid you sixty-six thousand dollars, you still couldn't get him in the sack, so you're both clean."

"You what!"

Shalimar's laughter rang out over the apartment. "I'm just kiddin'. Good God, Clea, you've got to get hold of yourself. I told them I was your sister, and I spelled my name so there wouldn't be any mistakes. And when they asked me if I knew about your affair with Brandon, I said, 'No comment,' just like you said."

"Are you sure?"

"Well . . . I might have said somethin' about how you were too much of a prude to ever sleep with a married man, and how you wouldn't have shot that dude in the balls if you were that easy. Somethin' like that."

Clea sank onto the couch, wishing the earth would open up and swallow her. "Shalimar, they'll print every word. You'll probably be on the evening news."

Shalimar's face brightened even more. "You think so? Oh, Clea, this is just workin' out great."

"Shally, my life is ruined. Don't you see what this has done to me?"

"Come on, Clea. Our mama didn't teach us to roll over and play possum. When the goin' gets rough, the rough get off their roonies and find the silver linin'. In this case, though, that linin' might be platinum. By the way, here's your thing."

Clea caught the envelope as Shalimar tossed it to her. It was unsealed, so she opened it and saw the key Brandon had placed there. "Thanks, Shally. I really appreciate your helping me after the way things have been between us lately. If you want to stay here while I'm gone, that'll be all right."

"Sounds good to me. This could be my big break, you know."

"How do you figure that?"

"Well, if they can't find you, they may start followin' me, instead. The more I can get these rosy cheeks on camera, the more chance I have for bein' discovered. You can't buy this kind of publicity."

Clea's stomach tightened. "Look, Shally, I know you almost always mean well in these crazy schemes you come up with, but this is serious. If you tell what you know, I could be prosecuted for fraud. It would serve no purpose."

"I know that," Shalimar said. "I've given it a lot of thought. See, I figure as the mistress, you're seen as a sexy mystery woman, which makes me look good. But if I spill my guts about all that other stuff, then you're a criminal, right? And I don't really want my name linked with a criminal. So you don't have to worry."

Clea started to mutter something about how nice it was that Shalimar had considered Clea's welfare in all this, but she decided to bite her tongue. As long as Shalimar was on her side, for whatever reason, Clea didn't want to antagonize her.

She leaned her head back on the couch and thought back over the events that had altered her life in the last few years. None of this was supposed to happen. None of it. And yet it had been a chain reaction from the beginning, all leading up to this moment. There was no turning back, no erasing any of it.

"You know," Shalimar said, propping her high-heeled feet on the coffee table. "I've been thinkin' about where you went wrong. I figure you shoulda never married John Carmichael. If you hadn't, maybe none of this would have happened to you."

"How do you figure that?"

"Well, maybe you'da been available for some nice guy who might have come along later, and instead of workin' like a dog, you'd have had a little help gettin' through school. 'Course then you wouldn't have wound up goin' out with that Mills guy. The poor kid's balls would still be intact, and you wouldn't have been desperate enough to take Tiffany's money."

"If, if, if," Clea said with a sigh. "Who would have believed my life could get so screwed up?"

"Well, I guess you're stuck with it. Only thing you can do is make the most of it."

"And how do you suggest I do that?"

"Do what Jessica Hahn and Donna Rice did. Capitalize on it. Get an agent, write a book, represent a line of blue jeans. The possibilities are endless."

Clea felt tears welling up in her eyes again, and she got up and started back to her bedroom to pack her suitcase. "Thanks, Shally," she said, "but I don't want to be like them."

"But you already are," Shalimar called after her. "The sooner you admit it, the better off you'll be."

Clea rejected the idea with all her soul, but as she packed, some voice inside her told her Shalimar was right. And she supposed that forgiving herself was going to be her biggest challenge yet.

34

Steven Donovan sat alone in his bedroom, the light from the television, which was set on CNN, bouncing off the walls. Over his lap sat a gooseneck lamp, casting down a heat that made him sweat. But it served its purpose. It shed plenty of light on the subject.

It had never occurred to him to turn on the overhead light, for he'd sat like this for hours, poring over every copy of every news story that had come out about Clea and his father that day. Today they were more famous than Romeo and Juliet, more scandalous than King Edward and Mrs. Simpson. The thought made him nauseous, but he brought his scotch to his lips and that helped ease the feeling.

He wondered if his mother was nauseous, or if she, too, had sought the comfort of a bottle of scotch, the way she had always done when things got ugly. He wondered if his father was off brooding somewhere about being caught. He wondered if he was in bed with Clea.

His heart burned with rage, and he ripped the picture out of the newspaper and went to the wall, grabbed a tack out of his pocket, and thrust it in. Stepping back, he examined the myriad pictures he'd acquired of her just that day. Three times more than he'd already had. Almost enough to cover the whole back wall of his bedroom.

He heard his father's name on CNN, and turned to see the same footage he'd watched already three times that day. The videotape of his father standing in the lobby of DC, looking at the incriminating pictures that were now in millions of American homes. Footage of his father turning and hightailing it away from the heat. Then he lowered himself to his chair and sat on the edge of his seat as they showed what they called, "the beautiful young woman who is being named in Tiffany Donovan's divorce suit. Clea Sands, formerly of Texas, is said to have a history of scandal, the most recent being one involving the shooting of a man in what she called a date rape. During that trial, it was disclosed that she'd had a longstanding affair with the banker, who was helping to finance her education."

He watched as the footage changed to Shalimar, standing outside her sister's apartment that morning. "My sister has decided to leave on an indefinite vacation, and has asked me to tell you that she and Mr. Donovan never, at any time, had anything resemblin' an affair, that their relationship was one of a business nature only, and that if anyone has proof of anything goin' on between them, they should come forward, because she's bettin' everything that there isn't anybody. Incidentally, I've lived with her for the last several weeks, and believe me, the woman lives like a nun. 'Course, she doesn't *look* like a nun, but it isn't her fault that she looks like a sexpot. My sister and I didn't ask to be given the bodies we got."

Steven cursed under his breath, and watched as Shalimar waved to the reporters before starting past the guard into Clea's building. Idiot, he thought. She thought she was a damn movie star all of a sudden.

But he bet she knew where Clea was.

He thought of going to beat the hell out of his father, but there were more pressing things first. He had to get to Clea. He had to be there for her. Maybe if he reached her in this time of extreme vulnerability, presented a caring shoulder to cry on, and helped her sort things out, he could, at long last, get her into bed.

But there was no way to get to Clea except through Shalimar. Something inside him told him she would know how to reach her sister. If he could get that much out of her, it might be worth sleeping with her for a few nights.

He picked up the phone, dialed Clea's number— since one of the twenty messages he'd gotten from Shalimar in the last week said she had moved back to the apartment—and rubbed his hand across his beard as he waited for the machine to pick up. "Hey, Shalimar," he said in a rumbling voice. "It's Steven. Give me a call when you get a chance."

Shalimar picked up quickly, and in a breathless voice, said, "Stevie? Is that you?"

He cringed at the name. "Yeah. Saw you on the tube."

"How did I look?" she asked. "Was the dress all right? It was one of Clea's, but she didn't care. She left all her nice clothes and said I could wear 'em."

"So where'd she go, anyway?"

Shalimar paused. "Now, Stevie, you know I can't tell anybody that. She's restin', that's where. Besides, I don't really know, anyway. She didn't even tell me." She was quiet for a moment, then asked, "Is that why you called?"

"No, of course not," he said. "I just wondered. This

whole thing is so unreal. It's got my head spinning."

"I know, honey," she crooned, "but you shouldn't let it bother you. I swear to God nothin' really ever happened between them. Your father's a saint. Truth is, Clea'd be perfect for him, but he is a married man."

"If nothing happened, then where did all this shit come from?" he asked.

"Hell, I don't know. Gossip? People love to make up things. You just got to learn to let it bounce off of you. As much as I hate to admit this, my daddy embarrassed my family a time or two. I just went with it, you know? Just acted like he was a rascal and that I was proud of his gall. It always worked for me. Even when he died in that woman's bed."

Steven rubbed his forehead and told himself that he really could endure her inane rambling just long enough to find out Clea's whereabouts. He sighed. "I called to see if maybe you'd like some company tonight. I could take you out to dinner, but we'd probably be hounded by photographers."

"I know," Shalimar said with glee. "Isn't it wonderful bein' famous?"

He couldn't bear to answer such a stupid remark. "I could order some Chinese food and bring it over. We could listen to the new Kenny G. CD, curl up and get cozy . . ."

Her voice dropped to a sultry level. "You play your cards right, Stevie, and you might just be able to have your way with me."

"That's what I'm counting on," he said. "I'll be there in a couple of hours. Is there a back way?"

"Yeah, but they still might see you. You'll have to wear a disguise or somethin'. Maybe it'd be better if I came to you. You haven't invited me into your house since we first met, you know."

He shot a look at the pictures of Clea on the wall, and shook his head. "No, I don't like that idea."

"Why not?" Shalimar whined. "Why don't I ever get to come to your place?"

"Because . . ." he said. "It's a mess."

"A mess? Don't you have a maid or somethin'?"

"I fired her," he said. "I don't like having people snooping around in my house. I'll just be over there. Don't worry about it. I'll get in somehow."

"Hey, I've got an idea. If you call me on your car phone before you get here, I could create a diversion. I have some pictures of Clea when she was a little girl that I meant to offer to some of the reporters. If I go down there with them, they'll be swarmin' around me, and you can slip right in."

Pictures, Steven thought. More pictures. His heart accelerated, and he said, "Yeah, okay."

"See you later, sweetie," Shalimar said.

After he hung up, he stared at some of the pictures of Clea on the wall, wishing he had just one of her nude. But there weren't any . . . he'd stake his life on it. Somebody needed to fix that.

He got up and thought of showering, but somehow couldn't make himself do it. Not for Shalimar, anyway.

But when he found out where Clea was staying, then he'd pull out every resource he had. And Clea Sands wouldn't know what had hit her.

The phone rang, and he jerked it up. "Hello?"

"Steven? It's me." It was his father's voice, and Steven's muscles grew rigid as he sat up straighter in his chair.

"What do you want?"

Brandon was quiet for a moment. "A chance to explain things to my son?"

"The press has explained everything anybody will ever need to know."

"They're all lies," Brandon said. "I never slept with Clea Sands."

"Pictures don't lie."

"Sometimes they do. Steven, can we get together to talk about this? I don't want to lose my whole family."

"Come on, Dad, she was probably worth it," Steven said. "A piece like Clea Sands? Young, supple . . . you probably had the time of your life."

"I told you nothing happened. Why can't you believe me?"

"Because it's unbelievable, Dad," Steven cried. "I've seen the woman. I know how many hours you spent alone with her in Georgia. I know all the late nights the two of you worked together. I even told Mother what I suspected."

"You did *what*?"

"I told her that I thought there might be something going on."

"Is that why she had me followed? Had pictures taken?"

"Probably," he said.

"Steven, how could you tell her that, when you didn't know if anything was going on or not? This isn't a game. This is my life."

"You should have thought about that before you put your hands all over Clea!" he said. "You should have considered what you'd be losing. And if I have anything to do with it, you're gonna lose a hell of a lot more than you think!"

Steven slammed the phone down and leaned back, and settled his eyes on the pictures of Clea again.

°　°　°

Brandon dropped the phone onto its cradle and covered his face with both hands. Steven hated him, and Tiffany was out for blood. He had lost his entire family, and he hadn't really done anything.

But deep in his heart, some distant voice told him that he had. He had wanted Clea. He had begun to fall in love with her, and that was probably a greater sin than sleeping with her.

His hands trembled as he picked up the phone and dialed his father. It was several moments before Peter Donovan answered.

"Dad?"

"Son, I've been trying to call you. The maid keeps telling me you aren't home."

"I'm not. I guess you've read all about it."

"I've read the trash the newspapers are printing. What part of it's true, Brandon?"

Brandon sighed and shook his head. "Dad, you won't believe this. Nobody believes it."

"Whatever you tell me, son, I'll believe."

Brandon's heart warmed a degree, and he clutched the phone tighter to his ear. "Dad, could I come up and stay for the weekend?"

"I was going to suggest it myself. Ida can make us your favorite apple pie, and we'll walk along the lake and you can tell me everything."

Brandon's eyes misted at the unconditional love that he hadn't found anywhere else in the world. "I'll be there in a few hours," he said.

"All right, son. I'll be waiting."

Tiffany was jubilant as she went through the records she had gotten from Brandon's office, the records she was giving to her father—who had agreed to represent her—that very afternoon. Brandon was worth even more than she'd hoped. And now she stood to win it all.

Life was about to become wonderful.

Abandoning the files, she strolled across Brandon's study, the only room in the house he'd insisted on decorating to his taste, which happened to be earthy, drab, and utterly boring—and checked her face in the gold plate on one of his plaques. She wondered what people would think when they learned she was remarrying so quickly after her divorce. It didn't really matter, she thought, once all the papers were signed and she had the money in her hand. Soon enough, gossip would fade and people would concentrate instead on how good she and her new husband looked together and how they had the world by its tail.

The doorbell rang, and Tiffany went to the door of the study and peered out as the maid let Steven in. Breezing out, she met her son. "Darling, how are you?"

"More to the point, Mother, how are you?"

"Oh, I've been better," she said, trying to appear despondent. "Where have you been? I've tried calling you at work."

"I've had it with that place," Steven said. "I won't be back. I don't want to be anywhere near my father."

"That's so sweet of you to defend my honor like that, darling. But you really should go back to work."

"For what?"

"To learn as much as you can about the business. You should know that I plan to sue your father for everything I can get. And when I do, I'll need someone to run DC."

Steven's bloodshot eyes changed. "Me?"

"As president at the very least. You deserve it, darling. I never agreed with his starting you at the bottom the way he did. A man of your caliber and education should be used where he can do the most good. That's what I plan to do if I win Donovan Concepts in the divorce settlement."

Steven went to the bar, poured himself a drink. "What do you think your chances are?"

Tiffany wanted to laugh, but she held herself back. "By the time I get through with your father, *he'll* be lucky to get a job on an assembly line somewhere. I've got plenty of proof, but I'll need your help."

"My help? What can I do?"

"You can testify that your father was in the room alone with Clea for several hours. If there were any gestures exchanged between them, touches, overheard whispers, kisses you might have seen . . . anything to indicate an affair was going on."

"You know I didn't see anything like that, Mother. We've already been through it."

"I know, darling, but I thought something might have slipped your mind. This is very important, and so much is at stake."

Steven sipped his drink, then ambled to the couch and dropped down. Was his mother asking him to lie?

"If there were something, that would surely nail Dad to the wall, wouldn't it?" he asked.

"It would be rather cut-and-dried," she said. "If you could say that she was in his room all night, or better yet, that you saw something. Something they might have done. Maybe if you had caught them at something—"

"But you know I didn't."

"Are you sure?" she asked. "Think, darling. Wasn't there anything?"

She *was* asking him to lie, he thought, but instead of repulsing him that fact amused him somewhat. He hated his father for being the one linked with Clea. And now, if he only said what his mother wanted him to say, he could wind up with the whole damn company. Clea would take notice of him then. But he didn't want to wait that long.

"I'll think about it, Mother," he said. "Maybe I can come up with something." He gazed at her for a long moment and realized that she looked better than she had in weeks. She was calm, unruffled, like a woman on top of the world. "I must say, Mother, you seem to be taking this incredibly well."

"I'm a fighter, Steven. You know that. Your father has shamed me irrevocably, but I'll get the last word. I don't like being made a fool of, and I can't bear having my feelings stepped on like they don't matter. He chose a younger woman over me, and there isn't a married woman in the country who won't realize the pain I'm going through."

"That's just the thing, Mother. You don't appear to be hurting at all."

Tiffany lifted her chin. "Just because I don't choose to parade my feelings around doesn't mean I don't feel the sting, Steven. But I can endure anything as long as I have a plan."

"Sounds like a plan, all right, Mother." He got up, set his glass back on the bar, and headed for the door. "Count me in."

"We're going to be better than ever when the smoke blows over," she said. "Just you wait."

Steven only lifted his hand in a wave as he went through the door.

35

"*I must tell you,* I'm a little confused." Theodore Holland dipped a shrimp into his cocktail sauce and brought it to his lips—lips that were couched in layers of fat. It didn't bother Tiffany that he was woefully overweight. He was still one of the most respected law professors in the country and had an unbelievable amount of clout. Besides that, he was a father who doted on his only daughter with every resource available to him. As long as Tiffany had her mother's looks, she could accept her father as he was.

"What are you confused about, Father?"

"About that letter you had me write for that Sands woman. I'd like to call a press conference and revoke it, just in case she's stupid enough to try and use it."

"No, Father. I don't want you to do that."

"And why not? The woman got you to hire her to work with your husband, then slept with him." He started to put another shrimp into his mouth, then stopped and looked up at her. "Which brings another point of confusion to mind. If you expected her to work for Brandon, why on earth would you be helping her to get into law school?"

Tiffany leaned back in her chair and focused on the ceiling, wondering just how much she should tell her father. He could forgive her almost anything, unless it meant losing money. In this case, he would probably applaud her. "It's a long story," she said. "And I don't suppose I'm entirely without blame."

"Oh?" her father asked.

She leaned forward on the table, and settled eyes that were calculatingly weary on his. "Father, I haven't been happily married for a very long time. There were incidents . . ." She let her voice crack, and pretended that she couldn't go on.

He reached out to pat her hand. "Go on, Tiffany. What incidents?"

"Brandon drank too much sometimes," she said. "Oh, nothing anyone else ever saw. Just at home, late at night, and when he did . . . sometimes he got physical."

"Do you mean violent?"

"Yes," she said, and tears came to her eyes, the way they always had as a child when she needed to persuade her father to see things her way. "He hit me several times, even bruising my face a time or two. I hid it with makeup. No one ever knew."

Her father slammed his napkin down on the table, scraped back his chair, and stood up. As he stood before her, he made a perfect Alfred Hitchcock silhouette. "You should have come to me. We could have prosecuted."

"But I couldn't prove it," she said. "There was no proof. I would have wound up losing everything . . ." She wiped her tear, paused to catch her breath, then went on as if she found it extremely difficult. "But then I figured out a way to get out of the marriage and *not* lose."

He frowned down at her. "Go on."

"I read about Clea in the paper, Father. About her trial, and how she had lost everything because of the publicity. She seemed beautiful and intelligent, and very bitter. So I called her."

Her father's brows rose infinitesimally. "Are you telling me that you instigated this whole thing?"

Tiffany nodded. "Money wasn't enough, though. She wanted a chance to finish law school, so I promised to get help from you."

"But didn't she realize after the publicity hit, no university would believe a letter from me would be genuine?"

"I don't think she realized just how infamous she'd become," Tiffany said on the edge of a laugh. "She thought I'd use her name in the trial but that the rest would be kept quiet. I may have agreed to something like that. But then she turned on me."

"What do you mean?"

"I mean she tried to pull out on me. Tried to give the money back and quit her job with Brandon. So I had to manipulate things a little to get what I needed."

"I see." He sat back down, crossed his hands in front of him, and smiled. "I'm proud of you, my girl. You would have made a brilliant attorney."

"Father, with the adultery case, I have a much better chance of getting the prenuptial agreement thrown out. I kept my vows, and he didn't. The judge will see that, won't he?"

"If I have anything to do with it, he will." He took her hand again and squeezed it. "Don't worry, darling. I'll handle your case myself. When we get through with Brandon, he'll know what it feels like to be beaten and left bleeding."

"I knew I could count on you, Father."

* * *

It was raining when Clea found the little cabin tucked just outside of Traverse City on the banks of Grand Traverse Bay, and she was soaked by the time she unloaded her car. She found firewood stacked near the door and matches on the mantle over the fireplace. The first thing she did was start a fire.

She changed out of her wet clothes and looked around at the simple furnishings that reminded her more of Brandon than the penthouse he lived in did. The sofa was soft and overstuffed, and there was a rocker-recliner in a corner, with a reading lamp close behind it. In the corner of the room was a double-bed, made up with a plaid country quilt.

She opened the cabinets and saw rows of canned vegetables, boxes of dried pasta, and packs of mix-to-make gravies, spaghetti sauce, and hot chocolate. For the first time in days, she smiled.

She fixed herself something to eat in the small microwave, which seemed Brandon's only concession to real civilization, then settled down in the recliner, watching the fire. The quiet wrapped itself around her like a warm blanket, reaffirming that she would find peace here.

And as she felt her soul being restored, she drifted off into a sleep more restful than any she'd had in days.

Clea heard the phone ringing from the lake where she sat in the sun the next morning, and she got up and ran barefoot into the house to answer it.

"Hello?"

"I was just calling to make sure you got there all right."

The voice was unmistakably Brandon's, and she smiled as she sat down. "I thought it must be you. Brandon, this place is wonderful. It's the most peace I've had in years."

"Good," he said. She noted the listlessness in his voice. "There are fishing poles in the little tack room in the back. You'll have to catch crickets or dig for worms for bait, but there's nice brim in the lake. Do you know how to cook it?"

"Yes. My stepfather used to fish a lot. Every now and then he'd drag Shalimar and me along with him."

"Drag?" he asked. "Didn't you want to go?"

"Not with him," she said. She felt her heart stirring again, resurrecting bitter memories, and she told herself it was time to lay them to rest. "How are things going? Is the press still raging about us?"

"Worse than ever. Apparently, your sister sold some pictures of you and her as children to CNN, and they've been showing them all afternoon."

"Pictures of me as a child?"

"Well, there were some from when you were a teenager, one in a bikini on the beach, and a couple of you in a prom dress."

"Why?" Clea asked. "Why would they care about any of that?"

"Well, I have to admit that the one in the bikini has been more prominently displayed than the others."

"I guess they want to show the profile of the femme fatale," she said. "Make me look cheap."

"You didn't, though. Even half naked, you still had class."

Clea smiled. "Thanks. But I'd prefer not to have my picture on America's television screens for any reason. Especially something like this." She grew quiet for a moment. "How are you doing?"

He shrugged. "I'm spending a few days with my father before the circus really gets underway. I've heard that Tiffany has gotten her father to represent her. I'll probably get papers any day now. The worst part is Steven."

"What about him?"

"He refuses to talk to me," Brandon said. "He's convinced it's all true. He's devastated by this."

Clea couldn't imagine anything short of a swift kick in the groin that would devastate Steven. "Don't underestimate Steven," she said. "He's a grown man."

"But he's my only son," he said. "I don't want to lose him."

"And you're his only father. I'm sure he doesn't want to lose you, either."

A moment of silence passed between them. "We used to go fishing up there on the lake," he said. "One year we caught twenty-two brim in one day. We froze what we couldn't eat and took them home, but Tiffany threw them out." He paused, thought for a moment. "You should walk up north of the cabin a ways if you get bored. There's an old church there and a little country store where you can restock. And a little farther up is a graveyard where I used to love to read the headstones."

"I will," she said. "I really love it here. Do you mind if I stay a couple of weeks? Until things blow over a little?"

"Stay as long as you want," he said. "I'll keep in touch with you. You're real easy to talk to, you know that?"

She smiled. "When will you go back to work?"

He didn't answer right away. "In a few days, I guess. Now I have to decide whether to unveil the car or not. It might be better to wait. All this negative publicity might detract from the car. I don't want that."

"I wish I could be there when you do," she said. "It's

going to be your crowning achievement, Brandon. Maybe it'll be just the thing to turn the negative PR around."

"Maybe," he said. "I'll give it some thought." He sighed, and she thought he was about to hang up, when he said, "Would it bother you if I keep calling? It means a lot to have a friend who isn't suspecting or condemning me right now."

"Call me anytime," she whispered. "As peaceful as it is up here, I can see myself getting lonely."

"Yeah, me, too," he said. "Well . . . I'll let you go."

"Take care," she said.

She listened as he hung up, then set the phone quietly in its cradle. Silence rang out like an orchestra around her, and it was a comforting sound. But that loneliness in her heart roused anew, and she wished with all her being that things could have been different. But they couldn't. She'd written her own script, and now she had to play the part.

She only wished that she'd had the sense to write a happy ending.

36

Shalimar lay limp as Steven rolled off of her, putting his face to the wall and closing her out completely. Damn him, she thought. He took as little time as possible getting his jollies, no matter how hard she worked to please him, then inevitably acted as if she wasn't even there after it was all over.

She got up and strolled out of the bedroom, not bothering to get dressed. It didn't really matter, she told herself. He was rich, after all. Rich guys could do almost whatever they wanted and get away with it. He seemed to like making love to her. Maybe he'd get addicted to her that way, then fall in love.

It sure wouldn't come through talking.

She went to the refrigerator, got out a container of yogurt, peeled off the top, and stuck a spoon in. They hadn't talked that much at all in the past few days that he'd been here. The only times he'd been interested in what she had to say was when she'd mentioned something about Clea. Then he'd hung on every word.

It was the story of her life. Clea was always the one

with everything. Looks, class, brains. Her hair was gorgeous, and she hardly ever worked at it, and her skin radiated a glow that makeup could do little to enhance.

She shrugged off the thought that Steven might be interested in her sister, and favored the idea that he just wanted to know more about the woman who was breaking up his family. That was probably why he was so distant. Because he was depressed. It wasn't easy for a person to watch his parents tear each other to shreds.

She went to the answering machine and rewound it, since she'd turned the phones off and the machine down so they wouldn't be disturbed. Then, plopping onto the couch and propping her feet on the table, she began eating the yogurt as message after message from reporters came across the tape.

It wasn't until one of them identified herself as an editor from *Playboy* magazine that she paid any attention. "We're trying to reach Clea Sands about the possibility of her posing for our centerfold. Please have her call us back."

She listened as the woman gave the phone number, and looked frantically around for a pen. Finding one, she hiked a leg on the couch and jotted the number on her thigh. "*Playboy*!" she shouted. "Oh, my God. This could be it!"

Cutting off the machine, she called the number and asked for the person who'd left the message. After going through several secretaries, she finally hit paydirt. "Uh . . . hey. I'm Shalimar Wilson, Clea Sands's sister? I thought I'd better return your call."

"Yes, Shalimar," the woman said. "We need to contact your sister right away."

"Well, good luck," she said. "She's nowhere to be found. But I am. You know, we have the same body structure, bein' sisters and all, and I have terrific boo—I mean, breasts. I'd be willin' to pose for you."

"No, we're only interested in Clea," the woman said. "Isn't there some way you could get a message to her?"

"Well, even if I did, she'd say no. She's such a prude."

"Tell her we're prepared to pay her more money than she could make in a lifetime."

"What?" Shalimar caught her breath, tried to breathe. "Hold on a minute."

She sat down, still naked, and tried to compose herself. "Okay. Did you say more money than she could make in a lifetime? Because she's got big-time earning potential, you know. She's got brains."

"Yes, we're aware of that."

"Oh, hell. She'll say no anyway. I know her."

"Well, if we could just talk to her, we might be able to meet her price."

"Meet her price? I love it!" She laughed aloud, ruffling her curls around on her head. "Look, the best I can do is hope she calls and give her the message. But I'm tellin' you, she'll never do it. She probably doesn't even get naked to take a shower. We're talking Victorian, here."

"She couldn't be too Victorian with her background," the editor said. "Sleeping with her banker, and now Mr. Donovan."

Shalimar wasn't sure if denying those rumors would diminish their interest, so she simply said, "Well, but she didn't do that in front of millions of people."

"Look, we have the picture of her in a bikini. If she posed for that—"

"My mother took that picture," Shalimar said. "It was about ten years ago. Did you notice the girl standin' by her? That was me. Before my boob job. Imagine the same girl with boobs."

The editor hesitated. "I'm sorry, but we're really only interested in your sister. Please have her call us. We'd like to get her in an issue very soon while interest in her is so high. We may even consider putting her on the cover."

"Damn," Shalimar said. "She has all the luck. Listen, don't you think the mistress's sister could sell a few magazines? You don't understand what this could mean to my career. I'm an actress, you know."

The woman almost sounded amused. "The best we could offer you is maybe a side shot with her if she decides to pose for us," the editor said. "The sooner she calls, the more receptive we might be to including you."

Shalimar assured the woman that she'd have her call as soon as possible, and she threw the phone down. "Oh, God, I've got to get to her!"

She hurried back to the bedroom and began riffling through the closet for something to wear. Steven sat up in bed. "What's going on?"

"*Playboy,* that's what," Shalimar said as she stepped into a pair of pantyhose. "They want Clea and me to pose for them. Can you believe it? I have to find her."

He sat up, suddenly more interested. "How can you do that if you don't know where she is?"

"I know the general area," she said as she slipped one of Clea's dresses, one of the ones she'd never worn, over her head. "How big is Lake Michigan, anyway?"

"It's huge," he said, beginning to get dressed. "Is that where she is?"

"Oh, hell, why didn't I make her tell me where she was stayin'?"

She threw him a glance, and grabbed her bra, then decided she'd rather not wear it. She wanted to keep remembering that she was sexy enough to do a *Playboy* spread. It all depended on Clea.

She grabbed the top of the dress up, slipped her arms in, and checked her hair in the mirror. "You didn't answer me. *How* big is it? Like, will I be able to drive around until I see her car, or what?"

"Is that where she is? On Lake Michigan?"

She glanced back at him. "Well, yeah. I'm pretty sure."

Steven got up and grabbed his clothes, and began dressing even faster than she. "Shalimar, don't be stupid. Lake Michigan runs along the whole eastern side of the state. Is she down on the south side by Holland or Saugatuck, or farther north, like around the Leelanau peninsula?"

"I don't know!" Shalimar shouted. "But I've got to find her!"

He buttoned his shirt and faced her, a little too breathless. But she didn't notice. "Is she in a hotel, or staying with friends, or what?"

"She wouldn't tell me. She just had a key and said she was goin' to see a cabin somebody was tryin' to sell her."

He stared off into space for a moment, and then it was as if a light bulb had snapped on inside his brain. "Did she say anything about Traverse City, Shalimar?"

"I don't know."

"Think, damn it!"

"I can't!" she cried. "Oh, why didn't I snoop around a little before she left. Damn it, they'll probably have some new scandal by the time she gets back, and *Playboy*'ll forget all about Clea and me!"

Steven was too preoccupied to commiserate. "I have to go," he said. "Shalimar, you have to stay here. She could call anytime. You can't miss that call."

"But where are you goin'?"

"Home for a while," he said.

"Why, all of a sudden?" she shouted. "You were lyin' in bed, for God's sake! If you're hungry, I'll feed you. Is it because of the *Playboy* thing?"

He shrugged her off as she clung to him. "Hell, Shalimar, I just need a little space, all right? Leave me the hell alone."

She dropped her hands and gaped after him as he hurried out of the apartment.

Steven reached his car and cranked it before he was even all the way in. He checked the gas gauge and realized that he had enough to get a good start toward Traverse City. Why hadn't he thought of it before?

The cabin. She was in the Donovan cabin. And Brandon was probably with her. He drove faster than his car had ever gone, dodging cars and skidding turns on the freeway, until afternoon turned into dusk.

It was dark before he reached the cabin, and just as he'd expected, he saw her car parked out beside it. There was no sign of his father's car, and for a moment, his heart leapt. Maybe Brandon *wasn't* here, he thought. Maybe she was alone.

Maybe now he had her exactly where he wanted her.

Clea watched the cork on her fishing line bob, and sitting up straight, she pulled the pole out of the water, revealing a flopping brim on the hook. She jumped to her feet and reached for the line, grabbed the fish and took it off the hook.

In her excitement, she didn't hear the footsteps coming up behind her.

"Some catch."

She swung around, dropping the fish, and saw Steven watching her. "Steven!"

"You gonna gut it or throw it back?"

"How did you know where I was?"

"It didn't take a genius to figure it out," he said. "All your sister had to do was let Lake Michigan slip, and I knew where you were. In my father's cabin." He looked around, his cold, brooding eyes taking in the landscape. "So where is he, Clea?"

"He's not here," she said. "He hasn't been here. He only let me come here to get away from the media."

"Right," he said, adopting a stance that she found menacing. "You expect me to believe that he's had the opportunity to spend days alone with you in a cabin, and nobody would have even known, and he turned it down?"

"Steven, I am not having an affair with your father." She got her fishing pole, bait, and the fish she'd already caught, and she started back up the hill to the cabin. Steven followed behind her, his step slower and more calculated. "I've been alone this whole time."

"Then you must be getting pretty lonely."

She reached the cabin, set down the pole and buckets, and started for the door. "Go home, Steven. You have no business here."

"It's my cabin, Clea. You're the one intruding. As a matter of fact, I'd think the press would be real interested in knowing where you're staying."

She stopped at the door and looked at him. "What do you want?"

"You," he said. "All I want is you." He opened the door and motioned her in. Bracing herself, she went inside, but placed herself beside the cabinet where she had put her gun.

She let out a deep sigh. "Why would you want me when you can have Shalimar?"

"Shalimar's a tramp. You're different." He came toward her, and she started to move, but he caught her and caged her with one arm against the cabinet. "Look at this hair, and your body, and that cold way you look through me, as if I was lower than trash. But you don't know me, Clea. We could be good together. I'd be even better for you than my father."

"I don't want you," she bit out through her teeth. "I'm not interested. Now go home."

She tried to duck away from him, but he slammed her against the cabinet, pressing his pelvis into hers. He was hard, and she realized that he hadn't come here to talk. He caught her mouth with his lips, and she shook her head away. "Steven, stop it. I'm not sleeping with you."

"Oh, yes, you are, Clea. One way or another."

She tried to reach behind her, to the drawer where she'd hidden the gun, but she was backed against it and couldn't pull it open. He thrust his tongue into her mouth and grabbed her hand, and forced her to touch him. Fury raged through her, and she closed her fingers over him as tightly as she could.

Pain shot through him, and he knocked her hand away and stumbled back. "You bitch!"

As fast as her trembling hands could move, she opened the drawer, found her gun, and aimed it at him. "Don't you come near me."

"You're nothing but a whore like your sister," he spat out. "You use your bodies like weapons, but they can be turned on you."

"I've used a gun before," she said. "I don't mind using it again. Now get the hell out of here."

"You'll regret it," he said. "I'll testify against my father in court. I'll tell them that I walked in on the two of you making love in Georgia. I'll even tell them that he was here with you in the cabin. That I saw him."

"Why? Why would you do that to your father, when you know it isn't true?"

"I'd do anything to get what I want," he said. "Now why don't you hand me that gun and be nice, so I don't have to destroy both of you?"

She thought for a moment, racking her brain to consider whether or not what Steven said was a bluff. Somehow, she doubted it. He could destroy Brandon in court, but if she slept with him . . . if she pretended to like him . . . maybe he'd leave his father alone.

She started to lower the gun, and thought what it would mean. Taking off her clothes, letting him take off his. Letting him touch her, enter her, explode inside her . . .

She hadn't held off Joe Don and shot Richard Mills only so she could let scum like Steven Donovan violate her.

Mistaking her quiet for hesitation, he let a smile tilt across his mouth. Slowly, he began to lower his zipper . . .

Her stomach churned, and she feared she would throw up and drop the pistol. Quickly, she raised it again to eye level. "I will never sleep with you, Steven. Never. You can say whatever you want in court. You can't prove it's true."

"Don't be stupid, Clea." He didn't bat an eye as she cocked the gun. "You know, I could so easily knock that gun out of your hand, throw you down, and rape you. Or I could follow you, wait until you're off guard, and use you until I'm sick of you. There wouldn't be a thing you could do. Nobody would ever believe you."

She felt sweat breaking out on her brow and held the

gun tighter. "On the other hand, I could pull this trigger before you even raised your hand."

His face reddened, and he cursed under his breath. "Why, Clea? It's just sex. What difference does it make?"

She thought back to a time not so long ago when she'd told herself the same thing. It was just sex. Why couldn't she do it?

"Because my body is not a toy. And if I have to die fighting you, that'll be just fine. If you have to die fighting me . . . well, that'll be even better."

He stood still, staring at her, not believing a word. Finally, she moved the gun and fired at the wall next to him. He jumped. "The next bullet has your name on it."

He started for the door, but turned back before walking out. "It's not over, Clea."

She swallowed back the bile in her throat as he slammed the door. She didn't lower the gun until she heard his car start and drive away.

Then, quickly, she ran around the cabin, gathering her things as fast as she could, and threw them into her car. She had to get out of there before he sent reporters to catch her, or worse, came back himself.

It was no more than twenty minutes later that she had locked the cabin and was on her way home. She held the gun in her lap all the way.

37

   Brandon washed the last of the dishes he and his father had eaten on that night and decided that in a little while he would call Clea and make sure she had everything she needed.

   Then he rebuked himself. He shouldn't call her. It wasn't appropriate.

   But damn it, she was the only one who understood fully the pain he was experiencing, for she was experiencing it herself.

   He heard the phone ring in the other room, and after a moment his father came to the door. "Son, it's for you. Tiffany."

   Brandon turned around, drying his hands. "Tiffany? Why?"

   "Talk to her. Maybe she's ready to work things out."

   A wave of dread washed over him, and dropping the hand towel, he went to the phone. He heard the back screen-door close and knew his father had gone out to give him some privacy.

   "Hello?"

"Hello, darling," Tiffany said, and he knew instantly from her sarcastic tone that this was not a reconciliation call. "This is your soon-to-be ex-wife."

"What is it, Tiffany?"

"I thought you might prepare yourself," she said. "You'll be served with divorce papers tomorrow."

He ruffled his hair, and let out a heavy breath. "Tiffany, we don't have to do this. Nothing has happened between Clea and me. Nothing at all. I've always been faithful to you."

"Yes, darling. And that's why she's been hiding out in your cabin, isn't it?"

"What?" The word came out on an astonished whisper.

She laughed again. "You're priceless, you know that? And careless. And your stupidity is going to cost you everything."

"Tiffany, you've got it all wrong."

"Tell it to the judge," she said. "I'm going to take you to the cleaners, Brandon. By the time I'm through with you, you won't even be able to afford the car you *drive*, much less your company."

"Tiffany, you've got to listen to me!"

The phone clicked in his ear, and he slammed it down and shouted a curse that reverberated through the house. He looked up and saw Peter standing in the doorway.

"It's over," he said, breathing hard. "My marriage is over."

Peter looked old as he came into the room and sat next to his son. Setting a hand on his back, he said, "You'll get through it, son. Maybe you'll be better off."

"I'm gonna have to go back to Detroit in the morning, Dad. My marriage may be over, but this war is just beginning. I have to gather my resources."

"Let me know what I can do, son," his father said. "I'll do anything I can."

Shalimar was sound asleep when Clea slammed into the house late that night, and after she dropped her things on the living room floor, Clea stormed back to the bedroom. She saw her sister lying there, oblivious to anything being wrong, and flicked on the light. "All right, Shally. Wake up, damn you!"

Shalimar stirred and slitted her eyes open. "Clea! You're back." Awareness dawned slightly, and she sat up. "Oh, my God. I've been hoping you'd call. Clea, *Playboy* called and—"

"How dare you tell him where I was?"

"Tell who?"

"Steven Donovan!"

"How could I tell him? I didn't even *know* where you were."

"He said you let it slip about Lake Michigan. How did you know I was on Lake Michigan?"

Shalimar suddenly looked hurt, and she stood up, her legs looking way too long beneath the skimpy negligee she wore. "You mean he found you there? What did he do? Drive up there?"

"Oh, yeah, he found me all right. Does the word *rape* mean anything to you, Shally?"

"Rape? He raped you?"

"No," Clea said. "But only because I had a gun, and he knew I wouldn't hesitate to use it."

Tears sprang to Shalimar's eyes. "Why would he do that? We had such a good time together. I thought—"

"He was using you, Shally. Now tell me how you knew where I was!"

"I didn't!" Shalimar wiped at her tears and shook her head. "You said somethin' about Lake Michigan, and he musta figured it out."

She sighed and tore a tissue out of the box on Clea's dresser. "Damn it. We've been together for days. I thought he really liked me."

Suddenly, Clea felt bone tired. She dropped down on the bed and rubbed her aching temples.

"What's wrong with me?" Shalimar asked on a whisper. "Why do I always wind up gettin' the short end of the stick? And why is it always you the men like? I'm younger, my breasts are perkier, I'm skinnier, and I'm always willin' to have a good time. But damn it, it isn't fair for you to have both of the Donovan men in love with you!"

"Neither one of them is in love with me," Clea said. "Brandon and I are nothing more than friends, and Steven has a screw loose. You should try telling him no a few times, Shally. Then he'd come after you with everything he's got."

"Hell, I can't tell him no. I'm usually the one doin' the askin'." The admission brought more tears, and she let a sob escape her.

Suddenly Clea didn't know how to be mad at her anymore. Shalimar was like an innocent puppy who kept running into the street. And she only had a conscience where her own welfare was concerned. She wasn't crying out of remorse for what she'd let slip, but because that sleaze ball liked Clea more than her.

But that very shallowness stirred Clea's heart, and she reached out and messed up her sister's already tangled hair. "Look, let's just get some sleep. I've been driving for a long time, and it's been an abysmal day."

Shalimar lay down next to Clea, tears still rolling down her nose. "Why doesn't he like me, Clea?"

She pictured the little girl that Shalimar had been, lying next to her in bed with her curls tumbling around her head and her thumb stuck in her mouth. As angry as she'd been, she couldn't help still loving her as she'd loved that child. "Why do you want him to, Shally? He's dangerous and mean, and he doesn't care about anybody but himself. He's Tiffany's son all the way through."

"But he's so fine lookin'," Shalimar said. "And so rich."

Clea felt that anger rising in her again, and she got up and changed into a gown. Then, slipping back beneath the covers, she said, "Let's don't talk about him anymore. He makes my stomach turn. Just go to sleep."

"Yeah," Shalimar said. It was quiet for a moment, then suddenly Shalimar sprang back up. "Oh, Clea! I forgot to tell you the reason I wanted to find you. *Playboy* called. They want you to pose for them. They're willin' to pay megabucks, and I'm tellin' you you could negotiate and get a fortune! I think we need an agent, so I spent all afternoon—"

"Wait a minute!" Clea cut in. "Why do they want me?"

"Because you're famous, of course. You're the billionaire's mistress. Everybody'll buy a copy."

"I'm not posing for *Playboy*! That's ridiculous."

"Why not?" Shalimar asked. "It's probably even more money than Tiffany promised you, and it could be a whole new beginning for you. It could start a new career, Clea. There are people who would kill for a chance like this!"

"Not people like me."

"Oh, Clea, don't be so selfish!"

"Selfish? How can you consider that selfish?"

"Because you're only thinkin' of yourself. If you pose, maybe you could add into the deal that you and I pose together in one of the shots. I need the exposure, Clea. Come on. It could be the best career move for me."

"No," Clea shouted. "I won't do it!"

"At least call them and talk to them tomorrow, Clea. Please! I sent them a video of myself today, just in case it came up in negotiations. So they'd know I'm no dog or anything."

"You sent them a video of yourself naked?"

She grinned. "Well . . . yeah. What else would you send? They have to know you don't have cellulite all over your butt, and that your boobs don't sag. I expressed it to them. Mention it when you talk to them."

Clea shook her head and fell back on the pillow, laughing. "Oh, Shally, you're hopeless! Where'd you get the camera, anyway?"

Shalimar swallowed. "Oh, I borrowed it from my boss at Hairem Scarem. And you're wrong. I'm not hopeless. I've got a lot of hope. This thing with you and Brandon could be the best thing that ever happened to me."

Clea's laughter faded, and that smothering melancholy fell over her again. "Well, I'm glad you're enjoying it. Because I'm pretty sure it's the worst thing that will ever happen to Brandon or me."

The next morning, Brandon was up at five and on the road by five-thirty. He hadn't slept a wink the night before. Failure, a concept he had never contemplated in his life, was now something he'd have to live with. He had failed at his marriage. He had failed at adulthood. He had failed at life.

But the failure had started years ago, not just now. He had known after a couple of years of marriage to Tiffany that he wouldn't have the kind of family with her that he had always wanted, but he had lived with it.

And for what? So she could manufacture a charge against him, then bleed him dry? What was the use in being faithful if you got blamed for things anyway?

And Clea's life, once again, was being invaded by newspapers and television cameras as if she'd done something wrong, when she too was just a victim. It wasn't fair. He hated putting her in this position when she'd done nothing to deserve it.

And where was she? He'd called her at the cabin three times after Tiffany called, but she wasn't there. Something must have frightened her away, he thought. But what could have happened?

He picked up the phone in his car, dialed her home number, then hung it up before she could answer. There would be a record of whom he'd called, he told himself. Tiffany could find a bill and use it against him. She'd be digging up every morsel of evidence she could. He had to watch his every move.

He raked his hair back from his face and told himself that it was going to get ugly for him. There wasn't much he could do about that except maintain his innocence. If he couldn't protect himself, at least he could do his best to protect Clea. And he could protect his son.

He wondered if Steven would talk to him yet. Maybe the initial anger had passed, and he had realized that the allegations the press had made against his father were ludicrous.

He dialed Steven's number and put the phone to his ear.

Steven picked it up and answered in a groggy voice. "What?"

"Steven," Brandon said. "I'm sorry I woke you."

"Who the hell is this?"

"It's Dad. I know it's early, and you're—"

The phone clicked off, and he was left with a dial tone humming in his ear. "Damn it," he whispered.

His heart hammered incessantly as he centered his sights on getting to Detroit and contacting his lawyer as soon as he could.

Clea hardly slept a wink that night as she replayed the events of the past few days over and over in her mind. Her life was out of control, and so was Brandon's. Somehow, she had to get the reins away from Tiffany. All night, she had racked her brain for someone who could help her find Tiffany out. She'd need a private investigator, someone who wouldn't be starstruck by Tiffany Donovan, someone who could keep his mouth shut.

Cliff Redin. The name had come to her out of the blue as daylight dawned, and quickly the face surfaced to match it. He'd been the PI that the firm she'd worked for during law school had used for everything from license-tag searches to actual crime solving. He was good at what he did, and moreover, he was discreet.

Quickly, she found his number and called it. When he finally answered, she faltered a little.

"Cliff? This is Clea Sands. You may not remember me, but I used to work for—"

"Bradstreet, Sinks and Dudmoore," he provided. "How could I forget? You're all over the papers."

Her chest constricted, and she found it hard to breathe. "Well, I guess that's partially why I'm calling."

Her voice dropped in pitch, and she glanced at the light beneath the closed bedroom door to make sure Shalimar wasn't listening. "I'm calling to hire you for a small job, but it has to be kept quiet. I mean, no one can know."

"Hey, I give that confidentiality to all my clients. No problem."

"Good." She let out a breath of air, and realized it was harder to get this out than she'd planned. "I want you to follow someone, someone who's famous and has to be very discreet about what she does."

"What do you want me to catch her at?"

"Anything." She caught herself, realizing how desperate that sounded. "Just . . . anything that could be used against her in court." Her voice fell off again, and she searched her brain for an explanation of why it would matter to her. "If there's a lover, I need to know who he is."

"Well, it shouldn't be too hard to get you just a name. I can probably keep it within your budget," he said. "Who is she, anyway?"

Clea was silent for a moment, and finally, she made herself answer. "Tiffany Donovan."

Cliff's low whistle was all the reaction she needed.

"Yeah, I know. She's pretty visible, all the time. But there are some things that don't fit. I think something may be going on."

"Do you want pictures, videos, a phone tap?"

Clea considered it a moment. "No, nothing like that. Just follow her for a day or two and see what you can come up with."

"Can do," Cliff said. "Where can I reach you?"

Clea gave him her number. "As soon as you learn anything, call me. And when you call, make sure you're talking to me. My sister lives with me."

"You bring a check by today, Clea, and I'll start on it myself this afternoon."

"All right," she said. "I will. I'll be there in an hour or two."

She hung up the phone and stared at it for a moment, wondering if she'd be wasting her money. What if he didn't find anything on Tiffany?

He had to, she thought. That was all there was to it. If he didn't, she'd have nothing to hang over Tiffany's head, and Brandon's life would be nothing more than vulture bait.

Cliff Redin was a man who did his job from the inside out, and from the moment Clea brought him a check that covered his first two days' expenses, he set out to follow Tiffany Donovan. She was all over the place that Monday morning, flitting around from hairdresser to nail salon, then to a meeting of some ladies' club she belonged to. It wasn't until her limo let her out a couple of blocks from the Westin Hotel, and he followed her around to the side entrance, that he thought, perhaps, he had something.

She was disguised, he realized as she cut through the cushy lobby of the plush hotel, without sparking any interest from people who ordinarily would have turned and stared. She wore her hair up, camouflaged by a large, smart-looking hat and huge sunglasses that hid half her face.

He followed her to the elevator, looking down, and Cliff waited with her, pretending not to notice who she was.

They were alone when they got on, and Cliff made sure he was closest to the numbers. He glanced at her with a tentative smile. "Which floor?"

"Fourteen," she said.

"How about that?" he said, pushing the button. "Me, too."

She threw him a glance, then cast her eyes down again. They came to the fourteenth floor, and he allowed her to get off first. Instead of following in the direction she went, he went the opposite way until he heard a door opening behind him. Then, stopping at the first door he came to, he pretended to be opening it as he glanced back up the hall.

He fixed his eyes on the door she had gone in, then when the door was closed, hurried back up the hall to get the room number. He jotted it down on the pad in his pocket and got his small pen camera ready, in case he was able to get something.

Ordinarily, he might have tried to pick the lock on one of the suites beside hers and climb out on the balcony to peer into her room and see if her lover was already there. Pictures were always worth a lot, but Clea hadn't paid him enough for that. All she wanted, she'd said, was the name of Miss Auto Queen's lover. That shouldn't be that hard, he guessed, for if the guy wasn't already there, he couldn't imagine him making a woman like that wait too long.

He paced the hall, then turned back each time the elevator bell went off and photographed each person getting off the elevator. Finally, a man in a black business suit got off and stuck his key in Tiffany's door.

Cliff snapped the picture, then headed for the elevator. Not bad work, he thought, dropping his camera back in his pocket. Half a day, and he was almost finished.

Smiling, he checked his watch and told himself he might have time for a few holes of golf this afternoon if he was lucky.

◦ ◦ ◦

Clea gaped at the picture Cliff had given her, and something miserable twisted in her heart. "Oh, my God," she whispered. "This will kill Brandon."

"You know him?" Cliff asked.

"Yes."

She swallowed and, with trembling hands, dropped the picture in her pocket. "I really appreciate this, Cliff. I can take it from here."

"You're the boss," he said. "It really wasn't that hard."

"No, I don't suppose it was," she whispered. "Poor Brandon."

Still in a haze, she left Cliff's office and went back out to her car, her mind reeling. Part of her wanted to bask in ecstasy, for it meant she had gotten what she needed on Tiffany. It was Brandon's ace. His way out of this mess.

But the other half of her knew what it would do to him when he learned who his wife's lover was.

There were too many things to think about, she thought, and too little time. Whatever she decided to do, she'd have to do it soon. Time was running out.

Somehow, she would do whatever was necessary to save Brandon. Saving herself would be her second priority.

38

Clea refused to honor Playboy's offer by returning their call, allegedly ruining Shalimar's career and only chance for happiness. But as soon as Shalimar finished pouting, she called the magazine herself and relayed the message that no amount of money would convince Clea to pose nude for them. Then, as Shalimar had expected, they upped the ante, making an offer that any normal mercenary mistress might have taken. But Clea didn't bat an eye.

Disgusted, Shalimar reminded them that she'd sent in a video. With a decided lack of interest, they told her they'd look at the video when they got around to it.

Shalimar called in sick that day in order to sit by the phone waiting for *Playboy* to call her back. After voicing as much protest as she could when Clea tied up the phone, she paced while Clea made an appointment with Brandon's attorney.

Though a few errant reporters continued to linger outside her building, hoping to get a picture of Clea, no one seemed to be stalking Jacob Fairbane's office as yet.

It was likely that word hadn't gotten out that he would be representing Brandon in the Detroit divorce of the decade, but Clea had assumed it from all the work he had done for Brandon while she was at DC.

When she walked into the office, in her most pristine dress and with her hair pulled back severely—so she'd look the part of Victorian schoolmarm rather than femme fatale—the secretary gave her a curious once-over and instantly picked up the phone.

In seconds, a man of about six feet three, with a head that was bald in the back but still prolific in the front, Buddy Holly glasses, and a pipe in his hand, confronted her from the doorway. "Miss Sands, how are you? Come right back with me."

She followed him back through the maze of law offices to one of the most lavish ones in the firm. Secretaries stopped their work and watched as she followed the lawyer, and when he closed the door behind them, she nearly collapsed into a chair. "Are you all right?" he asked, putting his pipe between his teeth.

"Yes," she said, bringing her fingertips to her forehead. "It's just . . . the way they all stared at me."

"You're quite an enigma, I'm afraid," he said without apology. "Now what can I do for you?"

She looked up at him, noting the rigid, matter-of-fact way he regarded her. Trying not to let his apparent disapproval distract her from her purpose, she said, "Two things. First, I want to testify on behalf of Brandon. I want to go to court and tell them that nothing happened between us. Nothing at all. Brandon has been faithful to his wife since the day he married her."

Mr. Fairbane adjusted his glasses. "I don't think that would be a good idea, Miss Sands. No one would believe it. They'd expect you to deny it."

"But Mr. Fairbane, how can he prove his innocence if you don't let me testify? His word alone isn't good enough. Not with those pictures—God knows how she got them—but they're misleading."

The man leaned forward, his elbows on his desk, and he took the pipe out of his mouth. "Miss Sands, I only got this case yesterday. I won't deny that the first thing that came to my mind was that I needed you to testify, and when you called this morning, I had every intention of asking you to. But now, seeing you today, I'm more convinced than ever that if you were to go into that courtroom, there isn't a judge in this country who would believe that Brandon spent hours and hours alone with you and never had a lustful thought."

"He isn't being sued for any lustful thoughts," Clea snapped. "He's being sued for adultery, which he did not commit. No one but he and I knows that for sure."

"I have to do what's best for my client," he said, leaning back with an air of finality. "And I'm sorry, Miss Sands, but bringing you into court will only complicate matters tremendously."

She dug into her purse for the photo she had brought with her, and looking down at it, considered whether to spring this on him yet. The picture the man alone wouldn't prove anything, but just the suggestion of an affair might start them on a search of their own. "Mr. Fairbane, you haven't—"

His phone buzzed, and he picked it up. "All right. Send him back." When he hung up, he dumped his pipe into an ashtray and put it away. "Miss Sands, I phoned Brandon when you made your appointment and asked him to join us. I hope you don't mind."

Something in her heart leapt, but she tried to restrain her expression. "No, not at all. Maybe *he* can convince you."

"I doubt it. More likely, he'll see it my way."

There was a knock on the door, and Jacob Fairbane stood and walked around his desk. He opened it, and Brandon stepped in, his eyes shooting straight to her. The air seemed immediately charged with something Clea couldn't name, something that she was sure Jacob Fairbane hadn't missed.

"Clea, why did you leave the cabin?" he asked softly. "Did something happen?"

Selfconsciously, she glanced at the attorney. "I had things to do," she said. "I decided I'd rested long enough."

Brandon wasn't buying, and when he sat down next to her, his eyes seemed to cut right to the heart of her. "Clea, Tiffany somehow knows you were there. I don't know what happened, but I know something did."

He glanced at Jacob, as if noticing him for the first time. "I lent Clea my cabin on the lake to get away for a few days, Jacob. I didn't go near it myself, so there was absolutely nothing going on."

Jacob dropped back in his chair, and shot them a look that seemed to ask what bomb they would drop next. "And Tiffany found out? How?"

Brandon looked at Clea, and she felt her stomach turning again.

"Steven," she whispered. "Steven showed up and found me there. Apparently he got the information from my sister."

"Damn." Brandon rubbed his tired eyes, and looking at him, she realized that he must not have slept in days. She had turned his life into a nightmare, and it was destined to get worse before it got better. She looked at the picture, but hesitated to bring it up just yet.

"Brandon, I came here to get Mr. Fairbane to let me

testify at your hearing." Her eyes grew harder, and her lips tightened. "But he refuses. If he truly believed that nothing happened between us, then he'd let me testify."

Jacob shook his head. "Miss Sands, I've known Brandon for a very long time. I've never seen him do anything inappropriate. He has quite a long list of other friends who could testify to that. We have a priest in his home church in Ann Arbor who will come and tell of his exemplary religious beliefs. We have business associates and employees who will add to it. We simply don't need you."

"But I'm the one he supposedly slept with! What will they think if we don't refute that?"

"We *will* refute it. *He* will refute it. That's enough."

She came out of her chair and turned to the back wall, fighting the temper rising inside her. Desperately trying to calm herself, she turned back around.

"All right, then. What about Tiffany? What are you going to do to discredit her?"

Fairbane frowned and gave a shrug. "What do you mean?"

"I mean, how much research are you willing to do on her? Are you going to have her followed? Are you going to have her watched? Because if you do, you're likely to find something. There's a reason why all this is happening."

"Miss Sands, I've been practicing law for a very long time. I know how to do my job."

"Then why the hell don't you know that Tiffany has been having an affair?"

Brandon's head shot around, and he gaped at Clea. "What did you say?"

She hadn't thought this out well enough, and this wasn't the way to break the news to Brandon. But no matter how it hurt him, she had to tell him. "Brandon, you have to know."

"Who?"

She met his eyes, and swallowed. "Lawrence Henderson."

"No!" He jumped to his feet. "That's not possible. Larry is my closest friend, and I trust him with everything!"

"Maybe too much," she said.

"No, you're mistaken. You misinterpreted something. They're good friends, because he and I are good friends. But nothing is going on with them. It never has."

"I swear it is, Brandon," she said, tears springing to her eyes. "But you don't have to believe me. Just check it out yourself. I had her followed, just long enough to find out who it was, but I couldn't afford the kind of proof you need."

Brandon seemed paralyzed, and Clea tried to harden her eyes, but the tears wouldn't dry. "Please, Mr. Fairbane. Have her followed. Watch Lawrence for a few days. I know you'll find something."

Jacob drew his brows together. "I'm sorry, Brandon, but I agree with her on this. I'll get a detective on it right away."

Brandon only stared off into space, and Clea realized she had delivered one more blow to knock him to his knees. She stood up and started for the door on legs that barely seemed to support her. "Please call me if you change your mind about my testifying," she said quietly.

Brandon didn't answer, and Jacob only nodded. She slipped out before either of them had broken the silence.

°   °   °

It was late that night, after Shalimar had given up on *Playboy* and decided to go bar-hopping, that the phone rang next to Clea's bed. Dreading whomever it might be, she let it ring until the machine picked it up.

"Clea, I need to talk to you. If you're there—"

It was Brandon, and instantly she jerked up the phone. "Hello?"

The machine beeped, then cut itself off, and Brandon hesitated a moment. "I'm calling from a pay phone," he said. "I'm getting a little paranoid about records of my activities."

"I understand," she said. "Are you all right?"

"Yeah." His voice was hollow and distant, and she doubted that he really was. "I've been thinking all day about what you said. You wouldn't make something like that up, would you?"

"No, Brandon," she whispered. "And I never would have hurt you by telling you, if it hadn't been so important. That's why she wants out of the marriage, Brandon. Not because of you. Because of Lawrence."

His voice was raspy, distant. "We play golf together," he said. "We go fishing in Canada two weeks out of the year. I stood up for him when he got married, and I helped him through his divorce." A long silence followed, and in a whisper, he asked, "How could he sleep with my wife?"

"You seem more surprised that he would do it than that she would."

He was quiet for a moment more. "I've been running this through my mind all day, and something has been replaying over and over and over."

"What?" she whispered.

"That maybe Tiffany used you to set me up."

Her heart suddenly seemed to obstruct her breathing passages, and she couldn't utter a sound. He knew. He knew what a fraud she was, that she could be bought, that she had been Tiffany's puppet. How could she have been so stupid as to think he wouldn't figure it out?

"I mean, if you think about it, it makes sense. She begged me to hire you, and I thought it was odd at the time. She's usually irrationally jealous. And then when you quit, she went into a rage. She's the one who found your number at your mother's."

"Brandon . . ." Her voice shook with fear, but he cut in.

"You knew, didn't you?"

Tears came to her eyes and spilled over, and she covered her mouth with her hand. "I was—"

"That's why you quit, isn't it? You figured it out before I did?"

She caught her breath. "Figured what out?"

"That you were being used. That I was being set up. If she wanted a divorce, and maybe wanted to have the prenuptial agreement thrown out, her best bet would be to find some unsuspecting young beauty to use against me."

Unsuspecting. He didn't think she was in on it. Her heart deflated, and she allowed herself to breathe again.

"But nothing happened," she managed to say, as if reminding herself would clear her of her own guilt.

"No, but she used it, anyway. And everyone believes her. Just your being there did the trick."

She closed her eyes. "Brandon, I'm so sorry. So, so, sorry."

"Me, too," he whispered. "I never wanted you to get hurt by knowing me. And if I'd seen it coming, I would have done what I could to protect you."

"Protect me?" she asked, astounded. "Why? It's you she's hurting."

"But I hate how it's falling back on you."

She tried to laugh. "Don't worry about me. I'm told that this is just a stepping stone to a brilliant career. *Playboy* has already offered me a centerfold." Brandon was quiet, so she hastily added, "I turned it down, of course. I'm not interested in being a professional bimbo."

"No, it doesn't suit you."

She wanted to shout that it *did* suit her, but she couldn't bear to take the heat. She could suffer the media, she thought, the censure from her mother, and the incessant phone calls and press reports she saw in the tabloids, but she could never survive Brandon's see-ing her for who she really was.

"I'd better go," he said finally. "Do you mind if I call you from time to time? I suddenly find myself with very few people to talk to."

"Call anytime," she said through trembling lips. "I want to know how things are going."

"All right. Sleep well," he said.

"You, too."

The phone clicked in her ear, and she held it to her heart for a little too long, and said a silent prayer that she wouldn't be found out, that her sins wouldn't be exposed for Brandon to see. And she prayed that he would rise above all this somehow. And that when the dust settled, maybe she'd have a real chance with him this time.

When Brandon got back to the hotel that night there was a message from the detective his attorney had hired that morning. He went up to his suite, took off his coat, and sat down beside the phone. Did he really want to know for sure that his wife and best friend were cheating on him? He had to know, he told himself. He had no choice.

He dialed the number, and a gruff-sounding man picked up. "Yeah, Tubbs here."

"Mr. Tubbs," Brandon said. "This is Brandon Donovan."

"Oh, yeah, Mr. Donovan. I got some news for you."

Brandon's fingernails dug into the arm of the chair he sat in. "All right, let's hear it."

"I followed your wife today and saw her and Mr. Henderson goin' into a hotel room at the Westin."

"Together?" he asked. "They went in together?"

"No," he said. "She went in first, and he followed about half an hour later. I was able to get some pictures you might be real interested in."

Something obstructed Brandon's throat, and he found it difficult to breathe for a moment. "Pictures? What kind of pictures?"

"The kind that could nail your wife to the wall in court. Pictures of them takin' each other's clothes off, pictures of them in bed, pictures of—"

"I get the message," Brandon cut in. His hand trembled as he brought it to his forehead. "Are you sure it was my wife?"

The detective laughed. "It's hard to mistake her. She's a real beautiful woman. I'd know her anywhere."

Brandon squeezed his eyes shut, trying to make some sense of this. "She wasn't even trying to be discreet?"

"Sure she was," Tubbs said. "But I'm real good at what I do. She came in with her hair up and sunglasses on, and didn't stop at the desk or anything. Went right up, so probably no one saw her. When they came out, he came out first, then she waited about twenty minutes and left through a different door. Pretty routine, like they do this a lot."

Brandon was mute as the information seeped like poison to his heart, and finally Tubbs spoke up again.

"I can keep followin' her if you want, tap the phones, hide some video cameras . . . As much as you want."

Brandon only sat clutching the phone to his ear, feeling as if someone had just pulled the floor out from under him, and he was falling . . . falling . . .

"Look, I just wanted to let you know what I found out. Do you want me to continue?"

"No. I mean, I don't know. I'll get back to you."

"Well, do you want to meet me to get you these pictures?"

Brandon closed his eyes and tried to escape the haunting image of Tiffany and Lawrence together. But the image was permanently branded on his mind. He didn't even have to see the pictures. "No," he said finally. "Take them to Jacob."

He dropped the phone in its cradle and stared into the darkness, wondering how on earth he could have been so cruelly betrayed by his best friend and his wife.

Sleep eluded him when he finally climbed into bed, and he found himself struggling against the longest night of his life. He couldn't just let this go without a confrontation, he thought. Tomorrow he had to tell Larry what he knew. Tomorrow he had to sit still as his best friend looked him straight in the eye and either admitted he'd screwed Tiffany or lied through his teeth.

Morning dawned as gray and dismal as the pell over Brandon's soul, and he went early to the office to wait for Lawrence to arrive.

An hour after all the other employees had arrived,

Brandon walked across the reception area to Lawrence's office. He started to walk in, but Lawrence's secretary stopped him. "Can I help you find something, Brandon?"

"No," Brandon said. "I'm going to be in here waiting for Larry."

"Well . . . he's kind of paranoid about anyone in his office when he's not there."

"I'm not anyone," Brandon returned. "I'm the founder and CEO of this company, and I own everything in that office, including the chair where he parks his ass every day."

"Of course you do, Brandon." She looked stunned at his outburst, and he thought of apologizing, but instead turned away and left her to wonder what had come over him. He went into Lawrence's office and looked around at the lavish surroundings, much more plush and extravagantly appointed than his own. He wondered how much the man had spent decorating this place. It hadn't mattered at the time. Brandon would have given him almost anything he'd asked for. But now it bothered him deeply that he took so freely what he wanted no matter whom it cost. And apparently, he wanted even more.

He went behind the desk and sat down in the deep leather chair, glancing around at the things on Lawrence's desk. There was nothing there to suggest that Lawrence was sleeping with Tiffany, that he laughed at Brandon behind his back. . . . Nothing at all to suggest that Brandon had misplaced his trust in him all these years.

He looked up, and through the double doors leading out of the office, he saw Lawrence at his secretary's desk. Taking his messages, he came in and fixed Brandon with a tentative smile. "Good morning, Brandon. Are you waiting for me?"

Brandon's expression didn't waiver. "As a matter of fact, yes. You're late."

"I had some stops to make." He paused, as if expecting Brandon to get up from his chair. Brandon didn't move. "What's up, buddy? You okay?"

"Those stops you had to make. One of them wouldn't have been at the Westin Hotel . . . or my penthouse . . . would it?"

Lawrence gave him a look that appeared genuinely confused, and if he didn't know better, Brandon would have sworn he was on the wrong track. "What business would I have at either of those places?"

"Oh, I don't know. A quickie with the wife of one of your best friends, maybe?"

"What the hell are you talking about?"

"I'm talking about why you're leaving Donovan Concepts," Brandon said in a calm, unruffled voice.

"You're firing me?" Lawrence went to the doors, closed them, and when he turned back, his face was as red as if he'd just played eighteen holes on an August day. "Oh, no, old boy," he said, setting his lips in a thin, straight line. "You can't fire me. It takes a vote of the board for that. What are you going to tell them? That you suspect I've been sleeping with your wife? You can't possibly have any proof. Besides, Tiffany herself is on the board. She'll convince them that it's sour grapes because of her suit, that you're at your rope's end, and that you're grasping at straws."

Brandon shook his head calmly. "There isn't going to be a vote, because you're going to resign on your own."

"Oh, am I really?" Lawrence asked.

"Yes," Brandon said. "Because if you don't, I'm going to countersue Tiffany for adultery, which will make it almost certain that she'll walk away from this marriage without a cent. I might throw in a conspiracy charge for her setting me up—"

"Setting you up? How?"

"By getting me to hire Clea," he said. "By encouraging me to be closer to her. She expected me to slip up, didn't she? But she didn't know me as well as she should have after twenty years. And I guess I didn't really know her."

Lawrence's face drained of all its color, and he dropped back into his chair.

"I'm also looking into a suit against you, Lawrence, old buddy."

"For what?"

"I don't know," Brandon said. "But I'll come up with something." He leaned forward and set his elbows on the desk. "What did you think, Larry? That you'd get to take my company away from me? That you'd get my wife and all my assets?"

Lawrence didn't answer.

"Well, you can have the wife, *old buddy*. But I'll lie down in my grave before I'll let you touch one cent of this company." He picked up the phone, called security, and told them to send up three guards. "You have fifteen minutes to clear your desk, and I'm going to watch you while you do it. Then I'll let the guards escort you out."

Lawrence's teeth clamped together. "You're going to regret this, Brandon. More than you'll ever believe."

"We'll see about that," Brandon said.

39

Lawrence didn't waste any time before calling Tiffany and asking her to meet him beneath the bridge a few blocks from his house. It seemed silly to her, all the secrecy, when they'd been doing just fine hiding their affair from everyone, but since he'd been so short on the phone, she'd done as he said. Something was obviously wrong.

The air was muggy as she sat in her car. She turned on her radio, flipped to the station that had Detroit gossip, and smiled as names of people she knew came across the air waves. Then it was Brandon's turn.

She bit her lip and smiled, and turned the radio up. "It seems Brandon Donovan was served with divorce papers yesterday," the gossip queen of Detroit said. "Word has it that Tiffany's getting him on adultery, and she's trying to have her prenuptial agreement thrown out of court. Friends of the couple are sitting on pins and needles waiting to see what happens to the company, which was set to unveil its new model sports car next month. Sources tell us that Brandon has put a hold on the unveiling until the divorce is final, and that both sets of attorneys are pushing for an early trial since there is a company and thousands of jobs at stake. Meanwhile, Clea Sands, the sexy young woman who's caused all this trouble in the Donovan household, refuses to talk to reporters. Word is out that she's been offered a *Playboy* centerfold, but it's not clear whether she has accepted it. This is Gilda Radcliffe saying, If mum's the word, we'll make sure you hear about it."

Tiffany laughed softly, and turned the radio down. A *Playboy* centerfold. Priceless. She was making the woman into a star, and she was too stupid to take advantage of it. But then she could hardly blame her. If Clea Sands thought she could hold out for Brandon and all his money, why would she go to all the bother of taking her clothes off for the world? She had to play the part of Pollyanna to hold Brandon's interest.

When she saw Lawrence's car coming down the hill to the clearing beneath the bridge she prepared to get out. But he only rolled his window down and pulled up beside her. "Stay in the car. We may have been followed."

"Followed? Why?"

He let out a deep breath, and she could see that he was shaken. "He knows about us, Tiffany. Brandon knows."

"What? He can't. We've been so discreet. He had no reason to suspect . . ."

"He knows, damn it," Lawrence repeated. "And this morning he demanded my resignation and had me escorted out of the building."

The cold hard fist of reality knocked the breath out of her. "Oh, my God. If he uses this in court, my case won't mean anything. What kind of evidence does he have?"

"I have no idea. But he knows about us and he knows you hired Clea to set him up, although I don't know if he realizes she was in on it. Proof—well, maybe he doesn't have any. That's why we can't be together for a while. If he doesn't have anything concrete, we can't give him the opportunity to get it."

Tiffany slammed her fist on her steering wheel. "Damn it, we had it all figured out. We were this close. Do you realize that I haven't got a leg to stand on if he sues me for the same thing I'm suing him for? The judge won't give me a dime . . . he won't even listen . . ."

"That's why we have to take drastic action."

"What?"

"We'll have to use Steven. I've been thinking about this all morning, and it hit me that Brandon would do almost anything for that kid. If we could somehow make him think that Steven is distraught over all this, that he can't take any more, that knowing his mother was having an affair might send him over the edge—"

Tiffany's eyes widened, and she sat straighter in her seat. "Yes. You're right. That might work."

"Something has to," Lawrence said. "Otherwise, this was all for nothing."

"It'll work," she said. "It has to."

"Meanwhile, we should stay away from each other for a while."

Tiffany's eyes filled with tears, but they still maintained that iciness that even he had never been able to melt completely. He supposed that was why he was so attracted to her. That and the money. "I don't like this, Lawrence. I need you."

"It's just for a while," he said.

"But I get lonely, Lawrence."

"I'll be lonely, too," he said. "But it can't be helped." He reached through the windows, took her hand, and kissed it.

"Will you call?"

"It's best if I don't. The phone could be tapped."

"Well, damn it, when will I see you again?"

"After the divorce is final, darling," he said. "That should be all the incentive you need to speed things up. Then we can be married."

She dabbed at her tears, as if the idea made her feel better. "And you'll be CEO of Donovan Concepts," she said, "and it'll be Brandon who's escorted out of the building."

Lawrence laughed aloud. "I look forward to it, darling. Just remember. We've come too far to lose it all now."

She watched as Lawrence drove away, and for a moment she sat alone in her car, her mind whirling, spinning, trying to formulate a plan. She could do it, she thought. With Steven's help, she could still win.

She started her car, pulled back onto the bridge, and picked up her phone. Quickly, she dialed Steven's number.

"Hello?"

"Steven, darling, I need to see you immediately," she said.

"Mother, I was just going out."

"It's urgent," she said. "Cancel your appointment and meet me at home in half an hour."

"Why?"

"Because our futures are at stake," she said. "Yours *and* mine."

He sighed dramatically and finally said, "All right, Mother. But this had better be good."

"I promise, Steven. It'll be well worth your time," she said.

◦ ◦ ◦

She turned the possibilities over in her mind as she drove home, considering whether it was in her best interest to tell Steven everything. Would he still side with her if he knew she had been sleeping with Lawrence? After all, he'd been so appalled about Brandon that he hadn't spoken to him since he learned of his supposed affair with Clea. But she couldn't help suspecting that that had more to do with Clea than it did with Brandon. Steven had shown more than a little interest in her.

And then there was the issue of whom to side with in the business. If he sided with Brandon, he started at entry level and worked his way up in the company. If he sided with Tiffany, he'd start as president at the very least. She had no doubt that that would mean a lot to him.

The other choice, however, was to try manipulating him without telling him the truth, but then she couldn't count on making him do anything drastic enough to get Brandon's attention. No, she thought. She had to tell him.

She parked her car and took the elevator to the penthouse, and found Steven already there, nursing a drink that she suspected wasn't his first of the day. "Hello, darling," she said, throwing him a kiss.

"What's so important, Mother?"

Tiffany poured herself a drink, took a big gulp that seeped through her muscles and relaxed her a little, and sat down across from him. "We've got a problem, Steven."

"With the divorce?"

"Yes. It seems your father thinks he has something on me."

Steven's brows arched. "Oh? And what does he *think* he has?"

Tiffany set down her drink, dusted off and straightened her skirt, and then met his eyes again. "He thinks that I've been having an affair of my own."

Steven's expression didn't change. "And why would he think this, Mother?"

"That's not important," she said. "The point is that if he uses it against me in court, it could ruin my chances of getting what I want."

Steven sat back, crossed his leg over his knee, and gave his mother a long, scrutinizing look. "Who is it, Mother? Who are you sleeping with?"

Tiffany's eyes snapped to his. "Why would you instantly assume that it's true?"

"Well, it is, isn't it? Otherwise, he wouldn't have enough to use in court."

"The point, Steven, is that if *I* lose, *you* lose."

Steven laughed. "No way, Mother. If you lose, I still have Dad. You see, I win no matter who loses."

"Do you really?" She leaned forward, intent on making him see. "And what if he wins, Steven, and he keeps his company? The best you can hope for is the same entry-level position that you just quit. Is that what you want? To work your way up like any other employee? But if you side with me, darling, and I win, you can start as president. Forget finishing school. There won't be any need for that."

She recognized the lustful sparkle in his eye and knew she was getting somewhere. "What do you want me to do?"

She smiled. "We have to make your father worry about your state of mind. We have to make him think the trial is wearing on you, about to push you over the edge."

"To what end?"

"To make him decide not to countersue. To make him stop fighting. If he's worried about you, he may try to settle to keep from dragging us all through the mud."

Steven didn't answer for a moment, and from the chilling way he stared at her, she wasn't sure if he was with her or against her.

"Steven, you were willing to lie in court to help me. You said you'd say you saw them making love. Are you still with me or not?"

Steven bottomed his glass, then stared at it with cold, dull eyes. "I'm with you, Mother. You know I am."

Tiffany let out a heavy breath of relief as she finished off her own drink. "That's wonderful, darling," she said on a sudden wave of laughter. "Let the games begin, and may the shrewdest player win."

40

The phone shrilled through the night, waking Brandon abruptly. His unfocused eyes shot to the clock. It was two-thirty A.M. Jerking up the phone, he grumbled, "Hello?"

He had barely gotten the word out before Tiffany shouted, "Brandon!"

Brandon sat up. "Tiffany?"

"Steven's in the hospital!" she cried. "I found him collapsed on his floor. It was sleeping pills, and Brandon, I think it was deliberate."

"Oh, God. Is he all right?"

"I don't know!" she wailed. "Oh, Brandon, please hurry!"

"I'll be right there."

He was at the hospital in moments, and found Tiffany pacing the floor, her makeup miraculously flawless despite the hour. "What happened?" he asked.

She looked frantic, but there was no sign of tears. Could she really be that cold, he wondered, that she wouldn't even cry when her son had attempted suicide? "He was with me when I got served with your cruel little countersuit today," she said. "And he went into a rage. I've never seen him like that." She paused, brought a trembling hand to her face, and tried to go on. "Well, he stormed out, and I was worried about him so I kept calling him. When he never answered, I finally went over to check on him, and I found him unconscious with an empty bottle of sleeping pills beside him."

"How many did he take?"

"I don't know," she said. "The doctors haven't told me anything yet. Brandon, what have you done to him?"

Brandon's heart shattered at the accusation, and he turned away. Was Steven that unstable that he'd rather die than watch his parents slug it out?

The doctor came out of Steven's room, and Brandon descended on him. "How is my son?"

"He's awake, but he's groggy," the young doctor told him. "Apparently, he didn't take as many pills as we feared."

"Are you sure it was a suicide attempt?"

"Positive," he said. "He even admitted it himself when he woke up."

"Can I see him?"

"Yes, but not for long. We're required to keep him overnight, and we'll be sending our psychiatrist in to evaluate him tomorrow. We can't release him until we're sure he won't try it again." He glanced at Tiffany, then back at Brandon. "Forgive me if I'm out of line, but if any of what I've been reading about you is true, it probably wouldn't be a very good idea for you to go in at the same time. It might make things worse."

"You go ahead, Brandon," Tiffany said. "I'll see him after you."

Rubbing his eyes, Brandon started down the hall to

Steven's room. Even the doctor blamed this divorce for Steven's suicide attempt, he thought. It was killing his only child.

He walked into the room and saw his son lying with an IV in his arm and a tube running up his nose.

Suddenly, Donovan Concepts lost all its significance.

"Steven?" he whispered, sitting beside him on the bed.

Steven's eyes opened—dull and heartless—and he fixed them on his father.

"Why?" Brandon asked in an anguished whisper.

Steven closed his eyes again. "I have nothing to say to you."

"But Steven, you have so much to live for."

"Like what?"

"Steven, you're young. You're healthy. You're talented. You have friends and girlfriends, and a bright future . . ."

"And a mother and a father who don't mind dragging everything they've ever had together through the mud, and making a mockery out of it all."

Brandon grew quiet, and he watched, horror-stricken, as Steven's eyes closed and his breathing settled into a slow cadence. He was right, he thought. It was all so senseless.

Slowly, he got up and started out of the room. Tiffany was waiting alone, and something about the calm on her face struck an angry chord in him.

"How is he?"

"Asleep," he said. "But go on in. When you come back out, I'll stay with him tonight. There's a couch in there . . ."

"No, I want to stay," she said. "I'm his mother. It's my place. Besides, he hates you right now. It would be better if I stayed."

"As long as *you* do," Brandon said. "Don't hire a nurse to do it."

"I would never do that."

"You've done it all his life," he spit out.

"Wait a minute," she hissed. "He's here because of you, not me."

"He's here because you're a liar and a whore," Brandon said. "And he doesn't like it that I have the capability to smear your name as badly as you've smeared mine. I don't blame him. It's not a pretty picture."

"Go home, Brandon," she said. "You aren't needed here anymore. You've paid your little mercy visit. Now you can go."

Brandon watched her sashay into their son's room, and for a moment, he realized that his capacity to hate was much greater than he'd ever dreamed.

Tiffany shook Steven awake, and he looked at her through a groggy haze and smiled. "How'd I do?"

"Terrific," she said. "You were wonderful."

"Damn, though. Those pills did make me sleepy."

"Then sleep, darling," she said. "You deserve it. Your father's terribly worried about you. There's just no telling what he might do. Before you know it, you'll be sitting in the president's office of Donovan Concepts."

Steven's eyes drifted shut again, and he whispered, "CEO."

"What, darling?"

"CEO," he repeated. "President isn't enough. I want to be CEO."

Tiffany's heart stopped, and she thought how impossible that would be. Lawrence was to be CEO, and there was no way he'd take a backseat to her son. "We'll see, darling," she said. "Now go back to sleep."

Brandon couldn't make himself go home, so instead he went down to the hospital cafeteria and drank a cup of coffee. Suicide. His son had attempted suicide.

He felt the first remnants of despair surging through him, and he knew if he didn't hold on tight, he would lose his grip entirely. But there was no time for that now. Steven was the one breaking down, and Brandon had no choice but to be strong.

He finished his coffee and went back up to his son's room. There was no sign of Tiffany in the waiting room. Even the lingering cloud of her perfume had gone now, and he wondered if she was in there with Steven. Somehow, he couldn't picture Tiffany sitting up with him all night, or trying to sleep on the couch in his room. It wasn't in her character at all.

A memory came back to him, faded and yellow, but as he thought of it it became clearer. Steven with a stomach virus when he was seven, when he couldn't stop vomiting. Tiffany had been with him the first time he'd let it go, then woke the maid to clean up the mess.

"I feel it coming again, Mother," Steven had cried, and instead of going to him and comforting him, Tiffany had darted for the phone. "Mother!"

Brandon had held him while he vomited into the maid's bucket, then wiped his mouth and face with a wet rag and looked at Tiffany. "What are you doing? Calling the doctor?"

"No, I'm calling Rebeccah," she said, referring to the nanny who cared for him during the day.

"Why? It's the middle of the night!"

"Because he's vomiting, Brandon. Somebody has to take care of him."

Brandon got up, took the phone from her hand, and laid it calmly back in its cradle. "I'll take care of my son," he said. "Just go back to bed."

Tiffany gave Steven one last look—a look that could have been either regret or revulsion. Brandon still didn't know which it was.

Suicide was even uglier than vomiting, and he wasn't sure she could stomach that any better. What if she'd gotten crazy and left him in there? What if he'd been abandoned again?

He'd bet on it, he thought. He'd bet everything he had that she had left Steven there alone.

He got up and went to Steven's door, opened it a crack, and peered in. Steven was sound asleep, and as he looked around in the darkness, he realized no one else was in the room.

His heart sank further, and he went in, closed the door behind him, and shrugged out of his coat. Then, sitting down on the chair beside his bed, he watched his son sleep.

" . . . he hates you right now . . . he's here because of you . . ."

Bitter, burning tears stung the backs of Brandon's eyes, and he tried to hold together, tried to keep from breaking . . .

My son, he thought. *My only son. What have we done to him?*

And as Steven's steady breathing percussed through the darkness, Brandon lost his grip. He buried his face in his hands, trying to muffle the sobs racking through him, and wept for all he'd ever had and lost, all he'd never had and wanted, all he'd allowed and all he'd accepted instead of fighting until it was right. Steven had been the victim in this charade of a marriage.

No one heard his sobs, and when he finally found calm, he wiped his face and managed to get a grip once again, and he made a decision. He would not play the game Tiffany's way.

No matter what it would cost him, he was going to let her win.

❖   ❖   ❖

The harsh light of dawn cut through the window, and Steven's eyes opened halfway. He breathed a curse, then reached for his head, which throbbed as if he had a hangover. Damn, he thought, looking at the clock. Those sleeping pills really worked. It was mid-morning, and he'd slept all night.

He looked around, and saw his father, rumpled and unshaven, propped up in a chair that he'd probably sat in all night. Just what he needed, he thought. A lot of heart-rending conversation about suicide and all he had to live for, when he hadn't even gone to the bathroom yet.

He laughed under his breath, then clutched his head as the headache's knives penetrated again. Pain or not, it really was funny, he told himself. Suicide. They had to be kidding. No way would he ever hurt himself over anything his parents decided to do.

He started to get up, to head for the bathroom, and realized he was connected to an IV. Damn thing, he thought, jerking it out. That was the only downside to all this. Needles and monitors and nurses checking him all the time. He'd be glad when he got out of here.

He started to the bathroom, and felt the last remnants of the sleeping pills weigh over him, and he staggered slightly and bumped the wall.

Brandon jumped.

"Steven, what are you—"

"I'm okay," he said. "Just wanted to take a piss. Is that gonna bother anybody?"

Brandon was beside him in an instant. "You're supposed to call the nurse before you try to get up."

"Well, if I'd seen a nurse that I wanted to watch me piss, I'd have called. But so far they're mostly over forty and fat." He stood over the commode, did his business, and turned back to his father. "What the hell are you doing here, anyway? Have you been here all night?"

"Yes," Brandon said, sitting back down and rubbing his stubbled jaw. "How do you feel?"

Steven went back to the bed. "Like a Mack truck has been making tracks over my head. And like I could sleep for another few days." He looked at his father, noted the concern in his eyes, and remembered his mission. *Might as well do it right,* he thought. "I wish Mother had never found me. I'd be dead by now."

"Don't say that!" His father's face reddened, and Steven noted the red rims around his eyes. Touching. The man was falling for it hook, line, and sinker. Steven almost wanted to laugh.

"Why, Dad? You want me to stick around for the grand finale? When you and Mother butcher each other in court?"

"There's not going to be any butchering," Brandon said. "In fact, there's not going to be any court."

"What do you mean?"

"I mean, I'm going to settle with your mother out of court. Get this whole thing over with."

"She wants DC, Dad. You gonna give her that?"

Brandon hesitated, and looked around, his face emotional and volatile and tired. Steven wished Clea could see him like this. Then she'd know he was too old and weak for her, and she'd turn to the better Donovan. "I told you, we're going to settle. Whatever that means. The bottom line is, I'm not going to let this divorce make your life any more miserable. It's going to be all right, okay?"

Steven was dumbfounded. Damn, he thought. His mother was right. It had worked. "All right," he said.

Brandon leaned forward, setting his elbows on his knees, looking into Steven's eyes. "Steven, I want you to know that you can come to me any time. Any time at all, day or night. If you need to talk, I swear, I'll drop what I'm doing and be there. You don't have to do anything drastic. It's not worth it."

Steven closed his eyes, trying to look moved, but what he really wished was that his father would go ahead and leave so he could quit acting sick. He was ready to get out of this place.

"Okay?" Brandon asked gently.

Okay, what? Steven wanted to ask, then realized his father wanted some kind of guarantee that he wouldn't put a gun to his head. He probably thought he was so desperate that he'd leave here and go jump off a bridge. The thought amused him beyond words. His mother would love it.

"I'll be okay, Dad," he said in his most despondent voice. "I just want to go home."

Brandon came to his feet, and Steven realized he'd never seen him look so tired . . . or so old. One glance at him and Clea would run the other way.

And when she found out that Brandon had lost his company, and that Steven was calling the shots, well . . . she'd come begging. It would be perfect, he thought. His father's company, his father's job . . .

And his father's mistress.

"I'll go check with the nurse about releasing you," Brandon said. "Just stay there until I find out if it's okay for you to get up."

Steven only nodded, for there was nothing that could be said to make the moment more perfect. The moment when he realized the world was his. Everything was within his reach. And he would have it all soon.

He couldn't wait to call his mother and tell her the good news.

41

To pay the bills, Clea took a job doing tele-marketing from her home, selling children's magazines. It paid barely enough to cover her rent and utilities, but thankfully, Shalimar developed a sudden sense of responsibility and began buying the food and contributing to household expenses. Clea attributed her sudden accumulation of money to her longer hours at the Hairem Scarem.

A few errant reporters still watched her apartment, ready to photograph her if she came out to breathe fresh air. So she never did. She stayed inside twenty-four hours a day, did her work at night, and let Shalimar do any errands that needed doing. And as Clea grew more and more inaccessible to the media, Shalimar grew more and more popular. She became Clea's "official" spokesperson, telling the media things about Clea's withdrawal from civilization, how she'd turned down a bid from *Playboy*, how agents had been calling her to sign her up, how publishers were offering her book contracts. She began to know the press members by name, and even had dinner—and, Clea figured, a few rolls in the hay afterward—with several of them. But as long as she didn't bring them home, Clea could live with Shalimar's exploitation of her bad fortune. As for Shalimar revealing too much, she didn't hesitate to remind her each and every day how disastrous it would be if the press got wind of the scheme she had joined Tiffany in executing. Because she still didn't trust Shalimar, she kept her frequent phone calls from Brandon a secret. Shalimar never knew they'd talked at all.

But that Wednesday night, a particularly lonely one when her heart yearned for the sound of his voice, she leapt up to answer the phone when it rang instead of letting the machine get it.

"Clea?"

It was Brandon, and a warm wave of relief came over her. "Hi."

"Hi." His voice was becoming a balm to her open wounds, and his confidences had drawn them even closer. He had told her about demanding Lawrence's resignation, about the nasty confrontations with Tiffany, about the divorce papers she had served him, demanding everything on the grounds of adultery. There was always something new going on, something terrible, but they didn't drag her down as much as the very connection between them lifted her up.

"I was hoping you'd call," she whispered.

"Have you heard?" he asked.

"About what?"

"Steven's suicide attempt."

Clea caught her breath. "No! Brandon, what happened?"

"Sleeping pills," he said. "After I had Tiffany served. Seems he couldn't take all this mud-slinging we were doing."

Clea found it hard to believe that Steven would have been affected at all. "Are you sure it was supposed to be a suicide?"

"Yeah," he said on a weary sigh. "Positive. He admitted to it."

"Oh, Brandon, I'm so sorry. Is he all right?"

"Yeah." She could hear the fatigue and soul-weariness in his voice. "He was real lucky." He was quiet for a moment, then said, "I thought I should tell you that I've decided to settle with Tiffany out of court. We're meeting tomorrow to slug it out."

"Why?" she asked in a horrified whisper.

"Because I'm sick of the sleazy publicity, and I'm sick of the fight, and I'm sick of what this has done to you. But most of all, I can't sit by and watch my son have some kind of nervous breakdown or worse because of his parents' stupidity."

"But Brandon, this is what she wanted. You can't just give her everything. You'll be playing right into her hands."

"What difference does it make, really? Even if it goes to court, I can't use her adultery against her. The pictures would probably wind up all over the papers, and Steven would have to listen to how his mother's a whore on top of his father's being a philanderer. The press would have a field day with it."

Clea felt a vise crushing her heart, threatening to squeeze the life out of her. "Brandon, you're making a mistake! Please don't do this. You've worked so hard. Your company means everything to you."

"She won't get everything, Clea, and whatever I lose I can rebuild. It's worth it to me just to get this over with privately. Nobody ever said divorce was a picnic."

Clea recalled her own divorce, and the fact that

they'd had nothing to divide, except a pizza and some bills. Still, she had grieved for months afterward, and in many ways, she supposed, she still grieved. Lost dreams were hard to find again, and broken-down hopes were almost impossible to rebuild. Especially when betrayal was involved.

"Brandon, whatever you have to do, you know I'll be here for you. I know what it's like . . ."

"I know you do," he said. "And I'm counting on you."

She heard the catch in his voice and knew he was on the edge of breaking. She wanted to reach through the phone, hug him, hold him, until the pain disappeared.

"When all this is over," he whispered, "and the divorce is final, would you consent to having dinner with me?"

She caught her breath. "I'd be honored."

"Are you sure?" he asked. "All I can promise you is your picture in the paper, a lot of malicious gossip, and reinforcement of everyone's belief that we're lovers."

"Then we'll do it in private," she said. "I'll cook for you."

He smiled, and the first warmth he'd felt in his heart all day began to spread through him. "I can't wait."

A tear dropped to her cheek, and she brought her other hand to the phone. "Brandon, I'm so sorry for my part in all this."

"You didn't do anything," he whispered.

"Yes, I did," she said. "Without me, none of this would have happened."

"Yes, it would. Eventually, she would have gotten me some other way."

She got quiet, for she knew he couldn't understand the extent of her guilt. And for the life of her, she could never tell him, not when there was hope of something

happening between them, something that wasn't dirty
or underhanded. Something that was sweet and
poignant and romantic.

Something that she would never deserve if she lived
to be a hundred. But she wasn't going to walk away from
it, not after all the pain and injustice she'd suffered in
her life, not after all she'd lost. As right as she knew that
would be, she wasn't strong enough.

Besides, he needed her now.

"I'd better go," he whispered. "I have a meeting with
my lawyer in an hour."

"Brandon, please let me know how things go. And if
there's anything I can do—"

"Say a prayer for me."

"I will," she said. "I promise."

The room was cold where Brandon sat across the
table from Tiffany, with Jacob Fairbane on his side and
Tiffany's father and two other attorneys on hers. His
soon-to-be ex-father-in-law shifted his Alfred Hitchcock
stomach so that he could lean forward and focus his
eyes on Jacob, as if Brandon didn't even exist.

"This settlement offer is a crock of manure," the law
professor who'd once been so proud to call Brandon his
son-in-law said. "My client wants much more than a
cash settlement, and you were well aware of that before
you came here today. Surely you haven't wasted all our
time to offer us this."

Jacob Fairbane gave Brandon one last beseeching
look, which Brandon knew was a final plea to make him
stop what he thought was nothing short of madness. He
had urged Brandon to go to court, use the pictures
against Tiffany, and fight her to the end. But Brandon

nodded for him to go on with the offer they had hammered out the night before.

"All right," Jacob said, adapting his most authoritative expression. "In the interest of keeping this divorce settlement as private as possible, and because my client doesn't see any good in dragging Mrs. Donovan's name through the gutter as she hasn't hesitated to do with his, we would agree to offer Mrs. Donovan the penthouse she now occupies, the cash settlement we've just discussed, and a third of Donovan Concepts."

"That's ridiculous," Tiffany said. "I already have practically that much of the company stock. Brandon would still have the majority of the shares, and he'd still have the deciding vote in the company. I won't agree to that."

"If you'd let us finish, you'll see that we've worked out something that you might find more attractive. Our offer is not for a third of the shares of DC, but your own company. Brandon is offering to literally cut out a third of the company to give to you. He's offering you the Donovan Signature division of DC. The Signature is one of DC's best-selling automobiles, with annual profits that would enable you to broaden your lines until your company could one day feasibly be as big as DC is now."

"You mean, I'd be his competitor instead of a partner?"

Brandon nodded. "That's right."

"I like it," Tiffany said, digging a cigarette out of her purse. She brought it to her lips, and one of her attorneys lit it. "But a third isn't enough. I want more. Half at the very least."

"That's impossible," Brandon said. "That would have to include more than one car. You start disassembling my product line, and DC will crumble."

"That's your problem, darling," she said. "The way I

see it, the more of DC's assets I get, the greater chance I have of making it all work."

"So how much do you think is fair?" he burst out. Jacob touched his arm, trying to shut him up.

Tiffany blew out a long cloud of smoke. "As I said, I want at least half of the company. I'll take the Signature line, the Executive line, and . . . the THD."

Brandon's fist hit the table. "You're full of shit!"

"Why?" Tiffany asked, amused. "It hasn't even made any money yet. It could turn out to be a gigantic lemon. I'd be taking a tremendous risk."

"Then leave it to me," he said. "That's *my* car. I've invested years of my life in it."

Tiffany's amusement faded, and her eyes took on a glint as cold as gun metal. "I want it," she said.

Brandon threw Jacob an agitated glance. "Out of the question."

Tiffany stubbed out her cigarette and began to rise. "Fine, Brandon. We'll see you in court, then."

Jacob Fairbane stopped Brandon from rebounding, and regarded Theodore Holland. "I don't think your client will want this to go to court," he said. He reached into the envelope he had lying in his briefcase, and pulled out the pictures of Tiffany with Lawrence.

Brandon turned his head, for he still hadn't been able to make himself look at them. But if it hurt him so to think of what was in them, how much sicker would it make his son?

Tiffany's face reddened, and she grabbed the pictures. Her father gave her an incriminating look, but she rallied. "You're despicable, Brandon. Our son tried to kill himself over the mere mention of my having an affair, and you're willing to splash these all over the papers just for a godforsaken car?"

"It's your choice, Mrs. Donovan," Jacob said.

She stared at Brandon across the table, and repulsed, he met her eyes. She was trying to decide whether to call his bluff, he thought. She was measuring him, just as he measured her.

"You can't win, Mrs. Donovan," Jacob went on. "The prenuptial agreement will stand as soon as we establish that the evidence for adultery is stronger against you than it was against him."

Something flickered across her face, and Brandon noted her hands trembling as she reached for another cigarette. "You don't know what kind of evidence I have," she said.

Brandon smiled. "I know what you don't have."

Taking a deep breath, she met his eyes again. "There is no way I'm walking out of this marriage with nothing. No way."

"Then take my offer," he said. "The Executive division of the company."

"I won't take anything less than the Executive, the Signature, and the THD," she said. "And if it goes to court, you can bet I'll use every resource imaginable. You won't even know what hit you. Steven has already agreed to testify that he saw you and Clea making love in the cabin on Lake Michigan, and that he walked in on you in Georgia."

Brandon's face fell. "Steven wouldn't lie about me."

"Who says he's lying?"

"If he says that, he's lying." He sat straighter in his chair, wishing he could get his hands on Tiffany's neck to throttle her. "How could you ask him to lie against his own father? When you know what he's been through?"

"I'll do anything to get what I deserve out of this marriage."

"Even use your son?"

"He volunteered," she said. "And you'd better believe I'll take him up on it."

"If he doesn't wind up dead first!"

"That's up to you," Tiffany said.

"You bitch."

Brandon covered his mouth with a shaking hand and racked his brain, trying to determine if she was bluffing. And suddenly it came to him that she wasn't, that she'd use her son or Clea or her father or anyone else to get what she wanted, and then she'd walk away without looking back. And if Steven wound up killing himself over it, she'd still have her company.

Several moments of silence filled the room, and finally, Brandon stood up. "Give it to her," he said. "Give her the Signature, the Executive . . . and the THD."

"But Brandon—" Jacob protested.

"For God's sake, just give it to her. My son's life is more important to me than that." He knocked his chair out of his way, then turned back at the door. "Then get me my divorce as fast as the law allows. The sooner I'm rid of that bitch, the better off I'll be."

He didn't look back as he strode to the elevator, leaving the vultures to tear his company limb from limb.

42

The day Brandon signed the papers finalizing his divorce and turning over more than half his assets to Tiffany, he felt more defeated than he'd ever felt in his life. The dissecting of his company had already begun, and half his employees were preparing to move out of the DC building into the one Tiffany had acquired for what she now called Holland Motors Corporation. They had worked out a plan to divide the manufacturing plants, and there was work yet to do to restructure the robotics for the cars she'd acquired in the divorce.

All joy was gone from his work, since the THD was no longer his, and he couldn't deny the burning in his gut every time he thought of Lawrence Henderson, who he was sure would play a major part in the structuring of HMC, profiting from the car that had been Brandon's baby for the last few years.

Not to mention sleeping with his wife. But the hurt was gone, and now he felt a fierce hatred in his heart toward her, an anger that wouldn't be quelled. He had confessed it, had prayed about it, had done penance, but still it kept spreading in him like a cancer.

The only thing that quelled it were his late night talks with Clea. Then, and only then, could he find a few moments of peace, a few moments of sincerity, a few moments of warmth.

The day the divorce was final, every network, both major and minor, and every cable station, reported it as if it was global news. But there were things he heard on the news that no one had told him. That Lawrence Henderson was being made CEO of Holland Motors, for instance. And that Steven would be president.

He tried to call his son at HMC, not certain what for, since he didn't know whether to congratulate him or lambaste him for choosing his mother's company over Donovan Concepts, but Tiffany intercepted the call.

"What do you want, Brandon?" she asked.

"I want to talk to my son."

"He's busy. He's got a big job on his hands. But I'll give him the message."

"What are you, his secretary?"

"No, I happen to own the company."

"Well, I noticed that you won't be making the decisions. You turned that over to your lover."

"You know I don't like being bothered with such things, Brandon. But I still have the majority of the stock. We all know who's in charge here."

"So what is Steven's job, or is he just a figurehead?"

"Oh, Brandon, you sound so bitter. It doesn't become you."

"Put him on the phone, Tiffany. I want to make sure he's all right."

"Why wouldn't he be? Do you think he's sitting in the dark somewhere brooding over our marriage? Think again, Brandon. He's living it up. He's never had it so good."

Brandon knocked a glass off the edge of the table, and brought his trembling hand up to rake through his hair. He tried to calm his voice. "Tiffany, don't forget that he's not the most stable person in the world. The pressure of a job like that could—"

"Oh, yes," Tiffany cut in. "I guess you're referring to the suicide attempt." She chuckled lightly. "Your son is sharp like his mother, Brandon. He's many things, but he never has been, and never will be, suicidal."

Brandon slowly sat down as her words sank in. "What are you saying? You're the one who found him."

"Yes. Exactly."

He held his breath, just as he held off the revelation she was inflicting on him. Was she telling him that his son had betrayed him, that the whole thing was a setup to get the company? Was she telling him that his only child had so much contempt for him that he'd deliberately set out to destroy him?

"Why?" he whispered.

"Why what, Brandon? Why does he hate you? I don't know, but he does."

"I haven't done anything to him. I've done nothing but what he wanted."

"Yes, but we can't always make people love us, now can we, Brandon? You ought to have learned that lesson by now."

The phone went dead, and Brandon dropped it. For a moment, he only stared, horrified, into space, assimilating what he had been told, what it meant, where it left him . . .

And then he stumbled to the wet bar in his suite, poured the tallest glass of vodka he could find, and began to drink.

He didn't stop drinking for the next three days.

* * *

The moment she heard the divorce was final, Clea waited for the phone call Brandon had promised, telling her when and where their dinner would be. But it didn't come.

She began to worry when she saw reports about HMC and Steven's part in it, and things began to make sense. From the footage she saw of him on television, Steven didn't look like a man who had attempted suicide just weeks earlier. He looked like a shrewd, conniving businessman who was willing to do whatever he needed to get on top the easy way.

She wondered if the suicide attempt had been part of a new hoax that Steven and Tiffany had cooked up. After all, Steven had everything to gain by helping her win part of Donovan Concepts. With his father, he was a low man in the executive lineup. With his mother, he was instantly at the top of the ladder.

Or almost the top. Lawrence Henderson was at the helm, and Clea wondered how Steven handled that. There were bound to be personality clashes. She wished she could have a front-row seat when that all blew up.

Now she only wondered whether Brandon had realized the extent of the betrayal. Was that why he hadn't called? Was he sinking in a mire of depression?

She waited three days for him to call, then finally decided that she had no choice but to go to him and see what was wrong. Putting her hair up in a Detroit Tigers baseball cap, and wearing black sunglasses, jeans, tennis shoes, and a sweatshirt, so that no reporters would recognize her, she drove to the Atheneum Suite Hotel, found a parking place two blocks away, left her car, and went in.

She found his door and knocked, but for a long time, there was no answer. She knocked again, waited, and finally heard a shuffling inside.

"What?"

It didn't sound like Brandon. She looked up and down the hall, making sure she was alone. There was someone crossing the hall to the elevators not too far away, so she lowered her voice and said, "Room service."

"I didn't order anything." The words were slurred and heavy, but now she was sure it was Brandon. Something was wrong.

Quietly, she checked the knob, but it was locked. She waited until she heard the elevator ring and the hall was empty.

"Brandon," she said as quietly as she could and still be heard, "it's me. Please open the door."

It took a moment for him to get there, and finally, the knob turned and the door opened. Clea stepped inside and saw him stagger back to a chair and drop into it. Around him were dirty glasses, wadded up napkins, and dirty clothes hanging over the chairs. The drapes were drawn, and there were four empty whiskey bottles lying on the floor.

"Brandon, are you all right?"

"Yeah," he said. "Fine." He opened his eyes slightly and looked up at her, and she noted his three days' growth of beard and bloodshot eyes that looked irreparably damaged. "What are you wearing?" he slurred.

She smiled and pulled off the sunglasses and cap, letting her hair tumble around her shoulders. "I didn't want to be noticed and start a whole new avalanche of news stories. But I was worried about you."

"I shoulda called."

"Brandon, how long have you been like this?"

"I dunno. What's difference?"

She knelt beside him. "Have you eaten?"

"Yeah . . . maybe . . . I dunno."

"You have to eat something," she said. She touched his face, made him look at her. "Brandon, look at me. What set this off? Was it the divorce?"

He shrugged, and shook his head. "Steven."

"What about him?"

He squeezed his eyes shut, rubbed them, and raked his hand through hair that looked as if it hadn't been washed in days. "It was a lie," he said. "She told me. They set it up."

"The suicide attempt?"

"All of it," he said. "To manipulate me. Worked."

An overwhelming surge of love burst through her, and rising up, she slid her arms around him. She felt how tired he was, how anguished. His body shook as his arms came up around her.

"You're going to be all right," she whispered. "I promise."

He pulled back and wiped at his eyes, as if he feared what might reveal itself to her if he let his grief take over.

"We have to get you cleaned up and feed you, Brandon. You have to sober up if you want to deal with this."

"Don't," he said. "Don't wanna deal with it. I'm sick of dealing with things."

"I'll help you," she said. "You're not alone."

Somehow, those words seemed to comfort him, and when she reached for his hand, he gave it to her. "Thank you, Clea," he whispered. He managed a smile, and added, "You're just as beautiful in that as any 'signer dress I've seen you in, know it?"

Smiling, she picked up the phone to dial room service.

An hour later, after she had forced Brandon to eat and was certain he could keep it down, and had poured three cups of coffee down his throat, she took him into the bathroom, started the shower, and began unbuttoning his shirt, which she suspected he'd had on for three days.

"What're you doing?" he asked.

"Making you take a shower," she said. "You're almost disgusting."

He smiled as she slipped the shirt off his arms, then went for his tee shirt. "Why don't you take it with me?"

She smiled. "You know, you wouldn't get away with that suggestion if you were sober."

"Then I better take advantage of my drunkenness," he said.

She pulled his shirt over his head, and found her heartbeat accelerating at the hard, healthy lines, the fit physique, the texture of his bare skin. He sat still, watching her, waiting for her to strip more off of him.

But she didn't. "You can do the rest yourself, I think."

His smile was daring, sexy, maddening. "I don't think I can."

She handed him a towel and backed away. "You're a real resourceful man, Brandon. I have faith in you."

She heard him laughing as she closed the door and turned her attention to the suite. His bed was still made, as if he hadn't slept in it in days, and clothes, empty glasses, and whiskey bottles were strewn everywhere. She heard him step into the shower and knew that he was feeling better already. Soon he'd be back to normal, but then he'd have to face the awful reality of his life. And she didn't know how to help him. Everyone in his life had betrayed him. Even her.

She was putting the dirty dishes outside the door for the hotel staff to pick up, when she heard the shower shut off. She heard Brandon brushing his teeth, and finally he opened the door. A cloud of steam escaped into the room, filling it with the clean scent of soap and shaving cream. He came out, his shoulders glistening with dampness, and a white towel wrapped around his waist.

Her heart stumbled. "Uh . . . I forgot to get your clothes." She started toward the bedroom, but he reached out and grabbed her arm to stop her. Their eyes locked on each other's, and a moment of longing passed between them, a jolt of desire so fierce that it scared her to death.

He dropped her arm, releasing her. "I can get them," he whispered.

She couldn't talk, for her heart raced out of control, and she felt herself trembling from her lips to the legs she stood on. She stayed in the living room as he dressed in the bedroom, but his scent lingered behind, luring her, teasing her, torturing her. Awkwardly, she sat on the edge of the couch, set her arms on her knees, and tried to decide what to do next. Should she leave now that she'd almost sobered him up? Or should she stay here, waiting for the sparks they'd already ignited to combust?

He was back in a few minutes, still barefoot but wearing a clean pair of jeans and a Michigan State sweatshirt. She offered him a shaky smile as he came toward her and sat down next to her on the couch. "My head's starting to hurt already," he said.

"It's gonna be bad."

He leaned back and massaged his temples. "Guess I have to go through with it sooner or later."

"Unless you plan to be drunk for the rest of your life."

"No, can't do that."

She looked up at him, saw the genuine pain on his face, and felt her heart swelling for him again. "You look tired, too," she whispered. "Maybe you should get some sleep. I should go, anyway."

"No," he said, opening his eyes and reaching for her hand. "Don't go. I like having you here. I don't know what would have happened to me if you hadn't shown up today. I probably would have just kept wallowing in my misery until I drowned in it. Self-pity is pretty disgusting, isn't it?"

She suppressed the urge to embrace him again, to hold him and show him how deeply her feelings went. She watched his fingers massage his temples, and finally she reached up to stop his hands. "Here, let me," she whispered.

He looked at her, his eyes still red and bloodshot.

"Lie down," she said. "I'll massage your head."

Complying, he stretched out on the sofa, and lay his head in her lap. She swallowed as she looked down at him and felt that same burst of love that had surprised her so often lately. The love that had made her so miserable. The love she had no right to feel. Slowly, she began to massage his temples.

And even more slowly, his hand rose up to slip through her hair, and he pulled her face down.

Their lips met in a shattering kiss, and she shivered and sighed. His mouth opened, and his tongue slipped between her lips, meeting her tongue in a sweet, poignant dance of love. It was a short kiss, but when she pulled her face back, he looked up at her, his eyes as serious, as pensive, as she had ever seen them.

"Clea," he whispered, "I may just be falling in love with you."

Tears filled her eyes, and her heart seemed to stop. "Say that to me again when you haven't been on a three-day drunk, Brandon, and I may believe you."

He took her hand, brought it to his lips, and kissed it, then moved it to his heart and held it there as he closed his eyes. She began to massage again with her other hand, until she could feel the tension slipping out of him and sleep overtaking him.

And she thought she would be content to sit there like that for the rest of her life, with his head in her lap and her hand next to his heart.

Brandon woke in the wee hours of the morning, with a headache that made him want to die. Then he looked up and realized his head was still in Clea's lap, and she was sound asleep with her head propped against the sofa back.

He got up, found three aspirin in his shaving kit, swallowed them, and returned to the couch. She looked so sweet sitting there, her hair splayed around her face and shoulders, and her lips slightly parted as she breathed out in a gentle rhythm. He walked over to the bed and pulled back the covers, then returned to her. Gently, carefully, he picked her up, marveling at how light she felt, and carried her to his bed. She stirred slightly as he laid her down, but then she curled up and fell deeper into her sleep.

He stood watching her for a long moment, wondering if God had sent her to him to help him through this grief he had been buried in. He didn't know what her purpose in his life was, but he saw her as a precious gift that he would never deserve as long as he lived.

Quietly, he crawled under the covers beside her,

slipped one arm beneath her neck, and draped the other over her so that she was encircled in his arms. His head began to stop hurting as he grew used to holding her, and he found that deep black hole in the center of his soul filling up with something he hadn't felt in a very long time.

And as he found the peace that accompanied that feeling, he fell asleep again.

43

Clea woke when the light of dawn peeked through the curtains and realized that she was lying in bed wrapped in Brandon's arms. A feeling of content, of rightness washed over her, and slowly, she turned over to face him.

His eyes opened slowly. He looked at her strangely for a moment, and then a soft smile came to his lips. "For a minute I thought I was dreaming."

"How did I get here?" she asked.

"I carried you," he whispered.

"But I was supposed to be taking care of you."

"You did. You took good care of me."

He didn't let go of her, and she lay relaxed against him, looking up without inhibition, for the morning was too new to tarnish with anxieties and selfconsciousness. He gazed down at her with a soft smile.

"How do you feel?" she whispered.

"Better." Silence fell like a comfortable, well-worn blanket over them. "Tell me something," he whispered. "You remember last night, when I was drunk, and I told you that I was falling in love with you?"

Tension began to seep back into her body, breaking the spell. "Yeah."

"I'm not drunk anymore," he whispered. "But I'm still in love with you."

Tears filled her eyes instantly. She caught her breath and stared up at him, her silver-blue eyes glistening with disbelief.

He rolled her on her back and, on his elbows, braced himself above her. When his lips caught hers, she felt all the injustices, all the pain, all the heartache of her life slipping away. Abandoning herself to his kiss, she clung to him as if she had stumbled purely by accident on the one good man left in the world. And she couldn't bear to let him go.

He began to undress her, quickly, urgently, then undressed himself, and their loving became a desperate diversion from the betrayals and deceptions that each of them had endured in their lives, to the hurt inflicted on them by people they loved, to the things they had lost that could never be regained. But together they were whole again, together they found completion, together they were strong.

And when their love was sated, they lay quietly in each other's arms, knowing that they had been bound together that day in more than just a physical sense. For they had found something that neither had ever known before.

True, sweet, pure, unconditional love.

And for a moment, Clea was able to forget that she had deceived him already.

He kissed her temple, then her nose, then slid gentle fingertips along her cheek, watching her with absolute reverence in his eyes. "I meant it, Clea," he whispered. "I love you."

She touched his stubbled jaw, and ran her finger along his bottom lip. "I've loved you for a long time, too," she whispered. "Since before I had a right to."

"It's okay now," he said. "I'm not a married man, anymore."

They lay in each other's arms for what seemed an eternity, before he decided to get up and shave and order breakfast. Then, they sat together in bed, she in her jeans and one of his shirts, he in a pair of jogging shorts and a tee shirt, watching "Good Morning America."

None of the news mattered, none of the segments interested them, for they were both so peaceful in their ecstasy of being together that they hardly noticed when Charlie Gibson came in live from the Detroit Auto Show. But when they heard the name Holland Motors Corporation, Brandon turned up the television.

They watched, silent, as Charlie Gibson interviewed Lawrence Henderson, with Steven Donovan brooding in the background, and Lawrence told them that the car formerly called the THD had now been renamed Meteor. He told them how he had worked primarily on the car during his last few years at DC, and how he had personally been a part of its development and evolution.

Clea reached for Brandon's hand as the cameras zoomed in on the finished prototype of the THD, and they could hear the applause that it received at the unveiling. His face went pale, his hand turned clammy, and she knew the pain that he must have felt in the pit of his stomach as Charlie Gibson explained how HMC expected the Meteor to launch the company as one of the most dynamic automobile manufacturers in the world.

Brandon shut off the television and stared straight ahead at the blank screen.

"Brandon," she whispered, "I'm so sorry."

He shrugged and tried to breathe a weak laugh. "I probably should have stayed drunk a few more days."

"There'll be other cars," she whispered. "You have other ideas."

He shook his head, waving her off. "That car was the reason I started DC in the first place. I wanted to build it at Ford, but it was too ahead of its time for them, so I started my own company. But I had to have a product base first, so we came up with more practical cars. The THD was my dream. It was my goal for the last decade of my life."

"I know," she whispered. "The worst part of divorce is always the broken dreams."

"Yeah," he whispered. He reached for her, as if she could ease the pain, and she snuggled against him. She lay her head on his shoulder, felt him squeezing her so tight that she didn't know if he'd ever let her go.

"I really do love you," he whispered.

"I love you, too," she said. "But I never meant to hurt you. I never meant for you to lose your family, your business . . ."

"Shhh," he whispered. "You know it had nothing to do with you. Lawrence was in the picture long before you were. He was probably using Tiffany, and she used you."

Tears seeped into her eyes and ran down her cheeks. "But I shouldn't have let her. I should have known better."

"How could you have known?" he asked.

She looked up at him, wishing desperately she could purge this last thorn from her soul, but she couldn't heap another betrayal on the mountain under which he was already buried. Besides, she thought selfishly, she couldn't let him go. If she told him what she had done, he would hate her. And that pure, sweet, absolute love would be nothing more than a cruel joke fate had played on her. Her punishment would be losing him, and that was more than she could stand.

"I should have known," she whispered.

He wiped her tear, kissed her again, and tightened his embrace of her. "There's a way to make it up to me," he said, urging her to look up at him through her tears.

She nodded. "Anything. I'll do anything."

"Will you marry me?"

Her heart jolted, stopping her breath, and her very life seemed to come to a halt. Had she heard him right? "What?" she managed to ask.

His eyes twinkled with a smile that seemed to come from his core. "Will you marry me?" he repeated. "Be my wife. Make me the happiest man in the world?"

She sat up straight in the bed, gaping down at him. "But Brandon . . . the gossip . . . they'd think everything was true . . ."

"They think it's true, anyway. I couldn't have lost more if it *was* true. So who cares what they say?"

"But Tiffany . . . Steven . . ."

Brandon's face fell a degree. "I don't give a damn what Tiffany thinks, and as for Steven, I can only hope that someday I can understand why he deceived me the way he did. I love him, and I want a relationship with him. But I won't make decisions based on his feelings anymore."

Clea found it hard to breathe, and she covered her mouth. "Oh, Brandon. I don't know what to say!"

"Say yes," he said, sitting up and beseeching her with his eyes. "Please, Clea, say yes."

"Yes!" she shouted. "Yes, I'll marry you!"

His laughter as he threw his arms around her was

lighter and deeper than she had ever heard. And as she let the sweet ecstasy of his love seep into her, she prayed that that sound would never end.

Three days later, Tiffany sat curled next to Lawrence, watching CNN in hopes of more news about HMC. But it wasn't Tiffany's company making headlines today, but Brandon and Clea.

She grabbed the remote control from Lawrence's hand as soon as they flashed the recently taken photo of the two together.

"A Donovan spokesperson has confirmed that Miss Sands has accepted Donovan's proposal and is now wearing a five-carat diamond solitaire."

They flashed to Shalimar, surrounded by reporters, smiling as if she were a movie star making a rare appearance outdoors. "You should see this rock," she told the reporters. "I mean, this baby glistens. And she's asked me to be the maid of honor in the weddin'. If I have anything to do with it, it'll be the knockout bash of the year."

Tiffany's ire rose and she flicked off the television. "Mine was only three."

"Your what?" Lawrence asked.

"My ring. It was only three carats."

"Well, he didn't have as much money when he married you."

"But damn it, that little harlot doesn't deserve that. She's walking away with everything, Lawrence. If it weren't for me, she'd probably be working as a waitress somewhere."

"Half of everything, darling. Don't forget that we got half, and the Meteor will make up the difference. We're going to make a fortune on that."

Tiffany sank back onto the couch, staring at the blank

screen. "But they're getting married, and we have to wait. Why do we have to wait, Lawrence?"

"Well, you were the one who thought it was the appropriate thing to do. But if you ask me, we're already home free. It really won't make any difference."

"But everyone already knows about them. If we got married right away, everyone would suspect an affair between us."

Lawrence laughed. "Ironic, isn't it? They didn't really do anything, and we did. Life can be so comical sometimes." He reached out for her, pulled her across his lap, and nuzzled her neck. "But the truth, darling, is that I don't want to wait a moment longer than necessary."

"Neither do I," she said, wrapping her arms around his neck. "Let's do it, Lawrence. As soon as they're married, we'll announce our engagement."

"All right, sweetheart. Whenever you say."

"You do understand that I'll need a ring bigger than hers," she said.

"Bigger than five carats? Darling, your hand will get tired wearing it."

"Well, if not bigger, at least more valuable. It's important to me, Lawrence."

He reached up and kissed her. "We'll see what we can do. Don't worry, darling. I won't embarrass you."

And as he pulled her into a tighter embrace, she tried to wipe from her mind the image of Clea smiling like the conquering princess, beautiful and young and about to become rich . . . and she tried to concentrate on her own happiness, instead.

Steven sat in his dark bedroom, in front of the wall that had Clea's face all over it, and watched the news report of Clea and his father. It couldn't be, he thought miserably. His father had lost over half of his assets, had lost the THD, had lost a great deal of his power. He might even lose what was left of his company, since many of his investors were becoming skittish about the direction of what was left of Donovan Concepts. Why hadn't he lost Clea?

It wasn't supposed to work this way. She was supposed to come after Steven now. She was supposed to have watched his rise to power, his growing fortune. But still she ignored him.

It was all Lawrence's fault, he thought. If Tiffany had made Steven CEO rather than Lawrence, Clea would be impressed. But everyone knew that he was nothing but a powerless figurehead in the company, and Lawrence was the one calling all the shots. He'd probably marry Tiffany soon, and the lion's share of the company would be his. It shouldn't have been so damned easy for him.

And it shouldn't have been so easy for his father to wrap this up with Clea. How could she be more interested in Brandon than in him?

He turned up the television and saw Shalimar describing the ring and the wedding plans, and something snapped inside him. Getting up, he knocked his television off its stand, and glass broke and scattered across his floor.

He had to do something, he thought. He couldn't stand by and watch this happen. There was still a chance of changing her mind, if he could only make her understand how much he wanted her. If he could only make her see that he could give her everything his father could.

He'd have to use Shalimar again, he thought. He'd have to get to Clea through her.

Clea studied the way the light glistened off her ring, bouncing in a brilliant display of color, mirroring the way she felt. It was all too good to be true. Any minute now, it could all blow up in her face. But it wouldn't, she told herself. It couldn't.

She listened to her answering machine as the *Playboy* editor who had telephoned relentlessly for weeks tried to entice her to call back again. But as the message went on, she realized that it wasn't for her this time. "We saw the video Shalimar sent us," the woman said, "and there's nothing wrong with her. It's just that she isn't you. But since we're not going to get you . . ."

Clea smiled, relieved that they had finally given up.

" . . . we've decided that Shalimar is worth an interview at least. We'd like for her to meet with us tomorrow morning at ten o'clock at the Airport Marriot. We can't use her for a centerfold, and we'll be using your name along with hers. 'Clea's bridesmaid,' or something of that nature."

Clea closed her eyes and cringed at the thought. As the machine clicked off, she wondered how she could coerce Shalimar into turning their offer down, but she couldn't imagine her doing it. She supposed she owed it to her to at least give her the chance. She dialed the number of the Hairem Scarem and asked for her sister.

"Stevie?" Shalimar said as soon as she came to the phone.

Clea hesitated. "No, it's me. Why did you think it was him?"

"Because he called earlier, said he'd call back. I was hopin' this was him."

"Shalimar, you aren't going out with him again, are you? He's dangerous."

"Not dangerous, Clea. Adventurous. I like that in a man."

Clea felt something tensing in her chest. "Shally, please be careful with him. And don't bring him here, okay? I really don't want to run into him."

"You got it, Sis. Now if you're through lecturing me, I'm manicuring the sexiest hand I've ever seen, on an Arab sheik who thinks I'm the cutest thing *he's* ever seen. Keeps undressin' me with his eyes."

"Wait," Clea said. "There's someone else who wants to undress you. *Playboy*."

"You're kiddin'! What did they say?"

"They want to see you tomorrow at ten o'clock at the Airport Marriot."

"To take my picture?"

"No. To talk to you. Probably to make you an offer."

"Oh, my God!" she squealed, then turned back to the others in the Hairem Scarem and shouted, "I'm gonna be in *Playboy*!"

Clea couldn't help smiling at the commotion going on behind Shalimar. Her sister came back to the phone breathless. "God, this is great! I can't believe it."

"Hey, Shally, don't call a press conference yet, okay? It'd be real embarrassing if you announce this and it doesn't happen."

"It'll happen," she said. "I can't believe it!"

Clea hung up the phone as she heard Shalimar's friends descend on her again and decided that maybe it was worth it to hear her sister so happy.

The phone rang beneath her hand, and she answered it right away, no longer fearing reporters since she'd recently had her number changed. "Hello?"

"Clea, honey, is that you?"

It was her mother, whom she hadn't spoken with

since Tiffany had launched her media attack. Clea felt a stirring of dread. "Hi, Mama."

"Clea, I heard about your engagement. Weren't you even gonna tell me?"

"Why?" she asked. "The last time I talked to you you practically disowned me."

"Oh, honey, you know better than to expect me to stay mad. You're my daughter. And I'm so proud of you now."

It hit Clea all at once that her mother couldn't consider her an outcast when she was marrying Brandon Donovan. She would want to be right in the middle of things. The women of Beaut would be green with envy, and her mother wouldn't miss that chance for the world. "Thank you, Mama."

"Honey, when is the wedding?"

"In three weeks," she said.

"I want to help. I can get the first flight up there this afternoon, and—"

"Mama, there's no need. It's not going to be a big deal. It's just going to be a quiet wedding in a judge's chambers. No reception, no wedding dress, no flowers . . ."

"Oh, but you must have flowers, Clea, and you have to wear *something*! My goodness, you're marrying one of the richest men in the country. You don't want to disappoint him."

"He wouldn't mind if I wore a sweatshirt and jeans," she said with a soft smile. "Really, Mama, he's not the pretentious type. The quieter, the better."

"But at least let me come and help you with *something*. It would mean so much to me."

"Well." She sighed. "I know he'd like to meet you. I guess you could come and spend some time, Mama. We're going to be shopping for a condo between now and then, and—"

"I'd *love* to help with that! Oh, Clea, this is so wonderful! How much is he worth now, since the divorce?"

Clea's fragile joy at her mother's enthusiasm collapsed. "I don't know. Why?"

"Well, I just wondered. Several people have asked. He's still a billionaire, isn't he?"

Clea felt that old familiar pain twisting in her heart, and she said, "No, Mama. Actually, he's decided to donate what's left of his company to charity, and we're going to be living in a one-room efficiency apartment and living off what we can grow on the patio."

"Clea, don't be ridiculous."

"*You're* being ridiculous, Mama. I'm not marrying Brandon for his money. I happen to be in love with him."

"Well, it's like I've always said, sweetheart, it's just as easy to fall in love with a rich man as a poor one, isn't it? Anyway, when do you want me to come?"

Clea bit her tongue and told herself that she needed her mother now and would take her back any way she could get her. "Uh . . . you could come this weekend."

"Great," she said. "I guess after you're married to Brandon I can come any time I want. With a rich daughter, money won't be an object anymore. I'll talk to you later, honey. I really am so proud of you!"

Clea hung up the phone and let out a long breath. Graduating summa cum laude from college had meant nothing to her mother, and neither had being in the top ten percent of her class in law school. But marrying a rich man . . . it was the accomplishment of a lifetime. As though it was something she had worked toward. Something she had planned.

In a way, she felt as if she had done just that, for her part in the scheme had gotten her there. She wished she could erase that one sin from her soul and never think of it again. It loomed over her like an impending disease, as though there were a tiny spot on an Xray that might grow and consume her. Her future with Brandon was only as stable as Tiffany's mood at any given time.

She didn't like being at Tiffany's mercy.

But that was the way it was for now, and she was glad to have him any way she could get him. Brandon was in love with her, and that made anything that came before all right.

Sometimes the end did justify the means.

44

Playboy *decided that Shalimar* was a natural, so they offered her more money than she'd ever seen and insisted on shooting her immediately. They put the fastest possible rush on, so that they could get her picture in before people stopped caring who Brandon Donovan married.

She was photographed wearing a pink wedding veil and a bridesmaid's bouquet, and a smile so sexy that Joe Don Wilson would have been proud. Her mother would have disowned her for the deed, but she was too busy creating a circus out of Clea's wedding. Besides, Shalimar avoided her mother as much as possible while her mother was there, because Steven Donovan had revived his interest in her and was taking her out to dinner—in public, no less—several nights a week. She still couldn't understand why he never took her home with him, but she didn't worry too much when he didn't mind paying for a three-hundred-dollar-a-night suite. The backseat of a car would have done her just fine.

Clea and Brandon had found a condominium that they intended to share after their marriage, and already

Clea had moved most of her things out of her apartment. But Shalimar still didn't risk bringing Steven there. Things were going too well, and she figured she'd have the place to herself soon enough.

He got fidgety the week of the wedding, however, and when she questioned him about it, he said he was frustrated that she never took him home anymore. She told him she could say the same about him. Ignoring her point, as men often did, he said that he had been thinking about perhaps moving in with her when Clea moved out. Shalimar beamed at the prospect, although she was disappointed that he didn't want to move *her* into his place. But there was no use rocking the boat. When he insisted on taking her housekey to be copied so that he'd have his own, she realized she couldn't have been happier if he'd put a ring on her finger. Wasn't that a commitment, after all?

Anxious for her spread to come out in *Playboy* and for Steven to move in with her the moment Clea moved out, Shalimar floated through the next few days, as if she were the one getting married instead of Clea.

The night before their wedding—which had grown to include all of Clea's relatives and step-relatives from Beaut, as well as some of her mother's "closest" friends, all of whom were flying in the next day, as well as Brandon's father and sisters, whom Myrna had insisted on meeting—Clea found refuge with Brandon in the home they would share together. He had already moved in, though they had spent the last few weeks decorating together, and now Clea felt as if she finally had a place of her own, a place where she could belong. She planned to go back to work at DC as soon as she was married, but she dreaded the encounters with his remaining employees, who thought she was the whore who had won another woman's man. Even if that woman was Tiffany.

"They'll love you as much as I do after they get to know you," Brandon said, pulling her off the ladder where she had been measuring for curtains. He hugged her tightly around her waist, and let her slide to her feet. "And if they don't, I'll fire them."

"Oh, that ought to score points." She stood on her tiptoes and slid her arms around his neck. "Oh, Brandon, my mother's turned this into such a fiasco. But it's like the dream of her life, and I feel like a heel when I try to stop it. Is all this really going to happen?"

"You bet it is." He kissed her then, something he seemed never to tire of doing, and she melted against him and felt her anxieties slipping away.

The doorbell rang, and Brandon broke the kiss and sighed with frustration. "Who could that be?"

"Not my mother, I hope."

"We could send her on an errand," he said. "Somewhere far away."

Clea laughed, and the bell rang again. "Answer it."

He groaned and went to the door, winked at her, and pulled it open.

Clea caught her breath as she saw Tiffany standing there, dressed like a million bucks, and wearing a smile that couldn't have been more smug if she'd worked at it. "Hello, darling," she said, strolling into the condo and looking around. "Well, isn't this quaint?"

"What do you want, Tiffany?"

Tiffany smiled and turned back to Brandon. "I had some business to finish, darling. But not with you. With Clea."

Clea's heart began to sink level by level, and she felt her mouth growing dry. "Tiffany, you and I don't have any business together," she managed to say.

"Oh, on the contrary," she said. "It seems I owe you one more payment."

Clea shot Brandon a look, and saw the confusion on his face.

Smiling with intense pleasure, Tiffany strolled forward, and handed her a check and a piece of folded paper. "Thirty-three thousand dollars, and that letter of recommendation to get you into law school." When Clea didn't take it, Tiffany feigned a pout. "Oh, Clea, now, don't be like that. A deal's a deal. You did your part, now I'm doing mine. I always pay my debts."

Brandon stepped between them, settling his startled eyes on Clea. "What is she talking about?"

Clea's eyes filled with tears, and she panicked. "Brandon, I . . . I wanted to tell you, but I didn't go through with it, and I—"

"What?" he asked. "What kind of deal did you have with her?"

Clea crumbled, and she turned back to Tiffany. "Why are you doing this? You got everything you wanted!"

"I asked you what you did!" Brandon shouted through his teeth. "Now, tell me, damn it!"

Tiffany's smile flourished. "Maybe I can help you, Brandon. You see, Clea was working for me when you hired her."

"She what?" Shaking his head, he turned back to Clea.

Clea wiped at the tears flowing down her face. It was over, she thought. There was no way to hide it now. "Brandon, she hired me to sleep with you so she could get you for adultery, but I wouldn't . . . I didn't! That's why I quit. I turned down the money she sent me and—"

"Turned it down?" Tiffany cut in. "Oh, I don't think so." She reached into her purse and pulled out two can-

celed checks. "I have the canceled checks right here.
Signed by Clea Sands."

"You bitch!" Clea shouted. "My sister forged one of
those, and I gave you back both payments."

"It's here, in black and white, Brandon," Tiffany said.

"Brandon, I tore it up and sent it back to her. But
while I was in Texas, she sent another one, and Shally
cashed it! Look—" She ran to her purse, pulled out her
checkbook, and showed where she'd recorded the check
she'd written for Tiffany's cashier's check. "Sixty-six
thousand dollars! I sent a cashier's check back to her—"

Brandon raked his hand through his hair. "She paid
you to seduce me?"

"But I didn't!" Clea cried. "You know I didn't do it!"

"You helped set me up! You helped her get what she
wanted out of the divorce!"

"But not because of anything she paid me to do. She
just used what she could after I refused to go on! Brandon, you've got to listen to me!"

"Yes, listen to her, Brandon," Tiffany cut in. "But she
won't tell you why she decided to quit. You see, she saw
that you were falling in love with her, and she told me
that she'd be crazy to settle for a hundred thousand dollars when she could marry you and have everything!"

"You lying bitch!" Clea screamed. "That's not true. I
was never going to see him again! I was moving to Texas,
for God's sake. I tried to get out of the picture entirely."

"And tomorrow you're marrying him."

Clea turned to Brandon, her face contorted in pain,
and he only stared at her, as if she were a stranger he'd
never even known.

"Best wishes on the marriage, darling," Tiffany told
Brandon as she started back to the door. "Oh, and by the
way, I wouldn't waste my time on a prenuptial agree-

ment, if I were you. She knows all the tricks." She opened the door and turned back one last time, with a smile so smug that Clea wished she could carve it off her face. "She's a real pro, Brandon. And she'll always know how to earn a buck. You've got a real catch there, darling."

Her laughter echoed in the hall as the door closed behind her.

The air in the room seemed swelteringly hot, and Clea found it impossible to breathe. Her face reddened and twisted with her sobs. She reached for a chair to steady herself, and tried to move toward Brandon. He lifted a hand to hold her back. "Don't come near me."

"Brandon, you have to hear the whole story! I never told her that. I made a mistake, but I tried to fix it. You have to listen to me!"

"Get out," he said.

"But Brandon, the wedding—"

"Get out! There's not going to be a wedding!"

"Oh, Brandon, please don't do this!" She tried to muffle her sobs, but the grief was too deep, too great, for it reached down to the bottom of her soul. "I love you. That's why I quit without giving her what she wanted! That's why I was leaving town!"

"Get out!" he screamed, his face reddening. "I don't ever want to see you again!" He took her arm and ran her to the door, opened it, and shoved her out into the hall. And as she turned back to him, he pointed a finger at her. "You and Tiffany accomplished everything you set out to do! Don't you ever come near me again!"

The door slammed in her face, and Clea hugged her arms around herself and crumpled against the wall. It was the eve of her wedding to the only man she had ever truly loved, and she found herself more alone than she'd ever been in her life.

45

Though the Detroit sun shone unseasonably bright for the next few weeks, Clea's days were dark and dreary. Steeped in depression and shame deeper than she had ever known, she secluded herself in her apartment, trying to sort through the hopelessness of her life. She had burned the letter of recommendation from Tiffany's father, which she knew would have been worthless in light of the publicity, but even if it hadn't been, she could never have taken advantage of it now. Law school would forever be a buried dream for her, something she'd come so close to realizing. Now she was living on a minimum-wage salary from the telemarketing firm where she was nothing more than a faceless voice on the telephone with a fake name. No real human connections had to be made, no trust was involved, no betrayals were imminent. It wasn't really life . . . just business.

Shalimar, on the other hand, had been soaring since her picture came out in *Playboy*. It had been too late to pull her spread when the wedding was called off. Shali-

mar had found a new, plush apartment of her own and
was now signed with an agent who promised to get her
into some local commercials. Steven, meanwhile,
dumped Shalimar again after the wedding was called
off, and Shalimar finally told Clea about her most recent
affair with him, hoping for a little compassion from her
sister. But Clea wasn't surprised nor was she particularly
sympathetic. Only she knew of the barrage of cards and
letters and gifts and phone calls she kept getting from
Steven, gestures that frightened her more with each
passing day.

Myrna had been humiliated and appalled by the
Playboy spread, but even that hadn't upset her as much
as the collapse of Clea's wedding plans. It took her days
to stop blaming Clea for trying to ruin her life, and finally,
she had packed her bags and headed back to Beaut.
Clea hadn't heard from her since.

Cable television was the only thing that kept Clea
tuned to the outside world, and she watched it avidly
when she wasn't working. She devoured reports of
HMC and DC, and watched as the first of the Meteors
rolled off the production line. She knew Brandon was
watching it, too, and blaming her for her part in costing
him his dream.

But it wasn't until she saw the report that Donovan
Concepts was considering bankruptcy, due to nervous
creditors who were calling in loans, that she realized she
couldn't sit in a cocoon anymore. Someone had to do
something before Brandon fell too far to be picked back
up. And she was the only one who could do it.

She made the decision easily, for every possible sce-
nario of her rescuing Brandon had played through her
mind repeatedly over the last few weeks, fast-forwarding,
rewinding, and replaying, and she had studied the possi-

bilities frame by frame. Only one answer became clear to her. To save Brandon, she had to sacrifice herself.

And as the first step in that sacrifice, she made a list of all the television stations, radio stations, and newspapers in town, then called a press conference for three o'clock that afternoon on the steps of her apartment building.

It was time, she thought, to tell the world everything. It might not accomplish anything except to clear Brandon of any wrongdoing—and might even bring charges against her for fraud or worse—but it would at least be the truth, something no one had yet heard.

She called Shalimar and asked her to be there to help her through it, then showered, pulled herself together, and sat down to write the statement that she knew would make the six o'clock news. The statement that would expose Tiffany Donovan for what she was.

The statement that would do Clea in once and for all.

Steven had quit showing up at HMC, and no one seemed to miss him. He still drew a nice paycheck, which his mother had deposited into his account every month, but he had lost all interest in work. Clea occupied his mind twenty-four hours a day, and he spent every moment manufacturing ways to get her into his bed now that his father was out of the picture. He designed elaborate scenarios, wrote entire scripts of how the evenings would go, even shopped for rings in hopes of finding a bigger and better one than his father had given her. He tried to call her, but each time she heard his voice she hung up. He left messages, which she ignored. He sent her letters, which came back unopened. At night, he went to her building, sat in his car outside it, and stared up at the light in her window. She never came out, but it didn't sway him from keeping vigil, nonetheless. He had a key, after all, and could go in when the time was right. Soon enough it would all pay off. Soon enough, she would be his.

Shalimar's calls had become a colossal nuisance, and he took to hanging up almost as soon as he heard her voice. But when she called to tell him to watch for her on television that day, because she would be beside Clea at the press conference she had called, Steven's spirits lifted. He would get the chance to see Clea. She was finally coming out.

He called Tiffany the moment he heard about the press conference, and with a smile on his face, said, "Buckle your seat belt, Mother. This ride's about to get bumpy."

"What do you mean?" Tiffany asked.

"Clea Sands has called a press conference for this afternoon."

Tiffany caught her breath. "A press conference? Why?"

"Her sister said she planned to spill her guts."

He noted his mother's dead silence, confirming the nagging suspicion he'd had that his mother hadn't told him everything. "What does that have to do with me?"

"I don't know," he said, "but there's not a lot around here that's making sense these days. She's probably going to expose you and Lawrence, among other things. Maybe tell the real reason she and Dad split up just before the wedding, which personally, I'd give my right arm to know."

"Steven, you've got to stop her."

"Me? I haven't even seen her in weeks. I can't get near her."

"But you have to," she said. "She can't have that press conference."

"Why, Mother? Is she going to tell something that even I haven't heard yet?"

"Just stop her!" Tiffany snapped. "I'm warning you, Steven, if she isn't stopped, we could lose everything."

"Sounds serious, Mother," he said. "Maybe *you* should stop her."

"Steven!" The phone clicked in Tiffany's ear, and panic bolted through her. Quickly, she dialed his number, but he didn't answer. "Damn it!" she shouted, then dialed Lawrence's house. He wasn't home. Someone had to do something fast, she thought. There wasn't much time, but Clea couldn't be allowed to tell everything.

She called information for Clea's new number, found that it was unlisted, then hurriedly called down for her car. She would go to Clea's apartment, offer her more money, threaten her . . .

She screamed at the driver all the way to hurry, and he drove at break-neck speed, weaving in and out of traffic and taking shortcuts to reach Clea's apartment. He had barely screeched to a halt when she got out of the limo, the first time she had ever not waited for him to open her door.

But at the door, two guards stopped her and refused to let her in. Clea wasn't seeing anyone until after the press conference. Especially Tiffany Donovan.

Dazed, Tiffany got back into the car and ordered the driver to take her to Steven's. He would help her again; she knew he would. All she had to do was make him see how vital it was to stop Clea. All she had to do was make him understand how drastically Clea had affected all their lives.

His car was gone, but hoping beyond hope that he was there anyway, she banged on his door. He didn't answer. Finally she dug through her purse for the spare key he had given her long ago. Unlocking the door, she went in. Maybe there was a clue as to where she could find him, she thought. Or maybe if she waited, he'd come home.

His living room looked like a fraternity house on New Year's morning, with plates and dishes and stale food sitting all over the room. Clothes were strewn everywhere, and a stagnant, rotten scent wafted through the house.

Horrified, she stepped further in and picked up a newspaper with holes cut out of it and a pair of scissors on the floor. Had he really been living in this filth when he could have had a host of servants cleaning up after him?

A sense of apprehension crept over her as she went slowly into the bedroom, as cautiously as a child caught in a house of mirrors. She stepped through the cut-up magazines and newspapers that littered the floor and saw the broken television lying on its side, and regarded the rumpled bed. A pair of women's panties lay on the pillow.

But it was the wall that startled her into dropping the scissors.

Clea's face covered it in every possible expression, every picture of Clea that had been printed in the last year, every public moment and even stills of videotapes of Clea with Brandon, Clea on the news, Clea dodging reporters.

Steven was sick, she realized with startling certainty, and he was obsessed with Clea Sands. That explained his sudden hatred of his father. That explained his willingness to do his father in to help her. She should have seen it earlier.

Rage filled her that this woman had caused so much trouble in her life, that she had exposed Tiffany's affair to Brandon, that she had kept her from getting all that she deserved, that Brandon had truly loved her, and that now she had snagged her son and driven him to the brink of insanity.

Running back to the car, she ordered the driver to take her to HMC immediately. She would find Lawrence, and he would know what to do, she thought. Lawrence could get them out of this.

But when she got there, Lawrence was out, and no one knew where to find him. And she was left with nothing to do but sit and wait for the walls to come tumbling down.

At the appointed time, Clea came down the steps of her apartment building and out into the harsh light of afternoon. She looked around her at the swarm of reporters and television cameras and microphones, and couldn't believe they had all come here for this. Dirty little stories sold really well, she thought. She saw the podium someone had set up for her, wired with so many microphones she didn't know how they'd ever get them all untangled. She felt herself swaying at the thought of facing them all. When she reached out for Shalimar, her sister took her hand.

It didn't bother her that her sister had dressed like a Hollywood starlet, complete with cleavage and as much leg as she could get away with revealing, because what counted was that Clea wasn't alone. Yes, Shalimar would love every minute of the spotlight, and she'd milk it for everything it was worth, but she would also be there to help put Clea back together if she crumbled. If nothing else, sisters were good for that.

Clea walked to the podium, holding her head as high as she could, despite the terror closing in on her. Shalimar walked up behind her, making sure that she stood in the cameras' lines of fire, as well.

The cameras began flashing, and as Clea cleared her throat, the crowd grew quiet. "Thank you all for coming today," she said, pulling her written statement out of her pocket and unfolding it on the podium. "A lot has been reported about me and my relationship with Brandon Donovan over the last few months," she said, "and most of it has not been true. I called you here today to tell the truth about my part in the breakup of his marriage, because I feel that no matter how this implicates me, it's time that the truth came out."

On the outskirts of the crowd, Steven stood unshaven and dirty, watching and listening as the story of his parents unfolded.

Across town, Brandon's secretary dashed into his office and turned on the television. "Brandon, I just got a call from my daughter. She said that Clea's doing a press conference. CNN is covering it live!" She flipped around, found it, and Brandon came to his feet as he saw Clea standing in front of her building with a swarm of reporters around her.

"I thought you might need to watch it," she said, "since she's talking about you."

"Thank you," Brandon said calmly, going to the screen and turning it up.

Evelyn backed out of the office and closed the door, and Brandon sat down slowly to listen.

"Earlier this year, I received a call from Tiffany Donovan, asking me to meet her at a local restaurant. Not knowing what she wanted, I met with her. At that time she told me that she wanted a divorce from her husband, but that she needed evidence of adultery. She offered to pay me a hundred thousand dollars and help me get back into a reputable law school if I would agree to go to work for Brandon and seduce him."

A gasp went over the reporters, and Clea's voice faltered. Rallying, she went on. "Because of several occurrences in my past, my bitterness, my need for money, and my desperation to fulfill my own dream that had been taken away from me, I agreed. The plan was that I would instigate an affair with Brandon and provide her with enough proof so that she could win in a divorce battle with him in court and have her prenuptial agreement overridden."

Brandon felt as if some acidic monster was eating at him from the inside out as he sat frozen, listening as she recounted how she had changed her mind and tried to back out, how she had never slept with him during that time, how she had resigned from DC to keep from giving Tiffany the chance to set him up further. She told how Tiffany had been having an affair with Lawrence Henderson for months, and how they had used Steven to manipulate Brandon into dropping the countersuit against them.

"Because of the injustices we had suffered in common, and all the lies that had been printed, Brandon and I became close only after his divorce. He is the kindest, gentlest, most genuinely honest man I have ever known, and he was never unfaithful to his wife in any way."

Tears came to her eyes, and her mouth began to tremble, and Brandon felt his own misting, as well. But whether his abysmal sadness was born of his pain *for* her, or *from* her, he didn't know.

"As you can surmise," she went on in a raspy voice, "my wedding with Brandon was called off when he discovered my part in this scheme, and I deserved it. I have no hope of a relationship with him in the future, but I feel it's time that the truth came out. Brandon Donovan did not deserve to lose any part of his company, and he didn't deserve to be manipulated and tricked in the ways that he has been. I realize that my part in this bordered on criminal, and I expect him to take some legal action against me. But if things can be righted because of my coming forward, if in some way some of what he has lost can be restored to him, then I will feel it's worth it. Thank you for coming."

Tears stung Brandon's eyes, and that old familiar rage swirled inside him, but he didn't know whether it was directed at Clea or Tiffany, or even himself. He watched as she stepped down from the podium, refusing to comment further as the reporters frantically threw out questions to her, and she disappeared into the building again.

His phone rang, and he ignored it for a moment, and finally, Evelyn came back to the door. "Brandon, you really need to take this call. It's Jacob Fairbane."

Brandon only nodded, for he couldn't speak. Weakly, he got up and picked up the phone. "Yeah."

"Brandon, did you see the press conference?"

Brandon cleared his throat and rubbed his eyes harshly. "Yeah."

"Did you know about this before?"

He tried to draw in a cleansing breath, but it did nothing to cleanse the festering lesions in his soul. "Not until the night before I was supposed to marry her," he said. "Tiffany told me."

"Why the hell didn't you tell me?" Jacob demanded. "Brandon, with this information, we can sue the hell out of Tiffany. You could get everything back, including the THD. We could prosecute her for fraud and conspiracy, and a number of other things I haven't even come up with yet. Don't you understand what this means?"

He was numb, he realized, and none of it mattered. It was all useless. "I don't want to drag all this shit back up," he said quietly. "I've had enough."

"So you're going to sit there and watch your entire company go under? There are people depending on you for jobs, Brandon, and if you don't fight back, you're letting every one of them down."

Brandon closed his eyes tightly and tried to make his brain focus. "You're right, I know you are," he said. "Yeah, okay. Let's talk."

"Be at my office in an hour," Jacob said. "I'm going to pull out all the stops, Brandon, and this time you're going to have your day in court. Tiffany and Lawrence will walk away with nothing."

Brandon dropped the phone and stared back at the blank television, feeling a hopeless emptiness in his heart that had known overflowing happiness not so long ago. And somehow, even knowing there was hope of restoring what was his didn't help him at all. The THD couldn't fill the void in him or restore the light to the long dark tunnel he'd found himself groping through.

Revenge would be little victory when he was entirely alone. But he had no hope that that would ever change again. The worst hurt of all was Clea's part in the betrayal. And he could never forgive her for that as long as he lived.

46

Lawrence came in before the press conference, just in time to watch Tiffany fall apart. Immediately he took her home and mixed her a stiff drink. Everyone knew what she had done, she thought. She was finished. "Lawrence, what do you think is going to happen?"

"Nothing," Lawrence said, though he'd worn a scowl since they'd turned off the television. "None of this is news to Brandon. If he were going to do something about it, he'd have done it by now."

"But before it was a secret. Now everyone knows. Everyone!" She clutched her drink tighter. She took a gulp, but it didn't help. "Lawrence, she made me out to be a conniving liar, not to mention a whore."

"Well, if the shoe fits—"

"What?" she asked, slamming down her drink and glaring up at him.

Lawrence turned around and tossed back his own drink. "You did lie, Tiffany, and you did cheat."

"And so did you!"

"But they can't prove I did anything but sleep with

you," he said. "Brandon can't prove I had any part at all in setting him up."

Tiffany stood up, her hair tousled and her makeup smeared, and she faced him with horror in her eyes. "So what are you saying? That I'm in this alone? That you're bailing out if it gets tough?"

"No," he said. "It hasn't come to that, for God's sake. I'm just saying how it looks to the world."

She gaped at him, suddenly not sure whether the ground she was standing on was steady, or whether it would fall out from under her at any moment. "Lawrence—"

The doorbell rang, cutting into her words, and she turned back to the monitor above the door and saw her son standing in the hall. Wiping her eyes and trying to restore some order to her hair, she flung it open. "Steven, my God, where have you been?"

He shoved her back from the door, and she caught herself on a chair. "Just tell me one thing, Mother," he sneered. "Is it true?"

"Steven, I—"

"No more lies, Mother!" he said, coming toward her with a lethal look in his blazing eyes. "Is it or isn't it true? Did you hire Clea to seduce my father?"

Tears smeared more of her mascara, causing it to drip like mud down her face. "Steven, I did it for you, darling. I wanted you to have more than your father was willing to give you. I wanted you to have your own company, something worthy of your intelligence and your talent."

"But you didn't give it to me, did you, Mother? You gave it to him!"

Lawrence made no move to come between them. "Steven, your mother and I are as shaken by all this as you."

"Well, I should think so," he said, whirling on his mother's lover. "It's no fun being exposed as a liar and a thief, is it? I hope my father nails your ass to the wall!" He went back to the door, opened it, and looked back. "If things get too bad, Mother, I know where you can get some pills. Just make sure you do the job right. No one will believe it's real unless you wind up dead."

The door slammed behind him, and Tiffany fell into Lawrence's arms. But the warmth that was usually there had left him, and suddenly she felt the chill of loneliness and abandonment. It was the first time in her life those feelings had been turned back on her.

Tiffany was served with papers the following day, informing her that she was being sued on the grounds of conspiracy to commit fraud. Brandon wanted back all of the assets she had taken from him, along with punitive damages.

Lawrence grew strangely distant in the weeks leading up to the trial, and she realized that all talk of marriage between them had ceased. She was filled with anxiety about the precarious state of her life. If she lost HMC, would he leave her? Was their relationship based on perks, or would it endure the hardships? All she knew for sure was that she couldn't stand the thought of going through the trial alone. Agony reigned foremost in Tiffany's soul for the next few weeks as she and her father worked on the case. They had to prove Clea was a liar and ruin her credibility, but there was no getting around the fact that she had nothing at all to gain by testifying about the scheme. Instead, she had everything to lose, and no jury could ignore that.

The day before the trial, she found Steven and tried

to make amends with him. She needed him, she told him. She loved him. He was her only son, and they had to stick together.

Steven only told her that he had better things to do than listen to his mother whine.

And on the day of the trial, Tiffany realized that everything she had done to Brandon was about to be done tenfold to her.

The courthouse swarmed with reporters as Clea got out of the car and pushed through to get to the court-room where she was to be the star witness in Brandon's lawsuit. She had been surprised to find that he had no intentions of filing suit against her, as long as she testi-fied against Tiffany in court. She hadn't communicated with Brandon since the day before their wedding, except through his attorney, and it had been impossible to learn anything about how he was doing.

As she shoved her way into the courtroom, her eyes met his. He looked tired, beaten, but he still exuded the same charisma she had fallen in love with. And she found that her love for him was just as strong as it had been before Tiffany had intervened.

He looked away, shattering her heart, and she blinked back the tears and went to the witness stand, to which she had been called the day before, just before the court had adjourned. The courtroom got quiet, she was sworn in, and Brandon's attorney began his questioning.

And she prayed that, somehow, what she did today would restore to Brandon some of what she had cost him for loving her.

* * *

Brandon watched her with dull, tired eyes, and tried not to note that she looked more beautiful than even his dreams had been able to recreate, or that her eyes looked more sad and remorseful, or that her voice sounded sweeter. He tried to ignore the logic in her explanations, the pain in her reasons for doing what she did, and concentrate instead on the crime itself.

Tiffany sat across the courtroom, trying to look as vulnerable and sweet as Clea, but it was a feat she could never pull off in a million years. He wondered how Steven was taking all this, but his son still wasn't returning his calls, so he had no way of knowing.

He told himself that as soon as this mess was behind them, he'd work hard on fixing his relationship with his son. Besides his father, Steven was about all he had left.

But even the hope of getting Steven back didn't feed the hunger in his soul. Brandon felt he was a fool of the biggest kind, for no matter what Clea had done to him, he couldn't make that hunger go away. And he doubted it would ever be satisfied again.

The jury deliberated for less than an hour, then found in favor of Brandon. The judgment ordered Tiffany to return HMC to Brandon, thus putting the original Donovan Concepts back together, and gave him a substantial monetary award for punitive damages.

A cheer went up in the courtroom as court was adjourned, and Brandon was suddenly surrounded by well-wishers congratulating him and reporters shouting questions at him. As he accepted the jubilation, his eyes met Clea's across the room. She was smiling, as if his victory was hers, as well. He watched as she held her head high and pushed through the crowd that descended on her. He saw her refuse to be interviewed, and watched as she managed to leave the courtroom.

His father broke through the crowd and embraced him shamelessly, and Brandon hugged him, but his eyes still watched the door.

"Congratulations, son," Peter said against his ear.

"Thanks, Dad," Brandon said. "Thank God it's over."

"It wasn't easy for her, you know," Peter said, still holding him. "But she came through for you."

He didn't have to ask. He knew his father referred to Clea. He drew back and looked into his father's eyes.

"She may have been a little misguided in the beginning, son, but she's got a good heart."

The reporters grew louder and more demanding around him, but as Clea disappeared, his father's words began to sink like balm into his heart.

Clea broke down in the car as Shalimar drove her home, and she sobbed as if her soul was an endless well of pain as they drove up to the back door of her building.

Shalimar reached over and hugged her, her face wet with tears of her own. "Are you sure you don't wanna come home with me?" she asked. "I'll wait on you hand and foot."

Clea shook her head and tried to wipe the tears, but they still kept coming. "No. I really need to be alone for a while. I've got to get out of here, Shalimar, but I don't have a clue where I'll go." She sucked in her breath, and tried to picture herself a year from now. "I should probably cut my hair short and change my name, and move to some place where no one would ever recognize me."

"Oh, now. You're not all that bad," Shalimar said. "Look at Donna Rice, Marla Maples, Jessica Hahn.

None of them are livin' in poverty right now. You should use this notoriety. Just go with it."

"I'm not like you, Shally," Clea said. "I can't feed off of this. I want to get away from it, put it behind me, not drag it with me for the rest of my life. That's not the kind of life I want to lead."

"Well, it's the kind I plan to lead," Shalimar said. "*Playboy* is gonna be my launchin' pad."

Clea sighed and wiped at her eyes. "I guess we've each had our fifteen minutes, haven't we?"

"It wasn't enough," Shalimar said. "I plan to have some more."

"And I hope I never have another second of it as long as I live." Clea opened the car door, but leaned over and pressed a kiss on her sister's cheek before she got out. "Thanks for helping me through this, Shally."

"Sure, honey. Listen, if you change your mind and want some company . . ."

Clea smiled. "I'll call."

Shalimar caught her hand as she started to climb out. "Sis? You're not gonna . . . well, you know . . . do anything drastic, are you?"

Clea tried to smile. "Don't worry, Shally. The things I've done in the past year are about as drastic as I'll ever get."

She closed the door and went into the back exit door of her building, and realized that she felt more physically and emotionally spent than she had felt in her life. She was at the end of her rope, but Shalimar had nothing to fear, for she had nothing to do but hold on. Suicide wasn't one of her options.

She started up the steps to her apartment, longing for the quiet and peace she had found at the lake. She needed those still waters, to wrap herself in quiet, in simplicity again. She needed to rest, to regroup, to find a way to start over, bury her past sins, and live.

She heard the sound of reporters gathering on the front steps and the guards effectively holding them back. They would rip her apart like starving vultures, if she'd only let them. But she wouldn't. She had to hold herself together.

She stuck her key in her doorknob, discovered that it was unlocked, and, frowning, pushed the door open. Had she been so shaken this morning that she hadn't locked it?

She opened it, stepped inside, and looked around. Satisfied that nothing had been disturbed, she closed the door behind her.

"I've been waiting for you."

Gasping, Clea whirled around and saw Steven, standing in the hallway of the apartment, watching her with eyes that seared into her, threatening unspeakable terror. "Steven!"

"Did they believe you this time, Clea?" he asked, coming toward her.

Clea tried to steady herself and took a step backward. "How did you get in here?"

"With a key," he said. "Shalimar gave it to me weeks ago."

He was coming closer, and she took another step back. "Then the guards know you're here?"

He chuckled softly. "Don't be silly. I used the back way. I've spent a lot of time here, Clea, while you were with my father. I know my way around."

She racked her brain for a way to warn the guards downstairs, but she wasn't sure they'd even seen her come home. "Steven, what do you want?"

Steven looked at her with those vacant eyes for a

moment too long, and finally said, "You, Clea. You know I want you."

The emptiness in Brandon's soul was profound as he allowed his driver to take him to his office. "Congratulations, Mr. D.," the man said from the front seat. "I never thought it was right, her getting everything like she did."

"Thanks, Butch," Brandon said.

The driver was silent for a moment, and finally, he spoke up again. "You know, Mr. D., I know it's none of my business, and if I'm outa line, just say so, but I always thought Miss Sands had a lot of class. She's a one-of-a-kind lady."

Brandon didn't say anything, for the words launched a string of thoughts in his mind, thoughts about how brutally honest she'd been in the courtroom, to the point of incriminating herself. And knowing Clea the way he did, he feared the publicity would destroy her. How had she stood it all these weeks?

He thought of the rumors he'd heard about her turning down a quarter of a million dollars to pose for *Playboy*, an offer to write a book, an option to use her life in the movies, and exclusive interviews with Barbara Walters, "Sixty Minutes," and the *National Enquirer*.

She had become a hermit over the last few weeks, and it had taken its toll. She looked pale, and thinner, and the expression on her face was now waiflike and fragile. Her part in Tiffany's scheme had probably cost her more than it had cost anyone else.

Much more.

He thought about Tiffany and Lawrence, and wondered how they were taking the news that he had won back everything. They had gotten everything they deserved. *What goes around comes around* . . . His father's favorite adage had miraculously turned out to be true.

But did Clea deserve to be left with nothing but shame and despair? She, after all, had been the one to save him. Anyone else Tiffany had recruited might have gone through with setting him up, might have lured him into sleeping with her, might have pushed the knife in even deeper than it already was. Anyone else would have kept the secret, run with the press, and reaped the profits of the whole dirty deal.

He glanced out the window, saw that he was only blocks away from the DC building, and sighed heavily. He wondered how Clea felt now. Was she crying? Was she celebrating? Was she defeated, or devising a way to move forward?

He didn't know, but suddenly he realized something he hadn't let himself admit in a very long time. Something that he knew had been with him ever since the night Tiffany told him everything.

He was in love with Clea Sands, and nothing, no one, was ever going to change that.

He wiped his eyes with a shaking hand, and cleared his throat. "Butch, turn the car around, please."

Butch shot him a strange look. "Well, okay, Mr. D. Whatever you say. You going home?"

"No," he said. "Take me to Clea's apartment. You do remember where it is, don't you?"

A slow smile crept across Butch's face. "Sure do. I took her to the airport that time."

"Go to the back," he said. "I'm sure the press is surrounding the front again."

"You got it," Butch said as he turned the car around.

✧   ✧   ✧

"I imagine it, you know," Steven said, coming toward her as Clea backed away, wishing from the depths of her soul that she hadn't left her gun in the bedroom.

"Imagine what?" she whispered.

"Making love to you," he said, his eyes growing duller the more he came toward her. "Undressing you myself. Feeling your skin. Having you slide against me . . . But always, when I'm thinking of it, it starts out being *me* with you, and then it changes to my father."

"Steven, this obsession you have with me, it's crazy," she said, her voice trembling. "You've got to stop this."

"I can't get it out of my mind, Clea," he said. His breath seemed to grow heavier as he came toward her. "You and my father making love . . . it's like a movie that comes on even when the tube is turned off. It's over and over and over in my mind, you arching against him, him touching you . . ."

"Steven . . ."

"But that can stop now," he said, "because you see, once it's me in his place, once you sleep with me, you'll be mine, and it won't be him anymore."

"I'm not going to sleep with you, Steven." Tears rolled down her face. "You need to leave now."

"I'm not going anywhere," he whispered.

She swallowed and tried to fight the terror rising inside her. "Steven, there are guards downstairs. All I have to do is scream and—"

"They wouldn't hear you," he said. "The reporters are too loud. Besides, you wouldn't scream. Because you know you want me as much as I want you."

"Steven, you're sick!"

Something in him snapped. He grabbed her arm and jerked her against him, slamming her against the wall, anchoring her with his body. "Don't ever say that to me," he spat out. "You know it's me you've wanted since the first day. But my mother was paying you, and there was nothing you could do except what she wanted. But it's all over now, isn't it, Clea? There's nothing left but you and me."

He tried to kiss her, but she jerked her face away, and instead, he redirected his mouth to her neck. His pelvis pushed against her, and she felt the urgency in his hold. His fingers dug into her back, holding her still, and she knew that if she didn't stop him, he was going to take what he wanted. But she wouldn't let him.

Summoning every ounce of strength she had, she brought her knee up and rammed it into his groin. He dropped his hold on her, and she reeled across the room and grabbed a lamp from an end table. His eyes blazed as he came after her, and she hurled the lamp.

He dodged it as it crashed to the floor, and she screamed, but she knew it was in vain. There was too much noise downstairs. No one could hear.

He grabbed her and wrestled her onto the floor, and she struggled with all her might, with all the anger and hatred and injustice and despair she had stored in her soul, fighting, scratching, screaming, kicking . . .

"You'll have to kill me to rape me, you bastard!" she cried.

But as Steven tore at her clothes, she realized that might just be what he had in mind.

Butch drove to Clea's apartment along the back streets behind her building, and maneuvered the car to the back door without any of the press seeing them. It would be just a matter of moments before someone spotted them, Brandon thought, but hopefully he'd be inside before they did.

"Good luck, Mr. D.," Butch said as Brandon opened the back door and started to get out. "Do you want to call me when you're ready for me to come back?"

"Yeah," Brandon said. "Just drive around for a while. I'll call you on the car phone."

He closed the door quietly behind him and went into the building. Through the front hall, he heard the din of the reporters waiting for one final statement to lay this whole drama to rest. But it wasn't over yet.

He started up the stairs, still unseen since the guards held the reporters off. Quietly, he climbed the steps to Clea's door.

He thought he heard a scream before he even reached the top step, and something crashed. Then another scream, and he knew it was coming from Clea's apartment.

He broke into a run and reached her door. Turning the knob, he threw the door open.

A man had her pinned down on the floor, and two lamps lay smashed on the floor around him. Clea writhed with all her might, and he heard the sound of ripping cloth and a muffled gurgling as the man tried to smother her screams with his mouth, while his hands worked at her clothes.

A venomous rage like none he had ever encountered overtook him, and Brandon bolted forward and pulled the man off of her.

It was only then that he realized it was his son.

A scratch was bleeding on Steven's face, and sweat dripped like grease from his nose, and his eyes were too deadly pools of vacancy that suggested that someone Brandon had never known resided in Steven's body.

Brandon froze, not knowing what to do with the

anger that needed direction but could not be directed at his own son.

And then Steven hit him, shoved him away, and turned back to Clea.

Her scream shook Brandon back to life, and he leapt onto his son, dragged him off of her again, and hit him with all the shattering force of the rabid rage that had spiraled inside him for months.

Steven stumbled back, and for a moment, Brandon thought he might black out. From the corner of his eye, he saw Clea huddling in a ball and weeping in the corner, shivering and moaning, and more fury pulsed through him.

His son didn't fall. Instead, he looked at his father, fully ready to do whatever was necessary to get him out of the way. But Brandon didn't hesitate to go after him again, and this time when he hit him, he felt his son's jaw snap beneath his fist. The momentum knocked Steven back, against the wall and down, until his head hit the floor.

Standing over him, Brandon grabbed his collar and jerked him back up to his feet. Pulling his son's face close to his own, he said, "Now get the hell out of here before I kill you."

Steven smeared the blood across his mouth with the back of his hand, looked at Clea one last time, then staggered toward the door.

Brandon watched as he ran out the back way, dodging the reporters.

He closed the door and fell down at Clea's side, scooped her up into his arms, and crushed her against him. "Are you all right?"

Only her shirt was torn, and clutching it against her, she sobbed against his chest. "Oh, Brandon, why did I ever have to meet you? Why did I ever get involved in your family?" Sobs racked her body, shaking him as he held her. "I'm so sorry. I'm so, so sorry."

He felt his own tears scalding his eyes, and he held her tighter and harder, as if some unpredictable force might come at any time and snatch her away. "I'm sorry, too," he whispered. "God, you don't know how sorry."

He stayed there with her, holding her into the night, nursing her through the trauma and misery that had assailed her after all she'd done for him.

When her tears were spent, and she lay weakly in his arms, she finally asked, "Why did you come here today, Brandon?"

He wasn't sure, he realized, but it had turned out to be the right thing. "I don't know," he whispered. "I wanted to thank you, I guess. Mostly, I wanted to see you. Touch you. I've missed you, Clea."

"Why?" she asked. "How could you? All I've brought you is heartache, financial ruin, despair . . ."

"I love you," he whispered, framing her face with his hands. "I haven't stopped loving you."

His kiss was the sweetest, most poignant, most tender she had ever experienced, and she fell into it with all the abandon of someone who thought all the light was gone from her life forever, only to have it come back even brighter than before.

They made love with that same abandon, then slept in each other's arms, alone and removed from the world, united in their love, and pure in the truths that had purged them both.

He woke in the middle of the night and opened his eyes to find Clea staring at the ceiling, tears spilling down her temples and wetting the pillow.

He pulled her back into his arms, and whispered, "What's the matter?"

"Tell me what to do to set it right, Brandon," she whispered miserably. "Tell me how to get rid of this pain and this guilt."

"Marry me," he said.

Stunned, she lifted up her head and stared down at him. "No. I can't, Brandon. We can't just forget what's happened."

"It took two of us to fall in love, Clea. Nothing I've gotten back is worth a damn without you. I asked you to marry me once, and I'm asking again."

Clea dissolved in his arms and, weeping her heart out, agreed to be his wife.

Tiffany watched the live local coverage of the couple emerging from the church just days later, adorned in bride and groom attire, as her lover packed his suitcase behind her.

"That's everything," Lawrence said, snapping it shut.

Tiffany looked up at him, her eyes too red and swollen for any amount of makeup to conceal. "I did it all for you, Lawrence."

"Well, it backfired," he told her. "You're no good to me now."

"But I have nothing!" she cried. "You're leaving me with nothing!"

"You still have your looks," he said. "Maybe some rich wife will hire *you* to seduce *her* husband."

Without a look back, he left her sitting there alone. Tiffany stared at the door, and her conversation with Steven the previous day played through her mind.

You had everything, Mother. Now it's all going to be hers. He'll be sleeping with her every night, having babies with her, flaunting her—and all because you were so damned greedy to have it all!

Hugging her arms tightly around herself, she tried to block out the memory of Steven's voice. Instead, she heard the elevator in the hall taking Lawrence away. Only then did Tiffany understand what it truly was to be alone.

The THD—whose name remained the Meteor since it would have been too costly and confusing to the public to change it after Brandon won back his company—was filled with white roses and champagne, and as the newlyweds were about to get into it to ride away, deliriously happy for the first time in months, Myrna stepped forward and caught Clea's arm. Clea turned and saw that her mother's eyes were filled with tears. "I'm so proud of you, Angel," she said. "You've finally grown into your name. I told him you would, you know."

"Who, Mama?"

"Well, your daddy, of course, God rest his soul."

Clea smiled and took the bait. "He's not dead, Mama."

"He will be someday, dear," she said with that familiar look of longing. "But I told him the name Clea wasn't too big for you, that someday it would fit. Today it does, don't you think?"

Clea only smiled and pressed a kiss on her mother's cheek.

"Now don't you forget your mama, you hear? Just because you're all rich and famous, doesn't mean you can just forget where you came from."

"Don't worry, Mama," Clea whispered. "I'll never forget where I came from."

Peter Donovan came forward, flanked by Brandon's sisters, and gave them both a final hug, then reminded Clea to toss the bouquet. "Get in there, Myrna," Peter urged her mother. "A pretty lady like you deserves to catch a bouquet."

Laughing like a teenager, Myrna joined the single women crowding around, poised like basketball players ready to catch the rebound. Winking at Shalimar— whose legs looked as if they were six feet long under the shrink-wrapped mini-formal she'd worn to the wedding— Clea tossed it. Shalimar took a dive for it, effectively knocking everyone else out of the way. When she caught it, a hundred cameras flashed, and she came up smiling victoriously.

Brandon and Clea got into the car, and it was only then that they saw Steven standing back away from the crowd, gaunt, bruised, and unshaven, watching.

Brandon's gaze collided with his, and his smile instantly fell. Clea touched his arm. "Go talk to him, Brandon," she said. "He needs help. He's sick, and you're still his father."

For a moment he only stared pensively, and finally he shook his head. "I'm your husband," he said. "I can't forget what he did to you."

A look of almost wistfulness passed over his eyes for a second, but then the hardness returned, and he forced himself to look away. The engine purred to life, and he shifted into gear.

"So where would you like to go for dinner tonight, Mrs. Donovan? Paris or Athens?"

Clea's smile blossomed across her face. "How about the hotel up around the corner?"

"Hmmm," he said, leaning over to kiss her. "If you're eager, I can accommodate you on the plane. I never got to show you the bedroom on the last trip, did I?"

Her laughter warmed the few cool places left in his soul. "No, you didn't."

"Then let's go. I think I might just take you to Paris *and* Athens. But I should warn you. We'll be flying for a real long time."

Clea laughed again as the Meteor shot out into traffic, and a cheer went up from the crowd behind them as they disappeared.

Steven didn't take his vacant eyes off them as the sports car pulled away, but Brandon didn't look back again.

A new life was dawning, Clea thought, one without deceit or corruption. And as they embarked on that new life together, they would leave their pasts—with all their scars and bruises—behind them. It was time now to heal. Time to love. Time to embrace the sacred trust they had inspired within each other . . . a trust that both knew would never be betrayed again.

AVAILABLE NOW

ONE GOOD MAN by Terri Herrington
From the author of *Her Father's Daughter*, comes a dramatic story of a woman who sets out to seduce and ruin the one good man she's ever found. Jilted and desperate for money, Clea Sands lets herself be bought by a woman who wants grounds to sue her wealthy husband for adultery. But when Clea falls in love with him, she realizes she can't possibly destroy his life—not for any price.

PRETTY BIRDS OF PASSAGE by Roslynn Griffith
Beautiful Aurelia Kincaid returned to Chicago from Italy nursing a broken heart, and ready to embark on a new career. Soon danger stalked Aurelia at every turn when a vicious murderer, mesmerized by her striking looks, decided she was his next victim—and he would preserve her beauty forever. As the threads of horror tightened, Aurelia reached out for the safety of one man's arms. But had she unwittingly fallen into the murderer's trap? A historical romance filled with intrigue and murder.

FAN THE FLAME by Suzanne Elizabeth
The romantic adventures of a feisty heroine who met her match in a fearless lawman. When Marshal Max Barrett arrived at the Washington Territory ranch to escort Samantha James to her aunt's house in Utah, little did he know what he was getting himself into.

A BED OF SPICES by Barbara Samuel
Set in Europe in 1348, a moving story of star-crossed lovers determined to let nothing come between them. "With her unique and lyrical style, Barbara Samuel touches every emotion. The quiet brilliance of her story lingered in my mind long after the book was closed."—Susan Wiggs, author of *The Mist and the Magic*.

THE WEDDING by Elizabeth Bevarly
A delightful and humorous romance in the tradition of the movie *Father of the Bride*. Emma Hammelmann and Taylor Rowan are getting married. But before wedding bells ring, Emma must confront not only the inevitable clash of their families but her own second thoughts—especially when she discovers that Taylor's best man is in love with her.

SWEET AMITY'S FIRE by Lee Scofield
The wonderful, heartwarming story of a mail-order bride and the husband who didn't order her. "Lee Scofield makes a delightful debut with this winning tale . . . *Sweet Amity's Fire* is sweet indeed."—Mary Jo Putney, bestselling author of *Thunder and Roses*.

COMING NEXT MONTH

LORD OF THE NIGHT by Susan Wiggs

Much loved historical romance author Susan Wiggs turns to the rich, sensual atmosphere of sixteenth-century Venice for another enthralling, unforgettable romance. "Susan Wiggs is truly magical."—Laura Kinsale, bestselling author of *Flowers from the Storm*.

CHOICES by Marie Ferrarella

The compelling story of a woman from a powerful political family who courageously gives up a loveless marriage and pursues her own dreams finding romance, heartbreak, and difficult choices along the way.

THE SECRET by Penelope Thomas

A long-buried secret overshadowed the love of an innocent governess and her master. Left with no family, Jessamy Lane agreed to move into Lord Wolfeburne's house and care for his young daughter. But when Jessamy suspected something sinister in his past, whom could she trust?

WILDCAT by Sharon Ihle

A fiery romance that brings the Old West back to life. When prim and proper Ann Marie Cannary went in search of her sister, Martha Jane, what she found instead was a hellion known as "Calamity Jane." Annie was powerless to change her sister's rough ways, but the small Dakota town of Deadwood changed Annie as she adapted to life in the Wild West and fell in love with a man who was full of surprises.

MURPHY'S RAINBOW by Carolyn Lampman

While traveling on the Oregon Trail, newly widowed Kate Murphy found herself stranded in a tiny town in Wyoming Territory. Handsome, enigmatic Jonathan Cantrell needed a housekeeper and nanny for his two sons. But living together in a small cabin on an isolated ranch soon became too close for comfort . . . and falling in love grew difficult to resist. Book I of the Cheyenne Trilogy.

TAME THE WIND by Katherine Kilgore

A sizzling story of forbidden love between a young Cherokee man and a Southern belle in antebellum Georgia. "Katherine Kilgore's passionate lovers and the struggles of the Cherokee nation are spellbinding. Pure enjoyment!"—Katherine Deauxville, bestselling author of *Daggers of Gold*.

Harper Monogram **The Mark of Distinctive Women's Fiction**

ATTENTION: ORGANIZATIONS AND CORPORATIONS

Most HarperPaperbacks are available at special quantity discounts for bulk purchases for sales promotions, premiums, or fund-raising. For information, please call or write:
Special Markets Department, HarperCollins Publishers,
10 East 53rd Street, New York, N.Y. 10022.
Telephone: (212) 207-7528. Fax: (212) 207-7222.